Praise for Brett McBean's novels

The Mother

"Brett McBean is, as far as I'm concerned, one of the most exciting writers in the genre today." - Horror Drive-In

"The Mother is one helluva read. Sleek, dark, and impossible to put down… The Mother did what every great book should do – it made me think." –Richard Chizmar, Cemetery Dance Magazine

The Last Motel

"The Last Motel is fun; a thrilling, white-knuckled suspense read. McBean's voice is one that should be heard - a hint of Laymon and Koontz, yet distinctly his own. Genuinely creepy stuff!"
–Brian Keene, author of The Rising and Terminal

"Brett McBean is as brash and brutal as a young Jack Ketchum. He visits the dark rooms inside us all. The Last Motel is the first stop on his way to the top." –Scott Nicholson author of The Manor and The Farm

"A thrilling read about fate, coincidence and murder. McBean pumps up the tension to unbearable levels, and then lets rip."
–Tim Lebbon, author of Fears Unnamed and Desolation

The Invasion

"Brett McBean remains a certified genre stud despite flying under the radar recently." - Matt Molgaard, Horror Novel Reviews

"'The Invasion' is THE best horror book that I have read in 2016"
- Ginger Nuts of Horror

"McBean paints a terrifying and realistic picture of brutality with this book, and I cannot wait to see what he has in store for us next."
- Matthew Scott Baker, Shattered Ravings

Also by Brett McBean

Novels

The Last Motel

The Mother

Wolf Creek: Desolation Game (w/ Greg McLean)

The Invasion

Novellas

The Familiar Stranger

Concrete Jungle

Neighborhood Jungle

Suburban Jungle

Dead Tree Forest

Buk and Jimmy Go West

Collections

Tales of Sin and Madness

THE AWAKENING

BRETT MCBEAN

ISBN-13: 978-0692730980 (Bloodshot Books)
ISBN-10: 0692730982

READ UNTIL YOU BLEED!

The Awakening

A Novel by Brett McBean

CONTENTS

INTRODUCTION

The best coming-of-age tales are those that captured the uncertainty of youth.

Oddly enough, I can remember the exact moment when I felt it – that soul-scarring certainty of what lies just around the corner.

When I was in the fifth grade I participated in something called the Safety Patrol program. It was a team made up of volunteers who each wore an orange belt across the width of his or her body, a cheap plastic badge, and a big cheesy grin. In a nutshell, we were officially-sanctioned goody-two-shoes, kids who helped others get to their classrooms (as if a few of them might suddenly forget where to go) or warned them not to run in the hallways when perpetrators went racing past our post.

I remember early one morning I was standing alone in the stairwell in my Safety Patrol gear, and I was overcome by an existential dread like nothing I had ever experienced before. I've felt it a few times since, but these days it's the awareness of how fast the years fly by, the understanding that the people I love won't be here forever and neither will I. An abrupt, almost smothering sadness descended upon me as I realized my childhood was nearly halfway over. It wouldn't be long before the happiest days of my life were nothing more than really cool roadside attractions left in life's rearview mirror. Keep in mind, this occurred when I was in the fifth grade—years before I had to worry about things like deciding what I wanted do for a living, moving out of my parents' home, adulthood. And yet here I was at just ten years old, feeling sorry for myself as if I had already lost my parents, as if within just a few short days I was about to start some back-breaking nine-to-five job that I would despise until the day I dropped dead.

I do have a point to this strange little anecdote (and I should mention that it was during Mrs. Burnette's fifth-grade class when I decided I wanted to be a writer . . . just in case you were starting to think this little intro was all doom n' gloom with no happy ending). As I said, I believe that the most effective coming-of-age tales are those that capture not only the glorious, carefree days of childhood—back when our only concerns were not being the very last kid to be picked for the softball teams during P.E., or trying to decide whether to spend your last few cents on the latest issue of Batman or The Uncanny X-Men— but those stories filled with an honest pathos as well. "The future's so bright I gotta wear shades," claimed one song that was popular during my seminal years. While there is truth to that statement, it didn't tell the whole story. The future was bright, sure, insofar as anything was possible, but I remember thinking it was pretty damned scary as well. I saw my parents bust their butts day in and day out, struggling to pay the bills, and I didn't look forward to following that same path. Adulthood, from the outside looking in, resembled some cruel punishment for past transgressions. I wanted those days of climbing the tallest trees, reading the best comic books, and sneaking peeks at Playboy to last forever . . . although I knew, even at the age of ten, that's not the way life works.

Throughout the novel you're about to read, you'll meet characters who know this too. Toby and his friends know about the darker side of childhood all too well. They see it in the fathers who have abandoned their families . . . in the mothers who smoke too much, hiding their pain with strained laughter . . . they see it in the bullies who don't waste their time with wedgies and "KICK ME" signs slapped on the backs of their victims, because these guys prefer hurting the weaker kids in ways that leave scars, assuming their victims even make it out alive.

In the end, when it comes to growing up, that's what we all hope to do, isn't it? We just hope we can make it out alive despite all the meanness around us.

Brett McBean's *The Awakening* gets that.

The Awakening is the kind of coming-of-age tale I would have been unable to put down even if there was no horror element. Take out the voodoo, the zombis, and the surreal nightmare sequences, and Brett's novel would have kept my attention nonetheless because it's honest. It's real. It's a scary tale even without all the "spooky stuff."

Childhood is scary. No doubt about it, for most of us those really are the best years of our lives, but there also comes a time when we realize it will all come to an end. I'm pretty sure it comes a lot later for most kids than it did for me, but it comes. Eventually we all have an "awakening" of our own. The good times are finite, we realize. And so we must appreciate them like the gift that they are.

Brett knows about the uncertainty of childhood. He's captured it here, the good and the bad and the everything-in-between.

You're in for a treat. Savor this one, because nothing lasts forever and stories this engaging don't come along too often.

James Newman

June 26, 2016

James Newman is the author of a diverse selection of horror and suspense tales, dark fiction told with a distinct Southern voice and more often than not with a hint of pitch-black humor. His published novels include MIDNIGHT RAIN, THE WICKED, ANIMOSITY, and UGLY AS SIN. When he's not writing, he enjoys watching horror movies (and showing off what he knows about the genre with the recent release of his first nonfiction book: 666 HAIR-RAISING HORROR MOVIE TRIVIA QUESTIONS), listening to loud rock n' roll, and even dabbling in some stage-acting every now and then.

In real life, James lives in the mountains of North Carolina with his wife and their two sons. Online, he divides his time between Facebook and www.james-newman.com.

CHAPTER ONE

In the small Midwestern town of Belford, an old man sat gazing out the window.

Dawn had once again greeted the world with her presence, casting a glorious orange haze over the pretty two-story houses, freshly mowed lawns and imposing elms that lined the street.

The man had witnessed this scene more times than any one person had a right to, and would no doubt see many more. But that was fine by him. He loved to watch the onset of dawn; it was the one joy left in his life. He had watched the sun rise every morning, ever since first stepping foot in this country over ninety years ago, and had continued to do so in every town and city he had lived in since. It was part of his morning ritual. With only a few cups of herbal tea to keep him company, he would sit by the bedroom window and watch the arrival of a new day, and then, later, watch as the kids made their way to school.

There was nothing perverse or sinister about his window gazing. Nor was it simply the ritual of a lonely old man. The reason was deeper, more personal, and almost childlike in its simplicity.

It represented freedom. For him, to be able to sit and watch the sun rise was a gift from the gods. He felt the same way about the children. They were freer now than they would be at any other time in their lives. The old man knew what the children thought of him, and though it saddened him, he forgave their mostly harmless pranks and tactless laughter—their cruelty wasn't pure, not like those people who had robbed him of his life and driven him from the people he loved; no, their cruelty was born from fear:

a fear of the unknown. He was, after all, a curious sight, what with his prominent facial scar which started on the left side of his forehead and cut a path all the way down to the tip of his chin, and his crooked neck which made him see the world sideways. Yet, for all their finger-pointing and snickering, the old man still thought of the children as the true miracles of this world. Their smiling faces and songs of laughter held only trust and purity and freedom.

Freedom.

Most people didn't understand the true meaning of the word. They took it for granted, didn't appreciate the little things in life, the simple pleasures—to simply be alive.

He knew all too well what it was like to live without freedom. To be shackled both in body and mind. Visions of his past constantly filled his head, but they no longer evoked anger or hatred in him. Such venom had died years ago. Now, if he felt anything at all, he felt sorrow. What kept him going was the hope that one day he would be reacquainted with those he had left behind.

Which could very well be soon.

For the past week, he'd had a sense that an old friend was near. This gut feeling, a tingling, like two magnets being slowly drawn together, was faint at first, but had grown stronger as the week ticked by. He thought maybe he was imagining things, but over the last couple of days the sense that his friend was close had grown too strong to ignore. Now, as he sat by the window on the last day before the kids of Belford began their summer vacation, he was sure the man for whom he had been waiting for ninety years had finally arrived.

Soon, he would be reacquainted with his past, soon he would be returning home.

Soon, it will be over.

The old man raised a gnarled finger to the ancient scar that served as a permanent reminder of a past filled with pain and loss. But the moment he touched the rough surface, he drew his hand back as if the scar was red hot.

He picked up the cup of tea with one wrinkled hand. Wisps of steam curled from the drink. Taking a moment to savor the delicate peppermint fragrance, the man placed the cup to his lips and took a sip. The warmth soothed his tired old body.

He never used to drink tea; always coffee. But ever since leaving Haiti a long time ago, he could no longer stand the taste of coffee—too many memories associated with the drink, he supposed.

He took another sip of tea and, nestling back in his chair, he watched the sky turn from orange to pink, light purple and finally to pale blue.

A new day had arrived.

Soon the old man heard the familiar din of kids' laughter.

Gazing out the window, he watched.

"Man you should've seen her. Tits out to *here*." Cupping his hands, Frankie extended his arms to almost their full length.

"I can't believe you actually saw Debbie naked," Toby said, munching on a frosted strawberry Pop Tart as they left Toby's house.

Frankie nodded, a proud grin blooming across his plump face.

There was a strong possibility that Frankie was lying, but Toby didn't care. He was more than happy to go along with Frankie's story. It was more fun to believe that Frankie had in fact seen Debbie Mayfour's breasts than it was to try and catch him in a lie—Debbie Mayfour was one of the hottest girls in town.

Toby Fairchild and Frankie Wilmont were best friends, had been their whole lives—a full fourteen years. Being that their parents were longtime friends, it was only natural, then, that the two boys (who were born only two months apart—Toby was the older of the two) also became good friends.

They had only walked a short distance up Pineview Road when Frankie tapped Toby on the arm.

Toby, mouth full of sweet pastry, mumbled, "What?" He was still thinking about Debbie and her generous assets.

Frankie nodded towards the old single-story house across the street. "He's watching us again."

Toby glanced over at the old man sitting by the window. "Yeah, so what else is new?"

Old Mr. Joseph had been sitting watching them every morning for as long as Toby could remember, so though he should be used to it by now, seeing him there never failed to give Toby the creeps. The weathered wood clapboard siding, dirty and flaking, cracked window panes, mossy roof tiles, garden hose lying on the brown and green patchwork grass like some giant sleeping worm, and shed out back that was always closed: it all reeked of normality. But what was living inside—a reclusive freak with a strange accent and even stranger features, who liked to watch the children go by every morning—was anything but normal.

Jack Joseph's neck was bowed to one side, like his head had been pulled as far as it could possibly go. And he had a jagged scar that ran down the left side of his face. Coupled with his blank, almost glassy eyes, he gave most kids in town the creeps, and there were more rumors floating around about Mr. Joseph than there were days in the year. Most concerned the origin of his neck and scar. One rumor had it that he got his bent neck from spying on all the kids—a sort of punishment from above. Another was that his crooked neck was due to a spell by an angry witch. The scar on his face generated just as much wild speculation, from a gunshot wound, to the mark of the devil. With each passing year, more rumors surfaced, while a whole new generation of kids elaborated on the old ones.

It was also said that he could be seen walking around town late at night. Toby had never seen him, he had never been outside that late, but other people supposedly had, and Toby often wondered what the old man did on those walks. Did he go somewhere specific? Did he have some hiding place where he performed his devil worshiping? Some people thought he walked around peeping into windows while everyone was asleep. This rumor in particular unnerved Toby, and he was glad he slept on the second floor.

"I don't know how you sleep living so close to that weirdo," Frankie said, and kicked at a pebble on the ground. The tiny stone skipped along the sidewalk before veering onto the road, where it rolled to a stop. "One of these days I'm gonna throw a rock through his window," Frankie said once they were safely past Mr. Joseph's house. "Teach that old freak a lesson."

"You're too much of a wimp to do that," Toby said, eying Frankie with an impish grin.

"Eat cow turds and die."

Toby punched Frankie on one doughy shoulder; not hard, but enough to make a point.

"Owww!" Frankie cried.

"See," Toby said. "You are a wimp."

"I could beat you anytime of the week," Frankie said, rubbing his shoulder.

Toby laughed. The two had play-wrestled many times during their fourteen-year friendship; not once had Frankie won, despite his considerable size advantage.

Despite being good at sports—he was a slugger in baseball, and was surprisingly good at basketball—when it came to fighting and wrestling, Frankie's lack of ability was mystifying.

"Well you'll have plenty of chances to demonstrate your superior fighting skills this weekend," Toby said.

"Yeah, I guess," Frankie said, sounding none too confident.

Today was the last day of school before summer vacation started—the best day one could possibly have at school. No homework, no assignments, and the teachers had nothing left to teach, most just as eager to leave school behind for a few months as the kids were. And in celebration of the start of summer vacation, Frankie was staying over at Toby's place tomorrow night—they were camping out in his backyard. Toby had wanted to camp out tonight as well as tomorrow, but his parents said no, they thought two nights was one night too many of not sleeping and eating too much junk food. Still, it was going to be great, just him and Frankie lazing up in Toby's tree house, gorging themselves on mountains of junk food; and afterwards, bunking down in the tent for the night—it would be almost like camping for real.

The tree house was legendary, at least in Toby and Frankie's mind. It's where they spent most of their time (when they weren't playing basketball or the Xbox, that is). Toby and his dad had built it three years ago. It had taken them months, working mostly on weekends, to finish the job, his mother standing by the back door shouting: "You be careful up there, Toby," and "Don't let him fall,

David." They built the tree house about fifteen feet off the ground, in the V of a massive elm tree, and it was big enough for five people to sleep in. Not that Toby's mother would ever let anyone sleep up there.

"Hey, I just remembered," Frankie said. "There's a new rumor going around about Mr. Joseph. I heard from Paul Rodriguez that the old freak keeps live chickens in his shed and every full moon he bites one of their heads off. And tonight is supposed to be a full moon—and it's Friday the 13th, so it's a double whammy."

"Paul Rodriguez is full of shit," Toby scoffed. "How would he know that?"

"Well, apparently, Paul's dad knows someone who works with a woman who one day overheard Mr. Joseph telling Mrs. Stein that he had to buy frozen chickens that day because there weren't any live ones left in his chicken coop. Or something like that."

Toby resisted the urge to peek over his shoulder at Mr. Joseph's house for fear that if he did, he would see the old man sitting by his window, munching on a live chicken. With a sudden bad taste in his mouth, Toby threw what little there was left of the Pop-Tart to the ground. "Yeah, well, I don't believe it. No one bites the heads off chickens. That's disgusting."

"Just because you choose not to believe it," Frankie said, "doesn't mean it isn't true."

"Believe what you want. I think Paul's full of shit."

They crossed over Bracher Road and continued along Pineview. Up ahead, other seventh and eighth graders were heading off to their final day of school (the elementary school was way over the other side of town, and there was no high school in Belford; instead, a total of five communities in the area combined to form Holt Middle School and Holt High School, the former located in Belford, the latter in Polksville, the second biggest town in the group, with a population of around 2,500). Toby's heart-rate quickened when he saw Gloria Mayfour in the group closest to him and Frankie—only a block away. Gloria was, in Toby's eyes, the prettiest girl he had ever seen, prettier even than her older sister. She haunted Toby's dreams, day and night; those sparkling emerald eyes, smooth tanned skin, hair like golden silk, and for a fourteen-year-old, she had one hell of a mature body.

Of course, Toby had never actually talked to Gloria, other than a few brief exchanges over the years. He simply didn't have the guts. He and Frankie often talked about Gloria, mostly crude, adolescent male talk, but sometimes, mostly late at night during a sleepover, when they had stopped all the fooling around and were both in a more serious, reflective mood, they would talk about what they would say to her if either of them had the courage to talk to her.

But until he turned those late-night chats into reality, he had to be content with admiring Gloria Mayfour from afar.

"Hey dorks. Drooling over Gorgeous Gloria I see."

Such a harsh, irritating voice could only belong to Warrick Coleman.

Frankie rolled his eyes at Toby.

Toby grinned and said, "Hey, Warrick."

"I would sure like to stick it to Gloria," Warrick said, forcing his skinny body between Toby and Frankie.

"You wouldn't even know where to stick it," Frankie said.

"Wrong Tubby. It just so happens I've done it before."

Toby cackled, blurted, "Liar, liar, pants on fire!" and immediately regretted doing so; wondered why he had even thought of the saying in the first place. He hadn't used that juvenile taunt since the fifth grade. And to make matters worse, it seemed Gloria and her friends had heard. They turned around and stared at Toby before turning back, giggling.

Toby's face burned with embarrassment.

"Nice one, Fairchild," Warrick laughed. "Way to make an idiot of yourself."

"Stick a knife up your hole, Warrick," Toby grumbled.

"Now now, lover boy. You're gonna have to control that temper of yours if you want to impress Gloria."

"Well at least Toby doesn't lie about having done it," Frankie said in Toby's defense. "You're so full of shit, Warrick."

"Well of course I've done it."

Frankie huffed. "As if. Who with?"

"With some girl you don't know. She doesn't go to our school. She's a friend of the family."

"Yeah, right," Frankie said. "What was her name?"

"Patricia," Warrick said. "Yeah, Patricia. Real hottie. Titties as big as balloons."

Frankie laughed and again said, "You're so full of shit."

Toby barely cracked a smile. He was still fuming over his embarrassing outburst—and it was all because of Warrick and his stupid lies.

You're the one who blurted it out, he reminded himself.

Toby glanced at Warrick, at his stringy hair that looked in need of a wash, face spotted with pimples and ears too big for his angular face.

Though he was a pest most of the time and had all the tact of a sledgehammer (he was crude even by fourteen-year-old boys' standards), Toby felt kind of sorry for this unkempt beanpole of a kid. Even though most of the kids enjoyed his goofiness and penchant for exaggerated stories, he had no real friends. Toby saw Warrick not as Holt Middle School's answer to John Belushi, but as a lonely kid, someone who felt the need to make up stories about himself and others, no matter how absurd, just so people would notice him. And he was certainly successful in that department. One time after school, in front of a hundred or so curious onlookers, Warrick attempted to eat a whole carton of raw eggs. He claimed that doing so would make him super strong, like Rocky Balboa. Warrick had downed half a dozen eggs before throwing up. Annoyed that all his *super powers* were gone, Warrick vowed to finish the rest, but one of the kids dared him to eat his vomit instead. Warrick probably would've accepted the dare and gone through with it if Mr. Hoshire, the science teacher, hadn't come and broken up the whole thing. Toby heard later that Warrick got pounded by his father that night—not for the stupid stunt, but for taking the carton of eggs without asking.

"So have you?"

Toby was pulled from his thoughts when he realized Warrick was talking to him. "Huh?"

"I said, have you ever stuck it to a girl before?"

Toby hesitated, unsure of what to say, for fear of looking like a fool.

They turned right into Dorsett Street, the final leg on their journey to school.

"Come on Fairchild, be honest. Tubby here reckons he once touched a chick's beaver."

Toby frowned. "You have not. That's crap."

Frankie shrugged. "I have too."

Toby knew it was a bald faced lie. Frankie was just trying to make himself look good in front of Warrick. Because in school, reputation was everything, and word spread like a forest fire around Holt Middle School, which would then ignite throughout the town, and Warrick was the spark.

"Well, then what did your hand smell like afterwards?" Toby said, curious to hear Frankie's answer.

Frankie didn't answer straightaway. "Fish," he said.

"Ha!" Warrick laughed. "You're the one who's full of shit, Wilmont."

Toby turned to Warrick. "You can talk. I bet you never did it with... what was her name? Patricia?"

"Did so," Warrick said.

"Okay, what did it feel like?"

Warrick pinched his face—he did the same thing in math class when asked to solve a calculus problem. "Mushy. It felt all warm and mushy," he finally answered.

"What was Patricia made of, mashed potatoes?" Toby said.

Toby and Frankie laughed, despite the look of indignity on Warrick's face. When the laughter died a natural death, Toby looked at Warrick and said, "Hey, relax. We weren't laughing with you; we were laughing at you."

Frankie chuckled.

"Yeah, well, I don't care what you guys think. I did do it with her." A grin split Warrick's face. "Hey, did you guys hear the latest about Mr. Joseph?"

"You mean about the chickens?" Frankie said.

"Yeah. Disgusting, huh? Bites their heads clean off. Bet you he drinks their blood, too. A regular Dracula. And he probably sticks it to 'em, you know, after they're dead."

Toby groaned. "Trust you to think of that."

Warrick grinned again, bigger this time, revealing uneven rows of horribly-stained teeth. "Well, I've gotta run. I'm teaching Mikey Porter how to fart Happy Birthday before school starts. See you dorks in class. Be on the lookout for big guys in hockey masks. And don't think I've forgotten, Fairchild."

"Forgotten what?"

"You still haven't told us how far you've gotten with a girl. Last day of school. Hell yeah!"

Without exchanging goodbyes, Warrick left, jogging off down Dorsett Street.

"What an asshole," Frankie said.

"I can't believe you said you have touched a girl's beaver."

"What else was I supposed to say? Tell the truth and say I haven't even kissed a girl? Yeah, I bet Warrick would have a real good time with that."

"Warrick's going to be at me about it now. He won't rest until I've answered him."

"Just lie and say you've felt some girl's tits. No big deal."

Toby shrugged and watched as Warrick bounded towards school, which was now visible in the distance.

When Warrick caught up with Gloria and her friends, he stopped.

Most of the time, Toby didn't think much of Warrick and his antics, but he had to admit, he did admire Warrick's fearlessness at being able to waltz up to anyone—guy or girl—and talk to them. Toby was even a little jealous of Warrick in this regard.

Watching Warrick, Toby wondered what he was saying to the girls. Were they talking about Mr. Joseph? School? Him?

Christ I hope not. Nerves started pecking at Toby's gut.

It wasn't long before cries of disgust rang out from the group of girls. Warrick cackled and then continued on his way.

"What a weirdo," Frankie said. "I wouldn't be surprised if he sticks it to chickens."

"Yeah," Toby said, gazing at Gloria up ahead, wondering what she thought of him now after this morning's episode. "Wouldn't surprise me in the least."

And they neared the final obstacle that stood between them and three months of freedom.

The bell rang. Every student started gathering their books and papers together with breakneck speed, like the bell was the starter's gun and all the kids were runners.

"I hope everyone has a great vacation," Miss Wilson, their eighth grade English teacher, hollered over the racket.

Sure will, Toby thought as he stood, flung his bag over one shoulder and waited for Frankie. "Hurry up, Frankie."

"Yeah, yeah, hold your horses."

Up ahead, Miss Wilson had moved over by the door and was saying goodbye to each student as they left the classroom, giving most of the girls hugs.

Once Frankie was ready, he and Toby headed for the door, where freedom awaited them: three glorious months of lazy summer days; of sleep-ins, sleepovers, playing baseball till the sun faded and they could no longer see the ball, and staying up late watching monster movies.

At the door, they shuffled past Miss Wilson, who had a smile on her young, pretty face, though Toby noticed that her eyes were a little teary.

"Have a great summer, boys."

"You too, Miss Wilson," Toby said, admiring her tall, slender body, and taking one last whiff of her perfume—which was fresh, honey-sweet, like a flower in spring.

"Yeah, thanks for being such a cool teacher," Frankie said, and together they stepped out into the hall. "Free at last!" Frankie exclaimed.

"Thanks for being such a cool teacher?" Toby said, smiling at Frankie.

"What? She is cool. She's easily the best teacher at this crummy place."

Along with a bunch of other kids, they swarmed out of the squat red-brick building, their home away from home for the past two years, and once outside, made their way across the front lawn.

"I wonder if we'll get a teacher as nice as her in high school," Toby said as they left the school grounds and headed up Dorsett Road, the afternoon sun forcing Toby to squint.

"What makes you think you're graduating from middle school?" Frankie said and he stopped to pick up a stick from the pavement. He continued walking, tapping the stick on the concrete, occasionally striking at the leaves of low-hanging branches.

"Because, I'm a genius. I have my doubts about you, though. You ain't smart enough for high school."

"It's *you're* not smart enough."

Whack! Brown and yellow leaves were knocked from their perch and fluttered to the ground.

"No shit, Sherlock. I was just testing ya. Here, give me the stick."

Frankie shook his head. "Uh-uh. This stick has special powers. No one but me can use it. I'm the stick master."

"You jerk-off," Toby said and he lunged for the stick.

Frankie snatched it away before Toby was able to grab it. "Too slow," Frankie said, grinning.

"I'll sock you in the stomach if you don't give it to me."

"Ha! You couldn't hurt me even if you tried."

With more swiftness and cunning, Toby again grabbed for the stick. This time he managed to yank it out of Frankie's grasp. "Too slow," Toby taunted, waving the stick above his head like a trophy. "Too slow."

"Big deal," Frankie huffed. "I didn't even want the stupid thing."

Toby continued where Frankie left off, swinging the stick at any leaves unlucky enough to be within reach.

As they walked, the afternoon sun pressing down on them like a giant's foot, Toby's mind drifted to Gloria, as it had done all day. The few classes he'd had with her were an adolescent boy's worst nightmare—a case of too much of a good thing. He found himself constantly staring at her, dreaming about what it would be like to kiss her, to touch her, to talk to her, glances that sometimes spilled over into longing gazes. He feared getting caught—either by a teacher, another student or, God forbid, by Gloria herself—but he couldn't help it. She was the headlights, he the poor defenseless deer.

It was during 4th period math when the inevitable happened.

He had been staring at Gloria, imagining them kissing, an erection pushing against his jeans, when Gloria turned and looked at him. He froze, unable to look away. His heart started thumping; his mind screamed, *Look away! Dammit, look away!* But rather than laughing at him like she and her friends had done this morning, or frowning in disgust, Gloria had just smiled the sweetest smile, then turned back to the front. That was the first time Gloria had smiled at him (well, the first time since the second grade when Toby had given her his last Strawberry Twizzler during lunch, but that didn't really count), and it caused his head to spin. He wondered—did she like him? Could it be possible?

It was Gloria's smile, and what it meant, that Toby was reflecting on when they came up to the intersection of Dorsett and Main.

"I'm hungry," Frankie said. "Let's stop off at Barb's."

"Yeah, let's stop off at Barb's for a change," Toby quipped.

Frankie always wanted to stop off at Barb's on their way home from school. Toby wondered why he even bothered mentioning it anymore.

But as they turned left and headed down Main Street, which led into the heart of Belford, Toby had a sudden hankering for a Butterfinger and can of Coke, so maybe stopping off at Barb's wasn't such a bad idea after all.

Barb's Convenience Store was located on the corner of Main and Belford. It had been owned and run by Barbara Stein and her husband, Alex, for thirty years—from its opening in 1967 until 1997, during which time it was known as Stein's Corner Store. Then, in early 1998, Alex Stein had dropped dead of a massive heart attack.

Toby had been four years old at the time, so he only had vague recollections of going to Mr. Stein's funeral. Two things he specifically remembered were: lots of crying, mostly from Mrs. Stein, and he and tubby little Frankie Wilmont conducting a covert farting contest (well, maybe Pastor Wakefield knew—Toby recalled the Reverend glancing briefly at the two boys during his prayer, but otherwise, no one, including their parents, seemed to know). In hindsight, it was a horribly disrespectful thing to have done, but death meant about as much to a four-year-old as the theory of evolution. Toby had won the contest, but how the winner was decided, neither boy could remember.

After the death of her husband, Barbara Stein decided to keep the business going, but she changed the name—too many memories associated with the old one, Toby supposed. Mrs. Stein was a strong-minded woman, with a burly body to match, but her touch was as soft as a kitten's fur. Toby and Frankie loved going to her store, because most of the time she would give the boys free candy. The only time he disliked being in there was when Mr. Joseph was working. Though fortunately, he usually worked weekdays, while they were at school, never weekends, so Toby and the other kids hardly had to see him in there stacking the shelves or lazily pricing stock.

By the time they reached the intersection of Main and Belford—the only two roads that ran all the way through the town, Belford going east/west, Main north/south—Toby had thrown the stick away and was aching to taste the sweet chocolate bar and sugary soft drink.

It was a typical Friday afternoon in Belford, with more people on foot than in cars; those who did prefer to drive cruised through town at a leisurely pace. Toby had spent his whole life in Belford, and though he hoped to one day break free and move to a bigger, more exciting city, like Cleveland or New York, his mother never failed to remind him how clean and safe the town was. The streets were tidy, the lawns well maintained, crime was practically nonexistent, and the sky was the color God intended it to be. Toby took his mom at her word, and as he and Frankie crossed over onto the other side of Main, he took a moment to admire his town's simple beauty.

Located in southern Redina County and surrounded by rolling farmland, Belford was a town with a population of around 3,200—large enough to have all amenities, but small enough for everyone to be on first name basis with each other. It was a pretty town, with wide tree-lined streets, lots of attractive single and double-story houses, most with a smiling face and an American flag to greet you on the front porch. But the main attraction was the centre square, a quaint, picturesque park with pine trees, towering maples and buckeyes, and a white gazebo situated squarely in the middle. It's what most of the stores lining Belford Road looked onto, including Barb's.

The bell jingled when they entered the corner store. Mrs. Stein looked up from behind the counter and smiling said, "Well, hello there, boys. How are we today?" Mrs. Stein had short gray hair and her wrinkly face was kind, familiar. Draped over a long-sleeved candy-striped shirt was the light blue shawl she always wore.

"Great," Frankie said. "It was the last day of school."

"Last day of middle school," Toby added.

"Which means summer vacation has begun."

"My, my," Mrs. Stein said with a click of her tongue. "You boys certainly are growing up fast. It seems like just yesterday your moms came in with you two in prams, crying your little hearts out."

Toby and Frankie smiled politely, and then headed for the confectionary aisle—their favorite and most visited aisle. Toby grabbed a Butterfinger, Frankie a packet of Twinkies and a Reese's Giant Peanut Butter Cup, and then they wandered over to the drinks fridge, where Toby grabbed a can of Coke, Frankie a Dr. Pepper.

They paid for their stuff (receiving a complimentary bag of Gummi Bears each), said goodbye to Mrs. Stein ("So fast," she said again as they left the store), and outside, sat on the curb and munched on their food and slurped at their drinks.

Toby was lost in thought, enjoying the junk food, when Frankie nudged him on the shoulder. "Hey, what did ya do...?"

"Look," Frankie said, voice low, nodding.

Toby looked down the street, to where Frankie was gazing, and saw a man ambling towards them.

Ordinarily seeing a man walking down the street wasn't a big deal, it certainly didn't call for a nudge on the shoulder. Even when that person was a stranger. Though fairly uncommon, it wasn't unheard of for someone from out of town to pass through. But this was no ordinary stranger.

The man walking in their direction was tall, at least six feet, and was as dark as the night. He was as thin as old Mr. Joseph, and had similar white wiry hair. But what was most striking about him wasn't that he was black, or that he resembled Mr. Joseph; he looked like a homeless man. His clothes were dirty and crinkled—they were barely one step up from rags—and he carried a bag in his hand, a large, soiled gym bag that Toby figured contained the old man's clothes and quite possibly every meager possession he owned. And it occurred to Toby then, as he sat staring at the man drawing closer, that he had never seen a homeless person before, not in real life.

"A bum," Frankie whispered. "A bum right here in Belford."

"Ssshhh, he'll hear you," Toby said.

The stranger walked with unhurried steps, and as he passed the boys, he turned his head and looked at Toby.

Toby froze. The gaze was piercing in its nothingness. The stranger frowned ever so slightly, like he saw something in Toby, then he nodded, turned his head back to face the front and kept on walking.

Toby eased out his breath.

Then flinched when Frankie said, "Creepy looking dude. What do you reckon he has in that bag?"

Toby's mouth was dry, so he sipped some Coke. "Dunno. Clothes, I guess."

"Maybe a machete, or an axe," Frankie said. "Or a severed head."

"As if," Toby said.

Toby turned and watched the stranger shuffle down the street. He noticed others watching the disheveled man; or rather, trying not to appear to be staring while looking at him.

"I'm surprised he didn't ask us for some change," Frankie said. "I bet he goes into Patterson's and tries to bum a burger and some fries."

When the stranger was a small blob in the distance, Toby turned back and continued eating his chocolate bar.

"Patterson will probably throw him out if he does," Frankie said, slurping his Dr. Pepper. "I can't imagine Patterson giving away food to some bum. Wonder what he's doing in Belford?"

Toby shrugged. "Who knows?"

"Maybe he's Mr. Joseph's long lost brother," Frankie laughed.

"Yeah, maybe."

When both had finished their afternoon sugar rush, they disposed of the garbage and crossed over the wide, empty street and started up Belford Road.

"You know what we should do," Frankie said as they meandered along. "We should play a prank on Mr. Joseph this weekend. Sneak over to his house late at night, like midnight, when your parents are asleep."

"And do what?"

"I dunno. Go up to his house and knock on the front door?"

Toby grinned. "He'd probably bite our heads off, then drink our blood if we did that."

"Then cook and eat us."

"Yeah," Toby said, and they both chuckled.

When they came up to Hanny Street—a short, narrow, unpaved thoroughfare—they turned left.

"Come inside, little boy," Frankie said, in a screechy old-witch type of voice. He angled his head, in a bad impression of Mr. Joseph's severely crooked posture. "I won't hurt you, my little chicken," he continued. "I just want to drink your blood." He was now starting to sound like Count Dracula.

"Very funny," Toby said. "You know if the wind changes, you'll stay like that forever."

Straightening up, Frankie said, "That's bullshit. It's kid's stuff."

"Then why did you straighten?"

"It was starting to hurt. Anyway, it's your expression that stays the same, not your posture."

Hanny Street ended. They came out onto Bracher Road and crossed over. The moment they were back walking on the sidewalk, Frankie said, "Wanna race?"

Toby nodded. "To my house?"

"To your house."

The two boys stopped. They often held short, spontaneous races. Most of the time Toby won, but Frankie was getting faster and stronger.

Toby got into position: body bent forward, arms poised like pistons about to fire, eyes staring dead ahead.

"On my count," Frankie said.

Toby glanced at his best friend; now his competitor—his body was tense, his eyes determined.

"One...Two..."

Frankie bolted. Toby, taken by surprise, watched in disbelief as his portly friend bounded down the street, arms pumping wildly, backpack jostling on his back like Pamela Anderson jogging without a bra.

"Three!" Came the distant, breathy final count.

"Hey!" Toby shouted, and took off after him.

Frankie had gotten a good head start, he was almost at Toby's street, but by the time Frankie turned left into Pineview (which had no pine trees at all—though Toby liked to think that once upon a time, when Belford was founded in 1818 by William S. Holt, who also founded Polksville, the area was littered with them), Toby was less than ten feet behind him.

Toby flew around the corner, his own backpack slapping against his back as he ran.

He saw her the moment he rounded the corner—she was standing looking back at Frankie jogging up the street—but there was no chance of stopping in time, nor dodging her. She faced Toby, her eyes widened, she drew in breath, and then Gloria Mayfour was knocked to the pavement. Toby followed her down. He felt the impact of Gloria hitting the concrete, heard her grunt and then smelled the familiar sweetness of Bazooka gum as her breath whooshed against his face.

Toby lay on top of Gloria for a few stunned moments, his face buried in her peach-scented hair. He knew he should get off, she might be hurt, yet he couldn't help liking the feel of her body underneath. But when he realized his right hand was clutching her left breast, he immediately rolled off her, hoping she either hadn't noticed where his hand had fallen, or if she had, assumed it had fallen there by accident.

Frankie came running over as Toby got to his feet.

"Are you guys okay?" Frankie said, panting loudly.

Ignoring Frankie, Toby said, "I'm really sorry, Gloria. Are you hurt?"

Gloria sat up. She looked pale and a little shaken. "I'm okay. Just a bit winded." She reached around to the back of her head.

Toby drew in breath. "Did you hit your head?"

She brought her hand back. Thankfully her fingers were clean.

"Not hard," she said. "My head's not bleeding. I'll probably have a nice bump, but I'll live."

Gloria started to rise from her sitting position.

Toby twitched. He wanted to help her, knew that's what they would do in the movies—the hero taking the beauty by the hand and drawing her up close, holding her in his arms—but he was no hero; he was just some bumbling fourteen-year-old kid. So he stood there feeling useless as Gloria got to her feet.

"God, I'm so sorry," Toby said again. "Really, I am."

Brushing leaves and dirt off her clothes, Gloria said, "Don't worry, it was an accident." She smiled shyly.

Is she talking about the collision, the accidental grope, or both?

Standing face-to-face with Gloria, having just knocked her down, having accidentally felt her up, all of Toby's adolescent insecurities came flooding to the surface. He was rendered speechless, his face burned and his hands went all clammy.

There was an awkward silence.

Say something! Toby told himself. He looked at Frankie; Frankie looked just as lost as he was.

"You're bleeding," Gloria said, breaking the tension. She pointed to his knees.

Toby gazed down and saw, through a tear in his jeans, blood seeping from a graze on his right knee.

"Oh yeah," Toby said, shrugging. "It's nothing."

"Well," Gloria said, looking self-consciously between Toby and Frankie. "I guess I'd better get going. I was on my way to the store. I wasn't home for two minutes when my mom says we're out of milk and asks if I could go down to Barb's and get some."

"Parents, huh?" Toby said, mouth feeling thick and dry, like it was full of sawdust.

"Yeah. Well, see you guys around."

"Yeah," Toby said. "See you around."

"Bye," Frankie said.

Gloria walked away, soon vanishing around the corner.

A few moments ticked by before Frankie muttered, "Holy shit."

Toby faced Frankie.

"I can't believe it," Frankie said, sporting a goofy grin. "You talked to Gloria Mayfour. You ran into Gloria Mayfour. You actually fell on top of Gloria Ma..."

"I get the picture," Toby said.

Toby couldn't share his friend's excitement. Sure, he had finally talked to Gloria, brief and uncomfortable as it may have been, had felt one of her breasts, even though he hadn't meant to and there was a fabric barrier between his hand and her flesh, but he was embarrassed—both for Gloria and for himself.

"Why so touchy? She wasn't hurt, it's all good."

"She was hurt a little, she hit her head. But that's not the problem. I'm embarrassed."

Frankie frowned. "Embarrassed, why?"

Toby told him about the accidental grope. "She had to have noticed. She must've been so humiliated."

"Screw that. You felt up Gloria Mayfour! Man, wait till I tell the guys about this."

"Don't you dare," Toby told Frankie. "I don't want anyone to know about this."

"Why? You talked to Gorgeous Gloria. Christ, you fell on top of her and touched one of her breasts! Every teenage guy in town would give their right nut for that privilege."

"I don't give a shit about every guy." Toby stepped up to Frankie; stood so close he could smell the sourness of his sweat, feel the hotness of his breath. "Don't...tell...anyone," Toby said through gritted teeth.

Frankie's brown moon-shaped eyes widened. He swallowed. "Sure. I won't tell a soul."

"You promise?"

"I promise."

"Cross your heart and hope to die?"

With one hand, Frankie made the sign of the cross on his chest. "Cross my heart and hope to die."

"If you tell even one person, I'll tell the whole town that you cried like a girl at the end of Titanic."

"Hey, I promised, didn't I? Jeez!"

Satisfied, Toby stepped away from Frankie and started walking towards his house.

Frankie caught up to him. "You aren't mad at me, are you, Toby? I mean, I was only joking around. I won't tell anyone. I promise."

Toby nodded. He fought hard to suppress a grin, but he lost the battle. "Yeah, I know."

They arrived at Toby's house—a charming two-story structure, the imitation wood vinyl siding painted a light pink with brown trim. The house sat proudly in the middle of a neatly trimmed lawn, which matched the neatly trimmed hedges that flanked both sides of the property.

Stopping at the edge of the front lawn, Toby turned to Frankie. "Go on, I'll meet you at your house, okay?"

"Why? I always come inside and wait for you."

"I have to clean my knee. It may take a while. I'll be around at your place in about half an hour."

Frankie sighed. "Okay, whatever. You're still staying for dinner and then watching the horror movie marathon later, though, right?"

"Of course," Toby said.

"Mom's working tonight, Leah will probably be out, and I don't want to watch *Psycho* all by myself."

"Don't worry, I'll be there to hold your hand."

With a nod, Frankie turned and started up the street, but stopped and looked back at Toby. He was frowning. "Hey, why was Gloria walking down Pineview? She lives on Cooper Avenue. She doesn't need to cut down Pineview to get to Barb's."

Toby hadn't given the matter much thought, but Frankie was right. Why was she walking down Pineview?

"Who knows?" Toby said, trying to act like he couldn't care less, but really he was churning inside with nervous excitement. "Maybe she was taking the long way to Barb's, or she was just out taking a walk, enjoying the sunshine."

Or coming to see me? Yeah right, in your dreams.

With a shrug, Frankie turned back around and continued meandering up the street.

Toby cut across the lawn and hurried up the porch steps, to the front door, where he pulled the keychain from his pocket. Though they lived in a small town, one with an almost zero percent crime rate, his parents still insisted on locking all doors and windows whenever the house was empty, so he singled out the front door key, unlocked the deadlock, and stepped inside.

It wasn't quite three o'clock and both his parents were still at work, so the house was quiet. The only sound was that low, almost undetectable hum he heard people refer to as white noise.

As Toby headed for the staircase, he wondered if Frankie had any inkling of the real reason he didn't want him coming into the house.

Most days after school, Toby and Frankie headed straight to Frankie's house, where they played basketball, computer games, or lazed around watching TV. And since Toby's house was on the way, it made sense for Frankie to wait if Toby needed to stop off at home first for any reason.

But not today.

It was true, he did want to clean the blood and dirt from the small wound on his knee and put a bandage over the graze, but that would only take a moment.

The real reason he didn't want Frankie coming inside had to do with Gloria Mayfour, how it had felt lying on top of her, and the softness of her breast.

For that, he needed privacy.

Toby bounded up the stairs, and into his bedroom.

CHAPTER TWO

Toby was feeling nice and relaxed as he rode his Rampit Red Schwinn BMX towards Frankie's house; the warm wind that fluttered his hair carried with it the glorious scent of flowers and freshly-cut grass, heightening his joy and sense of freedom (he usually only rode his bike when he was by himself—Frankie's old BMX died last year, and his mom didn't have the money to buy him a new one, so Toby preferred to leave his bike at home whenever he was traveling with Frankie).

Replacing his torn jeans was a long pair of shorts, and instead of a polo shirt he now wore an old Nike T-shirt. Completing the outfit was a pair of Nike sneakers, so Toby was all set for a sweaty afternoon of one-on-one basketball, finishing off with a lazy night of watching *Psycho, Frankenstein* and, depending on the time, *Bride of Frankenstein*.

When Toby arrived at Frankie's, he dumped his bike on the front lawn and headed towards the front door.

The Wilmonts lived in an unremarkable house. The single-story wasn't rundown, but the clapboard siding could do with a repaint and some of the boards on the porch were loose. Still, Frankie kept the front and back lawns short, and they did have a colorful and healthy array of flowers, thanks to Suzie's green thumb.

Frankie lived with his mother and older sister, Leah, who was a senior at Holt High. Frankie's dad had left before Frankie was born, so he had never known his father, had never even seen a picture of him because, apparently, Frankie's mom had burnt all photos of him when he left. Toby had trouble picturing Suzie acting in such a way—he knew her as a sweet and gentle person—but then Toby had never experienced such loss and hurt before.

Frankie hardly ever spoke about his father, and Toby couldn't recall the subject ever being brought up by either Suzie or Leah. All Toby knew of Frankie's dad was that his name was Brian and that he used to work as a laborer. If Frankie knew more, he had never told Toby.

Toby flung open the screen door, which, as usual, wasn't locked, and stepped into the house—practically his second home—and called out, "It's Jack the Ripper!"

"In the kitchen," came the reply.

Toby strolled down the hall, through the family room and entered the bright, modest-sized kitchen. Suzie was relaxing back in a chair at the kitchen table, arms folded, smoking her favorite brand of cigarettes, Camel Lights.

There was always the smell of cigarette smoke in the Wilmont house, and it never failed to catch in Toby's throat, even after all these years. He didn't hate it—it was a familiar smell now—but he didn't love it, either.

"Hey there Tobes," Suzie said, drawing on the cigarette in that casual, oh-so-cool way of hers.

"Hey Suzie." Usually, Toby found calling an adult by their first name strange. But Suzie, who worked as a home care aide, wasn't like most adults. Toby thought of her more as a big kid. She had a round face that always seemed to be smiling, and her body jiggled every time she laughed, just like Frankie's.

"How was the last day of school?" she said, blowing out smoke.

"It was all right. Glad to be on vacation. School's boring as hell." Suzie didn't mind people swearing. If he were to swear at home, even something as innocuous as crap, he would get a stern lecture from his parents on how swearing was wrong. As if he was some ten-year-old. Toby didn't see what the big deal was; his father swore all the time. Strange cusses like: "Son-of-a-cock's head," or "Damn monkey fuck."

Toby wished his parents were more like Suzie—relaxed, not so uptight. Also, Suzie treated him like an adult, unlike his parents, who still thought of him as a kid.

"Would you like a drink?"

"Sure. Thanks. I'll have a smoke, too."

Stubbing out the cigarette in the ashtray that was sitting on the table, Suzie smiled. "That'll be the day. I've already told Franklin that if I ever catch him smoking, I'll pound his ass raw. It's a disgusting habit." She hopped up and wandered over to the refrigerator. "What'll you have? Coke, Sprite, or Dr. Pepper?"

"Well, now that's a tough one."

"Let me guess. Sprite? Hmmm, no. Dr. Pepper? Nah, that's Franklin's favorite. I know, Coke!"

Toby grinned. "Yep, how'd you guess?"

Suzie chuckled, and Toby could see her whole body wobble, even though she was wearing a large, billowy dress, one so colorful it was like a rainbow had puked all over it. "Just lucky, I guess." She took out a bottle of Coke and poured him a glass, then handed the glass to Toby. "There ya go, Tobes."

Coke was his favorite drink. He had at least one glass every day. Suzie knew this, but she still asked him what he wanted to drink whenever he came over. It was a silly game they always played.

"Thanks." He took a long drink, following it up with a deep, gassy burp.

"Charming," Suzie said. "You've been spending too much time around Franklin."

"Yeah, tell me about it. Speaking of which, where is Frankie?"

"He's in his room, apparently getting ready to beat your ass in basketball."

"Well, he has got a much bigger ass than me."

Suzie patted him lightly on the behind. "Go on, get going. You've wasted enough time speaking to an old fart like me."

Toby nodded. "Yeah, but you're a sweet old fart." Leaving the kitchen and Suzie Wilmont's infectious laughter behind, Toby headed down the hall towards Frankie's room, towards the hard rock music thumping from inside. When Toby opened the door, the pounding sounds of Linkin Park grew to an ear-bleeding level. Toby stepped into the bedroom and closed the door.

"About time," Frankie shouted over the music. He was lying on his bed, reading one of his mom's old Maxim's—the one with Jessica Alba on the cover. Toby noticed he hadn't bothered taking off his shoes; at the ends of his stocky legs he wore the same smelly

Reeboks he had been wearing all day. He slapped the magazine down on the bed, reached over and turned down the music.

"I hope I wasn't interrupting anything," Toby said, grinning, but probably blushing as well, considering what he had done only a short time ago.

"You wish," Frankie said, swinging his legs off the bed and onto the floor.

"Yeah right," Toby said. "I pray every day that when I come over to your house, I'll catch you stroking your monkey."

Frankie stood, raised his arms to the ceiling and emitted one of those unintelligible noises that always accompanied a satisfying stretch. As he did, the South Park T-shirt he was wearing was raised, exposing his round, hairless belly. "Speaking of which, what took you so long?" he asked once he had finished stretching.

"I told you, I had to clean my knee. Look." Toby nodded to his right leg. There was a small bandage plastered over his bony knee.

"Oh, poor Toby," Frankie said, feigning pity. "Are you sure you don't need a doctor? An ambulance?"

"It didn't hurt, numb-nuts. I just didn't want it to get infected."

The sides of Frankie's mouth curled. "But even if it did and you had to get your leg cut off, it would have been worth it. Hell, it would have been worth it if you had cracked your head open and your brains were oozing all over the pavement, just to be able to lie on top of Gorgeous Gloria."

"I wouldn't go that far."

"I would," Frankie chuckled.

"Anyway, are we gonna get this game started? Or are you too scared you're going to lose?"

"In your dreams, man. And when you lose, don't blame it on your knee." Turning towards his desk, which was crowded with items such as old Matchbox cars, toy plastic dinosaurs and Star Wars action figures, as well as an assortment of baseball cards, half-eaten chocolate bars and empty chip packets, Frankie opened the top drawer and pulled out a bag of balloons. He turned around and held up the bag. "For when we get hot."

They were the water bombs he and Frankie had bought last weekend. The bag was all but full; the weather had been unusually cool last weekend.

"Now you're talking," Toby said. "You're going down, Franklin."

"You shouldn't have called me that. You're gonna pay big time, Tobias."

"We'll see." Toby picked up the basketball from the rubbish tip that was Frankie's floor, and cradled it under one arm.

"First stop, the bathroom," Frankie said and together, they left Frankie's bedroom.

By late afternoon the boys were exhausted, having played basketball non-stop for almost two hours, though the last hour was mostly spent shooting hoops rather than playing one-on-one matches. The bucket of water bombs was almost empty. Only two small balloons remained. The rest were littered about the back lawn like hundreds of tiny, multicolored bird droppings.

Frankie and Toby were sitting with their backs against a wall, their hair and clothes still slightly damp, but drying rapidly in the heat. They were about to head inside to see what Suzie was making for dinner, when they heard a car pull up nearby. It grumbled to a stop and then idled, a growling tiger rather than a purring pussycat like his parents' Honda.

"Sounds like Dwayne's car," Frankie said. He pushed the basketball he'd been lazily rolling on the ground away, and stood up. He moved to the front of the house and peered around the corner. When Frankie came back, he had a look of distaste on his face. "It is Dwayne, and by the looks of it, the rest of his idiot friends are with him. They're dropping Leah off. Debbie, too."

By 'idiot friends' Frankie had to have meant Sam Bickley, Rusty Helm, and Scotty Hammond. None of them were as tough as Dwayne, but bundle the three of them together, and you had a pack of sometimes very cruel thugs, with the cruelest thug of all as their leader.

Dwayne Marcos was a senior at Holt High, and a complete asshole, someone who reveled in humiliating anyone who was, in his eyes, below him: which meant pretty much everyone.

Toby and Frankie were no exception; they hadn't been spared Dwayne's wrath over the years. One time when Toby was sitting in Belford Library, working on an assignment, Dwayne and his goons had come over to Toby and yanked his chair out from under him. Toby had fallen to the floor, smashing his butt on the carpet. With tears stinging his eyes, Toby was as much humiliated as he was hurt (his butt was sore for a full week afterwards). As for Frankie, they had chased him home on numerous occasions, usually catching him, sometimes forcing him to do embarrassing stunts like running around the neighborhood in nothing but his underpants; usually they just took any money he had on him.

Toby had even heard of Dwayne and his gang dunking one poor kid's head in the school toilet—after it had been used by the four of them (depending on which version of the story you believed, the toilet was filled with either just urine, just shit, or a combination of the two).

But Dwayne was tough, good-looking and athletic, so even though he treated most people like they were nothing more than something stuck to the bottom of his shoe. Guys still looked up to him, girls still adored him, and anyone younger or smaller feared him. Which was precisely why he was going out with one of the best looking girls in town. Not that Debbie Mayfour was a sweetheart—sure she was hot, but personality wise she was a no-show. She wasn't overly bright, and could be a right bitch at times. It was a mystery how two girls, so totally opposite in personalities, could be sisters. Gloria was shy, sweet, and intelligent, whereas Debbie was dull and boring. So really, Debbie was the perfect match for Dwayne.

"God I hate that guy," Frankie said. "I heard Debbie and Leah talking about him last night. What a jerk."

Frankie's sister, Leah, was best friends with Debbie Mayfour, so not only did Frankie get to see a lot of Debbie, he also got to hear a lot of gossip. Toby knew Leah and Debbie would kill Frankie if they ever found out he eavesdropped, but so far they had yet to catch him. Sometimes Toby got lucky and Debbie would come to visit when he was staying over at Frankie's. Then he and Frankie would spend the night sneaking around, trying to listen in on the girls' conversations, hoping to catch a glimpse of Debbie in any state of undress. Unfortunately, he had yet to see her naked.

"Get this," Frankie said. "I heard Debbie tell Leah that Dwayne sleeps around with other girls. That he takes them up to Taylor's

Hill, screws them, and then leaves them up there to find their own way home."

Behind Belford Cemetery, which was located on the outskirts of town, was Taylor's Woods. A paved road running behind the cemetery thinned out into a narrow dirt road as it entered the woods, which then narrowed even further into a tiny dirt track that snaked deep into Taylor's woods for a mile or so, before coming out at a large clearing—Taylor's Hill. It overlooked the cemetery and the west side of town—which was mostly farmland—and during the day it was a cool place for kids to hang out, go exploring through the woods, or lie on the hill under the sun and just relax and day-dream. But come night it was a popular place for teenagers to make out and do other teenage type things. One would often find empty beer cans and not so empty condoms scattered around.

"No shit?" Toby said.

"Yeah. But get this, Debbie was actually laughing about it, saying she doesn't mind because it's Dwayne, saying how hot he is, and what a great lover he is. And what a huge..."

"Yeah, I get the picture," Toby said. He looked up at Frankie and smirking, said, "So was this before or after you saw Debbie's tits?"

"Screw you. I did see them. Now hand me a water bomb."

"Huh?"

"On second thought, give me both of them."

Toby reached into the bucket and pulled out the last of the jelly-like balloons. He hesitated. "I hope you're not doing what I think you are."

"Dwayne and his gang have been giving us shit for years. About time we got some payback."

"He loves that Chevy more than he loves himself. And that's really saying something."

Dwayne's one true love was his 1969 Chevy Camaro. His parents bought it second-hand for his sixteenth birthday and he had spent a year fixing it up to pristine condition, complete with original LeMans blue paint-job and white Z stripes. He had named it 'Bruce' after the shark in Jaws—not only was the paint-job reminiscent of a shark's color, but apparently Dwayne thought sharks were badass, the ultimate hunters.

"I know. That's the beauty of it. Quick, give me the water bombs before Dwayne leaves."

Toby sighed, considered hurling the balloons away and letting them splash safely on the lawn. But he finally relented. He handed the water bombs to Frankie. "What if they see you?"

"They won't. I'll make sure of that." Frankie took the water bombs, handling them like they were made from glass.

"But what if Dwayne finds out who it was? He'll probably run us over with Bruce."

"Nearly every house on this street has kids, and they've all been picked on by Dwayne or one of his gang. Sure he'll be angry at first, but he'll have too many suspects to bother doing any real investigating. Besides, it's only water. Imagine if we had these bad-boys filled with shaving cream?"

With a balloon gently cupped in each hand, Frankie again crept up to the front of the house.

Deciding this was too important to miss—it was sure to be all over town come morning—Toby got to his feet and followed, his gut clenched in a tight knot. He stopped behind Frankie.

"I'll wait till he starts driving away and is a little ways down the street before I strike," Frankie whispered.

"I hope you're a good shot," Toby said.

"Hey, you know I am. I didn't beat you today for nothing."

Soon the car revved, Toby heard voices, a female saying: "See you guys later," then a horn honked. When the car pulled away, engine roaring like something out of Jurassic Park, Frankie said, "Okay, I'm going for it."

Frankie drew back his right arm, then sent one of the round balloons sailing. He quickly followed it up with the second. "Come on," Frankie whispered and as they hurried around to the back of the house, they heard the car screech to a halt and then Dwayne shouted: "Who did that! Who the fuck did that!"

Their backs pressed up against the wall, safely hidden from view, Toby and Frankie fought bravely not to laugh. Their laughter ceased, however, when the car, instead of continuing up the street, seemed to turn around.

"We're gonna get you!" Rusty Helm bellowed, as the Chevy's engine grew louder.

"Yeah, you're dead meat!" Sam Bickley screamed. The car sounded like it was cruising past the Wilmont house.

"Come on, let's go inside," Frankie said. "Dinner's probably ready soon."

"Yeah, good idea."

With Dwayne still shouting obscenities and the car dangerously close, Toby and Frankie hurried through the back door. The aroma of ham, cheese, pepperoni and onion sizzling in the oven hit them the moment they were inside.

"You guys must have an amazing sense of smell," Suzie said, closing the oven door. "Pizza's almost ready." Her face was flushed and thin beads of sweat dribbled down her forehead.

"Smells fantastic," Toby said.

"Thanks. Say, what was all that yelling just now?" Suzie slipped a cigarette from the packet lying on the table and popped it into her mouth. With the lighter, she fired up the smoke.

Frankie and Toby exchanged knowing looks, which thankfully Suzie didn't see. "Dunno," Frankie said. "Just some teenagers playing around, I guess."

Just then Leah walked in with Debbie, who hung back in the hallway, twirling her hair.

"Some jerks just water bombed Dwayne's car," Leah said, and then her eyes fell on the boys and she huffed. "You again," she said and smiled thinly at Toby.

Leah Wilmont wasn't a beauty queen, not like the surly, but model-perfect cheerleader behind her. She had an earthier quality, bordering on Tom-boyish, and though some guys found her attractive enough, Toby only saw her as the big sister he never had.

Toby smiled back, and then he looked past Leah, to the tall blonde hovering in the background. When Debbie noticed Toby staring at her, she winked at him, and Toby quickly looked to the floor. He heard Debbie giggle.

"I've just come to tell you that I'm staying at Debbie's tonight," Leah said.

"And miss out on my famous pizza?"

"Yeah, well, I think we'll live."

"So what have you two got planned for tonight?"

"Probably going up to Taylor's Hill with some guys," Frankie said, puckering his lips and making kissing noises.

"Pervert," Leah huffed. Then to her mom: "I dunno, nothing much, just hang around, watch some movies. Nothing major."

"Well, have fun doing nothing major," Suzie said. "Remember, I'm working tonight, so if you need me..."

"I know. You'll be at Mrs. McGregor's." Rolling her eyes, Leah turned around. "Come on, Deb. Let's go pack my bag and get the hell outta here."

As the girls left, Debbie said, "Hey, Toby. Gloria says hi," and the sound of two seventeen-year-old girls giggling was like nails down a chalkboard to Toby.

Frankie chuckled beside him. Suzie drew on her cigarette, the hint of a grin on her face.

"Now Toby, does your mother know you're staying over for dinner?" Suzie said.

Toby sighed. "No."

"Go on, give her a call. You know how she worries."

"Where else does she think I am?" he muttered as he stomped over to the wall phone near the kitchen bench.

"After that, you boys go and get washed up," Suzie said, and took a deep puff of her Camel Light.

It was nine-thirty when *Psycho* ended.

Frankie blew out a long breath, picked up the bits of popcorn that had fallen on his shirt and into his lap, popped the morsels into his mouth and said, "Dude, that was a creepy movie. You see that corpse at the end?"

Toby nodded. "And that shower scene, very cool."

"Yeah. Wish they had used more blood, but still, pretty damn creepy." Frankie picked up the remote, turned down the volume on the TV.

"How you holding up?" Toby asked Frankie. "Think you can manage *Frankenstein*?"

Frankie huffed. "Of course. It's even older than *Psycho*. I won't be scared."

"Just like you weren't scared when that old woman came out of the room and sliced that cop's face? You jumped a mile."

Frankie shrugged. "So, you about shit yourself when the lady was getting slashed in the shower." Frankie smiled.

"As if." Truth was, Toby had been more than a little spooked by the movie. For an old black and white horror movie, it was eerily effective.

Frankie got to his feet. "Well, I'm getting some Dr. Pepper and some M&Ms. Gotta stock up for *Frankenstein*. You want anything?"

"A can of Coke. And I'll share your M&Ms. Unless they're peanut. You know how I hate nuts."

"Let me go check."

Frankie left the family room.

Toby remained sitting on the sofa, feet resting on the coffee table. If Suzie was home, she'd yell at him for having his feet up on the table—she hated the thought of dirty, smelly feet on any place where you put food and drink.

Without Suzie and Leah, the house was quiet. No wonder Frankie wanted Toby to stay for the horror movie marathon. These movies were creepy enough watching them with friends. He could only imagine what it would be like watching them alone.

And Toby knew that Frankie disliked being home alone. He would never admit it, but he hated it when his mom worked the night shift. Those nights, he was always extra persistent that Toby stay the night, or until as late as Toby's mom would allow him to stay.

"Bad news," Frankie said, poking his head around the corner. "We're all out of Coke and there's only peanut M&Ms. And it's a small packet of peanut M&Ms."

Toby pulled his feet off the table, placed them on the carpet and turned around. "What else do you have to drink and eat?"

Frankie made a face. "There's one can of Dr. Pepper, some grape juice, cherry Kool-Aid, and a bag of pretzels."

Toby groaned. "I hate cherry Kool-Aid. And pretzels. Man, we can't watch another movie without proper food and drink."

"We could always go to the Circle K. You got any money?"

"Yeah, a little. But Circle K's over on the other side of town. It'll take ages to walk there and back. We'll miss half the movie if we go."

"Yeah you're right." Frankie stood by the kitchen entrance, deep in thought. A grin broke across his face. "It'd be a lot quicker by bike."

Toby sighed. "Yeah, but you haven't got..." He stopped, noting the look on Frankie's face. "Oh, I see. You want me to do all the work? Typical."

"Hey, this way it should take you no more than half an hour to get back. And don't worry, I'll fill you in on the movie."

"How thoughtful of you." With a groan Toby got to his feet. "Well you'd better give me some dough. I haven't got much. I'm saving most of it for tomorrow." He slipped on his Nikes.

"Hey, me too. So I can only spare five."

Toby made a face. "Five bucks? That's all you can spare?"

"Hey, tomorrow's the main event, bro. We're gonna go nuts for our campout. I want us to have as much junk food as we can carry. And since, well, you know, I'm not exactly rolling in cash, I can only spare five bucks right now."

Toby sighed. "All right. But you had better come through with the goods tomorrow."

"I will, I will," Frankie said. He turned and disappeared. When he came back, he handed Toby five ones. "Get me another can of Dr. Pepper and a big bag of peanut M&Ms."

"Yes, Sir!" Toby took the money and stuffed the notes into his pocket. He started for the front door.

"I'll be sitting here in front of the TV, waiting for you, watching *Frankenstein*."

Toby stuck his finger up at Frankie. "Uck Fou," he said, and with the sound of Frankie chortling, headed outside.

Belford's one and only 24-hour convenience store was located on Redina Street, one of the three main roads leading out of town.

It took Toby ten minutes to reach the Circle K, its luminous red and white lights a startling contrast to the dark, sparsely populated farmland which surrounded the store.

Parking his bike out the front, he stepped into the bright interior and bought a can of Coke, a can of Dr. Pepper, and two packets of M&Ms—plain and peanut.

The Circle K was surprisingly empty for a Friday night, and when he stepped outside, bag in hand, he discovered the reason why.

As he walked over to his bike, he heard the end of a cell phone conversation.

"...Jinks Field? Fuck, this I gotta see," some older teenager said, standing by his car.

Instead of hopping on his bike and riding away, Toby hesitated, taking longer than was necessary to hang the bag over the handlebars.

What was going on at Jinks Field? he wondered.

The older teenager hung up, then speed-dialed a number. "Shaun, hey, it's Paul. You heard about what's going down at Jinks Field? You are? Yeah, I'm on my way there now. I know, apparently the old bum was perving on them. Fuckin' old perv. Okay, okay, see ya soon." Paul hung up, jumped into his car and sped away from the Circle K.

Old bum? Are they talking about that drifter me and Frankie saw today?

Toby knew he should just get on his bike and ride straight back to Frankie's.

But he was curious. What exactly was happening at Jinks Field?

And what was that about the old bum perving on some people?

With nerves tingling in his gut, Toby hopped onto his Schwinn and started pedaling towards Jinks Field.

Man, Frankie's gonna be spewing when he finds out he missed this.

Not that Toby knew what 'this' was.

The night grew dark as he left the lights of the Circle K behind.

He pedaled hard, legs pumping, sucking in the sultry night air through his nostrils.

By the time he turned onto Longview Road, he could hear the distant sounds of cars' engines and shouting.

What the hell's going on?

He reached Jinks Field, puffing and sweating. He skidded to a halt, stopping at the outer edge of the gathering, mostly teenagers standing around the large car park, or sitting and standing on the hoods of cars, shouting, drinking, egging on whatever was at the center of this show. Some of the spectators were throwing beer or soda bottles along with the cries of "Get him!" and "Give the pervert a welcome to remember!" A few were even throwing stones. At what, Toby couldn't see. His view was blocked by bodies and parked cars, their headlights pointing in all directions, giving light to the otherwise lightless area. He could just see movement through the throng of onlookers and stationary cars, could hear the roar of engines, and it looked to him like cars were going in circles, kicking up gravel and clouds of dust as they went.

Spotting Warrick standing on the hood of someone's car, Toby rode over to him. When Warrick saw Toby, he smiled and jumped off the car. "Hey Fairchild," he shouted. "I'm surprised to see you here."

Head starting to hurt from all the noise, the dust starting to scratch his throat, Toby said, "What's going on?"

Warrick motioned with his head and Toby followed on his bike.

They stopped a little way up Longview, where the noise wasn't so deafening.

"Man, is this crazy or what?" Warrick said, face dripping with sweat. His eyes held a wildness that was unnerving. And his breath smelled of beer.

"Yeah, I guess so. But what's it all for?"

Warrick ran a hand through his greasy hair. "Some of us are just... well, let's say giving that bum a nice Belford welcome."

With feet resting on the ground, Toby said, "What do you mean?"

"Well, apparently the old hobo was caught perving on Nate and Val. They were parked by Jinks Field, making out, when Val sees this face appear at the window. She screams, so Nate jumps out and, seeing it's that nigger bum, starts beating on him..."

Nate Jenkins was a senior in High School. Val, a junior, was his long-time girlfriend.

"...Anyway, he calls some of his friends, tells them what happened. They come right on over and get in on the action. Word quickly spread, and now..." Warrick turned and waved a hand. "Now it's a party."

Toby gazed at the wild scene below. "So those cars in the middle of the crowd, what are they doing?"

Warrick chuckled. "Circling the hobo, what else?"

"You mean he's in the middle of all that?"

"Of course Fairchild, what do you think I've been telling you?"

Toby watched some high school senior pelt a bottle into the middle of the circle.

Toby swallowed, tasted grit. "Jesus Christ," he breathed.

"I just can't believe Dwayne's missing all this. I called him before, told him what was going down, but he said he was busy, or some shit. Man, it's not like him to miss out on a scene like this. If he was here, he'd be throwing bottles the hardest. Nah, on second thought, he'd be in Bruce, circling that motherfucker like a... a..."

"Shark?" Toby said.

"Yeah, like a shark. Say, come down with me. You can see better standing on a car. If you're lucky, you can see the hobo through the dust, cowering like a baby."

Toby looked at Warrick, at his thin face glowing with bloody excitement.

"Well..."

Torn between curiosity and fear, Toby didn't know what to do.

"Come on Fairchild. Help us give this nigger pervert a proper welcome—and a proper sendoff."

"Okay," Toby said, and he immediately felt bad for wanting to watch this mob hurt and humiliate a complete stranger.

He was perving on some teenagers...

Toby rode back behind Warrick. Resting his bike and the bag of food and drink on the ground, he followed Warrick onto the hood of some guy's car. It buckled slightly under the weight. Once Toby was steady on his feet, he stood and looked out. He saw a ring of kids screaming and hollering with delight, raising their bottles to the night like flaming torches, while three cars raced 'round and 'round. The dust was thick, so Toby only caught glimpses of the man huddled in the middle.

Someone in the inner circle shook up a beer can and then sprayed the contents over the bum. Everyone laughed and cheered.

"What if the cars get too close and lose control?" Toby shouted in Warrick's ear.

Warrick didn't answer straightaway. "I dunno," he said. "We'll just have to wait and see." Then he screamed, "Get out of town, pervert!" Then he cackled.

The choking dust, the smell of sweat, exhaust and beer—it was too much for Toby. Starting to feel queasy, he nudged Warrick on the arm. "I've seen enough. I'm outta here."

Warrick said, "You don't want to stick around?"

"For what?"

"For whatever happens once everyone gets tired of this."

Toby shook his head. "No, I think I'll..."

A police siren cut through the mob's bloodlust and the cars' engines.

"Shit, the cops!" Warrick cried, and he jumped down to the ground, Toby following.

With the sound of car doors slamming and tires squealing, Toby hurried over to his bike, snatched it off the ground and hopped on.

Toby didn't even bother to look for Warrick; he just started pedaling up Longview, then across the street and into a patch of woods. There he stayed, hidden behind an elm, watching as two cruisers, lights blinking, sirens blaring, tore down the road, swerving to miss cars driving in the opposite direction.

Once they were past him, screeching to a halt at the parking lot below, Toby left, but not before scanning the area for any sign of the hobo.

He looked through the settling dust, through the cars and teenagers that hadn't been quick enough to make a getaway before the cops arrived, but saw no sign of the stranger. He gazed over to the field, the scene of countless baseball games, town picnics and Fourth of July fireworks. He looked to the bleachers, dark and shadowy. There was no trace of the hobo.

Must've made a getaway, Toby thought and then he rode away from Jinks Field.

"What took you so long?" Frankie said.

Toby walked around to the front of the sofa and fell into it. He placed the bag on the table, then proceeded to tell Frankie about what he had seen.

"No way," Frankie said afterwards. "Man, I always miss out on the fun."

"Serves you right for being lazy," Toby said.

Frankie reached into the bag and took out the can of Dr. Pepper. An empty can of the same drink sat on the table, along with the half-empty packet of pretzels. "Hey, this is warm."

"Sorry, want me to go down to the store and get you another one?"

"Would you?"

"Sure, right after I fly to the moon."

Frankie popped open the can and took a sip. "Ah well, warm Dr. Pepper is still better than no Dr. Pepper." He faced Toby. "So this bum was really in the middle, with cars driving all around him?"

Toby nodded.

"Wow."

Toby opened his can of Coke and took a sip of the lukewarm soda. On the television screen Frankenstein's Monster was reaching up towards a stream of sunlight which was shining through the roof of some old castle. "So, what'd I miss?"

"Oh, yeah, cool movie. Not as exciting as what you saw tonight, but still, for an old movie, it's all right."

Once Toby was up to date with the story, once both boys had their respective packets of M&Ms open and were happily munching away, Toby relaxed back and watched the rest of Frankenstein—his thoughts occasionally turning to what he had witnessed tonight, and wondering what had become of the stranger.

When Toby arrived home that night at eleven o'clock, he found his parents in the family room, watching TV—some war documentary, judging by the grainy black and white images of tanks on the screen.

"Hi hon," his mom said, turning around and smiling.

"Have a good time?" his dad said without averting his gaze from the screen.

Standing just outside the family room, feeling the breeze from the air-conditioner, Toby muttered, "I guess."

"Hey kiddo, come and sit with your old ma and pa for a bit. We haven't seen you all day."

Toby rolled his eyes and thought, *Great, a talk*, then shuffled over to the old wicker chair that sat adjacent to the couch his parents were on.

All Toby wanted to do was go up to his room and listen to some music, perhaps get started on the book he had borrowed from the library—a Stephen King novel called *The Shining*, which, according to some kids at school, was supposed to be super scary.

"So how was the last day of school?" his dad said, finally turning his attention to Toby when a commercial break came on. "Kiss any girls, beat up any guys?"

"It was all right. Though I did kiss some guys and beat up a few girls."

His dad laughed. His mom just shook her head.

"That's my boy. Got a sharp wit, just like his old man."

"You've got wit," his mom said, "but I don't think it's very sharp."

"Hey, you're getting funnier in your old age, my dear. I guess spending too much time around me has finally paid off."

"So my mother was right," his mom said. "You are a bad influence."

His dad leaned over and kissed his mom on the cheek. "You bet I am."

This was typical Fairchild conversation; most of the time it was about nothing, with the odd sprinkling of meaningful discussion thrown in for good measure.

His dad worked as a bank clerk at Belford Community Bank, a job he'd had since he was seventeen and which was, according to the man himself, as tedious as listening to their neighbor across the street, Mr. Klein, prattle on about how everything was so expensive these days, not like back when he was a youngster. But the job paid well, even if he didn't always get along with his boss, Rudy Mayfour.

His dad often bitched about Mr. Mayfour, calling him all sorts of colorful names, the worst of which he waited until he thought Toby was out of the room (but in reality, Toby was just out of view, not out of earshot).

Toby had occasionally heard people refer to David Fairchild as crude, even obnoxious, but Toby, who got along well enough with his dad, as well as any of his friends got along with their fathers, simply saw his dad as a bit of a comedian, someone who had no qualms about speaking his mind.

By contrast, his mom, who worked at Belford Library, was quiet, introverted—she and Toby were a lot alike in many ways. How she put up with his dad's crude humor baffled Toby, but they seemed to get along well. They hardly ever fought, or if they did, it was behind closed doors.

"But seriously," his mom said, "how does it feel finishing middle school?"

"Feels okay, I guess. I'm glad it's over and that it's summer vacation."

"We're very proud of you, you know."

"Just because I finished middle school? It's no big deal, Mom."

"My word it is," his dad said. "Our little man is growing up."

Toby shifted in the chair. He hated it when his parents talked this way. Why couldn't they be more like Suzie?

"Well anyway, we just wanted to say how proud we are of you. So what did you and Frankie get up to tonight?" his mom said, probably sensing Toby's discomfort.

"The usual," Toby sighed. "Why?"

"I only want to find out what my son's been up to, that's all."

"He's in a mood because we wouldn't let him camp out tonight as well," his dad said.

Toby sighed again. He hated it when his dad was right; or at least, partially right, in this case. "We played some basketball, then had dinner, then watched a horror movie marathon on TV. Happy? Am I free to go?" He decided to leave out the part about watching a mob of teenagers torment a hobo.

"Hey, don't speak to your mother like that," his dad said, deepening his voice. "She's only asking because she cares."

Toby really wasn't in the mood for a lecture or an argument, so he said, "I'm sorry. I'm just tired."

"Too much basketball," his mom said with a kind smile.

Toby shrugged. "Yeah."

"You do look tired," his dad said. "Okay, you're free to go."

Thank you!

Toby stood up from the chair.

"Good night," his mom said.

"Night, champ," his dad said, turning back to the TV. The commercial break was over. "Get a good rest. Big day tomorrow. Have to set up the tent."

"See you guys in the morning," Toby muttered and he shuffled out of the icy-cool family room, up the stairs and into his stuffy bedroom (while the family room, living room and kitchen benefited from air conditioning, the upstairs relied on the old fashioned method of cooling—opening the window).

It was true; he was tired, but he wasn't sure how much sleep he would be getting tonight—he had a lot on his mind, aside from the campout tomorrow. There was Dwayne and the water bombing incident, Mr. Joseph and his blood-drinking, chicken eating ways, and of course the unsettling events at Jinks Field; but mostly it was Gloria who occupied his mind. He knew he would lie awake in bed daydreaming about the events of today, wondering what, if anything, might happen during the next three months of summer vacation.

Toby jerked awake, momentarily confused. It didn't take him long to realize that he was in his bedroom. He lay in the darkness, heart pounding, until he was orientated enough to sit up.

What woke me up? The dream?

In the dream he had been in darkness. He had felt around—cold, hard wood. He realized he was in a box of some sort; a box that was as narrow as it was high. He had pushed, tried kicking, but he had little room for movement, and nothing gave way. He had screamed, but no sound came out. He was trapped, and then someone grabbed his hand, and that's when he woke.

Toby wiped his brow. His forearm came away wet.

He turned and the red numbers on his digital clock told him it was 2:28.

He was about to lay back down and try and get back to sleep, when he heard the sound of an engine outside; a deep, familiar growl.

Toby drew in breath. His genitals shriveled and his brain screamed one word: *Dwayne!*

Toby hopped out of bed and, dressed only in a pair of boxer shorts, stood at the bedroom window and peeled away the curtains.

Moonlight shone in the clear, starry sky, a pearly orb that streaked light into Toby's room. Any other night and he would've thought it a beautiful sight, but it wasn't the moon Toby was interested in. It was the car, cruising up and down Pineview, like a shark stalking its prey.

A blue Chevy, the white stripes that ran along its hood and trunk dull gray in the moonlit night.

Bruce.

Toby's insides went all squirmy, perspiration rained down his face and body—there was no air drifting in through the open window to cool him.

Shit, Toby thought. *Dwayne found out I was involved in the water bombing, and now he's come to pay me back!*

Should I wake up Dad? Call the police?

But when the Chevy stopped a few houses down, on the other side of the street in front of Mr. Joseph's, Toby's worries eased and he remained by the window, still cautious, but curious.

The Chevy's passenger door opened. Scotty Hammond hopped out, then three more figures followed.

One was Sam Bickley. The scrawny, buck-toothed high school senior was wearing dark shirt and pants, similar to Scotty, and in one hand he was holding a cage, which contained a clearly distraught chicken. The bird was savagely flapping its wings and hopping around inside the cage. In his other hand, Sam was carrying an axe.

The other two figures that had emerged from the car, also wearing dark clothing, were Debbie Mayfour and Leah Wilmont. Both girls appeared to be holding small canisters of some sort.

Oh no, Toby thought. What's Leah doing with these guys?

The driver's side window remained rolled up, and Toby pictured Dwayne sitting behind the wheel, dragging on a Marlboro.

As Sam and the girls hurried across Mr. Joseph's front yard, Scotty reached into the car and when he emerged he was holding some kind of long, thin box. He placed the box on the roof of the Chevy, then he leaned back against the car and struck up a cigarette.

Debbie and Leah crept up to opposite ends of Mr. Joseph's house and, shaking the canisters, started spray painting over the white walls of Mr. Joseph's house.

While the girls went about their business, Sam opened the cage and pulled out the chicken.

Toby's stomach twisted.

No way. Sam's a weird guy, but surely he isn't that sick.

It seemed he was.

Sam crouched, and holding the chicken down on Mr. Joseph's lawn, drew back the axe and with a single motion, chopped off its head.

Toby flinched. The headless bird twitched and flapped its wings, blood gushing from its neck-stump, until finally it lay dead on the bloodstained grass. Toby noticed Leah had stopped and was watching Sam; Toby could almost hear her thinking, *How in the hell did I ever get mixed up in this?*

Sam crept up the porch steps and placed the headless chicken by the front door. He dangled the head through the metal bars of the screen door, and then hurried back to the car. Leah and Debbie followed soon after. Once they were back in the Chevy, Scotty took the box from the roof and started throwing small white objects, and it came as no surprise to Toby to learn that those small objects were eggs.

He pelted them at the dilapidated house hard and fast; egg missiles that smashed against the house in slimy yellow bursts.

When the porch light flicked on, Scotty ducked into the Chevy, along with the carton of eggs, and the car sped away, tires squealing.

The front door opened, and old Mr. Joseph, wearing cream-colored pants and a white shirt, shuffled out. He gazed down at the dead chicken oozing blood on the boards, then at the head hung through the screen door. He stepped around the chicken, walked down the steps and shuffled to the edge of his lawn. He looked both ways down the street, looking almost comical due to his crooked neck, like his neck was locked in the one position, and he had to move his whole body.

Realizing there was nothing to see, that whoever had carried out this act of vandalism was gone, the old man turned towards his house and examined the mass of broken eggs that littered the lawn and peppered the front of the house, windows and even the roof.

The old man's shoulders slumped when his eyes fell on the areas where Leah and Debbie had written the graffiti. Gathering up the dead chicken and its head, Mr. Joseph headed back into his house.

Toby remained at his bedroom window until the porch light flicked off, then he hopped back into bed, where he remained awake for a good twenty minutes before finally drifting off to sleep.

CHAPTER THREE

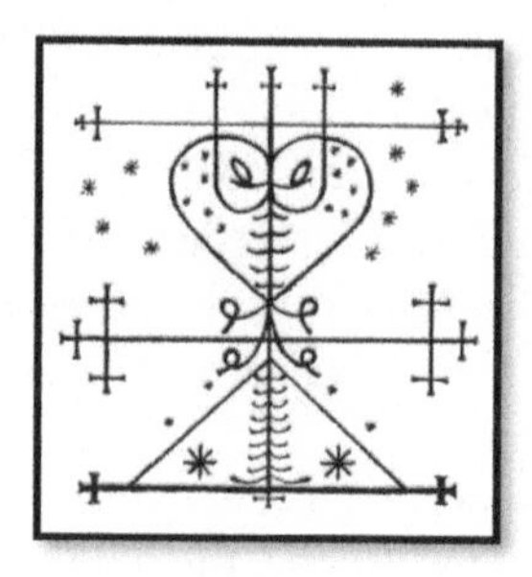

It was only a shade after eight o'clock, and already Toby was showered and dressed. Usually on Saturday mornings he didn't get up till at least nine, shuffling downstairs in his pajamas, eyes half-open and crusty from sleep, hair sticking up like he had stuck his fingers in a light socket.

But he'd had a restless night, so at around seven-thirty, wide awake and unable to fall back to sleep, he decided to get up and get ready. His restlessness was mostly due to the events of last night, but he couldn't deny that his excitement over getting ready for the campout was also part of the reason.

Also, he was still plagued by the dream.

He couldn't shake the feeling of being trapped, of being confined within a dark space and unable to escape. The feeling lingered with him like a bad smell.

"You're up early, champ," his dad said when Toby entered the kitchen. The Saturday paper was spread open on the table in front of him, open to the sports section. Next to the paper sat a plate of waffles and a mug of black coffee.

"Have a good night's sleep?" his mom asked. She was sitting opposite his dad, munching on her usual breakfast of toast and honey, sipping a cup of tea. Like Toby, she disdained coffee. To him, it tasted like runny, bitter mud.

Toby considered answering "No" and telling his parents about what he had seen Dwayne and the others do, but decided against it. His mom would only worry, and that might hurt the camping tonight. He could hear her now: There will be no fooling around after eleven o'clock. You didn't get a good night's sleep, young man. So there'll be no late night talking!

They were bound to hear about it anyway and besides, no real harm was done (aside from the killing of an innocent chicken). Also, Frankie's sister was involved, and he didn't want to get her into trouble.

So Toby answered "Yeah" to his mom's question as he headed to the refrigerator. There, he took out the orange juice and milk, poured himself a glass of juice, and took the juice and pitcher of milk over to the breakfast table. He sat down and grabbing the packet of frosted Cheerios that was already out on the table, tipped a mountainous level of the sugary cereal into the bowl that had been set for him, then coated it with icy cold milk. Lastly, he spooned a heap of sugar over the cereal.

"Isn't that cereal sweet enough without sugar?" his dad said, mouth full of waffles.

"You'll rot your teeth," his mom said.

"I will not," Toby said and shoved a heaped spoonful of Cheerios into his mouth. The cereal was sufficiently sweet. He washed it down with some juice.

"Toby, I was speaking with Suzie this morning, she told me about some trouble last night, over at Jinks Field. Do you know anything about it?"

Toby shrugged. "No."

"Well, apparently the police picked up a bunch of teenagers. They were drinking, bottles were smashed all over the ground, and the kids had been driving their cars all over the car park, causing all sorts of mess."

"Haven't heard anything about it," Toby said. "Did anyone get arrested?"

His mom shook her head. "Suzie didn't know, but she said most of the kids got away. Must've been a big party." She sighed. "I worry sometimes about the kids of today. No respect for public property, and too much alcohol."

Toby's dad huffed. "So some kids were drinking and playing around in their cars. That's nothing. Back in my day..."

"David," his mom said, shaking her head. "You'll give Toby bad ideas."

"All right, all right," his dad said. "So, you ready for the big campout?" he asked.

"You bet," Toby said, and the words had just passed his lips when there was a rapping at the back door.

"Gee, I wonder who that could be," his dad said, and forked the last of the waffles into his mouth.

Toby remained seated and continued to crunch away at his cereal. He figured his mom, who was sitting closest to the door, would get up and let Frankie in.

But his mom remained seated as the knocking continued. Toby glanced at his parents. Both were trying, though not very successfully, to refrain from grinning.

Annoyed at the interruption of his breakfast, Toby stood up. "I'll get it," he huffed.

"Would you?" his mom said. "I'm still in my dressing gown, and I haven't a clue as to who it could be. Why, it could be George Clooney for all I know."

"Or Catherine Zeta-Jones," his dad added.

Shaking his head, Toby ambled over to the back door, flicked the lock, then swung it open.

"What took ya so long?" Frankie said, panting. His face was a round red ball, teeming with sweat.

"No one wanted to let you in," Toby said and he turned and headed back to the table.

"Very funny," Frankie said. He picked up the backpack and sleeping bag that were sitting on the ground and stepped inside.

"Another atypically early riser," his dad said. "What is this, morning of the living dead?"

"And how are you this morning, Frankie?" his mom asked.

"Ah, you know. Can't complain."

"Then don't," his dad said, sipping his coffee. "We get enough of that living with Toby."

Toby ignored his father's remark and continued to plow through the gradually diminishing mountain of Cheerios. Frankie dumped his bulging backpack and sleeping bag on the kitchen floor and headed straight for the fridge. He flung open the door and pulled out the bottle of Coke.

"Yeah, help yourself," Toby mumbled through a mouth full of Cheerios.

"Thanks, I think I will." Frankie took down a glass from the cupboard and filled it with the cola drink. "Damn, it's already hot out there. I'm so thirsty I could drink a gallon of donkey piss."

"That's just charming, Frankie," his dad said. "This coffee tastes so much better now."

Frankie grinned and took a long drink of Coke, draining the glass in one hit.

"You know, you should be drinking water when you're thirsty," his mom said. "It's much better for you than that sugary stuff."

Frankie burped. "I can't stand water. It has no taste. I hate things that have no taste." He set the glass on the counter, then wandered back to his bags. "Where do you want these, Mrs. Fairchild?"

"Just put them in Toby's room," his mom said.

Frankie nodded, scooped up his bags and sauntered out of the kitchen, into the downstairs hallway and started up the stairs.

"You're in a bit of a grumpy mood this morning," his mom said, turning to Toby once Frankie was out of hearing range. She took a bite of her toast. "Are you sure you got enough sleep last night?"

"Yes. I slept fine."

"Then are you feeling all right?"

Leave me alone. Jeez!

"I'm fine."

"Well you can't blame it on PMS," his dad said with a chuckle.

"David," his mom sighed.

"Nothing is wrong," Toby said. "Honest."

His mom patted his left hand. "Okay. If you say so."

Heavy footsteps thudded throughout the house as Frankie made his way back down the stairs.

"Is it just me, or is that kid getting bigger by the day?" his dad said.

"David," his mom snapped. "Don't be so rude. He might hear you."

"Yeah, I think you're right, Dad," Toby said, smiling for the first time that morning.

"Both of you! Cut it out."

Frankie practically skipped into the kitchen; it seemed he was a lot happier with a belly full of Coke and no bags to carry.

"Come and sit down," his mom said.

As Frankie took a seat between Toby and his dad, his mom said, "I suppose you've had breakfast?"

Frankie nodded, and when his eyes fell on Toby's bowl of cereal, his eyes widened. "Jesus, that's more than I have."

"Yeah. Disgusting, isn't it?" his dad said.

"Yeah, well, speaking of disgusting, did ya hear what happened to old Mr. Joseph's house?" Frankie said.

Heat swept through Toby's body. His heart began to pound.

Why did he have to bring it up now? In front of my parents?

He knew they were going to hear about it sooner or later, but he would rather it have been later, when he wasn't around.

"What happened?" his dad asked.

"Somebody egged his house. There were eggshells all over his front yard. Also, there was graffiti all over his house." Frankie grinned, as if remembering some dirty joke.

"That's horrible," his mom said, a frown creasing her face. "Why don't kids just leave that poor man alone?"

"How do you know it was kids?" Toby said.

"Yeah, maybe it was that old bum," Frankie said, eyeing Toby.

"You mean that derelict everyone's been talking about?" his dad said.

"Now how do you know he's a derelict, David?" his mom said. "Have you seen him?"

"Well, no, but from all accounts, he looks like a bum."

"Probably just a drifter, someone backpacking across the country."

"He sure looked like a bum," Frankie remarked.

His mom frowned. "Have you seen him?"

"Yeah, me and Toby saw him down the street yesterday when we were sitting in front of Barb's. He looked dirty, he carried this old bag; he looked homeless."

"Well what did he do?"

"Nothing," Toby said. "He just walked past us."

"He was funny looking, though," Frankie said.

Toby tried to get Frankie's attention, wanting him to stop this talk; it was causing his mom needless worry. But Frankie was too caught up in the moment to notice Toby staring at him.

"Funny, how?" his dad said.

Frankie shrugged. "Just...strange. Kinda like Mr. Joseph."

Toby shivered, remembering the way the stranger had looked at him. He hoped no one noticed his tremor. "Anyway, like I was saying, why do people always blame these pranks on kids?"

"Because they always do things like that," his mom answered. "Especially to poor Mr. Joseph."

"He ain't nothing but a weird old freak," Frankie said, casually.

"Frankie," his mom said. "I'm ashamed to hear you say that."

"Well it's true."

"You do have to admit, he is a bit...unusual," his dad said. "He's basically a hermit. Never talks to anyone. I don't think we've exchanged more than a few words in all the years he's lived here."

"And he looks funny," Frankie added. "He just stares at you with those eyes, real creepy like, and the way his neck is all bent; and that scar...he is a freak."

"It's people like you two that make him too scared to come out of his house," his mom huffed. "No wonder he's a hermit."

"Have you ever talked to him, Nancy?" his dad asked with a smirk.

"That's beside the point," his mom stumbled. "Anyway, it still doesn't take away from the fact that somebody damaged his property. It's disgusting. I'm surprised we didn't hear anything."

"Did you hear anything last night, Toby?" his dad asked.

Toby looked at the table. He shook his head. "I slept like a baby."

"All this destructive behavior last night," his mom said. "Must be the end of school and the start of summer vacation. Makes kids go crazy."

"Last night? Oh, you mean what happened at Jinks Field?"

His mom nodded. "Your mom told you about that?"

Frankie opened his mouth to answer. Toby looked up from the table and glared at Frankie. This time, he noticed Toby's expression. "Ah, yeah, she told me something about it. Not much though."

"So what did this graffiti sprayed over Mr. Joseph's house say?" his dad asked Frankie.

"Eat this, and Freak, and..." Frankie stopped, shifted his gaze between Toby's parents.

"It's okay Frankie, you can say it even if it's rude," his mom said.

"Okay... Fuck off, nigger."

She winced, shook her head. "Horrible."

Hearing what was sprayed on the old man's house made Toby uncomfortable. True, the old fellow was a bit strange, but Toby couldn't share in Frankie's blasé attitude towards the graffiti. He almost felt bad for Mr. Joseph. Jokes between friends was one thing; what Deb and the others had done to Mr. Joseph's house was another. He would love to tell the cops who was responsible. But there was Leah to consider. And his own neck if Dwayne ever found out he had squealed to the cops.

"Let this be a lesson to you boys," his dad said in his most parental voice. "There is no excuse for ignorance and stupidity. Whoever did this to Mr. Joseph's house was both of those things. Treat everyone as equal, regardless of race or religious beliefs. That is, unless a person does something to you that is totally uncalled for, then you can treat them like dirt and beat the ever-loving crap out of them."

Toby and Frankie sniggered.

"Honestly, David," his mom said.

"What? It's the truth. Which reminds me, 'bout time I start teaching you boys how to fight. And I don't mean no pansy-assed wrestling, but real fighting. Boxing. How'd ya like that?"

All concerns regarding Mr. Joseph vanished and Toby was suddenly filled with excitement. For years he had begged his dad to teach him to box, but he had always responded with, "When you're older, son."

Now, it looked like it was finally time. Frankie, sitting beside Toby, looked just as excited.

Toby's dad used to be an amateur boxer. While studying accounting at university, he had joined the boxing team. His own father had taught him a few moves, so he already knew how to handle himself. But, as he had told Toby numerous times: "Fighting inside the ring is a lot different than fighting on the streets." Within a year he was State Amateur Middleweight Champion.

He had defended the title two years running. He reckoned he could've turned pro, but he was a strong believer in education, and, as he had drummed into Toby, strength and athletic prowess doesn't last; a good education and knowledge does. So, following his own advice, he stayed in college, continued to box as an amateur, but never tried to make it in the pro circuit.

Toby had heard the story countless times. Toby liked watching boxing on ESPN, though, unbeknownst to his dad, he was more inclined towards the martial arts, like Kung-Fu and Karate. Some of his favorite movies were the old Bruce Lee chop-sockys, and the newer Jackie Chan spectacles. He often day-dreamed he was a Kung-Fu master, one that could fly twenty-feet in the air and do a spinning round-house kick. Then he would show Dwayne Marcos who was boss.

But boxing was cool. Just as long as he learned how to punch properly, that was fine by him.

"How about we start tomorrow? After your big campout? That is, unless you men will be too tired."

"No way," Frankie said.

"Yeah, we'll be fine."

"Then it's settled," his dad said with a nod. "Tomorrow I'll start teaching you boys how to box."

"Hey, I thought you said we were men," Toby said.

"Well, you're not," his mom said. "And I don't want you two going around picking fights. Boxing is for self-defense only. It's not a license to fight."

"You're taking all of the fun out of it, Nancy," his dad said.

"Can we use the bag?" Toby asked.

"Yeah, can we use the bag?" Frankie repeated.

His father nodded. "I'll set it up today while you two are setting up the tent."

Toby and Frankie exchanged enormous grins.

"Come on," Toby said, getting to his feet. "Let's get down to the store."

Frankie nodded, skidding his chair back as he stood.

"You haven't brushed your teeth young man, or cleaned up this mess."

"I'll do them when I get back," Toby told his mom.

"Are you sure?"

"Yes."

His dad huffed. "I wouldn't count on Toby's word being any good."

"I promise I will brush my teeth and clean up when I get back."

"Well, that's good enough for me," his dad said.

"Okay," said his mom. "Just don't go buying too much junk food."

"We won't," Toby said. "We'll just get some carrots, a few apples and a pumpkin."

"And don't forget the bag of Brussels sprouts," Frankie chuckled.

"Pair of comedians," his dad said.

His mom couldn't hide her smile. Still, she was able to keep her voice even and semi-serious when she said, "I mean it guys, don't go overboard. And be careful of strangers."

"Jeez, Mom, we're not five years old," Toby said as he headed for the back door, Frankie following behind.

"I know, I'm sorry. But you heard me about the junk food? Not too much?"

"Yes," Toby said.

Once outside, Toby turned to Frankie. He grinned. "But I didn't promise."

Frankie wasn't kidding about the morning being warm. It wasn't quite nine and already the sun's heat was intense. Toby considered going back inside and retrieving his baseball cap and sunglasses from his room, but decided he couldn't be bothered.

Toby liked the heat, considerably more than he did the cold. Sure, winter had its charms—the snow, open fires, Christmas (which was his favorite holiday)—but the hot weather made him feel alive, eager to be outdoors, and glad to be at an age where nothing mattered except having a good time with friends. School was more of an annoyance than a major headache (though that might change come September), and girls were fascinating, sexy, and mysterious—the heartache was yet to come.

He had the freedom of a young teenager, without the worries of somebody a few years older. Toby couldn't see how life could get any better. He wanted to stay this age forever.

He was feeling these things, not consciously thinking them, when they passed Mr. Joseph's house. The old man hadn't yet cleaned up the mess. Must still be in bed, Toby thought.

Eggshells littered the front lawn, some were even plastered to the walls, stuck there by the now-dry yolks and mucous-like whites. Toby gazed over at the graffiti. ***Eat this!*** and ***Freak!*** were painted on the left-hand wall of the house. On the right was: ***Fuck off NIGGA!!!***

"What'd I tell you," Frankie said. "Cool, huh?"

"It's not cool," Toby said. "Why is it cool? Just because some stupid rumor was spread around doesn't give people the right to do this."

Frankie remained silent for a moment, his gently perspiring face staring intently at Toby. Then he exploded with laughter. A real belly whoop. "Goddamn, Toby! You sound just like your friggin' mother!"

"Fuck you, you tub of lard."

"Why don't you go over and clean the mess up for the old pervert? Then afterwards, you can suck his cock, which is probably crooked like his neck."

Toby felt anger and disappointment towards Frankie. He didn't mind the teasing. He expected it. Hell, he would've checked Frankie's pulse if he hadn't made some wisecrack in response to Toby's sentiments. No, he was upset at how cold Frankie was towards what had happened.

Sure, Toby was freaked out by the old man—had been his whole life. He had also done his fair share of teasing and rumor-spreading and been involved in more than a few harmless pranks over the years. And he did find it unsettling how the old man watched them from his window every morning. But there was something sad and pathetic about him, too. Kind of like some smelly old dog that nobody particularly likes, gets under everyone's feet, yet you still find yourself feeling sorry for it, at times wanting to go over and pet it. Still, you find yourself kicking at it all the same when its mangy body comes too close.

"Don't you think it's kind of mean what they did?" Toby said.

"Mean?" Frankie said. "They just threw a few eggs at his house and wrote some stuff. That's not so bad."

They also killed a chicken and left it on his doorstep, and hung its severed head through the screen door. Oh yeah, and by the way, your dear sister helped write those charming words.

They were a few houses past the old man's when Toby stopped.

"What?" Frankie said, stopping beside him.

Toby looked up and down the street. Pineview was deserted.

"If I tell you something, do you promise not to say a word?"

Frankie's eyes lit up. Whenever somebody started a conversation with the sentence, If I tell you something, do you promise not to say a word, you just knew something good was to follow.

"Yeah, I promise," Frankie said.

"I mean it. If you tell anyone, there's a good chance you'll get your head kicked in by Dwayne Marcos."

"Dwayne Marcos? What's he got to do with anything?"

Toby took a nervous breath. He had wanted all morning to tell somebody about what he had witnessed last night. Needed to get it off his chest. He knew he was taking a risk, but Frankie was his best friend. He told Frankie almost everything. "I saw who did all that stuff to Mr. Joseph's house," he whispered. "I watched it all from my bedroom window."

"I knew it," Frankie said. "I could tell you were holding something back from me. So who was it? Dwayne?"

Toby nodded. "And Sam Bickford and Rusty Helm and Scotty Hammond. Also..." He considered leaving Leah and Debbie out, but he figured Frankie would want to know. "Leah and Deb Mayfour were with them."

Frankie didn't seem surprised. "It figures they would be with those assholes."

"And that's not all," Toby said. "Not only did they throw eggs and graffiti his house, but, get this, they had a live chicken with them."

Frankie chuckled. "Why, so they could throw fresh eggs at his house?"

"No. They killed it."

Frankie blinked. "Holy shit! Why?"

Toby shrugged. "I guess to tie in with the whole biting-off-chicken-heads-every-full-moon rumor."

"What did they do with it?"

"Well, after Sam chopped off its head, he left its body on the front doorstep, then wedged its head through the screen door."

"Cool," Frankie said. "Disgusting, but cool."

"They killed a live chicken," Toby said. "That's fucking cruel."

"Hey, the old pervert was probably going to bite its head off anyway."

"That's bullshit."

"Well even if it is, how do you think the chicken you eat at dinner gets on your plate? Somebody has to kill it—and probably by chopping off its head."

"It's still wrong. Killing an animal just for a joke is wrong."

They resumed walking up the street, Frankie muttering, "Wow," and "Killed a chicken." Suddenly he said, "Hey, I didn't see any chicken."

"The old guy came out when he heard the eggs being thrown and after Dwayne and the others had left, he threw it in the garbage."

"Oh."

Toby saw no point in telling Frankie the truth, that the old man had in fact taken the chicken, including its head, inside. He could imagine Frankie's reaction upon hearing such a thing. The rumor about Mr. Joseph eating live chickens would be absolutely confirmed in his mind.

Hell, maybe that rumor is true, Toby thought.

"And you watched all this from your bedroom window?"

"Uh-huh."

"God, if Dwayne had caught you... if he knew you were watching..."

"That's exactly why you can't say a word to anybody. Because if you do, word will get around, and eventually the cops will find out. And then Dwayne will be really pissed—and not just at me, but at you as well."

Frankie's expression turned solemn. "Yeah you're right," he said. "Holy shit, Toby. I won't say a word."

"Good. I knew I could trust you. Though I can't believe you almost told my parents about last night. They'd flip if they knew what really happened and that I was there."

"Yeah, sorry, I wasn't thinking."

As they walked, turning from Pineview into Bracher, Toby again thought of last night's dream. "I had a weird dream last night," he said to Frankie.

"Yeah, I've had those. So who was it? Gloria? Jessica Alba?"

"I don't mean that kind of dream. I mean strange, like in scary."

"Oh. So what happened?"

"Well, I was in a box, like a coffin. It was completely dark. I tried kicking, but I couldn't escape, and when I screamed, no sound came out of my mouth. Suddenly a hand grabbed me. That's when I woke up."

"Yeah, that is weird. What do you think it means?"

Toby shrugged. "Who knows? Probably nothing. You ever have any dreams like that?"

"Can't say that I have. But you've always been the weird one, so it makes sense you would have weird dreams."

They took the shortcut to Barb's by going through the town square. They strolled along the path that wound past towering oaks and pines, past the white gazebo and park benches, and finally coming out at Main Street.

They were about to cross the street when Toby glanced to his right and saw the stranger. The tall dark man was sitting on one of the benches facing the street, his tatty old bag beside him on the bench. His clothes were dusty and looked to be torn in a number of places. He was just sitting staring at nothing. "I can't believe he's still here," Toby said. "I thought after last night he would've gone as far away from Belford as possible."

Frankie glanced over. "He stayed here in town? Wonder where?"

"By the looks of it, that park bench. Probably safer than staying at Jinks Field. Come on, let's get going before he sees us."

"Why, you scared?" Frankie chuckled as they crossed over Main.

"No, 'cos I hear he likes fat kids, so that leaves me in the clear."

"Ha ha, very funny."

They entered Barb's.

"Hi, boys," Mrs. Stein said from behind the counter.

"Hey, Mrs. Stein," Toby called, yanking one of the old wire baskets from the pile near the door.

"Hey," Frankie said, picking up a second basket.

"You two are in here mighty early. I don't think I've ever seen either of you in here before eleven."

"I guess there's a first time for everything," Toby said.

Mrs. Stein chuckled and went back to pricing stock.

Except for Mrs. Parker, over by the canned goods, the store was empty.

Toby and Frankie hurried over to their favorite aisle.

"Okay. How much you got?" Toby asked.

"Ten bucks," Frankie said.

"That all?"

Frankie shrugged.

"Okay, I have twenty. So that means we have thirty bucks to spend on junk food."

They looked at each other, avaricious grins on their young faces. This was as close to Heaven as fourteen-year-old boys got.

Both had earned money doing odd jobs: mowing lawns, painting fences (which was Toby's favorite job, *Tom Sawyer* being one of his favorite books), raking leaves, shoveling snow. Sometimes they got ten dollars for their day's work. Often it was only five. It wasn't much, but at their age they didn't have much to spend it on, aside from junk food and baseball cards.

"Let's begin," Frankie said.

Toby nodded.

As they started picking out their junk food of choice, the bell that signaled the arrival or departure of a customer jingled. Toby ignored it, figuring it was just Mrs. Parker leaving.

Toby had thrown a few Mr. Goodbars and Sugar Daddys into his basket when he heard Mrs. Parker say, very quietly, "Good morning, Mr. Joseph."

Toby froze.

"Morning," the old man replied in an even softer voice.

Toby gazed over at Frankie. He was busy scanning the assortment of confectionary, occasionally grabbing something off the shelf and dumping it into his basket like a girl picking flowers in a meadow.

There was another jingle as Mrs. Parker left the store. "Good morning," Mrs. Stein said to Mr. Joseph.

"Morning," he greeted Mrs. Stein.

Moving carefully, trying to make as little noise as possible, Toby set down his basket and crept to the end of the aisle. He peered around the boxes of Corn Flakes, saw Mr. Joseph disappear down the aisle two down from where Toby was standing—the one containing cleaning products.

Soon the old man reappeared, shambling up to the counter, basket filled with bags of cloths and various bottles. It never ceased to amaze Toby how large Mr. Joseph was. He wasn't fat or rippled with muscle; far from it. He was lean, wiry—but he was tall. He would've been even taller if his neck was straight.

"Hey, what ya doing?"

Toby jumped. He whirled around and put an index finger to his pursed lips.

Frankie frowned. "Told ya you're weird."

Toby turned back. At the counter Mr. Joseph and Mrs. Stein were chatting.

"Holy shit. When did he arrive?" Frankie was now peering over Toby's shoulder, his body pressed against Toby's back. "Wonder what he's buying. I'll bet it's stuff to clean the egg and graffiti off his house."

"Sshhh," Toby said.

Once Mrs. Stein had scanned his items, the old man paid, said goodbye to Mrs. Stein ("I'll see you Monday," Mrs. Stein said), and as he picked up his two bags and turned and headed for the door, Toby and Frankie scurried back to the candy aisle. Soon the bell jingled.

"That was close," Frankie said. "If he had caught us watching, we'd probably end up like that chicken."

Ignoring Frankie's comment, Toby continued filling his basket with junk food.

Soon they had what they estimated to be about thirty dollars' worth of chocolate, chips, cookies, soda and other assorted snacks.

When they dumped the contents of their baskets onto the counter, Mrs. Stein stared wide-eyed at the mountain of junk food. "You two are going to be sick if you eat all that."

"We'll manage," Frankie said, beaming. "Don't you worry 'bout that."

"Do your parents know you're buying this much junk food?"

"Of course," Toby answered before Frankie opened his trap and ruined everything. "They weren't very happy about it, but they said it's our money and our stomachs."

"Never mind those things. I'm worried about your teeth!" She began ringing up their items. "So would I be right in guessing that you boys are having a sleepover?"

Toby cringed at the word sleepover—it sounded so immature, so... girlie.

"Sort of. We're camping out in my backyard."

"I see. Perfect weather for it."

"Say, what did that old weirdo buy?" Frankie said. "Was it cleaning products?"

Mrs. Stein frowned. "That's none of your business, Franklin. And he's not a weirdo. Jack's a harmless old man. And he's a damn good worker, too"

Hearing someone refer to Mr. Joseph by his Christian name always sounded odd to Toby—it was like they were talking about someone else, someone... normal.

"You kids are just awful to him. I've heard about all the pranks; the late night phone calls, the trash left on his property, ringing his doorbell in the middle of the night." She clicked her tongue and shook her head.

That was just a few of the many things the kids in Belford had done to Mr. Joseph over the years. One time, when Toby was seven, a fire was lit in the old man's front yard. The blaze had burned some bushes and scorched the grass, but was put out before it could cause any real damage. They never did find out who started the fire.

Another time, about three years ago, somebody littered the old man's front yard with manure. They didn't just scatter a small pile over the grass—they covered most of the lawn and even some of the porch in shit. All of Pineview woke the next morning to the stench of fresh horse manure.

A junior at Holt High named Harold Watkins was nabbed for the offense when the jerk, who had done it on a dare, was found with his pickup littered with manure and stinking to high heaven. He confessed immediately.

"Yeah, but the old pervert deserves it," Frankie said. "Speaking of perverts, did you see that old bum sitting in the park?"

Mrs. Stein huffed. "He's just a poor man down on his luck Franklin. And yes, I saw him this morning as I was opening up. As a matter of fact, I went out and offered him something to eat and drink, poor man looked like he could do with a good feed, and a good wash, but he refused. He said thanks, but no thanks. I was shocked, let me tell you."

"Weirdo," Frankie muttered. "Refusing a free feed. What do you think he wants?"

Mrs. Stein shrugged. "He didn't say." She gazed over their heads. "Anyway, looks like he's gone now."

Both Toby and Frankie turned and looked out the window. Sure enough, the park bench the man had been sitting on was empty. They turned back. "He was there just before," Toby said.

"He must be moving on to the next town. Gypsies do that, you know."

Toby knew that gypsy was just a polite term for tramp, bum, or hobo.

"Anyway, your groceries come to $27.94."

Toby and Frankie handed Mrs. Stein the money.

After ringing up the sale, Mrs. Stein handed Toby the small amount of change and he pocketed the money—he had, after all, paid for the majority of the food and drink.

"You two have fun tonight. But don't go getting sick."

"We will, and we won't," Toby said and smiled.

Mrs. Stein smiled back. Toby noticed her yellow teeth.

They grabbed their bags of goodies, said goodbye to Mrs. Stein, and headed out of Barb's Convenience Store.

CHAPTER FOUR

"How are we going to get all this junk food past your mom?" Frankie said the moment they stepped outside.

Toby looked down at the two bags he was carrying, then at the bag Frankie was holding, the one containing the bottles of Coke and Dr. Pepper. One look at all this, and his mom would freak out.

"We should've thought about that before we left," Toby sighed. Instead, he and Frankie had been too eager to get down to the store to buy as much junk food as their slim wallets allowed. "You should've brought your backpack. We could've hidden some of the food in there."

"Well, we don't have my backpack, so what are we going to do? Your mom's going to be home all day, isn't she?"

Toby nodded. "Dad won't care. As long as we give him some chocolate, he'll keep quiet. But Mom, she'll probably take most of the food back to the store."

Standing in front of Barb's, it occurred to Toby that one of his mother's work colleagues might spot him and Frankie, who in turn would inform his mom how they had seen Toby and his friend down the street with bags full of junk food.

Sometimes he hated living in a small town.

As they stood, thinking, Toby noticed the Reverend Henry Wakefield strolling along the street. He had a kind smile as he stopped and chatted briefly to passersby, and when he saw Toby and Frankie he gave them a small wave. Toby waved back and the Reverend headed in their direction.

Toby liked the Reverend Henry Wakefield, he was one of the few adults he could share a joke with, feel relaxed around—surprising, considering he was a man of God. Toby had always thought all ultra-religious people were stale, boring old farts. He guessed Pastor Wakefield was the exception.

"Morning boys," the Reverend said, stopping just short of them, pleasant smile never faltering.

"Hey Rev," Toby said, smiling.

"Um, hey," Frankie said, facing the Reverend, a look of surprise on his face. Frankie never went to church; Suzie didn't have a religious bone in her ample body, so Frankie always acted nervously around religious people such as Pastor Wakefield, which Toby found amusing.

Henry Wakefield was a tall man, a few inches over six feet, and though he was lean, he was strong. His eyes were narrow-set, warm, and his nose jutted out just a shade too much for his angular face. He had short dark hair that was dusted with gray, though he still looked ten years younger than his real age of forty. This morning he was wearing loose fitting pants and a short-sleeved purple shirt.

"So what has got you two up this early? Helping your parents with the shopping?"

Toby shook his head. "No, me and Frankie are having a campout tonight in my backyard."

"I see. So buying too much junk food?"

"Yeah," Toby said, knowing this information wouldn't get back to his mom—the Reverend wasn't that kind of person.

"Well not that much junk food," Frankie said, stumbling over his words. "After all, gluttony is one of the Seven Deadly Sins, right?"

"Relax, Frankie, I'm sure God understands," the Reverend said. "Jesus was young once, too, though I don't think they had Ho-Hos back in His day."

Toby chuckled. Frankie laughed, too, though nervously.

"So, will I see you at church tomorrow?" the Reverend asked Toby.

"Yeah, I can't wait," Toby huffed.

"Good, because I'll be yammering on about sex and violence—you know, all the good stuff from the Bible."

"Really?" Frankie said.

Toby shook his head. "He was only kidding."

The Reverend raised his eyebrows. "You think so, huh?"

"I know so."

"Well, maybe Frankie had better come tomorrow and find out."

"Maybe I will," Frankie said. "If you're going to be talking about sex and violence, I mean."

The Reverend couldn't help but chuckle. "I'm sorry Frankie, I shouldn't laugh. But Toby's right, I was only kidding. I don't want you to start spreading nasty rumors that Christianity is full of sex and violence. That would only stir the natives, and we wouldn't want that."

"Huh?"

"He means, people would start thinking that all the Reverend talks about is sex and violence during mass."

"But that would be cool. I'd go to church if the Reverend talked about sex and violence."

"I'm sure we'd get a lot more people attending if that were the case. But I'm sorry to disappoint you, Frankie. All I talk about is boring stuff like plagues, and the fires of Hell, and people being nailed to crosses and left to rot out in the sun."

"Now I know you're jerking me around," Frankie said.

The Reverend winked at Toby, then he said to Frankie, "Guilty as charged."

"Yeah, if church was all about that stuff, think I would complain about going all the time?" Toby said.

Frankie shook his head. "Guess not."

The Reverend smiled. "Well, don't want to hold you guys up any longer. I guess you've still got to get ready for your campout?"

"Yeah. We still have to put up the tent."

"Good to hear. Idle hands and all that..."

"Hey, that was a cool movie," Frankie said. "Jessica Alba was smoking..." Frankie suddenly looked like he had just dropped the F bomb in front of his grandmother. "Sorry, Reverend."

"What for? I agree, Jessica Alba is smoking hot. Just don't tell my wife I said that."

"I won't," he said, earnestly.

Toby shook his head again.

To Toby, the Reverend said: "I'll see you tomorrow." To Frankie: "And I'll be seeing you next time I talk about Jessica Alba running amok around a summer camp with a chainsaw. See you later, boys."

The Reverend continued walking along the street.

"You know, for a priest he's pretty cool," Frankie said.

"Yeah," Toby agreed.

"I didn't make a complete fool of myself, did I? I always say stupid things when I'm around priests and nuns."

Toby looked at Frankie. "When were you ever around nuns?"

Frankie said, "I was around a bunch of nuns years ago. I remember saying something like, 'Hey, you don't waddle like penguins'."

Toby smiled. "Yeah, that sounds like something you'd say."

"So did I?"

"Huh?"

"Make a fool of myself around the Reverend Wakefield?"

"Yeah, but if you have to make a fool of yourself around someone, he's the one you want to do it around."

"Yeah, he is pretty cool. He almost makes me want to go to church. So," Frankie sighed. "What're we going to do about our problem? You're the brain, Toby. Do we try and sneak around to the tree house and dump the bags and hope your mom doesn't see?"

Toby set his bags down. "It's too risky. Do you have any more bags at home?"

"What, like backpacks?"

"Nah, like suitcases. Of course backpacks."

"Yeah, I think so. Some old ones. Why? You wanna go back to my place and put the food in another bag?"

Toby shrugged. "Might work."

"Yeah, but wouldn't it be suspicious? I mean, we go out to the store empty handed, and we come back with a backpack?"

"I guess you're right. For once."

"Hey, dorks. Whatcha doing?"

Toby groaned. He wasn't in the mood for Warrick this morning.

"Quick, let's run," Frankie muttered.

They turned and faced Warrick. "What are you, stalking us Warrick?" Toby said.

"Yeah, right. So you get away all right last night, Fairchild?"

"Sure. You?"

"Of course. It'll be a cold day in hell when the cops catch this little black duck. But it was a wild time, huh? Wilmont, you missed out big-time." Warrick sported a clownish grin, and in the bright morning sun, his army of pimples glistened like tiny rubies.

"Yeah, Toby told me about it."

"So where were you? At home, jerking off?"

"In your dreams, Warrick."

Still grinning, Warrick said, "Well, it was fun while it lasted. We showed that nigger a thing or two. Pity the cops had to spoil the party."

"Don't think the bum would agree with you," Toby said.

"Hey, that old pervert got what he deserved. Spying on a couple of teenagers. Anyway, he wasn't hurt—well, not badly. It was all in good fun."

Toby huffed.

Warrick frowned at Toby. "So anyway, you hear that a few people got charged?"

"With what?"

"Disturbing the peace, drinking while underage, drinking alcohol in public. Nothing major. The cops have no idea what really was going down. Nobody blabbed about the bum being there. Somehow he managed to escape. Lucky for him; the cops would've definitely placed him in jail for vagrancy if they had caught him. You know, if I were in charge of this town, I'd have kicked him out yesterday, when he first arrived. We don't need stanky bums clogging up our streets."

"You can't kick a person out just for smelling," Toby said. "If that were true, you would have been gone a long time ago."

Warrick gave Toby the one-fingered salute. "Still, I say one bum today, ten next week, and then before you know it, the whole town'll be overrun with hobos. Makes me sick just thinking about it."

"We think he slept the night in the town square," Frankie said.

"No shit?" Warrick glanced over towards the park. "I would've thought for sure he would've left town after last night."

"That's what I said," Toby told Warrick.

"Wonder if he's still in there?"

"He's gone," Toby said.

"How do you know?"

"We saw him sitting on the bench," Frankie said. "Before we went into Barb's. Now, he's gone."

"Probably waiting at your house, Warrick, so he can give you some career advice."

"Hardy-fucking-har, Fairchild. Anyone ever tell you you're about as funny as a heart attack? But shit, if he did sleep in the square, someone should've called the cops, then he would've been told to hit the road, or maybe even put in jail. Anyway, I just hope he got crapped on by pigeons." Warrick cackled.

"If someone had called the cops, then maybe the hobo would've told them all about what happened. You ever thought about that?"

Warrick shrugged. "Nah, he wouldn't say anything. Then it'd come out that he was perving on some kids. Besides, as if the cops would believe a stanky old nigger bum. They would think he was just crazy." Warrick nodded down at the bags Toby and Frankie were holding. "So when did you two get married?"

"Last week," Toby said.

"And I wasn't invited?"

"As if we'd invite you," Frankie said.

"Well I'm hurt. Really. So, which one's the butt-fucker, and which one gets his butt fucked?"

"Get lost, Warrick," Toby said.

"Let me think," Warrick continued, apparently as deaf as he was crude. "Who would be the male, and who would be the bitch. I reckon that Fairchild would be the prissy one, and Wilmont would be the big hairy macho fag."

"What the hell do you want?" Frankie said. "We've wasted enough time standing here listening to your bullshit."

"Yeah, what do you want?" Toby said.

Warrick placed the back of his right hand across his forehead and rolled his head back. "Oh, how can I go on?" he said in a high Southern accent. "Toby and Franklin don't wish to speak to little ole me."

"Finally he gets the message," Frankie said.

Warrick took his hand away from his head and nodded at the bags. "Seriously, what is all that food for? You guys having a party?"

"No," Toby answered, a little too quickly.

A wry grin spread across Warrick's bony, acne-coated face. "You're lying Fairchild. I can always tell when you're lying."

"Am not. This is for... ah..."

"Our parents," Frankie cut in. "They're having a barbecue tomorrow."

It was a good save on Frankie's part. Usually he wasn't very good at telling lies. But Warrick's grin remained, so maybe it wasn't such a good lie after all. Warrick shook his head. "Bullshit. Parents never eat that much junk food. And they always buy the food themselves. They never trust their kids to buy the right kinds of foods."

"Your parents maybe," Toby said. "But not ours."

Warrick sighed. "Ah, the stupidity of youth."

"You can talk. You're the poster child for stupidity."

Warrick scowled at Frankie. "Fuck you, Wilmont. I'm smarter than you any day of the week."

"As if," Frankie huffed.

The thing was, even though Warrick acted like an ass, Toby knew that under all that crudeness and sarcasm, he really was a smart guy.

"I'll tell you what. If you tell me what you guys are really up to, I'll tell you the latest bit of news."

This was Warrick's usual way of getting people to include him—and for people to be nice to him. If they didn't want to see his latest trick, or hear his latest dirty joke, he would bribe them, usually with gossip that, somehow, only he knew about.

"Are you talking about what happened to Mr. Joseph's house?" Toby said.

The air was knocked out of Warrick's bluster. "Um, yeah. How'd you know?"

Toby laughed. "I practically live right across the street to him, dumbass."

"Well, I bet you haven't heard the other bit of news."

"What other news?"

The smugness returned to Warrick's face. He waved an index finger. "Uh-uh. Not until you tell me what you guys have planned."

"We told you, our parents are having a barbecue," Toby said, hoping to call Warrick's bluff.

Warrick shrugged, started turning away. "Have it your way. But you guys are never going to believe..."

"Okay, we're having a sleepover," Frankie blurted.

Toby winced.

Good one, Frankie...

"That's more like it," Warrick said, turning back. "A sleepover, hey? How fucking gay." He smiled to himself.

"Yeah, well, now you know what we're doing, how about telling us this other bit of news?"

"All in good time, Fairchild. Now, where is this little fag party being held? Yours or Wilmont's place?"

"We'll give you one guess. If you guess right, we'll tell you," Toby said.

"Well, using my incredible powers of deduction, I'm guessing the sleepover is at Fairchild's place."

"Why do you think that?" Toby said.

"Not only is your backyard bigger, but you have a tree house, and I know you pussies will want to use it. So, am I right?"

"Yeah," Toby muttered. "You're a genius. Anyway, we've told you what you want to know. Now tell us this amazing bit of news."

"I don't know whether I want to, now."

"Come on, just tell us," Frankie said.

"Okay, I'll tell you. Only because I like you guys so much." Warrick liked being an asshole; but he liked spreading gossip more. He leaned in close. He smelled like cheese and pimple cream. "Dwayne Marcos and his gang got hit with water bombs yesterday after school. Well, it was Dwayne's car, but it amounts to the same thing."

Silence hung in the air like a lead balloon. Toby knew he had to speak before Frankie said something stupid like, "Yeah, we know. We were the ones who did it."

"No shit," Toby said, feigning surprise. "Are you kidding?"

"I spoke to Dwayne and the guys after it happened. They told me all about it. They were angry as hell, especially Dwayne."

Warrick was on good terms with Dwayne and his goons—about as good as a kid from junior high can be. They seemed to like his stupid antics and crude humor.

"Wow," Frankie said. "So he was really angry, huh?"

"Fucking A. Said whenever he found out who had bombed his car, he and his gang were going to make them pay. But he told me not to tell anyone about it, okay? He's kinda embarrassed about the whole thing."

Toby nodded. "Sure. I won't tell a soul."

"Frankie?"

"Me neither. You can be sure of that. So do they have any idea who did it?"

Warrick shook his head.

"Well, we'd better be going," Toby announced. "See ya 'round, Warrick."

Toby picked up his bags and turned to leave. He wanted to be away from Warrick Coleman, away from talk of the water bombing incident. He feared either Frankie would somehow let it slip that they were the ones responsible, or Warrick would pick up on their guilt—either way would land them in deep shit.

"Have fun at your little tea party," Warrick said. "Say, Fairchild, I didn't think your mommy would allow you to buy all that junk food?"

Toby turned back around. "Sure. As long as we pay for it, she doesn't care."

"Really? That's not the Mrs. Fairchild I know."

"What the hell would you know about Toby's mom?" Frankie said.

"I know she wears blue G-strings, and that she has a birth mark right above her pubic hair."

Toby felt a rush of anger and disgust. "Shut the hell up, Warrick."

“What’re you going to do? Run home and cry to mommy?”

For some reason, Warrick was being cruder and meaner than usual. Maybe he was spending too much time around Dwayne Marcos.

“Just fuck off and leave us alone,” Toby said.

“Come on, Fairchild, I was only fucking with ya. Don’t be such a crybaby.”

“Don’t be such a prick,” Frankie countered.

Toby didn’t need this. He didn’t want his day ruined by Warrick Coleman. “Come on Frankie, let’s go,” Toby said and they turned to leave.

Warrick said: “I can help sneak that food past your mom.”

Toby and Frankie halted. “What are you talking about?” Toby said, facing Warrick.

“I know your mom would never allow you to have all that junk food. So, you have a problem. Am I right?”

Toby hated it when Warrick displayed some of that usually dormant intelligence—it made him more dangerous. “So what if you are?”

“So I can get the food into your tree house without your mom finding out.”

Toby eyed Warrick with suspicion. “What are you proposing...and what do you want in return?”

“Who says I want anything? Other than to help out two of my best buds.”

“Cut the crap,” Frankie said.

Face bursting with cunning glee, Warrick said, “Okay, here’s what I propose.”

When Toby and Frankie walked into the kitchen, Toby’s mom was in the middle of making a pecan pie. It was his dad’s favorite. Toby hated pecan pie.

“Hi boys. What did you buy? Not too much junk food I hope.”

“Nah. Just a few things,” Toby said. He and Frankie placed the two bags on top of the kitchen table—which, Toby noticed, had since been cleaned. His mom rinsed her hands then wandered over, just as Toby was taking out the bottle of Dr. Pepper. He handed it to Frankie.

"No Coke?"

"We still have some in the fridge," Toby said. "I'll just finish that off."

"Good boy. Sensible thinking." She turned to Frankie, who was putting the bottle of Dr. Pepper in the fridge. "I don't know how you can drink that stuff. Tastes like cough medicine."

"Mom says the same thing," Frankie said.

His mom peered inside the second bag. "I'm impressed," she said. "I thought you two would've bought at least twice this much."

Toby and Frankie exchanged a knowing glance.

"So, have we passed inspection?" Toby said.

His mom smiled and nodded. "Sure. Now, after you go and clean your teeth like you promised, go on out and see your father. He's in the garage."

"You wait here, Frankie. I'll be back in a minute," Toby said and as he left the kitchen, he turned and said, "Thanks for cleaning the table, mom."

She smiled and shook her head.

"I've found all the tent parts for you," Toby's dad said when Toby and Frankie entered the cluttered garage. Tent pegs, poles and the tent itself were scattered over the concrete floor. "Saves you two from trying to find it all. God knows I had trouble finding everything." He wiped his hands on the sides of his jeans, straightened and nodded to the bag Toby was holding. "What's in the bag?"

"Just some food," Toby said.

"Ooh, anything for me?" His dad walked over. His face was smudged with dirt and his hair mussed.

Although they no longer had to bribe his dad, Toby figured they had more than enough food, so giving up a few chocolate bars wasn't too painful. Toby dipped into the bag and pulled out a Twix and a 5th Avenue. He handed them to his dad.

"Thanks kid. Now, there's a mallet on top of the toolbox. If you need any help putting up the tent, just give me a yell."

"We'll be fine, Dad," Toby said.

"Yeah, we're the tent experts."

"Okay. Well, I'll be in here putting up the punching bag if you need me," his dad said as he tore open the Twix bar and took a bite.

"Come on," Toby said and he and Frankie left the shadows of the garage and stepped back out into the brightness of the morning. They headed over to the elm that loomed like a sentry over the house. With bag in hand, Toby started up the ladder (which was really just a series of planks nailed to the trunk).

When he reached the top of the ladder, he pushed open the trap door, then climbed the rest of the way up, into the tree house. Frankie followed, closing the trap door as he climbed inside.

"Want me to bolt it?" Frankie asked.

"Nah, we won't be up here very long."

The bolt on the trap door had been his mom's idea—she didn't want the door left open for someone to fall through. But Toby liked her suggestion—it gave them more privacy.

Toby placed the bag of candy down as Frankie wandered over to the window overlooking the next door neighbor's yard. Toby and his dad had hung thick canvas sheets over the two windows, mostly to combat the rain, but also for privacy. Currently, due to the warm, dry weather, the canvas sheets were tied with ropes to metal pegs on either side of the windows.

"This is the life," Frankie mused and Toby knew exactly how he felt. The tree house was their own special place, a place where they could hide away from the world and talk about anything, without having to worry about the invading eyes and ears of adults. Toby felt a sense of place up here in the roughly-made house of wood and nails. He loved the fact that he and his dad had made it with their own hands—about five years ago now—and he loved that he could share it with his best friend. But of course he would never voice these feelings. So instead he squeezed out a fart.

"Bombing raid!" Frankie yelled. "Take cover!"

"And there's plenty more where that came from," Toby laughed.

A foul odor filled the tree house.

Standing by the window, Frankie scrunched up his face. "Jesus, Toby. That stinks! What did ya have for breakfast? Baked beans and rotten eggs?"

"I don't think it smells that bad," Toby said.

"Well, then you're fucked in the head."

"Talking about being fucked in the head, what do you think Warrick has in mind?"

"Who knows," Frankie said. "Probably have us do his homework all throughout high school or something."

"Well he can forget that. What he's doing isn't that big of a deal. It's not like he's saving us from getting beaten up by Dwayne."

"Yeah, well, after tomorrow, we won't have to worry about getting beaten up by Dwayne." Frankie threw a few clumsy punches.

"It takes a lot longer than one day to become a boxer," Toby said.

"Yeah but I'm super good. Like Muhammad Ali. I'm gonna float like a butterfly and sting like a bee!" He threw some more punches.

"More like float like an elephant and sting like a poodle."

"I bet I'm better than you."

"Yeah, we'll just see." Toby headed for the trap door. "Let's try and get the tent up before lunch."

Frankie followed. He stopped and glanced back at the bag. "You sure the chocolates will be okay up here?"

"Sure. This place keeps pretty cool." The elm gave good shade. "And if they do melt, we'll just make chocolate milkshakes."

As Toby headed back down the ladder, he heard Frankie drone: "Hmmm, chocolate milkshake," and Toby smiled.

It took them almost three hours to put up the tent. During that time the day had warmed up considerably and Toby's dad had long since set up the punching bag. Toby hammered the last peg into the ground and standing back, said to Frankie, "Finished at last."

"Thank Christ," Frankie said, wiping his brow.

"Blasphemy will get you everywhere."

Toby turned to see his dad standing behind them, admiring their work. "See? Told you we could do it."

"Yeah. And it only took you guys half the day."

"It's only one o'clock."

"Looks good, though, huh?" Frankie said.

Toby's dad nodded slowly. "Yeah, not bad. Not bad at all. Well done guys. Now come inside. You two deserve some food and a nice cold drink."

"Hey, that sounds good," Frankie said. "My stomach totally agrees with you Mr. Fairchild."

"Somehow that doesn't surprise me," Toby's dad said, and laughed.

Toby and Frankie were up in the tree house, polishing off the half a dozen ham and salad sandwiches that Toby's mom had made, when she called out: "Toby! Warrick Coleman is here."

Toby checked his watch - 1:30 on the dot. "He's right on time," he muttered. He stood up and leaned out the window that faced the back door. "Warrick? What's he doing here?"

His mom, standing by the back door, raised both hands in the air. "I don't know. Come over to play?"

His mom still used terms like "play". Sometimes Toby wondered if she knew he was fourteen years old, not four.

"Okay, send him out," Toby called.

His mom headed back inside. Toby sat back on the rug that covered most of the floor of the tree house. "Here goes nothing," Toby said and took a drink of Coke.

"I reckon we should grab the bag off him then push him down the ladder."

Toby chuckled. "You think he's eaten any of our food?"

"I bet you he has," Frankie said. "Maybe that's his reward."

Toby shook his head. "I doubt it. Warrick will want something more than free food."

"Hey! Are you guys up there?"

Toby flinched at the sound of Warrick's voice.

"Let's pretend we're not here," Frankie whispered.

Toby liked that idea, but he also wanted the food they had bought. So he stood up and headed back to the window. "Yeah, we're here." He left the window, strode over to the trap door and slid back the bolt, then sat back down.

"Let's try and get rid of him as quickly as possible," Toby said. "I don't want my Saturday ruined by him."

The trap door flung open.

"How nice of you to make it," Frankie said and tucked into the last of the ham and salad sandwiches.

"Frankie stuffing his face. Gee, what a surprise."

"Fuck you," Frankie mumbled, though it actually came out as: "Uck ou."

"That's no way to greet your new best friend. Especially after I brought you your food and all." Warrick was standing by the now closed trap door, a green backpack dangling from his right hand.

"Which I bet you ate most of," Toby said.

"Never," Warrick said. "When I make a deal with someone, I keep it."

"Not eating the food was never part of the deal," Toby said.

"Ah, right you are. But I am a man of honor and pride. Besides, how would I be able to get what I wanted from you boys if I went ahead and consumed the very goods I was making the deal with?"

Toby frowned. "You talk a lot of shit, you know that?"

Warrick shrugged and gazed around the tree house. "So this is the infamous Fairchild treehouse. It's smaller than I imagined. Where's the en-suite?"

"Get bent. Now, show us the food. I want to make sure that you really didn't eat any of it."

"Aren't you going to give me the grand tour first?"

Toby sighed. "Okay. There's a window. And over there is another window. And, oh look, there is the trap door. Which, if you don't hurry up and give us the fucking candy, you'll find yourself falling through headfirst."

Frankie chortled, spitting out bits of sandwich.

Warrick shook his head. "You're a regular Jim Carrey, Fairchild. Okay, I'll give you your food. But first, my payoff."

Toby looked at Frankie, grimaced, then got to his feet. Judging by Warrick's remark, Toby figured he wanted money. He faced Warrick. "We don't have much money, Warrick. And I'm not going to give you all of my savings."

"Or a blowjob," Frankie said.

Warrick grinned. "How did you know, Wilmont?"

"It's all over town. You love to suck guys' cocks."

"Well I can't very well suck girls' cocks, now can I?"

"You know what I meant," Frankie said, looking embarrassed.

"Enough of this shit," Toby said. "Tell us how much money you want, Warrick."

"My, my, aren't we touchy today," Warrick said. "Anyway, who said anything about money? I don't need any money. What I want I steal. What I don't want I steal. I have no use for money."

It dawned on Toby then that whatever it was that Warrick wanted in exchange for bringing the rest of the junk food was going to be bad. His gut went all squirmy and his heart started beating faster. Maybe, deep down, he knew what Warrick was going to ask. Maybe he had known it all along; he just couldn't bear to think about it.

"I want to stay tonight. Camp out with you two dweebs."

"No way," Toby said. "Not a chance. Forget it."

"Yeah, not on your life," Frankie said.

"I helped you guys by bringing your food over. You owe me."

"Yeah, we owe you," Toby said. "But not that much.

"So this is the thanks I get," Warrick huffed, "for risking my ass for you two."

Toby choked out a laugh. "Risking your ass? You sneaked some food over. The only person you had to worry about was my mom. The worst she could do was tell you off. And you think that's worth letting you camp with us tonight?"

"You're damn right," Warrick said. "Hell, it might even be fun."

"Not for us it won't be," Frankie said. "Anyway, why do you want to spend the night camping with us? We don't even like you."

Warrick's face saddened and for what Toby thought might be the first time, Warrick looked hurt. He actually resembled a human being with feelings.

Good one, Frankie. Why'd ya have to say that for?

Toby didn't want Warrick to stay any more than Frankie, but that didn't mean he hated the guy. "That's not true," he said and frowned at Frankie. Frankie shrugged and mouthed *What?* Toby turned back. "Of course we like you, it's just...we've had this night planned for a long time. Just the two of us. And besides, the tent is only big enough for two people."

Warrick still looked dejected. "Fuck you both. I brought your food over, helped you guys out. I have a mind to go to your mom and tell her..."

"No," Toby cried. "Don't tell my mom. Come on, Warrick. Sure you can be annoying sometimes, but that doesn't mean we hate you. Does it Frankie?" Toby glared at Frankie, hoping he'd get the message.

Frankie held an expression that said *Of course I hate him. Why do we care if he knows that?* But when he saw the look on Toby's face, he nodded and said, "Yeah, I was only kidding around. I don't hate you."

Warrick shrugged. "Whatever. Anyway, here is your junk." He zipped open the bag and started pulling out the various items of junk food, including the second bottles of Coke and Dr. Pepper.

Toby scanned the items—everything was accounted for. Warrick had been telling the truth when he said he hadn't eaten any of their snacks.

"Hey, thanks," Toby said. "We really appreciate it. Now, what do you want in return? Aside from staying over? Money? Your homework done? Hell, some of the candy?" Toby felt rotten. In the back of his mind he wondered if this was all a ruse put on by Warrick to get them to accept his proposition. But he had never seen Warrick this upset, so maybe he was for real.

"You guys know what I want," Warrick said.

"Anything but that," Frankie said.

The sides of Warrick's mouth curled. "Let me show you guys something that may change your mind."

"Nothing will change our mind," Frankie said.

Warrick dug into his open backpack. "I think this will."

Toby watched with a mixture of morbid curiosity and apprehension. Knowing Warrick, Toby expected just about anything to be inside that bag. Possible items that ran through Toby's mind were: Playboy magazines; a gun; a severed hand; evidence that old Mr. Joseph was in fact the devil. But what came out of Warrick Coleman's backpack was none of those things.

When the pale, skeleton-thin kid with the pimply face pulled out a six pack of Coors and placed it on the tree house rug, Toby exclaimed, "Wow!"

"Bitchin'," Frankie said, eyes suddenly the size of dinner plates. "Where did ya get that from?"

Warrick was grinning stupidly. Somewhere in Toby's mind was the thought: He had this planned all along. He knew we weren't going to let him camp out with us—that whole deeply hurt thing was just an act. But that thought was fuzzy. Other, more important thoughts crammed his mind, like *We have beer. Actual beer. Right here in my tree house.*

"That's not all," Warrick said, that familiar devilish twinkle back in his eyes.

"More beer?"

Warrick looked at Frankie and shook his head. "Beer is just for starters. To get us relaxed." He reached into his backpack. This time when he brought out his arm, he was clutching a packet of cigarettes. "Marlboro," he said, nodding, eyes darting between Toby and Frankie. "The coolest smokes in the world."

Toby wasn't so enthused about this offering. His parents, neither of whom smoked, had drummed into him how bad smoking was. Also, Toby found the smell of tobacco smoke repugnant. But, having never actually smoked a cigarette before, he was curious to see what all the fuss was about. Most of the older kids in town smoked, and they were considered cool, the rebels.

"For after tea," Warrick told them. "To have with your second beer."

"Very cool," Frankie said, although Toby thought he too sounded unsure. "So where did ya get all this stuff?"

"In a minute, Frankie, in a minute. I have one more thing to show you guys. You'll love it."

"You mean there's more?" Frankie said.

Warrick dipped his arm into the backpack once again. The smug grin on his face was a far cry from the melancholy of just a few minutes ago. It was as if he knew he had Toby and Frankie by the balls. And when he pulled out the bottle of Jack Daniel's, he effectively tore their balls off and crushed them in his hand.

"Holy shit," Frankie squeaked. "Is that real?"

Warrick nodded. "You bet. Grade A Tennessee whiskey."

Toby was flabbergasted. Beer was one thing—every high school kid drank beer. Whiskey was a man's drink. He had tried beer a few times—his dad occasionally let him have a few mouthfuls, but he had never tried whiskey before. Toby associated whiskey with hard-boiled detectives sipping the spirit in smoky clubs, where gorgeous women were slumped over fat musicians with guitars in their hands.

"I'm impressed," Toby said, trying hard to conceal his joy—he didn't want to appear too eager for the hard liquor.

"Come on, where did ya get all this shit from?" Frankie said.

Warrick displayed his jagged yellow teeth. "Never you mind that. Let's just say I have my sources. I have the stuff, so that's all that matters, right?"

"Wrong," Toby said. "It matters if you stole it. Did ya steal all this stuff, Warrick?"

"If it makes you feel any better, no, I didn't steal it."

"You promise?"

"Yes, I promise. Now, do I get to stay?"

Toby looked at Frankie. Frankie nodded. Toby turned back to Warrick. "Okay, you can stay."

Warrick's face lit up so suddenly and intensely, Toby was reminded of Christmas tree lights. "Fucking A!" he cried. "Thanks guys!"

"But no screwing around," Frankie said. "If you begin to annoy us, you're gone. Outta here."

"Yeah," Toby agreed. "This is my treehouse. Whatever I say, goes. And after me, Frankie is in charge. So if we both tell you to do something..."

"Or not to do something," Frankie added.

"You do it. Or else."

"Jesus," Warrick sighed. "Are we allowed to have any fun? Or is that against the rules?"

"Sure, we're gonna have fun," Toby said. "But our fun, not yours."

And Toby knew there was a world of difference between the two. He had a feeling he was going to regret his decision to let

Warrick stay. But with the temptation of beer and whiskey, it was hard to say no.

"Whatever," Warrick said. "But we are going to have fun tonight. Hell, we've got enough junk food to last us a week, plus beer, smokes and a whole bottle of whiskey. How can we not have fun?"

Toby had to admit, Warrick's enthusiasm and sense of adventure had the potential to be contagious—a dangerous notion, considering.

"So, you think your parents will be cool with me staying?" Warrick asked.

"Sure. They'll laugh at the fact there's gonna be three people sleeping in a two-man tent, but they won't mind."

With that signature twinkle in his eyes that usually meant trouble, Warrick said, "Who said anything about sleeping?"

And Toby thought for a second time he was going to regret his decision to let Warrick stay the night.

CHAPTER FIVE

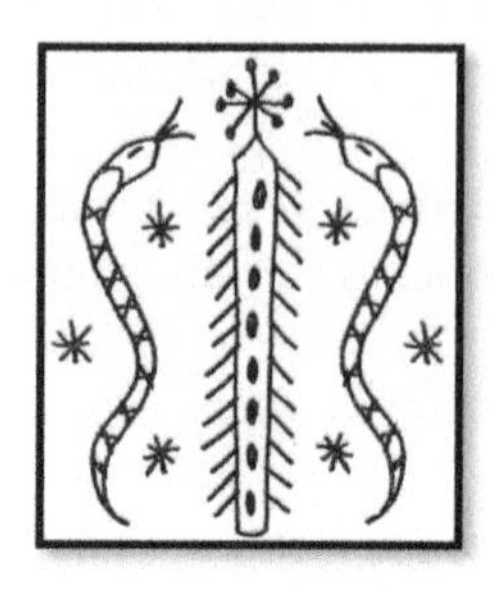

It was closing in on nine o'clock, and as the day bled into night, the sun sinking into the horizon spread glittering orange and pink over the land. The day's fierce bite had dropped away, there was a warm gentle breeze drifting in through the tree house windows, making it the perfect summer's evening.

"What'd I tell ya?" Warrick said as he slurped from his second can of beer. "Beer and fried chicken go together like dick and pussy."

On Warrick's suggestion, Toby had asked his parents if they could eat their dinner up in the tree house. They had been reluctant at first, but Toby told them that doing so would add to the overall experience of camping out, so they agreed. Of course, the real reason was so they could consume their first beer for the night during dinner. Because Warrick had assured them that beer and fried chicken went together like dick and pussy.

"I have to admit, they do complement each other," Frankie said, licking his greasy fingers and following it up with a sip of beer.

"Wow, that's a big word, Wilmont. Maybe it works the opposite with you."

"What works the opposite with me?"

"Well, alcohol is supposed to kill brain cells. But in your case, it seems to have made you smarter."

"Get fucked."

"I thought you'd be flattered."

"Well I'm not."

Toby, having almost polished off his first can of beer, was starting to feel the effects. His head was a little dizzy, but he felt good; relaxed and happy.

If this is what it's like to be drunk, Toby thought, *why does everybody always say it's bad to drink?*

He thought about his parents and how they'd flip out if they knew he was drinking. But he wasn't fearful of them finding out. They trusted him. They were fine with Warrick staying (though, as Toby predicted, they did laugh at the idea of three people sleeping in such a small tent, and his mom in particular was surprised at the inclusion of Warrick), and they promised not to continually check up on them, on the condition the boys were in the tent, asleep, by midnight. Plus, they had everything they needed—food, drink, flashlights, sleeping bags (Toby's mom dug out one of their spares for Warrick), roll mats, and pillows—so the three boys were free to do as they pleased, without worry of interruption.

"Hey Frankie, grab me a Twinkie, would ya," Toby said.

Frankie's eyes lit up. "Yeah, dessert. Good idea, Toby." He set his beer on the rug and being closest to the pile of junk food, reached back and grabbed one of the packets of Twinkies. So far they had barely made a dent in the mountain of chocolate, cookies and cakes. And as Toby had hoped, the shaded tree house had kept the food relatively cool; the chocolates were only slightly soft, not completely melted.

"Enjoying the beer?" Warrick asked Toby.

"You bet. A bit warm, but good."

"You tipsy yet?"

Toby shrugged. "I dunno. What does that mean?"

Warrick laughed. "You don't know what tipsy means? Shit. You're such a babe in the woods, Fairchild."

"So sue me," Toby said and burped.

"I think you are. How about you, Wilmont?"

Frankie was busy tearing at the Twinkies' plastic wrapping. Finally, he got the packet of Twinkies open, took one of the cakes for himself, then handed the packet to Toby. Toby grabbed the other and shoved it in his mouth.

Toby finished the Twinkie in three ravenous bites, licking the cream off his fingers afterwards.

"So, are ya Wilmont?" Warrick said.

"Tispy? I guess," Frankie answered, mouth full of Twinkie.

Warrick chortled. "It's tipsy, you moron. God, you two are unbelievable. Don't you guys know anything?"

"I know that you're an idiot," Frankie said.

"And I know how thirsty I still am," Toby said. He downed the last of the beer, then threw the empty can to the floor. It clanged beside Warrick's. "Hey, pass me another beer."

Warrick broke off a can and handed it to Toby. He popped the can open and tipped the tepid liquid down his throat. It was becoming easier to drink, which was good, since the beer had been bitter and not very nice to begin with.

"Hey, you'd better hurry, Wilmont," Warrick said. "Me and Fairchild are gonna leave you behind."

"Yeah, yeah," Frankie said. He placed the can to his lips and drank. And kept on drinking until he had drained the can. Frankie tossed the can down and let out a thunderous burp.

"Nice chug, Wilmont," Warrick said. "I bet you barf later on." He chuckled.

"Don't say that," Toby said. His parents were bound to hear one of them throwing up in the middle of the night. "Maybe you'd better slow down, Frankie. Take it easy, huh?"

"I'm fine," Frankie huffed.

Warrick picked up the pack of Marlboros. Toby got mildly excited. Earlier he had been apprehensive about trying the cigarettes. Now, that apprehension had all but vanished. Perhaps the alcohol had dulled his moral sensibility. Maybe it was knowing they wouldn't be interrupted by his parents.

Or perhaps he had finally caught Warrick's sense of adventure and daring.

"Time to light up," Warrick announced.

Toby's stomach tingled. It really did feel like butterflies were flapping around in his gut, desperately searching for an opening to the outside world. He looked at Frankie. His round eyes were staring at the packet as if it was a beautiful naked woman.

Warrick plucked a cigarette from the packet and slipped it between his lips, leaving it dangling there, like a fishing rod in a boat. He pulled a silver lighter from a pocket and lit the end of the cigarette. He puffed a few times, and when the tip of the cigarette was glowing and billowing smoke, he took the lighter away. After two long drags, he took the cigarette from his lips and blew a cloud of smoke. "That's how it's done, boys." He handed the pack of cigarettes and lighter to Frankie. "There ya go, Wilmont. Enjoy."

Frankie took the packet and lighter, yanked out a cigarette, then handed the pack of Marlboros to Toby.

Placing his can of beer down, Toby took the cigarettes. He drew the open packet to his nose and breathed in deep. There was a strong woody smell that was a lot nicer than the stink coming from Warrick's cigarette.

"You're supposed to smoke it, Fairchild, not sniff it. That's another drug altogether." Warrick chuckled.

"I know that," Toby said.

There was a sharp click to the right of Toby. He turned and in the fading light watched Frankie trying to light his cigarette. He fumbled, dropped the lighter. It took him three tries to finally light his cigarette.

"Amateurs," Warrick said with a shake of his head.

Frankie placed the cigarette to his lips and took a drag. His face scrunched up, as if he had just smelled something vile, and when he took the cigarette from his mouth he began coughing. "Ugh!" Frankie choked. "That's horrible."

"You'll get used to it," Warrick said. "Just keep on smoking."

"I don't know if I want to," Frankie said, face still looking like he had bitten into a lemon.

"Trust me. Smoking is like beer. The first sip might taste like piss, but keep on drinking it and by the end of the first can, you'll think it's the best thing you've ever drunk."

"Doesn't taste as good as Dr. Pepper," Frankie quipped.

"Or Coke," Toby said.

"You know what I mean."

Frankie shrugged and tried the cigarette again. He only coughed a few times, lightly. On the third puff he nodded his head. "You're right. This ain't so bad."

"Told ya," Warrick said. "Come on, Fairchild. Your turn."

Frankie held out the lighter.

Toby hesitated. His brain may've been slightly distorted from the beer, but he was still divided over whether or not to smoke. The sensible part of him knew it was wrong. It was asking him to consider what his parents would think of him if he went through with it. The other part, the slightly intoxicated teenager who wanted to be free from mommy and daddy's good boy image, was telling him to go for it. It was just experimenting—hell, his parents probably experimented with worse things back when they were growing up.

"Come on, Fairchild. Don't be a wuss. There's nothing to it."

"Yeah, once you get used to it, it actually tastes kind of...nice."

Kind of nice? I doubt that.

However, he had to admit, after the fried chicken, and now drinking the beers, he did feel like relaxing back with a cigarette. It seemed like the right thing to do.

Toby snatched the lighter from Frankie, popped a cigarette into his mouth, then lit the tip. He had less trouble than Frankie. After the second attempt, he had the cigarette alight. He sucked on the cigarette, felt a wave of smoke fill his throat, then his chest. It was all too much. He choked on the cloud of smoke and taking the cigarette from his lips, started coughing. Amid the spluttering, he heard Warrick laughing. "Fuck...you," Toby panted. He grabbed his beer from off the floor and took a drink. The beer seemed to calm the tickle in his throat and douse the fire in his chest.

"You okay, Toby?" Frankie asked.

Toby took a deep breath and nodded. "Yeah, just went down the wrong pipe, I guess."

"Bullshit," Warrick laughed. "You just can't handle it, that's all."

"Screw you," Frankie snapped. "So what? Everyone knows that smoking is bad for you."

"You're smoking."

"I'm just seeing what it's like, that's all."

"I'm fine," Toby said, annoyed he was being perceived as weak. Though his eyes were watering and the taste of the cigarette was vile, he took another puff. He still felt like coughing, but this time he suppressed the urge. "See?" he said, exhaling a cloud of smoke. "I can do it."

By the time Toby finished smoking the cigarette, his mouth tasted like the inside of an ashtray, he felt a tad queasy and Frankie and Warrick were dim shapes in the darkness. Flicking the cigarette butt away, Toby stood and switched on the larger of the two flashlights, positioning it on the floor so the light was directed at them and the pile of food. He sat back down and as he finished off his second beer, washing away the foul cigarette taste, he said, "Pass me the Snicker's, Frankie."

Frankie reached back, grabbed the Snicker's bar for Toby and picked up a Reese's Peanut Butter Big Cup for himself. Turning back around he handed the Snicker's to Toby. "Want anything Warrick?" he asked.

"Nah, I'm good." Warrick, having finished his cigarette, stubbed the butt on the boards, picked up the pack of Marlboros, lit another cigarette, then offered the pack to Toby and Frankie. Toby shook his head. "Maybe later," he said. Frankie accepted the offer, plucking out a second cigarette.

I hope Frankie doesn't get hooked on those things, Toby thought.

Toby had an uncle who died of lung cancer about eight years ago. He had apparently smoked two packets of cigarettes a day, as well as cigars and pipes. He remembered his mom telling him that his uncle started smoking when he was around thirteen. It was his long-dead uncle that Toby thought of when Frankie accepted another cigarette.

"So," Warrick said. "Here we are. Who would've thought, hey? Toby Fairchild and Frankie Wilmont sucking back beers and smoking cigarettes with ole Warrick Coleman."

"Yeah, but we were bribed, remember?" Toby said.

"It hasn't been too bad so far, has it?"

Toby, munching on the Snicker's, shook his head. "I guess not."

"What he means is that the beer and cigarettes are good," Frankie said, alternating between smoking the cigarette and eating the peanut butter cup.

"Precisely," Toby said, and laughed.

"Couple of comedians," Warrick said. "So anyway, now that we're the best of friends and a little loaded, let me ask you guys something." Warrick drew on his cigarette. "Which girls from middle school do you fantasize about? You know, which ones do you have wet dreams over? Which ones would you love to fuck till the cows come home?"

"That's easy," Frankie said. "Debbie and Gloria Mayfour. Imagine having a threesome with those two."

"Agreed," Warrick said. "You wouldn't believe the amount of times I've jerked off over that fantasy."

"You two are disgusting," Toby said. "They're sisters."

"Makes it all the better," Frankie said.

"Come on Fairchild, don't you think they're hot?"

"Of course," Toby answered.

"Well, then what's so disgusting about it?" Warrick asked.

Toby avoided answering by saying, "Well how about you, Warrick? Who do you like, besides the Mayfour sisters?"

"Well... Sara Hope's not bad."

Sara Hope had been in the same year as them. She was blonde, had massive tits, and was a complete snob.

"Yeah, I'd do her," Frankie said. "I mean those tits... ooh baby."

"You wouldn't stand a chance," Toby said.

"Hey, what's wrong with my looks?"

"Besides the fact that you're chubby, have a big nose and a dick the size of an ant?" Warrick said.

"Go fuck your mother, Warrick," Frankie snapped. "Anyway, it's a proven fact that men with big noses have bigger dicks. It's something in the genes."

"That's utter crap, Wilmont. Everyone knows it's big feet, not big noses."

"It's true," Frankie protested.

"Then prove it," Warrick said. "Pull down your pants and show us your enormous schlong."

"Okay," Frankie said. "I will." He stumbled to his feet. It seemed the one beer had gone to his head.

"Sit down," Toby told him. "I don't want to see your dick. Christ, here we are talking about which girls we like and you two end up talking about dicks."

Warrick frowned. "Yeah, I don't want to see your pint-sized cock, Wilmont. What are you, a fag or something?"

Frankie plonked back to the floor. "Hey, you're the one who wanted me to show..."

"Both of you, shut up," Toby said. He was now feeling the full effects of the two beers. He wasn't feeling sick; just the opposite. He felt happy, invincible, like he could do anything he wanted. "Okay, who else do you like, besides Sara Hope?"

"Okay, besides Sara Hope..." Warrick's eyes narrowed and he took a long draw of his Marlboro. "I've got it. Miss Wilson. Man, I would love to bang her brains out. For a teacher, she's one hot mamma. Great body, nice tits, and a gorgeous face."

"Yeah, she is pretty," Frankie said.

"Just pretty? She's more than pretty. She was the most fuckable woman in the whole stupid school. Don't you agree Fairchild?"

Toby, not wanting to reveal just how much he liked Miss. Wilson, said, "Yeah, I guess so."

"Are you two blind or what? Every guy in school was in love with her."

"I guess it never really occurred to me, her being a teacher and all," Toby said.

"Hey, you guys wanna hear something amazing?" Warrick leaned forward, eyes flicking from Toby to Frankie. He blew a cloud of smoke. "Dwayne Marcos has fucked Miss Wilson."

There was a moment of stunned silence. Then:

"What a load of shit," Toby huffed.

"Yeah, what crock," Frankie scoffed.

"It's true," Warrick said. "It happened last summer. He went over to her house to hand in some assignment that he was late in finishing, and one thing led to another, and they ended up screwing each other all day and night."

"And who told you this? Dwayne?" Frankie said.

"Yeah, so? I'm friends with him. The guy doesn't lie. Not about stuff like that."

"That's the kind of thing guys like Dwayne lie about the most," Toby said. "Miss Wilson would never sleep with a creep like Dwayne."

"Well Dwayne told me everything. He said that Miss. Wilson loves to go on top, and that her pussy tastes like beef jerky. He also said that she shaves her pubic hair."

"He's such a liar," Toby said.

"Jealous?" Warrick said.

"No, because it never happened."

"Well I think Dwayne did have sex with her," Warrick said, lighting another cigarette. He offered the pack to Frankie, but Frankie turned it down. "Suit yourself. Fairchild?"

"No, thanks."

"Anyway, all this talk about Dwayne and Miss. Wilson leads to my next question. No bullshit this time. And Fairchild, this time you answer. How far have you both gotten with a girl? And who was it?"

Toby groaned inside. He figured this question would come up sooner or later. Warrick's memory was like an iron grip.

"Well we all know that you've had sex before," Frankie chuckled. "With... what was her name again? Patricia?"

Warrick nodded, the cigarette perched between his lips. "Okay, okay. I admit it. That was bullshit. But I have felt a girl's pussy before."

"Yeah, your mom's when you were born."

Frankie laughed. "Good one, Toby."

"Yeah, ha ha. You're so fucking funny, Fairchild." Warrick took a long drag, puffed out smoke, then settled back. "But seriously, I have felt a girl's muff. It was last year, during the Christmas break. I went with my family to Connecticut to visit my cousins, and one night, while all the adults were out, the kids threw a party. You see, both my cousins are older. One's seventeen and the other is nineteen. Anyway, at this party I met this really hot chick. Don't remember her name, but I think she was about seventeen years old. She was drunk, I was drunk. We were in one of the bedrooms and we kissed for a while, tongues and all, and I even got to suck her tits. They were small and pointy, but I didn't care. I told her I wanted to fuck her, but she said no, she was Catholic, it was against her religion, or some shit like that. But she did let me take off her pants and feel her pussy. Man, it was fucking incredible. It was all wet and springy. She even let me stick my fingers up inside her. She was moaning and everything. Let me tell ya, I nearly shot my load right then and there. And I was this close to going down on her when she suddenly jumped up, rushed into the bathroom and threw up. Like I said, she was drunk." Finished with his story, Warrick had a proud look on his face and, Toby couldn't help but notice, an erection. But he couldn't laugh at Warrick, because he had one too.

"Cool," Frankie mused.

Toby and Frankie glanced at each other. Toby could tell Frankie was thinking the same thing he was. *I don't want to believe it, but I have a feeling it might be true. And if it is, damn I'm jealous. How did a scrawny, ugly kid like Warrick get to do that with a seventeen-year-old girl?*

Still, Toby didn't want to give Warrick any more satisfaction—he clearly had enough already. "So if it's true, how come you've never bragged about it before?"

"I don't brag about everything I do. Some things I like to keep private. Or until the time is right, like tonight."

Toby shook his head. "I still reckon you're making it up."

"Look, if I was making it up, wouldn't I say that she sucked my dick, or that I went down on her, or that I fucked her?"

"He's got a point," Frankie said.

"Maybe he's being smart. Knows that feeling a drunk chick's beaver is more believable than having sex with her."

Warrick huffed. "I can't win."

"Well I believe you," Frankie said. "So what did her snatch smell like? I mean, you must've smelt your fingers afterwards, right?"

A wide grin spread across Warrick's face. "Yeah, I did. And they didn't smell like beef jerky. It was a unique smell. Sweet, but with a sour tinge to it. Mixed with a bit of chicken."

"That sounds really convincing," Toby said.

"Well anyway, that's my story. Frankie, your turn. How far have you got with a girl? Seriously now, no bullshit."

Toby knew that Frankie had absolutely no experience when it came to girls. Like Toby, he had never even kissed one.

"Well, I've seen a girl's tits."

Oh brother, Toby thought. *Here we go.*

"That's all?" Warrick said. "Well, I guess it's better than nothing. So whose tits were they?"

"Debbie Mayfour's. I saw them Thursday night."

Warrick's interest suddenly perked up. "For real? How? I know she wouldn't have shown them to you."

"She was staying over at my house. I peeked into the bathroom while she was taking a shower. Well actually, she had just finished, she was getting dressed. Unfortunately, she had already put her skirt on, but I got to see her tits real well."

"And you weren't worried about being caught?" Warrick said.

"Nah. My mom was watching TV and Leah was in her room, yakking on the phone."

"I'm impressed, Wilmont. So how were they?"

"Big. Round and firm. Man, I just wanted to suck them so hard."

Toby couldn't fully enjoy Frankie's good fortune. He was too busy wondering why, if all this was true, Frankie hadn't divulged all the details to him yesterday.

Probably because he's lying, Toby thought. *Yeah, that must be it.*

"God, what I wouldn't give to suck on those tits," Warrick said, licking his lips. "I'd kill somebody for the privilege."

"Probably your own mother," Toby said.

"Hell yeah," Warrick said. "And my old man, too."

"Well you think that's cool," Frankie said, grinning, "Toby has touched some tits. And not just any old tits. . .Gloria Mayfour's."

Toby gasped. "Jesus Christ, Frankie! Can't ya shut your trap for once?"

He didn't want anyone to know about that incident, especially Warrick.

"What?" Frankie said. "You touched Gloria's titties. That's something to be proud of."

Toby shook his head. Maybe it was the booze—Toby wasn't in the most rational frame of mind, either—but Frankie had promised not to tell a soul about the run-in with Gloria, and no amount of alcohol should've changed that.

"Man, Gloria's even better looking than her sister," Warrick said. "I can't wait to hear all about it. But first..." With a groan he stood up.

"Where are you going?" Frankie asked.

"Home, I hope," Toby said.

"Sorry to disappoint, Fairchild. I'm busting for a leak. I hope your garden needs watering." He winked.

"You're disgusting," Toby said, but he much preferred Warrick to do his business outside than inside Toby's house. He figured if Warrick went inside to use the bathroom, there was a good chance he would run into Toby's parents. And they'd surely smell the alcohol and cigarette smoke on him.

"When I get back," Warrick said, sliding back the trap door bolt, "I want to hear all about Gloria's tits."

He flipped up the trap door and started climbing down the ladder.

When Warrick was gone, Toby thumped Frankie on the arm. "Why'd ya tell him about Gloria? That was supposed to be a secret."

"Lighten up, jeez," Frankie said, rubbing his arm. "I thought drinking alcohol was supposed to make you more relaxed."

"I was relaxed until you opened your big mouth. Now the whole town will know about what happened with Gloria. You've gone and fucked everything up. Gloria will never speak to me again. She'll think I bragged about it to all my friends."

"We'll just threaten to beat Warrick up if he tells anyone," Frankie said, reaching back and grabbing the box of banana flavored Mini MoonPies. He took one out and after ripping open the plastic wrapping, stuffed it into his mouth. "Relax, man," he mumbled. "Enjoy the food and drink."

"And cigarettes? You seemed to really be enjoying those."

"It was horrible at first. But once you get used to the smoke, I can see the appeal."

So did Uncle Bill, Toby thought.

"So do you believe Warrick about getting it on with that girl?"

Toby grabbed the box of Mini MoonPies, picked one out, tore open the wrapping and popped it into his mouth. He shrugged, mumbled, "I dunno."

"Well, I believe him. God, what a lucky son-of-a-bitch. Out of all the people..."

Warrick's scrawny, pimply face suddenly appeared. "Your roses are good and watered now," he said, then hoisted himself up into the tree house and slammed the door.

"Bolt it," Toby told him.

"Why?"

"Because I said so."

"You mean because your mommy said so."

"Just fucking bolt the door, Warrick."

"Yeah, or else Toby won't tell you about Gloria's tits."

Warrick promptly bent over and slotted the bolt into place.

"Okay, done," Warrick said and sat back on the floor. "Now, tell me all about it. Spare none of the details. I've had the major hots for Gorgeous Gloria ever since I was five years old." He spied the Mini MoonPies and grabbed one out of the box.

"It was nothing," Toby said, eyeing Frankie. "Don't worry about it."

Warrick stared at Toby with a look of disbelief. "Nothing? Are you a bona fide homo Fairchild?"

"What does bona fide mean?" Frankie said.

"I mean it wasn't what you think," Toby said. "So don't go creaming your pants just yet."

Warrick scoffed, took a bite of the MoonPie. "If it involves Gloria Mayfour and her tits, it's a big deal."

Toby knew there was no way out of this. The cat had been let out of the bag, and the cat was a great big Siberian Tiger, just waiting for somebody like Warrick to kick it squarely in the balls. But hopefully, by telling the truth, he would put to rest any rumors that would've undoubtedly started up if Toby had said nothing.

"Okay, I'll tell you. But you gotta promise not to tell anyone. I mean it Warrick. It doesn't leave this room."

Warrick rolled his eyes. "Yeah, yeah, whatever. Do you want to exchange blood too?" He finished the MoonPie.

"Fuck you then, I'm not telling you."

"Okay, I'm sorry. I promise I won't tell a soul."

"That's what Frankie said," Toby huffed.

"It's a good story," Frankie said. "Go on, tell him."

"Okay," Toby sighed. "Yesterday after school me and Frankie were walking home. We decided to have a race to my house. When we got to the corner of Pineview, I... I ran into Gloria."

Warrick frowned. "What, you mean you saw her standing there?"

Toby's face was burning.

Why am I still embarrassed about this? I thought alcohol was supposed to dull your senses.

"No, I ran into her—literally! I knocked her over."

Warrick giggled; it was high-pitched, totally uncool, but Warrick didn't seem to care. "You crashed into Gorgeous Gloria? Oh man!"

Frankie started laughing, too; a low chuckle that started in his wobbly belly and worked its way up and out through his nose.

"What the hell are you two laughing at?" Toby said. "It wasn't funny. She was hurt."

That put an end to Frankie's laughter. It took Warrick longer to settle down. "Sorry, Fairchild. It's just... that kind of shit could only happen to you. But she got hurt? Damn, that's too bad."

"Well, not seriously. Banged her head on the sidewalk."

"Is that how you got that cut?" Warrick asked, nodding to Toby's right knee.

He had taken the bandage off this morning; wearing a bandage over such a minor injury was fine around Frankie, but to be seen around town with one on was a major no-no—it wasn't the done thing among teenage boys. "Yeah."

"So how does feeling her tits come into all this?"

"Toby fell on top of her," Frankie said before Toby could answer.

Warrick's eyes lit up. "You fell on top of her? You lucky bastard."

Toby shrugged.

"So what, did your hand accidentally slip under her shirt or something? Did you kiss her titties all better after falling on top of her?"

"No," Toby said. "When we fell my hand just happened to land on top of one of her breasts—on the outside of her shirt. That's all.

It wasn't sexy or anything. All I could think about was that she might be hurt."

"Hey, it's a lot further than anyone else has got with Gloria. Believe me, a lot have tried, including me."

"Yeah, well, that's the story. Told you it wasn't much. I didn't touch her bare breasts or anything. She didn't let me touch them voluntarily. So don't go spreading any rumors about her letting me feel her up, okay?"

"Don't worry, I won't. But do you know what I think? I think you falling on top of Gloria deserves a drink." Warrick reached into his bag and took out the bottle of Jack Daniel's. He twisted off the cap and took a quick nip. "Woah, that's strong stuff," he breathed. He took another drink, this time leaving the bottle longer at his lips. He squeezed his eyes shut. "Holy crap," he said and when he opened his eyes, they were watering. He swiped the tears away.

Toby blinked. Jesus, what does it taste like, acid?

"Give me some," Frankie said. Warrick handed him the bottle.

"Careful," Warrick said. "Packs a real wallop. Don't drink too much of it at once."

"Have you tried whiskey before?" Toby asked Warrick.

He nodded. "A few times. Takes a long time to get used to it, though. Especially drinking it straight. It goes down easier mixed with Coke."

Frankie took a mouthful of the amber liquid. He swallowed and his face pinched, tears rolled down his cheeks. "Hell that's strong," he gasped. "Like drinking fire." He coughed. "Do all whiskies taste like this?" Frankie asked, passing the bottle to Toby.

"I guess so," Warrick answered. "I mean, I'm no expert. I'm sure there are some differences, but to amateurs like us, they basically taste the same."

Toby held the bottle as if it was some ancient artifact—some strange object of power and beauty, but one containing unknown dangers.

"That Mr. Daniel's must've had a throat of steel," Frankie said, grabbing the bottle of Dr. Pepper and gulping some down.

Toby licked his lips, placed the bottle to his mouth. The smell reminded him of a doctor's room—only slightly sweeter. There was also a hint of vanilla, similar to the vanilla essence his mom used in baking.

"Drink up," Warrick said.

Toby tipped the bottle up, took a small swill of the alcohol. It wasn't so bad at first—there was only a mild burning sensation in his mouth. Then he swallowed. It felt like a flame was scorching a path down his throat. His eyes began to water as the hotness spread to his chest. He sputtered and tightened his fists.

Water! Water! ran over in his mind. He wiped the tears from his eyes with a balled-up fist.

"Really warms you up, doesn't it?" Warrick said.

"Like a bonfire," Toby said coarsely and coughed some more. He grabbed one of the bottles of Coke to try to douse the fire.

"Hey Frankie, give me that half empty bottle of Coke," Warrick said.

"What are you doing?" Toby asked, still drinking from the other bottle of Coke.

"Now that you gentlemen have tasted whiskey in its purest form, let's dilute it so we can actually drink the stuff without feeling like we could piss fire."

Warrick twisted the cap off the Coke and carefully poured in the whiskey.

When the bottle of Coke was almost full, Warrick took the whiskey away, placed it down and screwed the lid back on. He did the same with the Coke, then gave the bottle a quick shake. "I think you guys are gonna like this," he said. He carefully opened the Coke bottle and when the liquid started overflowing, he put the bottle to his mouth and drank.

After a few generous gulps, Warrick took the bottle from his lips. "Yummy," he said. He held the bottle up. "To Toby and Gloria." He drank some more before handing the bottle to Frankie.

"To Toby and Gloria," Frankie said, and then swilled the whiskey and Coke mixture. "Hey, that's actually pretty good. A hell of a lot better than drinking it straight." He took another sip then passed the bottle to Toby.

"To me and Gloria," Toby said and downed a small mouthful of the beverage. He was pleasantly surprised to find that he liked the concoction. There was hardly any burning, and the syrupy sweetness of the Coke went well with the fiery whiskey. "Not bad," Toby agreed. "Not bad at all. I could learn to like this."

He took another, longer drink, then passed the bottle back to Warrick. It wasn't long before he felt the effects of the whiskey: his head felt funny, dizzy, almost light-headed and his body started tingling. He laughed for no reason.

"What's so funny?" Frankie said.

"Nothing. I just feel... good."

"Don't we all," Warrick said as he took another mouthful of Jack Daniel's and Coke.

"What we need," Toby said, "is music."

"Yeah, like Foo Fighters. Or that new band, Jeremy's Mom. They're cool."

"And women," Warrick added. "Don't forget the women."

"If only we had Gloria, Debbie and Sara Hope in here," Frankie said, "I'd be in heaven."

"Don't forget Miss Wilson," Warrick said. "Hey, maybe we should call Dwayne and ask him for her number."

"Can I ask you a question?" Toby said to Warrick.

"Shoot."

"Why do you hang around with Dwayne and his gang?"

Warrick swigged from the spiked Coke. "Because it looks good," he answered. "People leave me alone. It works out well. I mean, I know why he lets me hang around with him—because I'm good for a joke, a doofus who will do anything for a laugh."

"Don't you care that he uses you like that?" Toby asked.

"Nah. I'm protected, that's all I care about. They use me, I use them. Doesn't mean I like them. Tell you the truth, I can't stand those idiots. Especially Dwayne." He stared hard at Toby and Frankie. "You won't tell anyone what I'm saying, will you?"

Toby and Frankie shook their heads.

"Good. I mean, Dwayne actually thinks I like him. Idolizes him for Christ's sake. But let me tell you, he is one mean son-of-a-bitch. Hates everybody but himself. Even hates Debbie, only keeps her around 'cos he likes to fuck her. That's what he told me. I mean, here we are, three guys who would do anything to have somebody like Debbie Mayfour as their girlfriend, and that arrogant prick has her but treats her like shit. World works in funny ways. I tell ya, I would love to meet the guys who water bombed Dwayne's car. I would shake their fucking hands and kiss their feet."

A warm rush of pride ran through Toby. He turned to Frankie, who was staring at him with a wide, expectant gaze. Toby could see how much he wanted to tell Warrick, but the fear of upsetting Toby again was holding him back. But Toby didn't mind Warrick knowing this bit of information. He nodded, turned back to Warrick. "We'll take the hand shaking, but not you kissing our feet. That's just disgusting."

At first Warrick just smiled. He must've thought Toby was kidding around. But then his eyes grew wide and a look of astonishment almost completely overtook his bony face. "No way! You're fucking with me, aren't you?"

Toby shook his head. "It was us."

"Sure was," Frankie said. "What do ya think about that?"

Warrick's mouth hung open—for once it seemed he was lost for words.

"We were at Frankie's shooting some hoops. We heard Dwayne's car, we already had some water bombs made up, so Frankie got some and hurled them at his Chevy."

"Bulls-eye both times," Frankie said. "Bozos never knew what hit them."

"Wow," Warrick said, having regained the power of speech. "Holy Jesus, guys. I'm fucking amazed."

"But you can't tell anybody," Toby said. "Not a word. Dwayne would have our balls if he ever found out."

"Of course not," Warrick said. "I ain't that stupid." He shook his head. "Man, out of all the people I thought may have done it, I never even suspected you two. You should've seen how angry those guys were. Talking about how, when they found out who had done it, they were going to pound them into the ground."

"That makes me feel a whole lot better," Frankie said.

"Don't worry, Frankie," Warrick said. "They won't find out. Apart from us three, nobody else knows. So as long as none of us blab, they won't ever know who did it."

Toby nodded, feeling good about the whole situation. He grabbed the spiked bottle of Coke and took a drink.

"Say, you guys wanna know who did all that stuff to Mr. Joseph's house?"

"We already know," Toby said.

"You do?"

"Yeah, Toby saw it from his bedroom window."

"No shit? The whole thing?"

"Yep," Toby said.

"It was great, huh?" Warrick said. "Showed that nigger a thing or two. Taught that freak a lesson. And killing that chicken was pure genius. Don't suppose you know what Mr. Joseph did with it?"

"He took the head and body inside."

"Wait a minute. You told me that he threw the chicken into the trash," Frankie said. "You never said anything about taking it inside with him."

Toby shrugged. "I dunno why I told you that, Frankie. Probably so you wouldn't spread stupid stories about what he had done with the chicken."

"Well gee, thanks for lying to me."

"It makes you wonder, though," Warrick said, a mischievous sparkle in his eyes. "Why did he take it inside with him?"

"Maybe to use in some sacrificial ritual," Frankie said.

"Or maybe to have for breakfast," Warrick said.

Frankie nodded. "Yeah. Maybe he drank its blood, or even had sex with the corpse."

"That's disgusting," Toby said.

Warrick laughed. "Good one, Wilmont. Probably stuck his nigger cock up its neck. Got his rocks off 'cos he can't get a woman."

"Or maybe he knew that bum was coming, so he wanted to prepare a feast for him—raw chicken head for the main course, chicken entrails for dessert."

Warrick laughed. Toby didn't find it so funny.

"Speaking of that old bum, Billy Pierce's dad saw him walking out of town this evening—or at least, he thought it was him. Billy's dad was driving into town, and he saw someone who looked like the bum hobbling along the side of the road. If it was him, I say good riddance."

"Yeah, good riddance," Frankie said. "Still, I wonder why he came to town. I mean, it's not like Belford's a major city. Maybe he fell asleep on the bus from Chicago. He meant to travel only to Indianapolis, but ended up here, instead."

"He was probably so drunk he didn't know where he was. Maybe he stopped here to sober up."

"Well then why didn't he just take the bus to wherever he wanted to go? Why walk? I mean, there's nothing around here except farmland and more small towns."

"Maybe he didn't leave town; maybe he's still here," Warrick said. "Maybe he's on the run from the law and hiding out in Mr. Joseph's house. He murdered some kids back in Chicago, butchered them with a carving knife, and now he has to hide out in some small town in the middle of nowhere. And you know how niggers stick together—yeah, I bet that freak Mr. Joseph is hiding him. Or maybe they're lovers."

"You know, you can see Mr. Joseph's house from up here," Frankie said. "Maybe we can see something through a window or something."

"I'll go you one better; let's pay the freak a visit." Warrick's face gleamed with mischief. "If he is hiding the bum, we won't be able to see him from up here."

"No way," Toby said. "I'm happy to stay right here."

"Come on," Warrick said. "It'll be a blast. We might find out what happened to the chicken, too. Frankie, you'll come, won't you?"

"Count me in." Frankie pushed himself up off the floor, wobbling as he got to his feet.

"Come on, Fairchild," Warrick said, standing up. "We're going with or without you. But it'll be pretty damn boring staying here by yourself." He reached down and snatched the large flashlight from off the floor.

"What the hell are you going to do if you do see the stranger in there?" Toby said.

Warrick shrugged. "Who knows? But at least it'll liven up this little party."

Toby had to admit, the thought of sneaking over to the old man's house did send a shiver of excitement through his slightly inebriated body.

"Okay," Toby said, sighing heavily for effect. "I'll come. But first I need another drink." He grabbed the bottle of Coke and took a drink. Then he reached over, picked up the second, smaller flashlight and struggled to his feet.

With Warrick leading the way, the three boys climbed down the ladder.

"Let's be quick about this," Toby whispered once they were all on solid ground. He glanced nervously towards the back door—even though his parents had promised not to disturb them, there was always the chance his mom would pop out to check up on them, using some pretense like seeing if they needed any extra blankets or pillows.

"Relax," Warrick said. "This is going to be fun."

"Sure, fun," Toby mused, the sudden need to go to the toilet coinciding with their decision to sneak over to Mr. Joseph's house. "Wait here," he told Warrick and Frankie. "I gotta take a leak."

Frankie said, "I gotta go, too."

Toby sighed and with the flashlight leading the way, the two of them trudged down to a dark patch near some bushes. Toby stopped, clicked off the flashlight, unzipped and eased the pressure from his bladder. He heard Frankie splashing onto the grass nearby. "Hey Frankie, you sure you want to do this?" he whispered.

"Yeah," Frankie replied. "Why, you scared?"

"Course not," Toby said. "I'm just asking, that's all."

"It's exciting. I mean, what if we uncover something really cool. Really disgusting."

"Like what?" Toby said. "Dead bodies?"

"Yeah, or evidence of cannibalism or devil worship. Or maybe that bum really is a murderer and hiding out in there."

"Jesus, Frankie. Mr. Joseph's just some weird old man. He's not a cannibal, and he's not hiding any murderers." As Toby's urination petered out to the occasional spurt, Warrick whispered harshly from behind, "What are you guys doing? Sucking each other's peckers?"

Toby zipped his pants.

When Frankie finished, he sighed, "That's better."

Switching the flashlight back on, Toby and Frankie walked back to where Warrick was waiting, sly grin on his face. "All better, girls? We ready?"

Toby started forward, but Warrick grabbed him by the shirt. "Hey," Toby said. "What the hell are you doing?"

"Turn off the flashlight. It's what, only around nine-thirty? People might still be around. I don't want to be seen going up to the old man's house carrying flashlights." Warrick let go of Toby's shirt. "We'll turn them on when we need them." Warrick started off towards the street.

Toby glanced at Frankie. Frankie shrugged and together they followed Warrick alongside Toby's house.

When they reached the sidewalk, they stopped. Toby looked around the moonlit street. It was empty.

"Come on," Warrick whispered, and the three boys crossed Pineview, their footsteps quick. When they reached the other side, they halted again, gave the area another sweep, and satisfied they weren't being watched, continued towards Mr. Joseph's.

They had only taken a few steps when Warrick ducked left, into the front yard of Mr. and Mrs. Openshaw.

Toby and Frankie stopped. "Warrick?" Toby said. "What are you doing?"

They watched as Warrick crept alongside the hedge that separated the Openshaws' property from the Kleins'. Soon he was out of sight. Toby sighed. "Idiot," he said, and together with Frankie, followed Warrick.

They trekked down the side of the house, found Warrick in the backyard, crouched by the hedge. Toby and Frankie joined Warrick in the relative darkness, the Openshaw's two-story stucco looming over them. "This isn't Mr. Joseph's," Toby whispered. "What the hell are we hiding here for?"

Warrick huffed. "You don't just walk into the belly of the beast, you moron. You attack it strategically. What, you think we're just gonna walk up to the old freak's house, stroll up to the first window we see and look in? Hell, he could be sitting out on his front porch, a shotgun in his lap, just waiting for us. No, we can't go the front way, we have to go the back."

Toby shook his head. "So we're going to sneak through the Klein's backyard, into Mr. Joseph's?"

"You got it in one."

"What if he's waiting for us in the backyard with a shotgun?" Frankie said.

Warrick didn't answer straightaway. "That's a chance we're gonna have to take, Wilmont. Hopefully the old fart is out on one of his late-night walks, but we can't take that chance. So you guys ready?"

"No," Toby answered.

"I guess," Frankie said. "Wait, don't the Kleins have a dog?"

"Yeah, a little terrier," Toby said, getting the feeling that this whole expedition was a bad idea.

"Last one over is Mr. Joseph's bitch," Warrick said and then he leaped over the four-foot high hedge. Once over, he said, "See, easy. Just be careful of sharp twigs."

Frankie was next. But instead of bounding over the hedge like Warrick, he opted to step over. In the dim light, Toby could see him fumbling, struggling to get over the hedge. He got his left leg over, stumbled, then his right. Finally, he was on the other side.

"Come on, Fairchild. Get your ass over here."

Toby drew in a shaky breath. He didn't want to jump over and risk breaking a leg, so he wussed out and like Frankie, stepped over the hedge.

How the hell did we wind up following Warrick? Toby wondered. *First alcohol, then cigarettes, and now a stealth mission through the backyards of my neighbors.*

When Toby planted his feet on the Klein property, Warrick said, "About time."

"Yeah, well, you might do this sort of thing all the time, but I'm new to it. So fuck you." Toby looked around. Aside from a single light glowing through a second-story window, the rest of the Klein house was in darkness.

As they started across the moon-streaked lawn, nerves tingled up Toby's spine like there were a thousand tiny spiders scurrying across his back. They were half-way to the fence separating the Klein property from Mr. Joseph's, when there came a yapping from inside the house. A back porch light flashed on, and then the back door opened. The yapping grew louder.

"Shit," Warrick breathed, and the three boys darted forward, over to the far side of the house. Hidden by the wall, surrounded by darkness, they huddled, waiting, not daring to climb the fence for fear of being seen or heard.

"That's a good girl," they heard Mrs. Klein say. "Good girl, Sheeba."

Soon the white terrier trotted around to the side of the house where the boys were hiding. The dog stopped and stared at them.

"Fuck off fur-ball or else we'll feed you to Mr. Joseph," Warrick muttered.

Toby wanted to thump Warrick for talking, but he was too afraid to move.

Like it was hypnotized by their presence, the dog stared at them for what felt to Toby like the longest time.

"I think we're done for," Warrick whispered, and if Toby didn't know any better, he would've sworn that Warrick actually sounded amused, like he was on the brink of laughter.

How could he be finding this funny? Toby thought. *If we're caught, our night is ruined.*

"Come on, Sheeba," Mrs. Klein called. "There's nothing there, girl. Come on."

Yeah, listen to your mom, Toby thought.

The dog seemed to be thinking its next move over. It broke from its statue-like state and took a few steps towards them, growling as if saying, *Yeah, I see you. I know you're there. I just have to decide whether or not to be bothered enough with you to start barking.*

Toby drew in breath. He could see it now—the campout would be finished once Mrs. Klein told his parents of their nocturnal activities. Frankie and Warrick would be sent home and he would be punished—worse once the alcohol and cigarettes were found.

Toby felt ill. The night, possibly the entire summer, was going to be ruined, all because of a stupid little dog.

But the dog turned away and bounded back inside; either it was too scared, or too dumb, to bother with them. Either way Toby was relieved.

"What's the matter with you?" Toby snapped once both the dog and Mrs. Klein were inside, the porch light off. "If we had been discovered, we would've been toast."

"Or dog food," Frankie said, snickering.

"Relax, Fairchild. We weren't, so don't worry."

"Still, you're an idiot for speaking," Toby said, heart hammering.

"Whatever. I'm going over."

Toby heard Warrick's shoes scraping along the wooden fence as he climbed. There was some grunting, then a soft thud as he dropped to the other side.

This time Toby didn't delay. He scaled the fence, dropped to the ground on the other side, glad to be out of the Kleins' backyard.

Frankie was last to struggle over the fence. "I wish we'd just walked the front way," he panted. "Would've been so much easier."

"And less dangerous," Toby added.

"Well we're here, aren't we?"

The area along this side of Mr. Joseph's house was thick with shadows. Toby saw two windows: the one closest to the front was dark; the other, nearer to the back where they were, glowed with dull light from behind a yellow curtain.

"Hey, this is spooky," Frankie whispered.

Toby agreed.

It somehow would've been less unsettling if the old man lived in some monstrous castle—at least that would've been appropriate—but there was something unnerving about such a strange man living in such an ordinary house.

Warrick crept up to the lighted window.

"Can ya see anything?" Frankie said.

"Yeah, a meathook, a bunch of chickens in cages, and Leatherface sawing some poor dude in half," Warrick replied.

"Don't say things like that," Frankie whined. "I'm already scared enough. Toby, you go see."

Toby didn't particularly want to, but he also didn't want to look like a chicken, so he sighed, said, "Okay, move aside Warrick," and stepped forward.

Warrick moved and when Toby peered in through the window via a narrow gap in the curtains, he saw part of a kitchen. The kitchen looked small and very basic, with a stove that looked like something out of an old Western movie, a fat, round refrigerator, and a sink scattered with dishes. Moving his head to the left, he saw the right portion of the kitchen: a small wooden table, two rickety chairs and a doorway leading into darkness. He left the window. "It's just a scummy old kitchen," he told Frankie. "No meathooks or psychopaths."

"Well, no meathooks," Warrick said.

"Funny," Toby said. "So, what now?"

"We go into the backyard."

"Why?"

"I'm guessing his trashcan is back there somewhere. I wanna look inside it. You never know what you might find. Also, we might be able to see into other parts of his house, see if that homeless nigger's in there."

"Stop saying that word," Toby said.

"What, homeless?"

Toby shook his head.

"What about his shed," Frankie said. "Maybe the bum's hiding in there?"

"Yeah, good one, Wilmont. We'll check that out, too."

"You're both crazy," Toby said. "I'm not going down there and looking through stanky bins and breaking into sheds."

Warrick shrugged and switched on his flashlight. The sudden blinding light hit Toby's eyes. He squeezed them shut and turned his head away. "Get the light away, turd-brain. Jesus!"

The light went away, and Toby opened his eyes. "God, you're an idiot," he huffed. "I thought you said no flashlights unless absolutely necessary? What if the old man saw the light?"

"He'd probably slit our throats and suck out all the blood," Frankie said.

"Nice, Wilmont," Warrick said, grinning. "Just the image I want in my head when we're about to go into his backyard."

"Who's we?" Toby said. "I'm not going down there. This is as far as I go."

"Then don't," Warrick said. "Frankie's coming with me, aren't ya, Frankie?"

Frankie's eyes were glassy in the glow of the flashlight. "Yeah, count me in," he said.

Toby looked at Frankie. *It's just the alcohol, it's making him silly.*

"Great. You can stand watch for us then, Fairchild. If you see the old man come into the kitchen, come and get us."

"Whatever," Toby said.

Frankie followed Warrick down into the backyard. Soon they, along with Warrick's flashlight, were out of sight, leaving Toby alone and feeling exposed.

What's happening to Frankie? he thought. *We used to do everything together.*

He knew he shouldn't take Frankie going with Warrick personally—he knew it was just the alcohol influencing his decision. Still, it didn't stop Toby from feeling disheartened.

He was thinking about Frankie when he heard the sound of running water coming from inside Mr. Joseph's house. Toby crept up to the kitchen window and peered inside. The old man was at the sink, filling a tea kettle with water. The kettle was one of those old fashioned metal ones, the kind his grandmother used to have. He once asked her why she didn't just use an electric kettle like everyone else—she had simply chuckled and kissed him on the cheek.

Done with filling the kettle, the old man placed it on the stovetop, put the lid on, then switched on the front gas burner. From the pantry he got a box of tea and heaped three spoonfuls into a white ceramic teapot sitting on the counter. Then he moved over to the table, where he eased himself slowly into one of the chairs almost opposite the window and sat staring at seemingly nothing. Toby had never really looked closely at the old man, even though he had been living across the street from him his entire life. Like most people in Belford, Toby had only ever given Mr. Joseph the occasional backwards or sideways glance. Toby noticed him, occasionally stared at him, but had never really taken the time to actually see him.

But now, as he peered in at the old man, Toby saw past the crooked neck and nasty scar and saw for the first time the short, curly hair, like he had a bunch of cotton wool sitting on top of his head; the sparsely wrinkled face and thin lips. One could almost call it a gentle face, a kind face.

Except for his eyes.

There didn't seem to be any life in those eyes; no light, no sparkle—just two dark holes. He was reminded of the stranger's eyes. Toby shivered, despite it being a humid night.

After a few minutes, Mr. Joseph got out of the chair, slowly, like molasses pouring out of a jar, and shuffled over to the stove, where he poured boiling water from the kettle into the teapot. He stood waiting for a full minute before taking a cup down from the rack and filling it with tea from the teapot. He brought the cup to his lips, took a sip, and then turned to the sink and dumped the rest of the tea down the drain. He set the cup on the counter, reached down and opened a cupboard under the sink. He came up with a bottle of alcohol. He took it over to the table, sat down, and sunk back a long mouthful of the liquor.

Afterwards, he sat motionless, his gaze burning a hole through the table. Finally, he stood, hobbled back over to the counter and opened the top drawer. He pulled out a gun.

Toby sucked in breath.

Mr. Joseph stuck the barrel of the revolver into his mouth.

"Oh my God," Toby squeaked.

He had to do something—run and get help, bang on the window, smash the window, something, anything; but he couldn't move. He was frozen to the spot, terrified.

I can't just stand here and watch a man blow his brains out! Do something!

Mr. Joseph closed his eyes. It was crazy, but at that moment, Toby thought he looked almost... calm, happy.

But that was crazy, wasn't it? Surely just a trick of the light, or Toby's imagination.

A sudden crash startled Toby. He gasped, and for one horrifying moment thought the old man had pulled the trigger. But the crash had been too soft, too distant and Mr. Joseph was still standing with his head intact.

As Toby's heart-rate returned to a relatively normal pace, he watched Mr. Joseph take the gun barrel out of his mouth and place the revolver on the counter. Then he started towards the back door.

Yes, that's where the crash had come from, Toby now realized. The backyard.

Frankie and Warrick!

From off to his left, Toby heard the sound of feet slapping against the dry, hard ground.

"Did he hear us?" Warrick panted when he and Frankie reached Toby. "What's he doing?"

"He's going to the back door," Toby told them.

"Oh shit!" Warrick exclaimed. "Run!"

They all raced down the narrow pathway that ran alongside the house until they reached the sidewalk.

"Hold on, guys," Frankie said.

Toby skidded to a halt and turned around. "What?"

Toby watched Frankie bend down and scrounge around on the ground.

When Frankie straightened, Toby saw, clenched in his hand, a small rock. Toby groaned.

"Go for it," Warrick said, grinning like a demented skeleton.

Frankie drew his right arm back and then hurled the rock at the left-side front window. The rock smashed the glass, sounding like an explosion in the still night.

Toby winced.

Warrick searched the ground, found another, smaller rock, and threw it at the right-side window. "Take that, you fucking freak," he cackled.

In his mind, Toby saw a desperately sad Mr. Joseph looking crookedly at the broken windows. The image abruptly changed to the old man with the black metal gun stuck in his mouth like a deadly lollipop, empty eyes closed, and then...

"Come on," Frankie said.

Toby shook the image away.

"Hurry!" Frankie said, and took off after Warrick, who was already halfway across the street.

Toby followed.

When they joined Warrick in front of Toby's house, Toby saw that the front family room light was still on. "Be as quiet as possible," he told Frankie and Warrick. "My parents are still up, and if they catch us, we'll be toast."

With Toby leading the way, they crept down the side of his house, down to the backyard. Toby was relieved to see that neither parent was standing by the back door with their arms folded, a hard stare on their face. The three boys hurried over to the tree house ladder. Toby went up first, climbing it with blistering speed. When he reached the top, he threw the trap door open and scurried inside.

Soon Frankie and Warrick were back up inside the tree house. "Bolt it," Toby said, sitting against one of the walls.

Frankie, the last one in, bolted the trap door, then he leaned against the wall opposite Toby. Warrick rested against the wall between them, opposite the trap door.

"Wow, what a rush," Warrick said. "I'd love to see the old pervert's face when he sees the broken windows." Warrick grabbed the non-spiked bottle of Coke and took a long, thirsty drink. He then passed it to Frankie.

"So what the hell happened in the backyard?" Toby asked. When Frankie offered him the bottle, Toby grabbed it and guzzled the soda.

"Warrick saw a human arm," Frankie said.

Toby frowned. "What did you say?"

"In the old man's trashcan," Warrick said. "I was searching in there amongst all the rubbish and I pulled out an arm."

A laugh escaped Toby; a nervous laugh, but a laugh all the same. "You're kidding me? You expect me to believe that?" There was no way, after witnessing the old man contemplating blowing his brains out, that Toby could believe there was an arm in his trashcan. Maybe yesterday he would've believed it; but not now.

"No shit," Frankie said. "A real human arm."

"A mangled human arm," Warrick said. "It had bits of flesh hanging from it and you could actually see some bone. Man it was disgusting."

"And this was in his trash? Just thrown in there like some empty soda bottle?"

"Yeah," Warrick said.

"We was so freaked out that we knocked the trashcan over," Frankie said.

"You knocked the trashcan over," Warrick said. "You should've seen your face, Wilmont. The moment I told you what I'd found, you looked like you had crapped your pants."

"So you didn't see this arm?" Toby asked Frankie.

"Well, no, not exactly. I was at the shed, trying to see inside. But I couldn't. Suddenly Warrick cries, 'Shit, there's an arm,' and I guess I knocked into the trashcan as I bolted."

"Well, at least we now know what was in the bum's bag," Warrick said with a chuckle. He stood and looked out the window that overlooked Pineview. "I can't see him," Warrick said. "Reckon he heard the windows being broken?"

"I'm sure he already knows about the broken windows," Toby said. "Bet you he's already called the cops, too."

"Oh shit," Frankie groaned. "We're screwed if he calls the cops."

"Relax, Wilmont," Warrick said, sitting back against the wall. "He ain't gonna call the cops. He has an arm in his trashcan for Christ's sake. And a murderer in his house."

"Yeah, I guess you're right," Frankie said. "But what if he gets rid of the arm, hides the bum in the cellar or something, then calls the cops?"

Warrick chuckled, shook his head. "You're a riot, Wilmont."

"Well it's bullshit about the arm, there is no murderer hiding in Mr. Joseph's house, and breaking his windows was a stupid thing to do." Toby stood up.

"What?" Frankie said, a puzzled expression on his face. "He deserved it. Fucking freak."

Whether or not Warrick thought he saw an arm, or was just plain lying, Toby wasn't sure. Not that it mattered. After what Toby had witnessed tonight, seeing somebody moments from death, it really put things into perspective. He was upset at Frankie and Warrick for what they had done. If only they knew the truth about Mr. Joseph. But Toby couldn't tell them. Maybe one day he would tell Frankie, when they were older and living in a dorm room together, sinking back a few brewskies. Maybe then he would tell him about what he had seen tonight. But not now, not tonight.

Toby started for the trap door.

"Hey, where are you going?" Frankie said.

"I have to take another leak," Toby lied. In truth he needed some time away from these two.

As he unlatched then lifted the trap door and began climbing down the ladder, he couldn't shake the thought that at any moment he could hear the distant pop of a gunshot.

And only Toby would know what the sound meant.

CHAPTER SIX

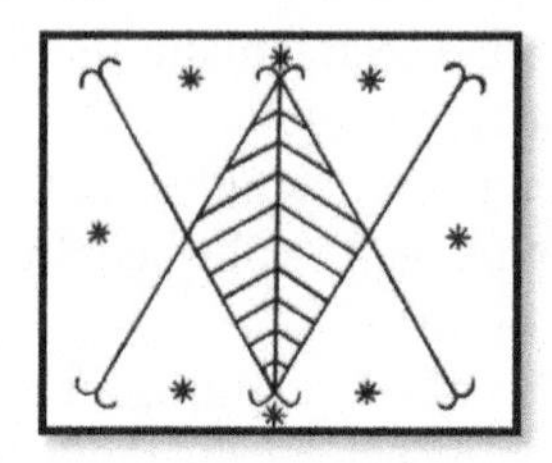

Toby stepped into the shower and immersed himself under the hot spray. After five minutes of standing perfectly still and letting the water cascade over his lean body, Toby grabbed the soap and began lathering up.

Having a long, hot shower always worked wonders whenever he wasn't feeling well. And this morning he was feeling terrible: monster headache, queasy stomach—he had already thrown up twice. He had woken early with a breathless start, mouth like sandpaper and tasting of old sweaty socks, the noise of a loud blast ringing in his ears, remnants from a dream (one that he couldn't remember anything about—other than it ended with a gunshot). Moments later he crawled out of the stuffy, crowded confines of the tent, sunlight pushing through the open flaps, and puked in some bushes. The second occasion was about an hour later, in the bathroom. Frankie had also puked upon waking, but not Warrick, although he did look pale and he complained of a headache.

After returning to the tree house from his brief respite, the three of them had sat and talked and drank for a while longer. Toby had vague memories of stumbling down the ladder and slithering into the tent. But he had no idea what time that was. He also couldn't remember whether Frankie and Warrick went with him, or if they came later. But they were there, lying cramped inside the two-man tent, when he woke feeling like a train wreck.

I'm never drinking again, Toby thought as he soaped his chest. *That was the first and last time.*

Why people drank to excess when in the morning you felt this terrible defied logic, in Toby's opinion.

Something else that defied logic was how Frankie could be downstairs gobbling down a large plate of waffles. Just the mere thought of food sent Toby's stomach in a spin.

At least Warrick had left; that was something to be grateful for. He had left about half an hour ago, after scarfing down a glass of orange juice and a Krispy Kreme for breakfast. The empty beer cans, bottle of Jack Daniel's and pack of Marlboros went with him.

So far it seemed his parents hadn't cottoned on about the smoking and drinking. Or if they had, they hadn't let it be known.

Probably waiting until Frankie leaves, and then they'll start in on the yelling.

That was the last thing Toby needed; his head would probably explode if his parents raised their voices any louder than a whisper.

His skin now a deep shade of red, Toby turned off the taps and hopped out of the shower. The bathroom was swimming with steam and after wrapping the towel around his waist, Toby grabbed his toothbrush and tube of toothpaste and brushed his teeth for the second time that morning. Then he headed into his bedroom, where he looked at his reflection in the wall mirror. He saw red, puffy eyes and a pallid face staring back at him.

With a sigh, he started dressing.

"Feeling better?" his mom asked when Toby entered the kitchen.

"I guess."

"Too much junk food." She was sitting at the table, sipping her tea, alone.

"Where's Frankie?" Toby asked as he shuffled over to the fridge.

"Out with your father learning how to box."

"Boxing?" Toby took the carton of orange juice out and poured himself a glass. How Frankie could manage any sort of physical activity this morning confounded Toby. He took a drink and winced. Orange juice and mint toothpaste weren't a match made in heaven, that's for sure. The second mouthful was better, and by the third, all trace of the toothpaste was gone.

"So, did you boys have fun last night? Didn't get up to too much mischief?"

"Aside from eating too much junk food, no," Toby said and offered his mom a sickly smile.

"I warned you, didn't I?"

Toby shrugged.

"Pastor Wakefield asked after you at church this morning. I told him you weren't feeling well. He said to give you his best and that he hoped you were feeling better. I don't suppose you feel like any breakfast?"

Toby finished off his orange juice and shook his head. "Think I'll pass." He rinsed out the glass and then dumped it in the sink.

"I want you two to take that tent down today," his mom said.

Toby sauntered towards the back door. "Sure," he answered and stepped outside.

He squinted against the glare, though the sunlight no longer felt like nails driving through his eyes and into his brain. He made his way to the garage. Inside, his dad was punching the heavy bag, puffing, sweat teeming down his face. Frankie was sitting on the garage floor, red-faced, looking like he had just run a marathon.

"Here he is," his dad said, stopping his workout. "How you feeling, champ?"

"Okay, I guess."

"You wanna have a go? I'll teach you some moves."

"Another time," Toby said. "I'm feeling too... tired."

"What? I spent all yesterday morning setting this thing up and you boys are too tired to use it?"

"Hey, I'm just getting my breath," Frankie said.

"You know it ain't good," his dad said.

Toby sighed. "What isn't good?"

"When a man almost three times the age of two teenagers is fitter than the both of them."

"Sorry Dad, I promise I'll have a go another time. Just not today."

His dad walked over and put a sweaty arm around Toby's shoulders. "Hey, that's okay kid. I know what it's like the morning after a party." He chuckled. "Believe me, I understand. How late did you boys stay up, anyway? Don't worry, I won't tell your mom."

"I don't really remember. I think it was around one o'clock."

His dad humphed. "That's not late. One time when I was a few years older than you two, I camped out in the woods with some friends. We all told our parents we were sleeping over at each other's places. Anyway, the only sleep we got was one induced from too much beer. I think we fell asleep around four or five in the morning. When we awoke we were not only sick, but covered in mosquito bites. We didn't realize it at the time, but we had camped near a swamp. Well, needless to say, our parents found out. Couldn't exactly hide all that itching. Let me tell ya, I got the hiding to end all hidings. My ass was sore for a week. What made it even worse, was that one of my friends, Michael, brought along his younger brother, and we got him drunk." His dad shook his head. "Strange kid, as I recall. Very quiet, would sometimes just sit and stare at us. What was his name? J-something. Jason? Johnson... Jackson! That's it, Jackson. Wondered what happened to him."

"And the point of the story is?" Toby asked.

He shrugged. "Dunno. Just felt like reliving old times."

Toby sighed. "Come on, Frankie, we've got a lot of cleaning up to do."

Frankie struggled to his feet, pulling off the old gloves he was wearing and tossing them to the concrete.

"Hey, watch it. Those old gloves won me a championship."

"Sorry. Say, thanks for the lesson Mr. Fairchild," Frankie said as he and Toby left the garage.

"Anytime, Frankie. But next time, try to get more sleep...and try not to drink so much booze."

The boys froze. Toby felt like he had been kicked in the stomach. He glanced at Frankie; his face was all squished up, like he had the runs.

Toby's mind whirled with excuses, pleads of ignorance, and heartfelt apologies. He was mere seconds away from having his summer taken from him - no more staying up late, no more staying over at Frankie's, no more campouts. He knew he had to come up with something good to worm his way out of this, and fast.

He and Frankie turned, faced his dad, but instead of seeing a stern look of disappointment, his old man was laughing.

Laughing?

"It's okay, guys. Relax, you look like you're about to face the firing squad."

Toby and Frankie frowned at each other. Was this some sly adult ploy to try and get them to confess to more than they would otherwise?

Toby's dad strolled over to them, sporting a wide grin. "For a full year I was fourteen. Bet ya guys didn't know that. Hell, I had my first drink when I was twelve. Puked it all up, just like you two. Felt horrible the next day, and the day after that, come to think about it." He glanced back at the house. Facing the boys, he whispered, "Your mom doesn't know about it. I didn't tell her. She's a bit... naïve when it comes to matters such as these. Doesn't understand what being a young man is all about."

"You mean, you're not mad?" Toby said.

"Nah, not really," his dad said. "It's all a part of growing up. As long as you don't abuse it, get hooked on the stuff or start stealing bottles, one night of drinking isn't the end of the world."

"You can be cool sometimes, Mr. Fairchild," Frankie said.

Toby's dad threw back his head and laughed. "Gee, I'm glad you think so, Franklin."

"So you won't tell Mom?" Toby said.

"Or mine?" Frankie put in.

His dad shook his head. "Secret's safe and all that. Go on, get going. You've got a lot of cleaning and packing up to do." He turned around and headed back into the garage.

"I can't believe that just happened," Frankie said. "Holy shit."

"Yeah, neither can I," Toby said. It didn't seem right—or real. His dad knowing about them drinking, yet acting like it was no big deal. It was very strange. Hell, he didn't even punish Toby. Very strange indeed.

"Well at least he doesn't know about the smoking," Frankie said.

"And I want to keep it that way, so keep ya mouth shut," Toby said. "Come on, let's clean the tree house."

An hour later, Toby and Frankie had disposed of all the empty candy wrappers, chip packets, soft drink bottles, cigarette butts (Warrick had neglected to take them with him; it was lucky Toby's parents hardly ever ventured up into the tree house), had stowed away all the leftover junk food, and were in the middle of taking down the tent. It was slow going, not only because of the heat, but because they both still felt like it had been them hanging up inside the garage instead of the punching bag.

They were taking a much-needed break under the shade of the elm tree, when Toby's mom came walking towards them, arms folded—her usual 'not happy' pose.

"Here comes trouble," Frankie whispered.

"Shut up," Toby said. So much for his dad keeping his promise of not telling her about them drinking.

"How's it going?" she said, stopping just short of the two boys.

"Slowly," Toby said.

"Lunch is almost ready," she told them. "You two hungry?"

"Starving," Frankie said. The day Frankie didn't answer "starving" to that question, even after getting drunk for the first time the night before, was the day that Frankie was well and truly sick.

"Yeah, a little," Toby said. The thought of food no longer made him want to throw up.

"Can I ask you boys something?"

Here it comes.

"Earlier when I walked to the store, I noticed that Mr. Joseph's windows were broken. Both front windows. He was out there cleaning up when I walked back. Poor man, he looked so...awkward. I was just wondering if either of you saw or heard anything last night?"

Toby was relieved she didn't come out here to lecture them about the evils of alcohol, but he couldn't relax—he was worried Frankie would let it slip that they were the ones responsible for the broken windows.

"We didn't hear anything," Toby said. "Must've happened after we had gone to sleep. Right, Frankie?"

"Ah, yeah, we didn't hear nothin'."

His mom nodded slowly. "Well, just thought I'd ask. I think it's awful what the kids in this town do to that man. Now he'll have to pay for the windows to be replaced—and he doesn't look like he can afford to replace two broken windows." She sighed. "Let me know if you boys need anything. Lunch will be in twenty minutes." With arms still folded across her chest, she turned and walked away.

Once she was inside the house, Frankie said, "I don't know how she can feel sorry for that freak."

"Don't you feel bad?" Toby asked. "You broke one of his windows."

"He deserved it."

"Oh, that's right. The severed arm in the trashcan."

"You got it."

Well, at least I know the old man is still alive. Yeah, and cleaning up the mess we made.

"Okay, let's just get this tent down," Toby sighed. "I'm hot and I feel like crap."

They left the shade of the elm and continued dismantling the tent.

After lunch, the tent dismantled and packed away (stuffed would be the more accurate term, considering the way the bags bulged), Toby and Frankie were lazing up in Toby's room, Toby relaxing on his bed, Frankie slumped in the chair by the desk. Their bellies were full of tuna and salad sandwiches and iced tea.

"You don't think your mom could ever find out who smashed the windows, do you?"

"Nah, of course not." Toby paused. "Unless somebody saw us last night."

"You think somebody saw us?"

"I don't think so," Toby said. "But it's not out of the question."

Gently swiveling in the chair, Frankie furrowed his brow. "I don't think anyone saw us. I mean, they would've told your mom or Mr. Joseph by now. Right?"

"Sure," Toby said. He hopped off the bed and wandered over to the open window. It was from here, just two nights ago, he witnessed Dwayne and his goons deface Mr. Joseph's house and kill a chicken. Now as he looked down, he saw Mr. Joseph outside, body hunched, methodically going through the bushes, presumably picking out broken pieces of glass. Watching him, Toby felt sad, angry, and responsible. He may not have thrown any rocks, but he let Warrick lead them over there. He didn't try to stop Frankie or Warrick from smashing the windows.

How did Mr. Joseph sleep last night? Toby wondered. *It was a warm night, sure, but still... maybe he didn't sleep. Maybe he sat up all night with the gun in his mouth...*

The image of Mr. Joseph sucking on the gun barrel flooded Toby's mind. He closed his eyes and literally tried to shake the image from his head. He heard his mom's voice: *I think it's awful what the kids in this town do to that man. Now he'll have to pay for the windows to be replaced—and he doesn't look like he can afford to replace two broken windows.* When he opened his eyes, the image was mercifully gone, but he knew what he had to do.

"Is he still out there cleaning up?" Frankie said.

Toby turned from the window and faced Frankie. "Look, I'm still not feeling well. Matter of fact, I'm suddenly feeling quite sick. Maybe you should go."

"Go? But...it's summer vacation."

"Yeah, I know, but all I feel like doing is sleeping. And maybe some more puking. No point in you hanging around for that."

Frankie, looking a little wounded, muttered, "Okay. Sure, whatever." He stood, picked up his backpack and sleeping bag.

Toby rarely lied to Frankie. The few times he had, he had felt terrible afterwards. But now, as he looked at Frankie's melancholy face, he felt nothing. No remorse, no guilt. After all, it was Frankie who had instigated the rock throwing, so really, it should be him going over to Mr. Joseph's instead of Toby. But there was no way Frankie would conceive, let alone carry out, what Toby had in mind.

"Sorry, Frankie, but I don't think I'd be much fun today."

Frankie, backpack slung over one shoulder, said, "Well, guess I'll see ya tomorrow."

"Yeah."

Frankie shuffled out of the bedroom. Toby closed the door, laid back down on his bed. Soon he heard talking and then the front door bang shut. Then, just as he expected, he heard footsteps pattering up the stairs. There was a knock at the door.

"Toby?"

"Yeah?"

The door opened and his mom came in. "What's wrong? Frankie told me you weren't feeling well. That you told him to leave."

Toby sighed. "I didn't tell him to leave exactly. I just suggested that it would be for the best. It won't be much fun for him to watch me sleep all day."

"Are you feeling that bad?"

"Just tired. And a bit headachy. Nothing serious."

His mom wandered over to the bed, placed a hand across his forehead. "You do feel hot."

That's probably because it's a hot day, and my room is like an oven, Toby thought.

"Maybe I should call Doctor Hampton."

"No. I'm fine, really. I just don't feel like climbing any mountains today, that's all."

His mom smiled. "Okay. Well, get plenty of rest and drink plenty of water."

"See, who needs a doctor when I've got you."

She patted his arm. "Smart guy." She kissed his forehead then left.

Toby waited for his mom to walk back downstairs before hopping off the bed and shutting his door completely (his mom never closed his door all the way). Then he went to his closet, pushed away clothes and putting aside his tennis racquet, baseball gloves, and pairs of shoes, he pulled out the old shoebox. He sat down on his bed, flipped off the lid and gazed down at all the money he had left in the world—$120. He thought of all the lawns he had mowed, fences and walls he had painted, and he hesitated. Was it really his responsibility? Was any of it his fault? What if the old man really was some kind of pervert or devil-worshipper? Did he really want to give away all his hard-earned money to such a person?

Damn Frankie and Warrick. They should be the ones paying for the windows.

But he knew they would never give a cent to the old man.

Taking a deep breath, he reached in and took out one hundred dollars. He figured he should keep some back for himself—after all, he needed some spending money for the summer. That left him with twenty dollars. Twenty measly dollars. He pocketed the money, placed the lid back on the shoebox, then hid the box back behind the tennis racquet and shoes.

I'm gonna have to work all summer to get that money back, he thought, and his shoulders slumped.

Next Toby grabbed a sheet of paper and a pen and wrote—

To Mr. Joseph.

I'm sorry about your windows. Here is 100 dollars so you can pay for the replacements. I hope 100 will be enough.

Toby left the note unsigned, though he was tempted to sign either Frankie's or Warrick's name.

He folded the note and placed it inside an envelope, along with the money. He scribbled *Mr. Joseph* on the front of the envelope, tucked it into one of his pockets, then headed for the bedroom door.

Toby managed to avoid his parents as he slipped out the front door—he heard his mom in the kitchen and he figured his dad was still out in the backyard.

Back out in the sunshine, he crossed the street and made his way down Pineview. As he passed the Klein house, he chuckled to himself about their close encounter last night with Sheeba the killer terrier.

Wasn't so funny at the time, Toby thought, and then he was at the old single-story. He looked out for any sign of the old man. He had decided that if Mr. Joseph was still outside cleaning up, he would walk casually on by and keep walking and maybe go to the corner and wait until the old man went inside.

But there was no sign of him, so Toby stopped. Nerves pecked at his stomach.

Why am I so scared? Toby wondered.

All he had to do was drop the envelope in the mailbox. Simple. It should take no longer than a few seconds.

In the sober light of day Toby could see the broken windows; both front windows had large holes in them, with cracks spider-webbing around them.

Toby looked around, just in case someone was watching. He didn't want to be associated with the broken windows.

But the street was empty, so Toby reached into his pocket and pulled out the envelope. With slippery hands, he aimed the envelope at the narrow mail slot.

He was just about to slip it in, when Mr. Joseph's front door began to open.

Toby gasped. His hand froze, his grip tightened on the envelope. He was too scared to run. Instead he just watched the door widen until there stood old Mr. Joseph.

Toby's breath caught in his throat.

"Bonswa," the old man called.

"Huh?" Toby breathed, and was amazed he could say anything at all.

"Bonswa means good afternoon."

Toby swallowed. "Oh."

Mr. Joseph had a surprisingly high voice, not feminine, just not the deep, thick voice Toby would have expected. Also, he spoke with an accent—kind of like those guys in that movie, Cool Runnings. The accent wasn't strong, had probably lessened over the years, but to Toby's all-American ears, it stood out like the hairs in an old man's nostril.

"Can I help you?" Mr. Joseph said.

Toby blinked. "Um..."

"Looks like you've got something for me. Come closer. I won't bite."

Toby almost laughed, but thankfully the laugh got stuck in his throat. He managed to take a step forward, followed by another.

He shuffled up the path, up the porch steps, stopping in front of Mr. Joseph. Wearing cheap, grimy tennis shoes, loose fitting jeans and a long white shirt, Mr. Joseph looked less frightening up close, but Toby's hand still shook as he handed him the envelope. Toby just hoped the old man didn't notice his trembling hand.

Taking the envelope, Mr. Joseph said, "Mèsi, Monsieur Fairchild."

He knows who I am? Toby thought. And then, *Of course he does.*

The old man flipped open the envelope, pulled out the money, then the note. He held the piece of paper at a slight angle and his eyes flicked over the words.

Toby watched nervously; he desperately wanted to turn and run.

When Mr. Joseph was through reading the note, he looked at Toby. He was frowning, and though it wasn't a mean scowl, more of a confused look, his expression still sent chills down Toby's back. "You broke my windows?"

Toby muttered, "Yes." He wanted to tell him the truth, but really, what purpose would that serve? And would he believe Toby even if he did tell him the truth? After all, Toby was the one giving him the money. "I'm sorry. Really. It was...an accident."

"An accident?"

Toby nodded.

"Well, boys will be boys. Here." He held the money out. "I can't take this. You must have worked hard to earn this."

Toby didn't know what to do or say.

"Go on," the old man urged.

Toby took the money. For a fleeting moment, their hands touched. The old man's skin was like ice. Toby jerked his arm back and clumsily pocketed the money. "Ah, thanks," he said.

"Well, thank you for coming around," Mr. Joseph said. "Orevwa." Flashing a brief, melancholy smile, the old man turned and headed back inside.

So that's the man we've been scared of for all these years? Toby thought. Still a little shaken from the encounter, Toby left Mr. Joseph's and headed home.

That night, Toby dreamt he was on stage. The stage reminded him of something out of one of those old black and white movies he and his parents often watched Saturday nights—old wooden boards, heavy curtain behind, balconies on either side, and rows upon rows of hard, creaky seats before him. But these seats were empty. Suddenly the lights blinked out, there was momentary darkness, and then a spotlight flicked on, hitting him square in the eyes. He squinted, went to shield his eyes, but found he was unable to. It was like his arm was tied to something. He tugged, but his arm wouldn't move. He tried the other, but it, too, wouldn't budge.

Music started playing, some jazzy number, and Toby expected clowns to appear on stage, or a line of dancing girls.

But he remained on the stage, alone, squinting against the bright glare of the single light.

"Dance!" someone cried out from the audience. "Go on, Dance!"

It sounded like Miss Wilson.

But weren't the seats empty just a moment ago? he thought.

"Yeah, come on, give us a good show!"

Was that Dwayne Marcos?

There was an audience out there now?

Suddenly his left arm started jiggling.

Huh? Toby breathed, and then his head was turned to the left. He saw his mom off stage, pulling on a string that was tied to his left wrist. She was smiling, gaily moving the string up and down, side to side. Toby wanted to stop her, but it was like he didn't have any control over his own body.

His head was moved to the right, just as his right arm started to flail, not of his own accord. He saw his dad maneuvering his right arm. He too was grinning, seemingly lost in his own enjoyment of making his son's right arm dance.

Then his legs began to jerk and he wanted to cry out for it to stop, but his mouth no longer worked. His head was shifted down, to where Suzie and Leah were lying on the floor, pulling his legs to and fro. All his limbs were now moving independently of one another; flailing in an uncoordinated dance number.

The audience he couldn't see clapped and laughed and whistled, seemingly enjoying Toby's bizarre dance routine.

Toby wanted to scream *let me go, stop making me dance, I look like an idiot*, but he couldn't.

His parents, Suzie and Leah continued to pull the strings.

Suddenly his head was jerked down, and if it were possible, Toby would've gasped at the sight of his naked body.

More laughter from the audience.

Oh my God! Toby screamed inside his head, mortified.

His pale, skinny body jumped and jerked, the jazz music kept on playing, and just as the drummer started his solo, a syncopated rhythm on the tom-toms, Toby noticed there was a string tied around his member. It, too, was being pulled, though it didn't appear to be in time with any music; it was simply tugged for the sole purpose of getting him hard.

Toby didn't want to see who was on the other end of this string, but he had no say in the matter. Just as the drummer crescendoed into the wild crashing apex of his solo, Toby's head was maneuvered a little to the left and he saw Gloria squatting on the stage, a shy grin on her radiant face, tongue poking out, tugging on the string.

Nooooooo!!! Toby cried and as the drummer finished his solo and the band came back in with the chorus, Toby's head was lifted, up, up, and he knew he was about to see who it was that was controlling his head.

While his body continued to dance, Toby's head was pulled back as far as it could go, and he stared up at rafters high above, but darkness lay beyond, swallowing the person sitting up there, pulling on the head-string.

Who are you? Toby cried

But the dream ended and Toby never got to find out.

CHAPTER SEVEN

The day that was to change Toby's life forever started out like any typical summer morning.

He slept in till almost ten and then unhurriedly made his way downstairs (with images from the truly bizarre dream last night rolling around in his head).

There was a note on the fridge door from his mom. It read:

> *You looked dead to the world, hon. Didn't want to wake you. When you do finally get up, can you please see that the front and back lawns get mowed sometime today, preferably before your dad and I get home? Thanks a bunch.*
>
> *Love, Mom.*

Recovered from the hangover and feeling back to normal, he'd had a relaxing breakfast of pancakes (made from a pre-mix of course; Toby didn't have the slightest clue how to make them from scratch), toast and orange juice and afterwards relaxed in front of the TV for an hour, watching cartoons. It was during this time his dad called and told him he was not only to do the mowing today, but sweep the leaves from the gutters and tidy his room. When Toby had protested, in his sulkiest little boy voice he could muster, his dad countered with, "If you don't want your mom to know what happened Saturday night, then you'll do these chores, and you'll do them with a smile. And if they're not done by the time I get home from work, then your summer may not be as fun as you had hoped. Understand?" His dad usually wasn't one to resort to blackmail, but Toby figured he had gotten off lightly regarding the drinking, so if this was his only punishment—one day of chores—then he could count himself lucky.

When midday came without any sign of Frankie, Toby figured he also was having a lazy morning, so Toby decided to get the mowing over and done with. That way, when Frankie did show up, he could maybe talk him into helping tidy his room and clean the gutters.

Dressed in old sweatpants and a ragged Metallica T-shirt that was more holes than fabric, he headed outside and over to the shed. He loved going into the shed. It was a whole other world, full of familiar smells such as old oil, grass, petrol, paint; they all merged to form one great big nostalgia-fest of a smell, one that reminded him of long weekends as a kid helping his dad with the gardening or the mowing. The shed had seemed a thousand times bigger back then, a massive tome where spiders lay in wait for little boys, but where his daddy was always there to protect him.

Now, it was just a shed—small, murky and completely harmless.

Still, Toby couldn't help but grin as he entered the shed and pulled out the mower. There was a time not so long ago when he wasn't allowed to help his dad with the mowing unless supervised; the pouring of the gas into the tank; the starting up of the mower's engine; the whirring of the blades underneath—these were all potentially hazardous for a young boy, and positively terrifying for any parent.

Now, he often mowed the lawn on weekends while his mom and dad went about their daily chores, or his dad watched baseball on television. He didn't mind doing it; if truth be known, it was probably his favorite chore (except when it was cold or raining; then mowing was the worst chore on earth. But on days like today, when the sun was a round burning flame in the clear blue sky, then it was his favorite chore).

The tank was full, so, slipping on the protective goggles that were dangling from the handle, Toby started up the mower. It took him two pulls of the cord to get her going. As exhaust spewed from the engine, Toby started pushing the mower over the green and yellow grass.

As he mowed, his mind floated from Gloria, what she might be doing right now, to Mr. Joseph and what Toby had seen two nights ago while staring into another person's private world.

He was almost finished mowing the backyard when Frankie came strolling over.

He was looking much better than he did yesterday; he had a spring in his step and his face had regained its color.

Toby killed the engine, slipped the goggles off his face and said, "Hey."

"So am I allowed to see you today?" Frankie said with a lop-sided grin.

"Yeah, sorry about that. I really wasn't feeling that great. But you must've been feeling the same way? You looked sick enough."

Frankie shrugged. "Yeah, I guess so. Anyway, I feel all right today. So, whatcha doing?"

Toby huffed. "What does it look like?"

"No, I mean, what are you doing after you're done with the mowing? There's a baseball game starting at two o'clock. You wanna come and play?"

Nothing said summer vacation like an all-day game of baseball. Toby loved baseball, even more than he did basketball. But he sighed. "I really should get this done."

"Come on, do it later. Or tomorrow. Hell, you've got all summer to mow the lawns. But there's not a game of baseball on every day. It's gonna be a big one. Guys and girls from junior and high school are playing. Come on Toby, you gotta come. After Leah, you're our best pitcher."

Toby sighed again, a heavy, 'woe-is-me' sigh. Sure it was vain, but no teenage boy hated being told he was a great baseball player and the team would be worse off without him.

"Sorry dude, no can do. I have to clean the gutters and tidy my room after I'm done with the mowing. It'll probably take me the rest of the afternoon."

"Since when did your parents become slave drivers?"

"Since my dad found out about us drinking Saturday. This is my punishment. He said if I don't do these chores, not only will he tell Mom, but he's gonna make this summer hell. Which probably means not letting me out after six and no staying over at your place. Which means no watching late night creature features."

Frankie sighed. "That sucks. I thought your dad was cool with us drinking?"

"Yeah, well, my parents aren't as cool as your mom."

"Are you kidding? If she ever found out about the drinking, she'd pound my ass raw and then ground me for the next ten years."

Toby smiled thinly. "Anyway, as much as I would love to come and play baseball, I just can't. If I get these chores done by this afternoon, then I'll be a free man for the rest of the summer. And I'm sure there'll be more games. Hey, you never know, I may get the chores finished quickly, and then I'll come over and watch the rest of the game. See you fumble the ball and lose it for your team."

"Screw you. Are you sure you don't wanna come and play? Risk getting grounded for a week? It's gonna be a killer game. Oh, and, ah, Gloria's gonna be there," Frankie added.

Toby blinked. "Gloria?"

Frankie nodded. He smiled; a smug, 'I've got you now' smile.

Why Frankie didn't offer up this vital piece of information earlier Toby didn't know. Still, Gloria or not, if he didn't get these chores done by the time his dad got home, there'd be hell to pay. "Sorry, you're gonna have to play without me. Say hi to Leah for me, and tell her to hit a home run for me."

Frankie nodded. He looked disappointed. "Only if you're sure."

Toby considered his options one last time; the thought of seeing Gloria for the whole afternoon was mighty tempting. But so was a summer free from strict curfews and his parents breathing down his neck. "Yeah, I'm sure. I'll try and get these chores done as quickly as I can. Unless you wanna help and then I'd get it done in half the time?"

Frankie huffed and he kicked at a pile of mowed grass. "Yeah, right. And miss out on the game of the summer? Have fun Toby. Oh, and I'll be sure to say hi to Gloria for you, too."

"You do that," Toby said and reaching down he scooped up some of the freshly cut grass. It felt like cotton wool in his hands. He dumped the bundle over Frankie.

"Hey!" Frankie cried.

And they spent the next ten minutes scattering mowed grass all over the lawn as they waged a fierce grass-throwing battle.

Toby worked harder and faster than he ever had in his life. By four-thirty the front and back lawns had been given the short back and sides treatment; the gutters were free from leaves and grime; and his room was neater than it had been in years. Toby could picture his parents' faces when they got home—they were probably expecting him to do a half-assed job. But there was no way Toby was going to let his summer be ruined by something silly like not doing some simple chores properly.

So the way Toby saw it, he was free. He had paid his debt for Saturday night.

And so, after a quick shower and a change of clothes, he rode his Schwinn over to Jinks Field.

When he arrived, the game was at the top of the ninth inning—the blue team, which included Frankie, Leah and Warrick, was down by two runs, losing to the red team, which included Paul Rodriguez, Rusty Helm and Scotty Hammond.

Toby rested his bike alongside the others against the chain link fence and then strolled over to the bleachers, glancing over at the parking lot as he walked—it seemed all bottles and broken glass from Friday night had been picked up, leaving no trace of what had taken place.

The stands were crowded with kids and teenagers, all cheering for one side or the other. Toby smiled at the familiarity of it all: the roar of the crowd, the smell of grass, dirt and sun block; but the smile was tainted with a touch of sadness as he looked out at the make-shift baseball field, wishing he was out there, playing. Leah was currently pitching, the reds were two out. He spotted Frankie out in left field, and when Frankie noticed Toby, he waved. Toby waved back, then turned to the bleachers.

His spirits lifted when he spotted Gloria sitting about halfway up the stands. She was sitting with Emma and Danielle, two of her best friends, and she looked a picture of beauty—her hair was tied back in a ponytail, she was wearing a baby-blue sleeveless top, which showed off her slender, lightly tanned arms, and light-colored shorts.

Toby's breath was sucked back into his throat. Suddenly the sun was too bright and his mouth too dry.

Get a grip. She's only a person. No need to get so worked up.

Toby looked around, saw plenty of empty spots where he could sit. There was one beside Emma, or there were plenty behind the three girls.

He desperately wanted to be near Gloria, but there was no way he could sit next to Emma—he'd have to make small-talk, and he just knew he would fumble and make an idiot of himself. And besides, Emma was a rude, stuck-up cow. So that left either behind Gloria—or somewhere else entirely.

His decision was made easier when Emma and Danielle got up, said something to Gloria, then started down the bleachers.

Toby swallowed.

This is it. Come on, make a move.

Toby waited until the two girls were gone, then he started up the stairs, walking casually, scanning the rows of seats like he really was looking for somewhere to sit and didn't already have somewhere in mind.

He said absent hellos to some of his classmates as he walked up the concrete stairs, and when he reached the bench where Gloria was sitting, alone, he took one more step, and then turned into the row above her.

He walked in front of kids and teens, all screaming, either in joy or disappointment, depending on who they were rooting for—Simon Hunter had fallen prey to one of Leah Wilmont's trademark fastballs, making the reds three out.

When Toby reached the appropriate spot, he sat down.

Just below him Gloria was sitting with arms in her lap, her blonde hair like spun gold in the afternoon sunlight.

Beside Toby were two kids, both slightly older than him, and to his left were a few empty spaces; so if he made a fool of himself, there wasn't too many people around to witness his humiliation.

Waiting for the cheering, clapping and booing to die down, as the teams swapped over for the second half of the last innings, Toby sucked in the hot June air and said, "Hey Gloria."

Gloria flinched and when she turned around, she had a look of surprise on her face. Then she smiled and said, "Oh, hey Toby. How are you?"

Toby shrugged. "All right. Enjoying the game?"

She shrugged back. "Yeah, I guess. Baseball's never been my favorite game. But Emma and Danny wanted to come. I thought you would be playing?"

"I had to do chores."

"No, really?"

Toby nodded.

"All day?"

Another nod.

"That sucks."

"Yeah, that's what Frankie said."

There was silence after that, as they exchanged nervous smiles.

Come on, say something! Don't let the conversation die so soon. You were getting somewhere! Don't blow it!

"So... where are Emma and Danielle?"

"Gone to the bathroom."

"Oh."

Out on the field, Warrick was batting, while a sophomore (soon to be junior in a few months) at Holt High by the name of James Ogilvy was pitching.

"Look, about the other day," Toby said. "I'm sorry about knocking into you. I hope you didn't have a bad bump."

"Well, my hats look lopsided now when I wear them, but apart from that, I'm okay." Gloria chuckled, Toby followed, and then they both laughed good and hard.

Afterwards, the ice having been broken, Gloria said, "Mind if I come up and sit with you? Who knows how long Emma and Danny will be, and baseball's kinda boring watching it by yourself."

Toby clenched his teeth, for fear that if he opened his mouth, he would expel a big, fat, embarrassing "Yippppeee!!" So he nodded, and watched as Gloria got to her feet and, with a tiny handbag laced over one shoulder, stepped over the bench she had been sitting on. When she was on Toby's level, she turned and sat beside him, smiling shyly.

Toby took her in, every line and contour of her face, noticed the small sprinkling of freckles across the bridge of her nose; breathed in her smell—vanilla—all in the space of a few seconds, before averting his gaze to the baseball game.

"So," Gloria said, her breath smelling of root beer. "What chores did you have to do? Not vacuuming or washing the dishes I hope. They're the worst. I hate doing those."

"Nah," Toby said, turning back to Gloria. "I had to mow the lawns, clean the gutters and tidy my room."

"What did you do to get stuck with those?"

"You really want to know?"

"Sure," she answered. She smiled. Her teeth were white and straight, her lips cherry red.

Toby felt the beginnings of an erection, but using every ounce of his willpower, he managed to subvert the potentially mortifying incident. "Well, Frankie and Warrick Coleman came over Saturday night. We camped out in my backyard. Warrick brought over some whiskey, and well, we all got drunk. My dad found out, and as punishment, he made me do those chores."

"Bummer. So how'd he find out?"

"I think he sorta figured it out while I was busy puking my guts out in the rose bushes."

Gloria laughed. "You were that drunk?"

Toby nodded. "But never again."

"That's what they all say," Gloria said. "Deb's always coming home drunk. And every morning she says never again. Then a few nights later, she comes home drunk again." Gloria shook her head.

All around them the crowd cheered and bellowed, but Toby barely noticed; he didn't even bother looking to the field to see what was happening. Gloria looked, briefly, but Toby could tell she wasn't interested.

"Look, Toby, I have something I want to say to you." Gloria turned to Toby. She looked nervous.

Toby's already sweaty palms grew even sweatier.

Oh no, what's she going to say? Is she going to tell me she knows what happened when I fell on top of her? Or that, sorry, but she finds me boring and she has to go? That my breath stinks?!

Toby tried smiling, but his lips quivered, so he spoke instead. "Um, yeah?"

Gloria sighed. "It's a little embarrassing," she said.

He just knew it was about him touching her breast—he wanted to run away and hide.

He was close to interrupting her and telling her it was all an accident, he didn't mean for it to happen, that he got no enjoyment out of it (not so, but he couldn't tell her the truth), and that he didn't even realize what he was touching until...

"I wasn't going to the store on Friday to buy some milk. I was coming to see you."

Toby frowned. "You were?"

Gloria nodded. "I felt bad about, you know, about laughing at you that morning. I wanted to apologize, but I chickened out. I was heading back home when we ran into each other."

Toby didn't know whether to be happy or embarrassed. "Oh," he said. "Okay. Thanks?"

Gloria shook her head. "I knew I shouldn't have mentioned it. You're embarrassed now."

"No, I'm not. I'm just..."

"Your face is red."

"It is?"

She nodded.

"Oh. Well, yeah, I guess I'm a little embarrassed. It was a stupid thing to say. Childish. I don't know why I said it. It just came out."

"We all say silly things sometimes. I shouldn't have laughed. None of us should have. But I don't think Emma and Danny are as sorry. They still think it's funny."

Toby rolled his eyes. "Well, apology accepted."

"Thanks," Gloria said. "I can relax now."

After that, they sat and watched the rest of the game, chatting about what they had planned for the summer, occasionally commenting on the game—both were rooting for the blue team—so it was nice to cheer together and boo as one.

Just before the game ended, Emma and Danielle came back, and Toby noticed their expression when they first saw Toby and Gloria sitting together—one of disgust and surprise, respectively. But they pretended not to be, as they said, looking up from the row below, "Hey Toby," in almost perfect unison.

Toby nodded.

"Where were you guys?" Gloria said. "You were gone for like fifteen minutes."

Thank God, Toby thought.

"We got chatting to some guys," Emma said. She paused, flicked her eyes at Toby before adding, "Some high school guys. Well, they'll be going to college next year."

"Oh, really," Gloria said, sounding none too impressed—which pleased Toby immensely.

"Yeah, anyway, a bunch of us are going to Patterson's for some burgers and shakes," Danielle said. "Chip's giving us a lift there, so come on, he's waiting."

Gloria frowned. "Chip Donovan?"

"Yeah, so?" Emma said. "Chip's cool. He's gorgeous, too."

"Gorgeous? Don't think Drew would be too happy hearing you say that."

"He's away for most of the summer, won't be back until just before the start of school. I'm allowed to have some fun. After all, he's only my boyfriend, it's not like we're married."

Gloria sighed. "Okay, whatever." She turned to Toby. "Say, you wanna come?"

Toby raised his eyebrows. "Me?"

"Yeah, you and Frankie. Are you hungry?"

Toby hadn't given the matter much thought—he had been too preoccupied with Gloria. But now he thought about it, his stomach did feel empty. "Sure, that'd be great."

"Well he can make his own way there," Emma said, sounding bored. "There's not enough room in Chip's car."

"Oh," Gloria said.

"That's okay," Toby said. "We'll just meet you there."

"No, you guys go on ahead," Gloria said. "I'll go with Toby."

Toby looked down at Emma and Danielle—they looked as shocked by Gloria's decision as Toby was.

"Are you sure?" Danielle said.

"Yeah," Gloria said. "What's the big deal?"

"Whatever," Emma said with a sigh. "Come on Danny, let's go."

"See you there," Danielle said and as she and Emma left, she gave Gloria a I hope you know what you're doing look, which didn't go unnoticed by Toby.

"You could've gone with them," Toby said once the girls were gone. "I'll just go with Frankie."

"It's okay, really. I hate Chip Donovan. He's so sleazy. I'd rather go with you. And Frankie," she added as an afterthought.

"Okay."

The game ended—the red team won by one run—and so Toby and Gloria made their way down to the field, where they met up with Frankie.

Frankie, his clothes dirt and grass-stained, took one look at Toby's companion, and his mouth literally dropped open. Toby itched to tell him to shut it, that he looked like one of those amusement park clowns.

"I'm sorry you guys lost," Gloria said. "It was a close game, though."

Frankie looked to Toby, then back at Gloria. "Ah, yeah, thanks," he said.

"A bunch of people are going over to Patterson's for something to eat," Toby said.

"Yeah, I know," Frankie said. "I heard Leah talking about it with some of the others."

"You want to go? Me and Gloria are heading over there now."

Frankie nodded. "Sure, sounds good. I'm starved. I could really go for a burger, some fries, some onion rings, a chocolate shake and a sundae."

"I feel sick just hearing you say that," Gloria said.

"Yeah, and I bet ya he won't even share any of his fries."

Frankie made a face at Toby, then said, "Hey, I'll see if Leah can give us a lift."

“I don’t mind walking,” Gloria said.

“It’s okay, Leah’s heading over there anyway. Besides, I’m beat. I don’t think I could walk all the way into town on an empty stomach.”

Frankie left to find his sister.

“Boy loves his food,” Toby said with a shrug.

Gloria smiled. “So I noticed.”

Toby checked his watch; it was just after five o’clock. His mom should just be getting home from work.

“I wonder if Leah would be able to swing by my place,” Toby thought out loud. “I should tell my mom I’m not going to be home for dinner.” He added, “She worries.”

“Don’t you have a cell?”

Toby shook his head. “My parents don’t want me to have one until I’m sixteen. They say until then, I shouldn’t need one. I know, stupid, huh? I mean, every kid I know has one. Except for Frankie.”

Toby immediately regretted adding that last part. It had nothing to do with responsibility that prevented Frankie from owning a cell phone—Suzie simply couldn’t afford to give Frankie one. Leah had a cell, but she paid for it herself.

“You can use mine to call your folks if you want.”

“You sure?”

Gloria dipped into her purse and pulled out a pink cell phone. She flipped it open and handed it to Toby.

“Thanks.” He dialed home. As he put the phone to his ear, he thought of all the times the cell had been against Gloria’s own ear, all the times her breath had blown against the end of the cell as she talked, perhaps her mouth occasionally touching it.

Toby swallowed, had the urge to lick the end of the phone, but thought better of it.

After speaking to his mom, he handed the phone back.

“Everything okay?”

Toby nodded. “She said to have fun and not to eat too much.”

“You should pass that advice onto Frankie.”

“Yeah.”

Soon Frankie came jogging back. “It’s cool,” he puffed. “Leah will drive us. But we have to hurry. She wants to go home and get cleaned up first." Frankie rolled his eyes. "Chicks." And then, as if suddenly remembering it wasn't just Toby standing there, Frankie said, "Oh, sorry."

"Hey, I'm a chick, I know that," Gloria said. "No need to be sorry."

Toby laughed; Frankie simply looked embarrassed.

"Hey, what about my bike?" Toby said as the three of them left the field and headed towards the car park.

"Just leave it here, it'll be all right," Frankie said. "We'll come back for it later."

"But I didn't bring the lock with me."

"Relax, nothing's going to happen to it. Who would want to steal your bike anyway?"

Toby looked over at his beloved BMX, leaning against the fence in the distance, now very much alone. He hated leaving it, but as his mom had so often pointed out, it was a safe, virtually crime-free town.

"Okay," Toby said.

As they neared Leah's car, Toby looked at Frankie. Frankie glanced at Toby, and mouthed, *I can't believe this is happening*, and Toby shrugged, mouthed, *Me either*, and they both grinned stupidly, but stopped before Gloria caught them.

Patterson's Diner was located on Main Street, a few stores up from the corner of Main and Longview Road. It was run by a stocky fellow by the name of Luke Patterson, a gruff, straight-talking man of about fifty. Patterson's had been an institution in Belford for twenty-five years. It had the best burgers in town, and the shakes were all homemade, using only the freshest of ingredients—at least, that's what the sign above the counter claimed.

It was a simple, bare-bones kind of eatery. No fifties nostalgia theme, no kitsch adorning the walls. Mr. Patterson scoffed at such things. There was just a whole lot of red vinyl booths circling the perimeter of the inside of the diner, a lot of free-standing tables and chairs in the middle, ten stools at the counter, and half a dozen tables and chairs outside.

The mornings were always packed with the breakfast-crowd and kids wanting an early morning hit of milk and sugar before school; the nights were usually as crowded as the mornings. On this particular Monday evening, the place was brimming with the laughter and screams of delight from a roomful of hormonally charged teenagers, full mostly of the day's baseball game's players and spectators.

Toby, Frankie and Gloria arrived at Patterson's at around six, managed to grab a table inside, and for almost half an hour had sat and shared a basket of chili fries and onion rings, washing the grease down with vanilla malt, chocolate and strawberry shakes, respectively. The conversation had been comfortable, if at times a little strained, but nice all the same. At six-thirty Danielle and Emma came up to their table and pulled Gloria away—Gloria rolling her eyes at Toby and Frankie, saying, "Sorry guys, won't be long." That had been almost two hours ago.

Not that Gloria was being intentionally rude—Toby and Frankie both understood that it was nothing more than a popular girl spending time with other popular people, including her two best friends. They were grateful for the time they spent with Gloria, and in truth, Toby was amazed she lasted as long as she did—people kept on coming up to Gloria, guys as well as girls, and asking her to come and sit with them, or telling her that so-and-so wants to talk to you.

Such was the life of a pretty, popular teenage girl, and Toby was more than happy to sit back, relax with Frankie, and take it all in.

Because this was a new world for them. Sure they often hung out at Patterson's, sometimes meeting up with Paul Rodriguez, very occasionally Warrick Coleman tagging along, but they had never been invited to hang out with the cool crowd from middle school, let alone the cool older kids from high school—it was all a little overwhelming for them.

Which was why it didn't upset Toby when Gloria was whisked away—it gave Toby and Frankie time to breathe, to not have to worry about keeping up the conversation, just enjoy their burgers and second round of shakes (Toby opted for another vanilla malt, Frankie a strawberry), and goof around, like old times.

At around nine o'clock Dwayne Marcos came in.

Toby and Frankie had just polished off two bowls of coffee flavored ice cream and were arguing about who would win in a fight—Arnold Schwarzenegger or Sylvester Stallone (Toby reckoned Stallone, said he knew how to fight and was a real bad-ass, Frankie reckoned Schwarzenegger, giving the obvious reasons that he was simply bigger and had more muscles)—when the older teenager burst into the diner. A hush fell over the diner, all eyes turning to Dwayne.

Toby could tell right away Dwayne was drunk, it didn't take a genius to figure that out, what with the way he was staggering and the glazed look in his eyes. Toby shrank down in his seat.

Turning back around, Frankie also sank down in his chair. "He doesn't look happy."

Toby nodded.

Mr. Patterson took one look at Dwayne staggering over to the booth housing Debbie, Leah and a few other junior and senior high school kids, and he stormed out from behind the counter. "Get out, Dwayne," Mr. Patterson growled. "I'll have no intoxicated people in my diner."

"I just want to speak to Debbie," Dwayne said, voice slurry.

Toby glanced over at Debbie. She looked annoyed and when Dwayne said, "Come on, honey. I'm sorry, okay?" She turned her head and faced the wall.

"Trouble in paradise," Frankie muttered.

"Out, Dwayne!" Mr. Patterson ordered. His voice was firm and even. Mr. Patterson may have been pushing fifty, but he was still as fit and strong as anyone Toby knew. "You're lucky I don't call the cops and report an intoxicated minor. So just leave."

"Fuck you," Dwayne said. And then to Debbie, "Come on babe, just give me one more...hey!"

Mr. Patterson had grabbed Dwayne by one arm and was pulling him towards the door.

"I warned you, Dwayne," Mr. Patterson said.

Only Luke Patterson would have the balls—and the strength—to throw Dwayne Marcos out.

"Abuse!" Dwayne cried. "I'm gonna report you to the cops!"

Mr. Patterson pushed Dwayne out the front door; Dwayne stumbled, almost toppled over onto the sidewalk, but somehow managed to keep himself upright. "I'll bust your head in with my baseball bat, then I'll call the cops if you ever come back in here drunk again."

That seemed to shut Dwayne up—at least for a few moments.

As Dwayne staggered to his car, parked out the front, he cried: "Debbie, I love you, you'll see, I'll get you back," and then he hopped into his Chevy, the engine grumbled to life, and then Bruce sped off.

"Wow," Frankie said.

Toby glanced over at Gloria, sitting in one of the booths with Danielle and Emma; she was looking over in Debbie's direction, a concerned look on her face.

Mr. Patterson sighed, said, "Sorry 'bout that folks. We're closing in about twenty minutes, so now's a good time to finish what you've got and start getting out those wallets."

As Mr. Patterson headed back to his place behind the counter, the diner continued to buzz with talk and laughter.

Twenty minutes later, as people were starting to leave, Gloria stopped by their table. "Hey guys. Some scene before, huh?"

"Yeah," Toby said.

"That guy's crazy," Frankie said, finishing off his third shake for the evening—another chocolate.

"Say, everyone's heading up to Taylor's Hill. Keeping the party going, you know? A sort of a celebration for the official start of summer vacation. I was going to head up there, you guys are more than welcome to come."

Toby and Frankie exchanged looks: a combination of fear and excitement.

They had never been to Taylor's Hill at night, aside from a few times when they were younger and had ridden their bikes over (this was back when Frankie had a bike, before it broke) to try and catch some of the older kids making out—or better yet, having sex. But they had always hidden behind trees, keeping well out of sight.

"Come on, it'll be fun," Gloria said. "There'll be heaps of people there."

All kinds of thoughts ran through Toby's mind, good and bad: people drinking, people doing drugs, people making out—he and Gloria making out—Dwayne crashing the party; it all flooded

Toby's mind and he didn't know whether to say yes, no or maybe. After all, he knew his parents would never agree to him going to such a party; neither would Suzie. And he was already on thin ice with his father.

"Hurry up, Gloria," Emma called. "Chip's leaving."

Gloria sighed, said, "Yeah, I'm coming," then turned back to Toby and Frankie. "So, how about it?"

"Um, well..." Toby stumbled.

"Yeah, sure, we'll be there," Frankie said.

Gloria smiled. "Great, well, see you guys there." Her gaze lingered on Toby before she turned around and hurried out of Patterson's, along with her friends.

"Why'd you say yes for?" Toby said. "I mean, it's Taylor's Hill...at night...our parents..."

"Don't need to know. Relax," Frankie said. "We're going to high school in a few months, about time we had some real fun."

Toby jumped when Warrick, appearing out of nowhere, draped an arm around Toby's shoulders. "She likes you, man," he said, grinning. "Gorgeous Gloria likes you. Holy shit!"

Toby flung Warrick's bony arm away. "She does not," Toby said, his defenses firing. "She's just being friendly."

Warrick slapped Toby on the back. "Duh, that's because she likes you! So you guys coming up to Taylor's Hill? Gonna be a wild time." He nudged Toby's arm. "A real wild time, hey Fairchild. Say, you got some rubbers? You might need them..."

"Get lost," Toby said, springing to his feet. "That's all you ever think about."

Warrick paused, a frown plastered on his face. "Yeah, what's wrong with that? Isn't that what all guys our age think about?"

"We'd better hurry if we want a lift up there," Frankie said. "I'm sure Leah's going, and I don't feel like walking all the way over there."

"Too late, your sis already left," Warrick said.

Frankie stood and scanned the diner, which had thinned out considerably. Sure enough, there was no sign of Leah Wilmont. "Oh, man," Frankie groaned.

Toby left the table and walked up to the counter, Frankie and Warrick following.

Once they had paid for their meals, they headed for the door.

Outside the night was humid, thick with the smell of possibilities. "Well I ain't walking to Taylor's Hill," Toby said.

"How else you gonna get there?"

"By bike," Toby told Warrick. "I left my BMX at Jinks Field." Toby looked at Frankie. "You wanna come? Or else you can go with Warrick and I'll meet you guys up there."

Frankie turned to Warrick.

"Hey, don't look at me. I've already got a lift. And there's no room left in the car."

Frankie sighed. "Okay, I'll come with you."

Toby nodded and together they started down Main Street.

"See you guys there," Warrick called out. "And watch-out for old perverts! Paar-tyyyy!"

"I reckon Warrick has been drinking," Frankie said.

Toby shrugged. "Hadn't noticed."

Frankie sighed again. "Man, can't believe Leah ditched us. Now we have to walk all the way to Jinks Field, then get all the way out to Taylor's Woods."

Jinks Field was a fifteen-minute walk from Patterson's, and from there it was about twenty minutes on foot to Taylor's Woods.

"I wish I still had my bike, then we could both ride up there."

"Well we don't have to go to the party," Toby said. They turned left and started up Longview Road. Away from the store lights and street lamps, the night was dark—their only light now came from the full moon.

"You don't want to go? Hell, I was thinking mostly of you when I said yes."

"I can think for myself."

Frankie huffed, loudly. "Warrick was right, Toby. Gloria likes you. God knows why, but she does. It's obvious to everyone but you. I mean, she comes and sits with you and talks to you at the baseball game, then comes with you to Patterson's instead of going with her friends, and then she invites you to go to Taylor's Hill. Could it be any more obvious?"

"First of all, I came and sat near Gloria at the baseball game; she was just being polite when she came up and sat with me. Secondly, she came with you, me and Leah to the diner; her sister is best friends with yours, remember? And lastly, she invited us both to Taylor's Hill. Hell, maybe she likes you. You ever thought about that?"

"I wish," Frankie said. "But come on, we both know that ain't the truth. I saw how she was looking at you. She's into you, man. But hey, if you don't want to go to Taylor's Hill and spend some time with her, then that's fine with me. I don't care either way. I'm just as happy to go home and play some Xbox."

Toby stopped. Frankie halted, turned, and in the moon's glow, Toby saw him frown. "What?"

Toby drew in a deep breath, and then expelled hot air. "I'm scared," he said. "Okay? I'm scared."

"About what?"

"About everything. About Gloria liking me, about going up to Taylor's Hill. I mean, of course I want Gloria to like me. It's all I've dreamt about for as long as I can remember. But now that it may actually be happening..." He shrugged. He didn't know how to put into words exactly what he was feeling. He and Frankie told each other almost everything, but they rarely discussed their feelings.

How could he tell Frankie that he was scared about growing up? That he was scared about starting high school, about leaving behind all that was familiar and safe? He liked the idea of staying at home playing video games with his best friend, or watching horror movies late at night. He liked doing those things; they were what he was used to. He wasn't sure whether he was ready to go to Taylor's Hill at night, not with a bunch of high school kids, not even with Gloria. What if he made a complete idiot of himself? Embarrassing himself in front of Frankie, or even Leah, was one thing, but in front of a girl he liked so much it hurt, in front of a bunch of older kids, most of whom would be attending the same school as him come September?

That scared him.

But Toby didn't have the words to express these feelings to Frankie. He just hoped Frankie felt the same way, and understood where he was coming from.

"Yeah, well, you always were a scaredy-cat," Frankie said and smiled, and in that smile Toby knew Frankie understood.

"Come on, we'd better get moving," Toby said. "It's gonna be late enough by the time we get up there. I told Mom I'd be home by eleven at the latest. And she'd flip if she knew where we were really going."

"We don't have to stay long," Frankie said, ambling beside Toby. "Just an hour, tops. I mean, Gloria is expecting us... you... so we'll just go, see what's happening, and then, if we don't feel comfortable, we leave."

Toby nodded. He was already feeling better about the situation.

They walked in silence for a bit, the nighttime sounds of owls hooting, cicadas buzzing and dogs barking loud around them. Then Frankie said, "You remember the dream you told me about the other day? The strange one about being locked inside a box?"

"Yeah."

"You remember you asked me if I had ever had a strange dream like that? Well I had one last night. A real weird dream. It still creeps me out thinking about it."

Remembering his dream last night, the one where he was naked on a stage, being controlled by other people, like a marionette, Toby shivered. "What happened?"

"I dreamt I was drowning. But it wasn't just that I was underwater and couldn't get to the surface; someone was holding me down. Actually had a hold of my legs and was pulling me down further. I kicked and struggled, but they wouldn't let go. There was someone up above, I could just see them through the murky water, but I wasn't sure if it was my mom, or just some stranger. I couldn't see them properly. But I felt like they were calling me to swim to them. I tried, man how I tried, but I just couldn't break free from the person's grip. Man I was scared. But you wanna know the weirdest part of the dream?"

"What?"

"When I looked down to see who was holding my legs, I saw you."

Toby shook his head. "Yeah, that is weird."

"When I woke, I had trouble breathing. It took me like ten seconds before I could take proper deep breaths and not feel like I was drowning. It was freaky, man."

"Yeah, I bet," Toby said, and he was about to tell Frankie about his latest dream, but they arrived at Jinks Field. So Toby decided to wait until they were on their way to Taylor's Hill.

Toby was relieved to see his BMX still resting against the high chain link fence.

Guess Mom was right, after all, Toby thought.

The night was suddenly eerily quiet, with only the faintest hint of a breeze. The field was a dark, empty wasteland, the bleachers a big black blob nearby.

It was a stark contrast to Friday night, with all the noise and thick amalgam of dust and exhaust fumes.

Toby's gut tightened at the memory of all those teenagers hollering and laughing, eyes wide with excitement as they harassed and assaulted a perfect stranger.

What did Warrick call it? Giving the bum a nice Belford welcome.

As they walked towards Toby's bike, there was a sound, like a car door thumping shut somewhere in the distance. Frankie paused and glanced around. "You hear that?"

Toby shrugged. "Yeah, it was a car door. Big deal. Now look who's the scaredy-cat." Toby stepped up to his bike.

Standing back, Frankie chuckled nervously. "Hey, maybe it's that bum. Maybe he didn't leave town, after all."

"Yeah, maybe he's come to get more arms for his collection," Toby said, meaning to sound jokey, but instead his voice was shaking as much as his hands were.

Watch-out for old perverts...

As he reached out and gripped the handlebars he heard footsteps behind him, coming up fast.

He thought it was Frankie, but then he smelled a sour smell, like sweat mixed with beer, and his mouth went dry.

Frankie screamed. It sounded like a knife scraping through ice.

Toby started to turn. Something heavy struck the back of his head. He grunted, and bright flashes danced before his eyes. The pain was overwhelming, and as the second blow hit, Frankie stopped screaming and Toby heard a weight drop to the ground. As another blow struck him, the world began to spin and he felt like he was going to throw up.

He dropped to the ground.

And saw Frankie sprawled in the grass nearby, his head painted with blood, his eyes closed, and before Toby blacked out, he tasted blood in his mouth, heard the sound of voices, somebody laughing (laughing?)—a horrible high-pitched cackling—and felt his body being pummeled.

And then...

In the dream he was half-dead. Blood was spewing from his head like a geyser. One arm was numb and dangling from his shoulder like a stuffed toy that had had one of its arms almost pulled off...

He was staggering through darkness, pain was eating away at him like termites through wood, and he wanted desperately to sleep, just to lie down and sleep...

He heard screaming—Frankie, Frankie is that you?—and then he saw trees, but they were dark, like shadows, and then somebody lumbering over to him...

A voice, soft and kind, "You'll be all right."

Darkness.

A small light, like a candle's.

A room, a strange room filled with color and drawings and bottles.

And then the same soft voice:

"Papa Legba, ouvri barriè pour moin, agoè!

"Papa Legba, Attibon Legba, ouvri barriè pour moin passé!"

The voice fades, the light fades.

The voice comes back:

"Passé Vrai, loa moin passé m' a remerci loa moin, Abobo."

Then a prayer, and he thinks, I know this, it's from the Bible.

He sinks again into silent darkness, pain eating him up; the sound of a rattle, like a baby's rattle, brings him back, and the candlelight reveals a strange figure dancing, shaking the rattle, and then:

"Zo wan-wé sobadi sobo kalisso."

More darkness, a voice, distant, says, "Guédé Nimbo, please, I need your help..."

Then a figure, dark as the night, hovering above him, his old black hat flickering in the candle flame, a smell like whiskey, but different, floats over him, and thick cigarette smoke, and then another voice, more nasally than the last, but jovial, says, "I'm here to help you, ti moun..."

A warm sensation, a tingly sensation, and then...

More voices, more pain, more screaming, some crying, flashes of too-bright light...

And then darkness...

ONE MONTH LATER

CHAPTER EIGHT

A knocking at his door woke Toby. Groaning, he sat up, glanced at his clock radio and saw it was almost eleven o'clock.

"Jesus," he muttered.

Another knock. "Toby?"

"Yeah, yeah, I'm up."

The door edged open and his mom poked her head in. "Sorry to wake you, but Gloria's here."

"Okay," Toby said. "I'll be down in a moment." He remained sitting up in bed, head still foggy.

His mom entered his room, walked over to the window and flung open the curtains.

"Can you shut them?" Toby groaned, squinting his eyes against the sudden brightness.

"Sunshine is good for you. It's a beautiful day outside. You and Gloria should go out, enjoy the sun."

"Playtime for the invalid, huh?"

His mom shook her head. "You're not an invalid, Toby. And I don't think Gloria wants to spend another beautiful Sunday listening to you feeling sorry for yourself."

"Whatever," Toby mumbled. He flung off the sweat-stained sheet and planted his feet on the ground.

Toby stood and pain shot through his right side. He gritted his teeth. Mornings were always the worst. His body was stiff, like a rusty machine. He longed for the day when he could walk around without feeling like his whole body was on fire.

"I'll go and fix you some breakfast," his mom said. "What would you like?"

"To be free from this pain," Toby sneered.

And to have Frankie back, he thought.

"Come on what do you feel like? Oatmeal? Granola? Fruit? Pancakes?"

"Just a cup of coffee," he said.

"Are you sure? You need your strength."

"I'm not hungry."

His mom sighed. "Coffee it is." She left his bedroom.

Toby slipped on the same shorts and T-shirt he had worn yesterday and then hobbled over to the window. He looked out. It was a typically beautiful summer day in Belford: still, clear and hot. The sort of days he and Frankie loved the most.

The kind that Frankie would never see again.

Toby began crying. It hurt his body to do so, but he couldn't stop the tears from coming.

He cried almost every day. The pain—the deep, invisible kind—was still strong and would take a long time to heal, longer than the bruises on his ribs, longer than his broken nose and fingers had.

When the crying eased, he wiped the tears away and looked down to see Mr. Joseph out in his front yard, doing some much-needed gardening.

Mr. Joseph.

"Are you decent?"

Gloria's sweet voice.

"Yeah," Toby answered, still holding his gaze at the window.

"Being a Peeping Tom is a crime, you know." Gloria came and stood beside Toby. "Oh," she said, softly. "Here's your coffee."

"Thanks," Toby said, turning away from the window and taking the mug from Gloria. He took a sip. It was good and strong.

Gloria was wearing a short denim skirt and white shirt.

Toby's groin stirred.

"So how are you this morning?"

"The usual. Had a rough night."

"You know, that's something we could do today. If you felt up to it."

"What's that?" Toby said.

"You could go over and say thanks."

"Why would I want to do that?" Toby said, knowing full well the answer.

"I know he's... a bit weird and all, but you do owe it to him to at least say thanks. He did save your life, Toby."

"Yeah, I know that," he said.

As if he needed reminding of that fact. He thought about it every moment he wasn't thinking about Frankie.

"Well why don't you...?"

"I'm not thanking him for you," Gloria said. "You know that. So, how about it?"

Toby shrugged. "Maybe."

"I don't understand why you're so afraid to speak to him," Gloria said.

Toby shuffled back over to his bed. He sat down and sipped more of the coffee. It was strange, but ever since the attack he had grown fond of coffee.

"You should be up and moving around," Gloria said. "Especially in the mornings. You need to work the stiffness out of your body."

"I know, I know. But if it's a choice between being a little stiff or walking around in pain, I think I'd rather be stiff." He chuckled. But it hurt, so he stopped.

Frankie would've liked that one.

Gloria sighed. "Suit yourself." She started for the door. "So you coming down?"

"I need to have a shower first. I'll be down in about ten minutes."

"Okay, but hurry."

"Why?"

"Because we're going outside today and enjoying the sunshine."

Toby said, "You're starting to sound like my mother," and Gloria grinned as she left the room.

"I thought you were never going to finish in the shower," his mom said when Toby walked into the kitchen.

He limped over to the table and sat opposite Gloria. "And miss out on a day full of pain and sorrow?"

His mom hopped up, poured him a fresh mug of coffee, and brought it over to him. "Now Toby, don't be smart."

Toby took the mug and sipped the coffee. "Me? I'm as dumb as they come."

He could hear the lawn mower growling out back. The sound brought back a time when he was happy, his world normal.

"So what are the plans for today?" his mom asked.

"Toby and I are going for a nice walk, aren't we?" Gloria said, smiling at Toby.

His mom's face brightened. "Really?"

"I don't know, maybe," Toby mumbled.

"Why don't you go over and see Suzie? I'm sure she would love to see you. Only if you feel up to it, of course. You know what the doctor said about taking it easy."

"Suzie comes around practically every day," Toby said.

And drunk, to boot.

It was true, Suzie did pop around nearly every day, but that wasn't the reason Toby was hesitant in going over to her house. He hadn't been there since getting out of the hospital, and the thought of entering the place where Frankie used to live, where they had spent so much of their youth, terrified him. He feared the moment he stepped inside, saw all the familiar surroundings, the memories would be too overwhelming and he'd fall into a sobbing mess on the floor.

"I suggested we go over and see Mr. Joseph," Gloria said.

"That's a wonderful idea. You still haven't thanked him for what he did."

"Why does everyone insist I go over and thank him? I'll just send him a note or something."

His mom flashed Gloria a worried glance, said, "Well, I'll leave you two alone," then left the kitchen.

"I wish she would just leave me alone," Toby sighed.

"Your mom just loves you, that's all," Gloria said. "She worries about you." She paused and looking down at the table, said, "Like I do."

Heat washed through Toby's body. They had become good friends in the month since the attack, but Gloria had never said anything like that to him before.

Gloria got to her feet. "Mind if I get a drink?"

"Ah, no, help yourself."

Toby continued to drink his second mug of coffee as Gloria walked to the fridge. An uncomfortable air of silence hung between them when Gloria sat back down, a can of Coke in her hand. She popped open the can and took a long drink. The constant whir of the mower purred in the background.

Gloria broke the silence by saying, "This is your last can of Coke, sorry. I'll go down to Barb's and get you some more."

"You don't have to, you know," Toby said.

"I don't mind. The walk will do me good. Maybe you can come?"

"No, I mean you don't have to spend all your time with me. You have other friends."

Gloria stared at Toby. He could almost hear her thinking, *Yeah, but you don't.*

"I like spending time with you," Gloria said. She leaned over the table and pecked him on the lips. When she pulled back, they stared at each other.

Toby's heart was racing.

"Sorry," Gloria said.

"What? Don't be," Toby stammered.

Didn't she know how much he cared for her? How much he wanted to kiss her, hold her, touch her?

"So, um, I'll come with you to Barb's, if you want."

Gloria nodded. "I'd like that. Only if you're feeling up for the walk."

"Sure. I'll just let Mom know. I'll meet you out front."

Gloria nodded, finished off her drink, hopped up from the table, then headed for the back door.

When she was gone, Toby eased out a shaky breath. For the first time in a month he had something else on his mind, besides the attack.

She kissed me! Gloria kissed me!

It might've simply been a friendly gesture—after all, she had become his closest friend in such a short amount of time—but he felt there was more to it than that.

She was the one who came to see me after the attack. She made the first move. She must care about me, must have feelings for me.

After finding his mom and telling her that he was going with Gloria down to Barb's, Toby hurried outside, where the day was bright, and the heat pressed down like a hot iron.

Gloria got up from her seat on the porch when Toby shut the front door.

She looked radiant in the sunlight. Toby thought about the kiss and heat spread through his body once again.

Gloria took a hold of his hand; her skin felt soft, warm, and was slightly damp with sweat.

"Come on," she said and they walked hand-in-hand up Pineview. "Are you sure you don't want to make a quick stop at Mr. Joseph's? We're going past his house anyway."

"Well..."

They stopped opposite the weathered old house. The old man was no longer in the front yard doing the gardening.

Thank God for that, Toby thought.

"You would only have to see him for a minute or so."

Toby stared at the house across the street. "Maybe tomorrow," he said. And sighed.

"Okay," Gloria said and Toby detected a hint of disappointment in her voice.

They continued up the street.

Toby was downstairs watching TV when the doorbell rang.

"Would you get that?" his mom said, voice sleepy. She was sitting in the seat beside him, eyes closed.

Toby hopped off the sofa, wandered to the front door and pulled it open.

"Hey Tobes," Suzie said, and kissed him on the cheek. She smelled of perfume and whiskey. Toby let her in and closed the door. "Whatcha doing?"

"Nothing. Just watching TV."

"Anything good?"

Toby shrugged. He had no idea what he had been watching. His mind was on other matters, namely what had happened today with Gloria.

Suzie chuckled. Her body no longer wobbled like it used to. She had lost a frightening amount of weight in the month since Frankie's death, and sometimes Toby had trouble accepting that it was the same person.

"Come in, have a seat."

Suzie followed Toby into the family room. She sat in the old wicker chair, Toby sat back on the couch.

"Hi Suzie," Toby's mom said, sitting up and rubbing her eyes.

"Hi yourself. Sorry to wake you"

"I was only dozing. Toby, turn the television down."

Toby picked up the remote and turned the sound down.

"Thank you," his mom said. "So how are you?" she asked Suzie.

Suzie smiled weakly and shrugged. "It wasn't too bad today. Not good, but not terrible."

"Well you're looking well," his mom said, and Toby could tell she was lying.

"Bullshit," Suzie said. "Thanks, but bullshit."

Apparently so could Suzie.

"She does, doesn't she Toby?"

"I guess," Toby said and glanced at Suzie. She winked at him.

Thankfully Suzie wasn't too wasted tonight. Some nights, and occasionally days, she would turn up at their house drunk off her face, rambling about men, how the good ones always die and the bad ones live.

He hated it when Suzie was drunk. He loved her, but it annoyed him.

"Where's David?" Suzie asked.

"At his Sunday night poker game."

Suzie nodded. "So, how are you feeling, Tobes?"

"All right," he told her.

"He walked all the way to Barb's and back today," his mom said, proudly.

"No kidding?"

"It was nothing," Toby said.

"Speaking of Barb's, I saw Mr. Joseph in there today."

"Working?"

"No, he was buying some kind of alcohol, rum, I think it was, and some herbal tea."

"Is that right?" Toby's mom said, trying her hardest to sound interested—after all, the old man had saved her son's life.

"Yeah, quiet man. I said hi, and he just nodded."

"Did he buy any chicken?" Toby asked.

"What sort of question is that?" his mom said.

Suzie furrowed her brow. "No. Not that I recall. Why?"

Toby shrugged. "No reason."

"He can be a strange boy sometimes," his mom said, reaching over and patting Toby on the leg.

"No stranger than the rest of us," Suzie said and smiled at Toby. Toby smiled back, and the need to cry suddenly overwhelmed him. Holding back the tears, he stood and headed towards the kitchen.

"Where are you going?" his mom said.

"Drink," he squeezed out. "Anybody want one?"

"No thanks," his mom said.

"I'll have a coffee, if you're making one," Suzie said.

Toby nodded and hurried into the kitchen, where he stood by the sink and wept.

Get a grip, you crybaby, he told himself, but the tears continued to flow like water from a busted faucet.

He went about making the coffee, and by the time he had finished, the tears had stopped. "Here ya go," he said, handing the steaming mug of coffee to Suzie.

"Thanks darling. Isn't he just the sweetest kid?"

"He sure is," his mom said.

"Can I be excused?" Toby said.

"Are you feeling okay?" his mom asked.

"Just a bit sore and tired."

"Sure. Get some rest."

"Night, Tobes. See ya tomorrow, unless you've got plans with Gloria." She grinned. "Oh, and by the way, Leah says hi."

"Well, say hi back."

"What is Leah up to tonight?" his mom asked.

Suzie huffed. “Doing god-knows-what with Debbie and Dwayne, most probably.” She said the names Debbie and Dwayne like they were rat poison on her tongue.

“I’ve told her time and time again that they’re a bunch of no-good losers. Sluts and criminals. But you think she listens? I think she’ll...”

Toby left the family room, missing the rest of the conversation. He headed straight upstairs and into his room.

Toby couldn’t sleep. His ribs ached and the heat was oppressive, but these weren’t what kept him staring up at the murky shadows of the ceiling.

He was thinking about the attack.

Toby only had the vaguest recollections of that night. He remembered walking to Jinks Field with Frankie, going over to get his bike, but everything after that was a blank. The next thing he remembered was waking up in the hospital the following day, wondering why his parents’ faces looked so old, puffy and sad. It didn’t make sense; Toby wasn’t dead, he was lying in hospital looking up at them, so why were they so sad?

He learnt of Frankie’s death a few moments later when his mom broke down and told him how sorry she was, how very, very sorry, but there was nothing anyone could’ve done, he had been too badly beaten, and Oh Toby, I’m so sorry but Frankie’s dead...

He hadn’t believed it at first. How could he? There was no way that his best friend in the whole wide world was dead. Things like that just didn’t happen, not to him, not to Frankie, not in their quiet town. But when he looked up at his dad, at a face that had aged so strikingly, Toby was almost fooled into thinking he was looking at his Grandpa who had been dead three years, Toby knew it was true.

“I’m so sorry son,” his dad had said, voice trembling. Then he had turned around and sobbed.

The week that followed was a blur of tears, anger, guilt and pain. Toby had never cried so much in his life and at one point he was truly scared that he would run out of tears and start crying blood. He had never been so angry, either, though he couldn’t fully express that anger due to his own injuries, which included: a busted hand and two broken fingers; a broken nose; broken ribs, head lacerations and a mild concussion.

He found out from various sources what happened that night; from his parents, Gloria, the cops—he pieced it all together and this is what it amounted to: at around ten to ten on Monday, June 16, a person or persons had attacked Toby and Frankie at Jinks Field. The attack had been swift and brutal. Nobody saw anything, no weapons were found at the scene, and due to the baseball game earlier, the ground was covered with too many footprints, the nearby parking lot rife with too many tire tracks to know which, if any, belonged to the attacker or attackers. If who the majority of the townsfolk believed to be responsible was true, then he most certainly came by foot—a suspicion that was confirmed when, a few days after the attack, the mysterious stranger was found dead in some woods about five miles out of town, a gun clenched in his hand, the back of his head a gaping hole where skull and brains used to be.

Toby had his doubts about the drifter being the culprit (but then Toby had no idea who else it could be—the only name that was even remotely possible as a potential candidate was Dwayne and his gang, but the police had questioned them and they apparently had solid alibis; and besides, Dwayne may be a bastard and a bully, but he had never done anything as violent as what was heaped upon Toby and especially Frankie). But since nobody had confessed to the attack and he hardly remembered a thing about the night—other than an occasional hazy flash of a memory—Toby guessed the stranger was as good a contender for the attacker as anyone. Because it also came out a few days after the attack what really happened that Friday night at Jinks Field. Valerie Parsons broke down and told the cops everything—the real reason for the gathering at Jinks Field. She told them about how she saw the old bum peering through the car window, about how her boyfriend, Nate, had beaten up the old man as a result. About how once Nate called Billy Pierce and told him what had happened, to "Get your ass down here and help me teach this pervert a lesson", word quickly spread and soon there was a whole bunch of angry, excited, drunken teenagers all bent on "teaching the old bum a lesson".

And this, according to the police and nearly everyone in town, gave the old hobo motive for the attack.

Again, Toby wasn't convinced, but who was he to go against popular opinion? Even Billy's dad, who told people he had seen the drifter walking out of town a few days before the attack, started doubting his own eyes, claiming he was wrong, it probably wasn't him he had seen leaving.

After the attack, Toby had lain unconscious for about an hour, and then, dazed, had managed to stagger back to Pineview, but had collapsed before making it home. Fortunately, Mr. Joseph was out on one of his late-night walks, and found Toby collapsed on the sidewalk. He had taken off his shirt and used that to bandage the head wounds, and if not for his actions, Toby might very well have bled to death from his injuries.

His parents had gotten the fright of their life when, at a little after eleven-thirty, Mr. Joseph knocked on their door and told them Toby was down the street, badly injured.

An ambulance was called, and the rest, as they say...

Toby glanced at the clock.

12:40

He thought about what Doctor Hampton had said at the hospital: "You were very lucky that Mr. Joseph found you. You probably wouldn't be here with us now if it wasn't for him. I think you owe him a big thanks."

Yeah, well, guess what Doctor, I haven't thanked him yet. I'm too chicken. How's that for gratitude?

They found Frankie at midnight. When he hadn't turned up at home, a search by the Belford police soon discovered the beaten, bloody body of Frankie Wilmont lying in the grass by Jinks Field. Paramedics were called, but he was pronounced dead at the scene.

Toby didn't know how Suzie reacted to the news, but he knew how she looked when he left the hospital a few weeks later and she came to his house to visit (she hadn't been up to a hospital visit, his mom had said). She had lost about twenty pounds, her face was pale and the bags under her eyes were big enough to take on an overseas trip. She smelled of whiskey and her hands trembled when she reached out to hug him.

They had cried together for hours; it almost turned into a contest of who could cry the longest.

The funeral was held on the second Tuesday following the attack, but Toby, still in hospital, hadn't attended. There was talk of postponing the service until Toby was well enough to go, but Toby had said no, it was all right, they could go on without him and give Frankie a grand send off.

Toby wouldn't have wanted to go even if he was well enough. He knew people cried and stuff at funerals, but Toby feared he would go beyond mere crying; he feared he would jump onto the coffin as it was lowered into the ground, screaming, real dramatic, like he had seen in various movies over the years.

Toby smiled up at the shadowy ceiling. *Bet you would've got a kick out of that, huh Frankie?*

It was good that Toby was at least able to smile now. And he knew he had Gloria to thank for that.

He couldn't have gotten through these last few weeks without Gloria. Not that she was a replacement for Frankie—she wasn't around every day, she didn't shoot hoops with him, and they didn't stay up late watching TV or playing video games—but she was just the kind of person he needed around at the moment; kind, understanding, a good listener. She had a way of making things seem not so dire; sometimes all it took to lift Toby out of a self-pitying funk was one of her gentle smiles.

Like last week, during the Fourth of July celebrations. Toby hadn't wanted to go to the town barbecue, instead staying up in his room, window open, listening to the distant sounds of the band, and, later, the fireworks, tears rolling down his cheeks. It used to be one of his and Frankie's favorite holidays, and as he lay up in his room, his parents downstairs watching the TV, he could almost smell the hotdogs and hamburgers sizzling, taste the blueberry lemonade and fudge pops.

It was during the playing of "My Country, 'Tis of Thee" that the doorbell rang and shortly thereafter, Gloria came into his room, holding a bunch of red, white and blue balloons. Wearing the same color streamers in her hair, she looked a picture of American pride. Smiling, she held out the balloons, and Toby, wiping his cheeks dry, had smiled back and seeing her smile almost made up for the fact that this was the first year he and his parents hadn't celebrated Independence Day, the first Fourth of July without Frankie.

His parents had been great throughout the ordeal, too, giving him space when required, consoling him when needed; although Toby was starting to worry about his dad. He was looking too thin, and tired, like he wasn't sleeping well; it seemed almost losing his son had really hit him hard. And to make matters worse, it was possible that whoever had attacked Toby and Frankie was still out there, possibly still in Belford. This was one of the many things that kept Toby awake at night, and, he guessed, so too his dad. In Toby's case, not being able to remember the attack itself plagued him as much as the possibility of the murderer still being out there. He had to wonder—if those elusive flashes of memory started becoming actual cohesive recollections, would the attacker suddenly be revealed? Did he actually ever see his attacker? Or would that bit of information forever remain a black hole in his memory?

Toby lay in the darkness, thinking, and eventually he drifted off to sleep.

CHAPTER NINE

Toby was upstairs in his bedroom, glaring at the scars and sickly yellow bruises that covered his body.

Christ I look like a monster, he thought and wiped tears from his eyes.

The doorbell rang. He turned away from the mirror, slipped on his T-shirt and took his time going down the stairs. The doorbell chimed again.

"Yeah, hold your horses," Toby muttered. When he reached the front door he tugged it open.

Paul Rodriguez was standing on the porch, a forced smile on his face. "Hey Toby," he said. "Um, how's it going?"

Toby shrugged. "All right, I guess."

Paul nodded and looked down, kicking his sneakers against the boards.

Toby was used to these awkward visits by now. Every kid who had come to see him since he had gotten back from the hospital had acted nervously, unsure of what to say. Everyone that is, except Gloria.

"What's up?" Toby said.

"Just wondering if you wanna come and play some baseball? Nothing big, just a few of the guys getting together for a hit. It would be good if you could come and play."

Poor kid was trying at least, which was more than Toby could say for a lot of the kids in Belford.

Yeah, like Warrick.

Toby had neither seen nor spoken with Warrick since the night of the attack.

"Thanks, but I don't think so," Toby said. "Maybe another time."

"Come on Toby, it'll be fun," Paul said, looking back up.

"I said no. I'm still sore, I couldn't play even if I wanted to."

"Then come and watch."

"No," he snapped.

"Okay, whatever," Paul said and then he turned and trod down the porch steps.

Toby slammed the door.

Baseball. Why'd it have to be baseball?

Toby headed into the family room, where he sat staring at the TV, even though there was nothing on he wanted to watch. But then he could stare at the television screen all day and not care that life was carrying on without him.

Aside from Gloria visiting every few days, he was by himself from morning till just after five when his mom came home from work.

His mom suggested she take more time off from work and stay home, but Toby had reminded her that the doctor had given him the all clear, so he was fine to be at home, resting, alone. He didn't need a babysitter (though that didn't stop his mom from ringing two, sometimes three times a day).

Toby didn't mind being at home, but he had to admit, the endless days of watching mindless day-time television was starting to wear thin.

He had tried playing video games, but doing so only reminded him of Frankie, so he couldn't even waste time doing that.

He had also tried reading, but that was no good either. His mom had brought home a stack of books from the library for him to read, but he just couldn't get into any of them. He would start to read, and his mind would drift to the night of the attack, or things he and Frankie used to do, silly things, like the time they built a cubby house constructed from sheets in Toby's bedroom when they were young. It was an elaborate network of small rooms and tunnels and they played in it all day, until his mom got to wondering where all her spare sheets were, and then they were forced to demolish the white and floral-patterned cubby house. Or the time they stood in Frankie's backyard and threw stones. They had simply hurled the stones as hard and far as they could, in all directions, and then listened. When they heard glass shatter on Frankie's fourth rock-throw, they high-tailed it into the house, scared that whoever's window they had smashed would somehow know it was them and would come over and tell Suzie, and then they would be in all sorts of trouble. But no one had come, and they later learnt that it had been Mr. Kirk's window they had broken.

Toby would think of such memories and then the words would get all smudged from his tears and he would throw the book against the wall in frustration. His mom had taken a look at the stack of library books a few days ago and, frowning, said, "I don't remember them being this damaged when I got them out for you." Toby had assured her they had been.

Toby switched off the TV and threw down the remote. The constant wall of noise buzzing from the set was getting on his nerves.

Toby sat there, wondering what to do. It was only midday, still the whole afternoon ahead of him.

He couldn't call Gloria—she was spending the day with friends.

You could always go over to Mr. Joseph's...

Toby owed the old man his life, and yet he couldn't muster the courage to go over and tell him thanks.

I'm a coward, Toby thought, and the phone jangling was like a jackhammer in the silence.

Toby hopped up off the couch and answered after the fifth ring.

It was his mom, wanting to see how he was doing.

As per usual, he told her he was fine, that he was just relaxing, watching TV, and no, he didn't feel faint or sick (just sick of you calling all the time...), and yes, the cell was charged and he would use it if he started feeling faint or sick and wasn't able to get to the regular phone (his parents had bought him a cell phone upon returning home. It was to be taken whenever he went out, and used solely for emergencies. He finally had a cell, and it was only because he had been attacked and his parents were afraid of him suddenly slipping into a coma).

After talking to his mom, Toby headed outside. The sun was hot, the sky clear. He made his way over to the treehouse. It used to be his refuge, his place to hide away from the world whenever he was feeling lost or upset. He hadn't been up there since the day after the campout, and now, as he stood under the massive elm, he wanted nothing more than to climb up, bolt the trap door and never come down. He always felt safe up there. Things never seemed as bad, and he was always able to think more clearly hidden away in his own private sanctuary.

So, heaving a deep breath, he stepped up to the ladder, gripped one of the wooden planks, and started climbing. Immediately pain ripped through his side, his breath was sucked out of his body. He dropped to the ground, sweat teeming from his brow, tears streaming down his cheeks.

"Damn it," he whimpered.

Wiping tears away, he gazed up at the wooden structure, at the window overlooking the back door.

He half expected Frankie to pop his head out and laugh at him, telling him how much of a pansy he was that he could no longer climb the ladder.

But of course, he didn't.

With a shake of his head, Toby turned and headed back inside.

A few hours later, Toby was up in his room, standing by the window.

Outside, the grass was dry and summer scorched, the trees thirsty, tired—mirroring his mood.

Go on, just do it.

He had to go over and see Mr. Joseph. There was nothing else to it. If he didn't do it soon, his dad would probably drag him over by the ear. His parents had been around to see the old man, to thank him and to update him on Toby's progress, so why couldn't he?

Because I'm afraid.

Also, there was the guilt. How could he stand and face the man he'd teased for years, thought of as a freak and a weirdo, and say thanks? Thanks for saving my life, oh, and by the way, I always thought you were some strange old man whom I enjoyed teasing and playing pranks on...

Toby felt low. Petty, childish and low.

"Toby?"

The voice was a soft echo; he thought for a moment it was a ringing in his ear.

"Toby?"

No, the voice was definitely real, and feminine.

He turned from the window and left his bedroom. "Gloria?" he called.

"Yeah, I'm in the kitchen."

Toby walked down the stairs and when he entered the kitchen, saw Gloria standing by the back door.

"I rang the doorbell, but nobody answered. So I tried the back door, found it was unlocked—hope you don't mind."

"No, I don't mind."

Gloria was wearing a white tank top and shorts, and her hair, tied back in a ponytail, was damp. "I thought you were spending the day with friends?"

"I've been at Emma's all morning, swimming, but I'd had enough, so I thought, I've got nothing better to do, why not see what Toby's up to."

"Gee, I feel so special," Toby said.

Gloria smiled. "So, you feel up to doing something?"

"Like what?"

Gloria shrugged. "I dunno. Maybe just walk around?"

"Anyplace you had in mind?"

"Well, we could always..."

Toby gave her a look, and she stopped mid-sentence. "Okay, where do you wanna go?"

He considered a few options—none of them particularly interested him. Then, like a baseball cracking against a bat, an idea struck him. "I know," he said.

"What?"

He hadn't felt up to going before, but with Gloria by his side, he couldn't think of a better time to visit his best friend.

Toby patted his pocket, making sure his cell was sitting snugly—it was—and then said, "Come on." He started for the back door.

"Would you mind telling me where we're going?"

"You'll see when we get there," Toby said.

"You can be strange sometimes," Gloria said.

As Toby stepped outside, he turned around and smirked. "I know."

Toby stood in front of the chain link fence, breathing deeply, sweat trickling down his face and neck.

"You okay? You want to take a minute before we go in?"

He nodded. "Yeah, just a quick breather." Aside from feeling fatigued, his ribs ached—Toby hadn't gotten much exercise of late, so the twenty-minute walk to Belford Cemetery had been a struggle.

With Gloria standing beside him, he looked through the fence into the sea of headstones. He'd only been inside this cemetery twice in his short life. The first was to bury Mr. Stein. The second was two years ago, when ten-year-old Jimmy Skiburn died. He was in the back seat of his older brother's car, when Mike Skiburn—who was drinking, along with a friend in the passenger seat—lost control and ran off the road and into a tree. Mike and his friend survived, though the friend became a paraplegic; little Jimmy died instantly. The Skiburn family moved from Belford shortly thereafter.

Neither the Fairchilds nor the Wilmonts were close to the Skiburn family, but they still attended the funeral.

Toby remembered the crisp Fall day well. He and Frankie had stood next to each other, quoting lines from Night of the Living Dead. "They're coming to get you, Frankie." "Toby, you're acting like a child."

Toby wasn't sure why they always joked around at funerals. It wasn't out of disrespect. Maybe it was simply their way of dealing with death.

Not that death had been close to either of them—they hadn't been close with either Mr. Stein or Jimmy Skiburn, so the few times Toby had been inside the cemetery, he had been more of an observer than a participant.

Unlike now. This time was very different, very real. Somewhere beneath the shortly cropped lawn, among the sparsely populated trees, lay his best friend.

Toby breathed in the sultry air, exhaled and turned to Gloria. "Okay, I'm ready."

He took Gloria by the hand. She smiled. Together, they walked through the gate and into the cemetery.

They wound their way past headstones, the silence heavy. They passed the mausoleum, which Toby had always thought was an ugly thing. He couldn't remember whose tomb it was, now.

"Do you think it's colder in here?" Toby said as a shiver passed down his spine.

"I dunno," Gloria said. "Maybe."

Finally, they stopped.

Toby stared down at the patch of earth Gloria had led him to. Unlike most of the other graves, Frankie's hardly had any grass covering it.

So that's where you are, Frankie?

Toby's throat constricted. "Nice headstone," he said. In truth, it looked just like any of the hundreds of small white markers that littered the graveyard.

Gloria looked at him, sadness in her eyes. "Yeah. It is."

"Not quite as elaborate as Jimmy Skiburn's," Toby said. "But still, it's a nice headstone." He read the inscription: Franklin Scott Wilmont. Born November 12th, 1993—Died June 16th, 2008

Under that: You were a special person, taken far too young. We miss you. We'll always love you. May you rest in peace. Mom and Leah

Toby looked across at Gloria. She was staring at the headstone, eyes glimmering with tears.

"Sorry," she said.

"Don't be sorry," Toby said. "I'm sure Frankie would love it that you were crying over him."

Gloria smiled, wiped her eyes.

"So, how was the funeral?" Toby asked. "Mom and Dad told me about it, but you know how parents can be. How was it really?"

"It was a nice service. It really was. A lot of people were sad that you couldn't go."

"Yeah, well..."

"Do you want to say something?"

Toby frowned. "What do you mean?"

"Talk to him. I dunno, might help, like closure or something."

Toby nodded. "Okay." He cleared his throat. "Hey buddy. How you going? Getting some good rest? Well, I'm here with Gloria, in case you're too lazy to wake up and see. Sorry I didn't come to your funeral. But I was still in hospital. But don't worry, even if I was there, I wouldn't have said anything stupid or played any stupid games like we used to. Ah, let's see. Your mom misses you heaps, of course, but she's doing okay. So is Leah. Oh, and you'll never believe it, but Mr. Joseph saved my life. He found me wandering up the street, all bloody and dazed. Can you believe it? Yeah, old Mr. Joseph. They still haven't caught whoever attacked us, but most people think it was that hobo, you remember? Yeah, apparently he was some vagrant, killed himself a few days after the attack. It makes sense, I guess. Anyway, I'm sure you're busy trying to chat up all of those hot angels, so I'll leave you alone. Take care, Frankie. I miss ya."

Toby wiped the tears away. He turned to Gloria. "How was that?"

"He would've liked it," a voice said from behind.

Toby and Gloria turned around and faced Suzie. She was standing a few feet away, a bunch of flowers in one hand, tissues in the other. Her face was pale, her eyes red and teary. She was wearing tracksuit pants and an old T-shirt that was in need of an iron. Toby had never seen Suzie in tracksuit pants before.

"Suzie," Toby said. "I didn't know you were there."

"Sorry, didn't mean to sneak up on you guys. I try to come at least twice a day if I can. It's good to see you here."

Suzie stepped up to Frankie's grave, placed the flowers by the headstone. She stood silent for a minute or two, staring at the headstone, tears falling from her eyes. Finally, sniffling and wiping at the tears, she turned and said, "You guys wanna come back to my place for some drinks? I'd like the company."

Toby's hands grew clammy.

He looked to Gloria, hoping she'd say, "Thanks, but we really should be getting along," but instead she smiled and nodded. "Sure, that sounds good Ms. Wilmont."

No!

Didn't she know he hadn't been inside Suzie's house since Frankie died? That the thought of venturing into that place sent waves of fear through him?

"Toby?" Suzie said.

He swallowed, wanted to answer, "No, I can't, not now, maybe later." But he nodded and said, mouth dry, "Okay."

"Good," Suzie said. "Car's parked just outside."

They followed Suzie out of the cemetery.

Suzie came back from the kitchen, handed Toby a can of Coke and Gloria a Sprite.

There had been no silly guessing games like there once was, just: "I know you want a Coke, Toby, but Gloria what'll you have?"

Suzie sat down in her old chair and picked up the glass of whiskey.

It was only two o'clock in the afternoon.

"So, is Leah really at your house?" Suzie asked Gloria as she took a quick sip of whiskey.

"I don't know. I haven't been home all day." That was the first time Gloria had spoken since arriving at Suzie's—other than "Sprite, please."

Toby guessed she couldn't believe that anyone could drink so early in the day. But the glass of whiskey in Suzie's hand was proof.

"Well that's where she told me she was going. Probably lied to me. She's probably off getting drunk or high. I mean, who knows what they get up to when they're with Dwayne and his lot. Speaking of which, how is the charming young lad?" Suzie continued sipping her amber drink, seemingly unaware of how hypocritical she was being.

"He's fine, I guess," Gloria said, softly.

"I'm sorry, hon. I know she's your sister and all. But I really don't know what she sees in that creep. I really don't."

Gloria flashed a smile. She looked almost as uncomfortable as Toby felt.

Being inside the Wilmont house was worse than he had expected—but for an entirely different reason. It felt foreign, like he had never been in here before. And it wasn't just that the house smelled dirty, like ash, old liquor and sweat, or that there were clothes strewn over the floor and mail piled high on top of the coffee table in front of them, unopened. No, the house itself felt different, like it had morphed into some bizarre parody of its former self. Toby felt claustrophobic and he couldn't wait to leave.

"So, how have you been, Tobes?"

"Fine," Toby muttered. He was tempted to remind Suzie that he had seen her only yesterday, but he kept quiet.

"Hmmm, that's good. Say, have you gone around to Mr. Joseph's and thanked him yet?"

Toby glanced at Gloria, gave her a look; she offered a slight shrug, and then he turned back to Suzie. "Um, no, not yet."

Suzie tipped the rest of the whiskey down her throat.

Toby winced, remembering how fiery the drink was. He watched her grab the bottle of Jack Daniel's and with shaky hands, pour herself another glass—half, no ice, no water, not even Coke. Then she fired up a Camel Light and took a long, thirsty drag.

Toby opened his mouth to protest her drinking, but he clamped his mouth shut. Was it really his place to speak up? Suzie was an adult, she could do what she pleased in her own house. Toby just hated seeing her wasting away like this.

"I don't blame you for not wanting to go over and talk to that man," Suzie said, breathing out smoke.

Toby frowned. "Sorry?"

"Well he is weird, Tobes. You have to admit that. I know what he did for you. And we're all grateful for that. But it still doesn't hide the fact that he's... well, a freak."

Toby was shocked. Was Suzie really saying this? His Suzie?

"But I thought you liked him?" Toby said. "You were always one of the few people who treated him with respect."

Suzie cackled. Tipped more whiskey down her throat. "The only person I feel sorry for is Frankie. My dear Frankie. Not some deformed freak who couldn't even save my little boy. Not him!"

Toby felt like a steam train had crashed into his body. Suzie used to be a kind person, with warm, clear eyes to match. Now, her eyes held fire, her face cruelty, even hatred.

"Oh sure, he saved your life," Suzie spat. "He found you and made you all better. While my poor little Frankie lay dying. Where was he then, huh?"

Toby flinched when Gloria took a hold of his hand.

"Ms. Wilmont," she said. "Please, don't talk like that."

Suzie's eyes were now runny with tears. "Why not? It's my house. I can talk however I want! Don't tell me what to do."

Toby was dumbfounded.

"Where's my Frankie now, huh? Dead! That's where. Why couldn't that nigger freak save him as well? So don't talk to me about respect, Toby. I spit on that black freak. And I spit on the black fucker who killed my boy. I shit on him!"

"We don't know for sure it was that stranger," Toby muttered.

"Well of course it was that nigger! Who else could it have been? The cops think it was him, and so do I. Well fuck him! And fuck Mr. Joseph! Fuck the black nigger freako motherfucking-nigger-fu..." Her words trailed off as she buried her head in her hands and wept, her glass of whiskey dropping to the floor, liquid spilling over the carpet.

"Come on, we'd better go," Toby said and pulled Gloria to her feet.

They left the Wilmont house. Suzie's sobbing was cut off when the door closed.

Outside, surrounded by half-dead flowers and thirsty-looking shrubs, Gloria said, "Toby? Are you okay?"

Toby shook his head. "I'm sorry you had to see that."

"I can't believe Suzie said all those things," Gloria said.

"She was drunk. She didn't mean any of it. Once she sobers up, she'll come around and apologize."

They walked away from Suzie's house, a place he'd been too afraid to venture into, for fear the flood of memories would be too much. He needn't have worried—all traces of the once cozy, familiar house were gone. All those memories were now safely locked away inside Toby's head.

"You look tired," Gloria said.

"I feel all right," he lied. He was tired, and in pain; he felt like crawling into bed and sleeping for a week.

"You're a bad liar, Toby Fairchild. I think you should go home and get some rest. It's been a big afternoon."

He sighed. "Maybe going home isn't such a bad idea," he admitted. "Okay, I'll go home and rest. On one condition."

"What's that?"

"I get to walk you home."

Gloria smiled. "Okay.

They took their time walking to Gloria's house.

Hand-in-hand they walked, chatting comfortably about nothing much of importance, but it felt good, it felt right, and when there were silences, they weren't filled with unease.

"So, that was quite an afternoon," Gloria said as they approached her house, a large white double-story colonial. "I would say let's do it again tomorrow, but I promised Emma and Danny I'd spend the day with them. Sorry."

"Hey, don't be sorry," Toby said. "They are your best friends, after all."

"You're my friend," she said, in that wonderful shy way of hers that Toby found irresistible.

Sometimes Toby could hardly believe that he and Gloria were friends. "But why?" he asked. "You have so many friends, you're one of the most popular girls in town, yet you still spend time with a busted-up dork like me."

They stopped on the sidewalk in front of Gloria's house.

"I spend time with you because I want to," she said. "Because I like you. A lot. And because..." She stopped, cast her eyes to the ground.

"Because you feel sorry for me?"

"No," she answered. "Well, a little, I guess. It's just, when I heard about what happened, I felt so sad. About Frankie, sure, but I admit, I felt even worse for you. You had lost your best friend, you were all beaten up..." She stopped to take a breath. "When I came over and saw you lying there..." She tried to smile, but the tears got in the way. "I couldn't imagine how you must be feeling. I've never lost anyone that close to me before. I felt for you. But I also wanted to be your friend. I've always liked you, thought you were cute, but I was too shy to do anything about it."

Toby blinked.

Gloria's always liked me?

"You were too shy to do anything about it?" he said. "I didn't think girls got nervous around guys. I thought we had that market cornered."

"Well you're wrong." She looked up and smiled at Toby, a wonderful, glowing smile. "Girls are human, too, you know."

Toby hadn't thought about doing it. All of a sudden he found himself leaning in towards Gloria. He planted his lips on hers. She seemed taken by surprise; her lips were initially tight, but they soon loosened and then her mouth parted and her tongue slipped into his mouth.

Toby's head went giddy; a bulge grew in his pants. He slipped in his tongue and soon they were kissing with their mouths wide apart, their tongues exploring.

She pulled Toby closer. So close their bodies were pressed up against each other, which embarrassed Toby; he was sure Gloria could feel his erection. But she didn't pull back. Toby in turn could feel her soft breasts pushing against his chest, and the heat radiating from her body.

It was the most incredible moment of Toby's life, and he didn't want it to end. Unfortunately, it did end, and sooner than he hoped.

"Hey lovebirds."

Toby and Gloria pulled away fast and turned to see Debbie up on the porch, leaning against the doorframe. She was wearing a tight halter-top and especially short cut-off jeans that showed off her long slim legs.

"I hope you're not trying anything dirty with my little sister," Debbie said, her lips smacking as she chewed gum.

"Deb," Gloria sighed. "What are you doing, spying on us?"

"As if. I'm just looking out for my little sister. I know what guys are like." She glared at Toby. "All guys."

"Well Toby's not like all guys," Gloria said. "So why don't you just go back inside and leave us alone."

"All guys are the same. They're all cheating, lying pricks. Why should young Mr. Horn-bags be any different? They only want one thing."

"Let me guess, you and Dwayne had another fight?"

"What do you reckon," Debbie huffed. "So anyway, what have you kids been up to? Nothing too naughty, I hope."

"I was just walking Gloria home," Toby said, trying hard not to stare at Deb's body.

"Looks like you were doing more than walking her home," Debbie said, sporting a wicked grin. "You know you're her first boyfriend, don't ya, Toby? Little princess has never been with another guy."

"Get lost, Deb," Gloria said. "Leave us alone. Just because you're angry at Dwayne, doesn't mean you can take it out on us."

"Ohhh. Little sis is talking back. Trying to impress your little boyfriend, huh? And I'll bet he is little, if ya get my drift." She laughed and her ample breasts jiggled.

"Shut up!" Gloria said. She faced Toby. Her eyes were narrow, her mouth pinched tight, her cheeks were flushed. "I'm sorry. I'll call you tomorrow."

Toby nodded and then Gloria turned and stormed up the path, up the porch steps and when she reached her sister, she stopped, said, "God, you're pathetic. Just because your relationship is hopeless doesn't mean you have to ruin mine," then stormed inside.

Debbie winked at Toby, blew him a kiss, then followed her sister inside, slamming the door as she went.

"Bitch," Toby said. He sighed.

Though his embarrassment at being caught lingered, as he turned and started home, all embarrassment vanished as he thought about the kiss. It was his first real kiss; a proper, tongues and all kiss, and it was everything he had dreamt it would be.

If anyone were to walk past, they'd probably think he was slow in the head due to the lop-sided grin painted on his face and the stiff walk.

It had turned out to be the best day so far since the attack and as he neared his house, he felt, for the first time in a long while, good. Not great, not healed in every sense of the word, but still a lot better than yesterday, or the day before that.

He arrived home, was about to make his way inside, when the idea occurred to him. He stopped at the edge of his front lawn. He gazed over at the beaten down old house across the street.

He had put it off for too long, and he figured if he was going to do it, then today was the day.

Why not make Mom and Dad—and Gloria—proud and go over and see him? Say thanks. You wouldn't have to stay long.

He glanced back at his house, thought about how, if he chickened out and went inside, it'd be that much harder to muster up the courage to leave the safety of his nest and go over and see Mr. Joseph.

Toby ran a hand through his hair.

Come on. If you don't do it now, you'll never do it.

He blew out hot, tired air.

He turned away from his house and crossed the street.

The warm fuzzy feeling from the kiss had been replaced with a nervous tingling sensation.

He arrived at Mr. Joseph's, and as he started up the short path leading to the porch, he licked his lips in an attempt to lubricate his dry mouth.

This is the man that saved your life, buddy-boy. He's not the scary monster from your childhood; he's just a harmless old man who did a good deed; a very good deed. There's nothing to be nervous about.

Then why had he put off doing it for so long? Why were his hands suddenly slimy with cold sweat and his heart pounding?

He walked up the porch steps, remembering the night he had seen Dwayne's posse deface the house and kill a chicken. He looked to the boards, but saw no traces of blood.

At the front door, he paused and gathered his composure.

Maybe he's working today. Yes, that would be a relief... No, it wouldn't. I just want to get this over and done with.

He reached out, plucked back the screen door and knocked.

He waited and soon he heard footsteps from inside.

Not at Barb's, he thought.

He licked his lips once again, and when the door eased open, he smiled thinly at the ancient head that snaked around the edge.

"Monsieur Fairchild," the old man said. He sounded tired, like he hadn't slept in days, and Toby immediately smelled the stink of booze on the old man's breath.

Is everyone drinking today? Toby wondered.

"Ah, hi," Toby said, and noticed his own voice sounded shaky. "Is this a bad time? I can come back some other..."

"No, no, it's fine, please." The old man eased the door the rest of the way open. And there he stood, Toby's savior and lifelong boogeyman. Mr. Joseph wore long white pants and a Hawaiian shirt; his curly white hair looked unkempt.

"I, ah, well..." Now that the time had come, Toby didn't know what to say. A simple thanks didn't seem enough.

"Would you like to come in?"

Toby hesitated. He knew that once upon a time, if such an offer had been put forward to him, he would've screamed and ran away, thinking how close he had come to having his head bitten off and the blood drained from his body.

But that was nonsense. Toby knew that now. It was the stuff of kids' fears, not reality. And in reality, Mr. Joseph had saved Toby from death, so if he was some blood-drinking devil worshipper, then he would've seized the opportunity that night a month ago and Toby wouldn't be standing here before the man himself, appearing rude at not answering his question...

"Sure," Toby said, and Mr. Joseph stepped aside, letting Toby take the first, and hardest, step into the nest of a very strange and foreign bird.

The screen door banged shut, and when the wooden door closed behind him, Toby flinched, and he immediately regretted doing so and hoped Mr. Joseph hadn't noticed.

"Please, follow me."

Toby followed the old man as he shuffled down the hallway.

The hallway was bare, except for two large bookcases filled with old books, most with spines creased and torn. A quick scan of some of the titles garnered no familiar names; a few even seemed to be in French.

Toby followed Mr. Joseph into the family room, which was almost as vacant as the hallway: only an old style TV, its screen like a pregnant woman's belly, one ratty looking chair draped in a red and blue quilt, and a chipped wooden coffee table. And that was it. There were no pictures of family hanging on the walls, there wasn't even a DVD player or a VCR.

The house was nothing at all like what he had imagined.

He'd imagined it to be filthy; a smelly mess of a place, piled high to the ceiling with old food containers and papers dating back fifty years. (His idea of what Mr. Joseph's house looked like mostly stemmed from photos he once saw when he was about ten—old black and white pictures of a filthy, crowded farmhouse of some serial killer named Ed Gein. One of the kids at school had a book, and the photos in that book had unnerved Toby—especially the one of a naked woman strung upside down from the roof of a shed, like a deer waiting to be skinned; which is what he had always imagined would be found inside Mr. Joseph's shed if it was ever opened.)

All those notions seemed ridiculous now; it was just a house, as boringly normal as any other.

Mr. Joseph led Toby into the kitchen, where an image of the old man standing by the kitchen bench, lips wrapped around his gun, flashed through Toby's mind. He glanced at the window he had peered in through a month ago and felt a surge of guilt wash over him.

"Please, have a seat," Mr. Joseph said, taking a bottle of rum off the table and placing it on the kitchen bench.

There were two chairs parked at the table. Toby pulled one out and sat down. The chair was hard, creaky, not at all like the cushiony ones at home.

"Would you like a drink? All I have is water or green tea, I'm afraid. Oh, and rum, but I can't offer you that."

Toby smiled politely; his lips quivered. He was having difficulty dousing his nerves. "Water's fine," he said.

The tap ran for a bit and then Mr. Joseph came over and sat down, placing a glass in front of Toby.

"I'm glad you came over," Mr. Joseph said. "I hadn't seen your parents in a while, so I was wondering how you were getting along."

Toby looked sideways at Mr. Joseph. The old man looked intensely sad, troubled, his eyes glazed. Toby glanced over at the bottle of rum—something called *Barbancourt*—and he shifted awkwardly in the chair. "Look, if this is a bad time, I can come back tomorrow."

Mr. Joseph frowned. "Why do you say that?"

Toby shrugged. "I dunno."

Mr. Joseph nodded. "You mean the bottle of rum? Well, that's just an old friend who keeps me company. So, to what do I owe this honor?"

Toby took a long drink of water. He wished it was whiskey and Coke instead. Despite making him gravely ill, he remembered how the drink had calmed him early on in the night, how it had made him feel tingly and weightless and carefree, like he was fearless and could do anything.

That's how he wished he was feeling now, instead of a giant ball of nerves. "Well, I thought it was about time I..." Toby cleared his throat, took another sip of water. "I just wanted to say, you know, thanks, for what you did for me. You must think I'm rude, not coming over here sooner, but I really appreciate what you did."

Toby groaned inside. That 'thank you' had sounded so lame, so trivial compared with the magnitude of Mr. Joseph's act.

But Mr. Joseph smiled thinly and nodded. "You're very welcome Monsieur Fairchild. I'm just sorry I couldn't help your friend."

Toby shrugged. "There was nothing you could've done. Frankie was... well, there was nothing you could've done."

"Hmmm," Mr. Joseph said, looking down at the table. "I guess not."

There was a moment of silence between them, and Toby noticed then how quiet it was inside the house; there was no clock ticking, no TV or radio humming in the background—it was too quiet. Toby shifted again in the chair.

So, is that it? Can I go?

"So, how are you feeling?" Mr. Joseph said, looking up. "Are your injuries healing okay?"

Toby nodded. "Yeah, they're healing fine. I still feel a little stiff and sore, but I can walk around now. In fact, I walked all the way over to the cemetery today. To visit Frankie's grave."

"Was that the first time you had visited your friend's grave?"

"Yeah. Pretty lame, but I just couldn't face going there until now, you know?"

Mr. Joseph gazed at Toby, and it was like the old man was staring straight through him. His eyes were like black marbles and Toby was taken aback at how deep with nothingness they were. "Yes, I know," Mr. Joseph said.

Toby blinked. "You do?"

"I know what it's like to lose a loved one. I know how it feels to leave loved ones behind and the fear of wanting to go back to them, but being afraid to face them at the same time."

Toby finished off the glass of water. "Yeah," Toby said, tears welling up, though he tried his hardest to stop them.

"Would you like another drink?" Mr. Joseph asked.

Toby looked to the empty glass. Answering no would probably put an end to this conversation and he'd most likely get up and leave; answering yes would indicate Toby wasn't ready to leave yet.

Toby chose his words carefully.

"Yeah, I guess," he said, and noticed the gentle surprise in the old man's face.

Mr. Joseph took Toby's glass, got to his feet and shuffled over to the sink. When he came back, he not only brought the full glass of water, but the bottle of rum and a second, empty glass. He sat down, placed the water in front of Toby. He was about to pour rum into his glass when he stopped. "You don't mind, do you?"

Toby shook his head. "Not at all. It's your house."

Mr. Joseph half-smiled. "This isn't my house. A house is a home. And my home is..." He stopped, glanced at Toby and poured a tall glass of white *Rhum Barbancourt*. He took a sip, closing his eyes and shuddering as he did. When he opened them, he said, "Rum is like water where I come from."

"Where's that?" Toby asked.

"Haiti," Mr. Joseph said, and darkness swept over his face. "Haiti is where I'm originally from."

"Where's Haiti?"

"It's near Cuba, it's part of the Caribbean."

"Oh," Toby said, unsure exactly where Cuba was. He knew it was somewhere near Florida, but he couldn't picture where in relation to Florida Haiti was. It sounded like a strange, exotic place. He pictured palm trees and beaches and beautiful women wearing hardly any clothing.

So Mr. Joseph is from Haiti. He thought of some of the places he and the other kids used to speculate Mr. Joseph hailed from: outer space, man-made from some mad scientist, even from the bowels of Hell itself.

"It's only a tiny country," Mr. Joseph continued. "Together with the Dominican Republic, it makes up the island of Hispaniola."

"Oh," Toby said again, wishing he had paid more attention in Geography class. "Sounds beautiful," he said.

Mr. Joseph chuckled. It was a low, throaty sound, almost dusty, like it hadn't been aired in years. "Sorry, I'm not laughing at you. It's just... to hear Haiti being called beautiful... I guess it is beautiful; some parts of it, anyway. Do you know what a Third World country is, Monsieur Fairchild?"

At least he didn't have to look like a complete dweeb. He nodded. "Like Somalia?"

"Right," Mr. Joseph said. "Well, Haiti is a Third World country, one of the poorest in the world. A lot of it has to do with..." Mr. Joseph smiled, took a nip of rum. "Well, it's a long, complex history, Monsieur Fairchild. Trust me, it'll bore you to tears."

Toby smiled back, grateful for Mr. Joseph's thoughtfulness; he wasn't in the mood for a history lesson. But he was curious about a few things. "Why do you keep calling me mis...mis...?"

"Monsieur? It means mister in French."

"Is that what they speak in Haiti?"

"Well, they mostly speak Creole there. It's like French...only slightly different."

"Oh. So which part of Haiti are you from?"

"I was born in a small town called Pignon. That's roughly in the middle of Haiti. Look, I'll show you."

With one bony finger, Mr. Joseph drew an imaginary diagram on the table.

"Haiti is like a crab's claw. The south is the longer pincher. See?"

Toby nodded.

Mr. Joseph jabbed his finger a few times on the table. "I lived here. Slightly north of the middle."

"What's it like in Haiti? Desert?"

"Oh no," Mr. Joseph said. "Mountainous. There are mountains all over. But there are also plains, farmland where they grow a lot of rice and coffee. The area where I lived is known as the central plateau region. There's a lot of farms there, where they grow produce and raise cattle."

"Is that what you did? Grow produce?"

"Yes. I started working in fields, helping my papa, when I was twelve."

Toby's eyes widened. "Twelve? Why did you start so young?"

"I had to. We were poor. Most kids in Haiti work. It's a lot different country than America, Toby. A lot different. I worked as a farmer for almost sixty years. It's where I met Mangela, when I was thirty-four."

"Who's Mangela?"

Mr. Joseph lowered his gaze. "My wife," he said, softly.

Mr. Joseph is married?

This was news to Toby. He had never heard anyone mention Mr. Joseph having a wife—was she the loved one he had left behind?

"I didn't know you were married," Toby said.

Mr. Joseph nodded. "A long time ago. Her family moved from Hinche, that's a little further south than Pignon, to a small plot of land near the town when she was twenty-one. I got to know her family, and I fell in love straightaway. She was more than ten years younger than I was, and beautiful." His face turned to stone. He stared at the glass of rum for a long time before snapping out of the trance-like state. He downed the rest of the alcohol, poured another glass and said, "But you don't want to hear about all that. So let's see, we got married when I was thirty-five, we had a daughter a year later, Felicia. We bought our own plot of land just after Felicia was born, where we grew lots of produce and raised some cattle."

"Did you like farming?"

"Oh my, yes. Mangela and I both loved it. So did Rachel." Mr. Joseph glanced at Toby and added, "She was my granddaughter."

No wonder the old man always looked so sad, so lonely, Toby thought—he had family waiting for him back in Haiti.

How many people in Belford knew about Mr. Joseph's life back in Haiti? Toby wondered. Did anyone?

"Can I ask you something?" Toby said, finishing off his second glass of water.

"Of course, Monsieur Fairchild."

"I don't want to seem rude or anything, but why did you leave Haiti? If you have a wife and daughter, I don't understand why you're living here?"

"Had a wife and daughter," Mr. Joseph said. His eyes closed and Toby expected to see tears wash down his cheeks. But they didn't come. "They're both dead. As is Rachel."

Toby's breath caught in his throat. "I'm sorry," he said.

Mr. Joseph's eyes remained closed. He poured what was left in his glass down his throat.

Toby winced, imagining the alcohol tasting like turpentine or white hot fire.

"I think, maybe, it's best you go now," Mr. Joseph said.

Toby got up from the table.

"Thank you for coming around. It meant a lot to me. Now I can be at peace. Goodbye Monsieur Fairchild."

When Mr. Joseph neither opened his eyes nor got up to show Toby out, Toby said, "I guess I'll see you around," and then he left Mr. Joseph's house the way he had come.

Outside, he sucked in the balmy summer air and taking one last look at the decrepit old house with the equally decrepit old man living inside, drowning his sorrows in a bottle of rum, Toby started across the street, unaware until he felt the warm tears flowing down his cheeks that he was crying—and unsure of the reason why.

That night, Toby dozed in fits and starts, never in slumber for longer than half an hour before something—a dream, a nightmare, a memory (still more indecipherable flashes from the night of the attack—splashes of blood, a baseball bat—though he now felt like something was trying to push its way to the surface of his memory, something important)—would wake him with a jolt and then he would lie awake, staring at the ceiling, wondering if he would ever fall into a deep sleep and stay there.

At around two-thirty, drifting somewhere between sleep and wakefulness, he heard a faint *pop!*

His eyes sprang open. His breath got stuck in his throat. He lay in bed for a few startled moments before he was able to breathe.

Toby had never heard a gunshot before; at least, not in real life, only on TV and in the movies. So the noise could've been a car backfiring.

But what he had seen the night of the campout while peering in through Mr. Joseph's window jammed itself into his head and wouldn't leave.

Toby sat up, flung the sheet off his body and hopped out of bed. With heart hammering inside his pale, sweat-soaked chest, he walked over to the window, pulled back the curtain and gazed down at the darkened street.

He saw the light immediately. It was the only one on—back side window; the kitchen. With the curtains drawn, the light was muted.

Toby gulped down a nervous breath as the sound of the distant pop echoed in his head.

What if it was a gunshot? What if Mr. Joseph has...?

Toby shivered as he turned away from the window.

He thought back to how sad and defeated Mr. Joseph had looked yesterday *(Goodbye, Monsieur Fairchild)*. He desperately hoped the noise was just a car backfiring, or some kids setting off firecrackers, but his gut told him otherwise.

What should I do? I can't go back to bed and try and sleep, not after hearing that noise.

He wondered—should he wake his mom and dad and tell them of his fears? No, he wasn't five years old. He couldn't run to his mommy and daddy every time he was scared or unsure. It was high time he started taking charge of things himself.

Besides, telling Mom and Dad would mean admitting that I had sneaked over to Mr. Joseph's that night, that I had spied through his window.

No, there was no need to cause any needless alarm or worry just yet. He would cross that troublesome bridge only when he deemed it necessary.

But I have to know if Mr. Joseph is all right.

Toby was certain that if he were to peer through the kitchen window, he would see Mr. Joseph sitting at the table, drinking tea, or maybe rum, his head intact, no smoking gun lying on the floor. But there was that nagging voice that wondered: what if he wasn't?

With a deep sigh, Toby bent down and plucked a T-shirt off the floor and slipped it over his body, then pulled on his sneakers. He crept up to the door, opened it slowly, wincing as the hinges squeaked, and then slipped through the narrow gap.

Out in the dim hallway, Toby tread carefully, the window at the far end of the hallway shedding enough light for him to see where he was going. When he reached the staircase, he glanced back at his parents' room. The door was half open, darkness lay beyond, so he started down the stairs, taking each step one at a time.

He kept as close to the edges as possible, hoping doing so would stop the boards from creaking, and when he stepped onto the floor at the bottom, he breathed a soft sigh of relief and then headed for the kitchen.

Moonlight streamed through the kitchen windows, lighting the room so he was able to tip-toe to the back door without banging into the table or chairs. When he reached the door, he clicked the lock, turned the knob and eased the door open.

A crisp breath of wind slapped him in the face. It had rained for most of the night, dousing the worst of the heat. The rain had stopped now, but the shower had left the pre-dawn air fresh and smelling of wet grass.

Toby closed the back door gently and then made his way along the side of the house, to the street.

This is crazy, Toby thought as he crossed the street and started along the sidewalk, eyes darting between the dark houses and shadowy trees. He had never been outside at this hour; had managed to stay up this late only once before, last summer when he and Frankie had stayed up to watch a *Friday the 13th* marathon. They had waited until Toby's parents were asleep, and then had sneaked downstairs. Keeping the volume on low and sitting almost nose-to-screen, they had watched the second half of *Friday the 13th Part 2*, all of *Part 3*, and Toby alone had watched *Part 4*. After watching a young Corey Feldman hack Jason to death, and deciding that was enough blood and slaughter for one night, that staying up till three o'clock was a good effort, he had woken Frankie and together they had headed back upstairs, Toby's parents none the wiser.

The early morning was deathly quiet, it seemed even the night animals were asleep; the only sound was leaves scraping along the sidewalk, and as he continued towards Mr. Joseph's, the image of a madman stalking teenagers around a campground suddenly seemed all too real.

He inched along the pavement, passing the Kleins' sleeping house, soon arriving at the very much awake and ominous house of Mr. Joseph.

Toby stopped, glanced around, saw no one (unless someone is watching from an upstairs bedroom window...) then headed down the side of Mr. Joseph's house, trying to be as quiet as possible, though certain that Mr. Joseph could hear his footsteps, or even the beating of his heart.

He passed the first window, the family room, which was bathed in darkness, stopping when he reached the second. Toby closed his eyes and inhaled deeply.

Do I really want to look? he thought. *What if I see him sprawled on the floor, blood and brains splattered everywhere?*

Nerves fluttered inside his gut like angry butterflies were trying to escape.

I have to look. What if he's hurt? After everything he did for me, I at least owe it to him to look. If he's hurt, then I'll go and wake up Dad. Who cares about all the trouble I'll be in for sneaking around at this time of night, or how I even knew that the gunshot had come from Mr. Joseph's in the first place.

Toby opened his eyes and stepped up to the kitchen window.

Found he was staring at a wall of pale yellow curtain—this time, he was unable to peek through any gaps.

What now? he wondered.

Did he risk knocking on the door?

What if Mr. Joseph is perfectly fine? What will I say when he opens the door? "Hey, I saw you put a gun in your mouth last month and I thought I heard a gunshot so I came over to see if you had blown your brains out..."?

Toby sighed.

He considered heading back home, back to the safety of his bed, back to the safety of ignorance.

But he knew there was no way he could do that now. He couldn't turn around and go back to bed without finding out if the noise had come from Mr. Joseph's.

So Toby headed around to the back of the house, hoping to be able to see inside from one of the windows there.

The backyard was littered with garbage, the grass was knee high, the small shed shrouded in darkness, but Toby didn't study any of it too closely. He was much too nervous.

The back door window curtain was also drawn, but not all the way, so Toby stepped up to the door and peered in.

He drew in breath.

Mr. Joseph was on the floor, one arm raised, clutching at a chair, trying to drag himself up off the floor. The other chair was on the ground, legs pointed at the ceiling like a dead animal that had gone belly up.

"Oh my god," Toby breathed.

He's hurt, was Toby's first thought. And then: *What if he's had a heart attack? Or a stroke?*

Toby didn't hesitate. He grabbed the knob, turned, found it unlocked. He pushed open the door and stepped into Mr. Joseph's kitchen.

The first thing that hit Toby was the smell: like whiskey, only sweeter. And underneath the alcohol was the smell of smoke; well, not smoke exactly, not like cigarette smoke, but a smoky odor.

An empty bottle of rum was tipped over on the table, its contents spilled over the wooden surface and dripping to the floor in a steady drip... drip... drip... There was a pool of clear liquid on the floor near the table.

"Mr. Joseph, are you all right?"

A tired, strained voice answered: "Toby?"

"It's okay, Mr. Joseph. Hang on."

"No," Mr. Joseph said. "Toby, go away." He sounded exhausted, on the verge of a breakdown.

Toby was about to step forward and help the old man up. But then Mr. Joseph turned towards Toby. Toby froze, a scream caught in his throat.

His head fogged and his eyes watered.

A flap of skin with wiry white hair attached hung down near Mr. Joseph's right ear, like his head was a banana with some of its skin peeled away. It jiggled as he struggled to get to his feet. But it was the hole, about the size of a golf ball, and what was visible within—a glistening, gray-pink mass that looked like a bunch of worms had been stuffed inside the old man's head—which caused Toby's heart to momentarily stop.

Strangely, hardly any blood was pouring down Mr. Joseph's face, just a trickle, nor was there much blood sprayed on the linoleum; just some meager streaks, along with some white shards that looked like pieces of skull, and Mr. Joseph's gun.

Toby blinked away cold tears. "Ambulance," he breathed. "I have to call an ambulance."

"Monsieur Fairchild," Mr. Joseph said, managing to get both arms up on the chair. "Oh Monsieur Fairchild, what are you doing here?"

"Where's your phone?" Toby said absently, unable to deal with how a man could have a portion of his head blown open, and still be alive. All he could process at that moment was that a man was badly hurt and that Toby needed to call for an ambulance.

But he remained glued to the spot, his body numb.

There was a smashing of glass and Toby gasped. The empty bottle of rum had fallen onto the floor as Mr. Joseph pulled at the table to ease himself into the chair. Once seated, he reached up and gingerly touched the open head wound.

"There's no need for an ambulance," Mr. Joseph said.

"Of course there is," Toby said. "You're hurt, we have to get you to a hospital."

"If you want to help, get some bandages, gauze and some tape from the bathroom."

A crazed laugh almost escaped from Toby's mouth. "Bandages? Tape? Mr. Joseph, your head..."

"Toby, please, either get me those things, pick up the gun from the floor and finish the job. Or just leave. But please, believe me when I say you don't need to call an ambulance. You don't need to save me."

Toby blinked and, in a small, frightened voice, said, "Where's the bathroom?"

"Down the hall, it's the first door on your right."

Toby stepped forward, dodging the mess of broken glass and spilled rum. When he passed Mr. Joseph, Toby glanced at the wound, at the flap of skin, looking like a large hairy horse's tongue, and in his mind he screamed:

It's impossible... how can he still be alive?... what's going on?.. what's... going... on??

A small voice in his head told him to get out, run on home and hide under the covers, pretend he wasn't seeing this, pretend this was all some horrible nightmare.

But he headed into the bathroom where he found the bandages, a roll of gauze and tape in the cupboard under the sink, and then headed back into the kitchen, where Mr. Joseph was mumbling, "I'm a failure. I can't do anything right."

Toby swallowed, said, "Here we are Mr. Joseph."

Mr. Joseph didn't move. He just sat there gently weeping, babbling to himself. After a few minutes of standing there watching, Toby cried, "What the hell's going on? Tell me!" Toby was also crying, but instead of swiping away the tears, he just stared at the old man until finally Mr. Joseph turned and looked up at Toby. He looked devastatingly sad, though, surprisingly, his face and eyes were dry.

He reached up and took Toby's free hand.

Mr. Joseph's skin was cold, icy cold, but Toby didn't pull away.

The old man rested Toby's open palm against his chest.

"Tell me, what do you feel?" Mr. Joseph asked.

Breathing in rapid spurts, unsure exactly what he was asking, Toby answered, “Just your shirt.”

“No, beyond that. What do you feel?”

Toby swallowed. Tried to clear his mind. He concentrated on what he felt beneath the thin layer of fabric.

He answered without giving it much thought. “Nothing.”

Mr. Joseph nodded. He let go of Toby’s hand and closed his eyes. “Exactly,” he said.

It didn’t click straightaway. Toby stood breathing heavily, sweaty palm pressed up against Mr. Joseph’s bony chest, his brain a hazy fog of confusion and emotion.

But then it dawned on him, as his own heart thumped in his chest and throbbed in his ears.

Mr. Joseph had no heartbeat.

Mr. Joseph wasn’t breathing heavily; there was no rum-soaked breath blowing against Toby’s face. Mr. Joseph wasn’t breathing at all.

Toby snapped his arm back. He shook his head at the realization. “Impossible,” he breathed.

“You weren’t supposed to find out,” Mr. Joseph said, eyes still closed. “Nobody was supposed to find out.”

“You’re...you’re...” Toby stepped back, suddenly finding it hard to breathe.

“Toby, please, you don’t understand.”

“...dead,” Toby whispered. His head started spinning and he feared he would either throw up or, worse, faint.

As Toby backed towards the kitchen door, he heard Mr. Joseph say: “It’s not what you think, Monsieur Fairchild. Please, let me explain. If you just let me explain, you’ll see, I’m not a monster.” The old man’s voice was distant, tinny. With tears streaming down his face, Toby staggered outside, turned and hurried along the side of the house, away from Mr. Joseph.

With confusion and fear crashing over him, he stumbled home and made it up to his room without waking his parents.

He jumped into bed and pulled the covers high over his head. It would be dawn in a few hours, but all Toby saw was darkness.

Curled up in bed, he squeezed his eyes shut and tried to block out the millions of thoughts that were rolling around in his head.

He wished he was ten years old again, free from any real problems, where the biggest decision in life was chocolate, vanilla or strawberry.

Hell, he'd settle for rewinding life back just a few months. That way, Frankie would still be alive and Mr. Joseph would just be the strange old hermit who lived across the street.

Damn it, why do things have to change? he thought, and by the time the sun rose, the pre-dawn incident almost seemed like a bad nightmare.

Almost.

CHAPTER TEN

Toby sat at the kitchen table, the letter from Mr. Joseph open in front of him. He had read it three times. He was still trying to process it all.

He felt numb and utterly drained, like he'd just finished running ten miles, then climbed up and down a mountain, all while battling the flu. He hadn't slept a wink, instead lying under the covers, trying to digest what had happened last night. When his door opened at around seven and either his mom or dad looked in on him, he pretended to be asleep.

It was only when, an hour after hearing the front door bang shut for the second time, and his bladder straining to the point of agony, he hopped out of bed, eased his pain and, throat parched, headed downstairs.

When Toby entered the kitchen, he found two items of mail waiting for him on the table: one was a note from his mom. It said:

> *Hope you're feeling better today. Rest easy. See you tonight.*
>
> *Love Mom.*

Toby scrunched up the note and threw it into the trash. *Rest easy, sure.* He wasn't hungry, the mere thought of food turned his stomach, so he poured himself a tall glass of orange juice and sat down at the table.

He downed the orange juice in three big gulps, taking with it two aspirin, then poured himself another glass. He was unbelievably thirsty.

He then picked up the second piece of mail—an envelope with his name written across it. Toby tore open the envelope and slipped out the sheet of paper.

His breath hitched, his stomach tightened when he saw who it was from. Toby had been tempted to throw it into the bin as well, but he was curious to know what it said. So, despite the sickness in his belly, Toby had read:

Dear Toby.

I'm sure you don't want to hear from me, but I feel I need to explain some things to you. I didn't get a chance to last night. First, I understand how scared and confused you must be. You were never meant to find out about me. Nobody was ever supposed to know about me. But, now you know. Or at least, you think you do. I can only imagine what must be going through your mind, what you think I am. Most of your assumptions will have come from the movies you've watched, or the books you've read. Forget it all, Toby. Reality is much different than the movies. It's a lot more complex. What I am now isn't who I always was. I was a normal human being, once. But it's too complicated to explain in a letter. I'm sure you think of me as a monster, and I understand your feelings. It must've come as a big shock to you.

I will understand if you feel the need to tell someone. The police, your parents. I've always feared that someone will find out my secret, and to be truthful, I'm amazed nobody has in all the time I've lived in this country. But I was resigned to the fact that my discovery was always a possibility, and have prepared myself for it. So, armed with this newfound knowledge, I leave it in your hands to do what you think is right.

My door is always open to you, Toby. If you ever want to come back, I will explain in greater detail about how I came to be the way I am. Maybe then, you will see that I'm not so scary after all.

Best wishes,
Jack Joseph

Afterwards, Toby had sat staring at the letter, unsure of what to do or think. So he read it again and again, hoping that by doing so would help him begin to understand or at least come to terms with the situation. But reading the letter three times hadn't helped. He was still just as confused and his head still pounded. He guessed there was only so much pain a headache tablet could take away.

When the phone jangled, it felt like a jackhammer hammering into his skull. He didn't want to speak to anyone, considered letting the machine pick up the call, but he was sure it was his mom and he knew she'd keep on calling until he answered, so he got up, strode over to the phone, snatched the mouthpiece off the cradle and mumbled, "Yes?"

"Well aren't you in a good mood?"

Toby sighed. "Sorry. I didn't get much sleep last night."

"So I figured," Gloria said. "Are your ribs causing you problems?"

"Yeah, my ribs," he said.

There was a pause. "Are you sure you're okay, Toby? You sound... different."

"Different? How?"

"I dunno. Like you're annoyed that I called. Like you don't want to talk to me."

Toby sighed again.

Tell her, a voice told him. *Go on, tell her everything.*

"It's got nothing to do with you, Gloria. Really, I'm just tired, I've got a headache and..."

Go on, spill your guts. You know you want to. You have to tell someone!

"...I've got a lot on my mind."

Another silence. "Do you want me to come over?"

Toby closed his eyes. Part of him wanted to say yes; he did want to see her, he never grew tired of looking at her, he loved being around her, she made him feel alive. But ultimately he felt like being alone. He didn't know yet whether he was going to tell anyone—even Gloria—about Mr. Joseph; Toby wasn't sure what to think about any of it.

"Toby? You still there?"

Toby snapped out of his thoughts. "Huh? Oh, yeah. I'm still here."

"So do you want me to come around? I'm supposed to go visit my grandmother in Akron, but I can probably get out of it."

"No, it's all right. You go, I'll be okay."

"Are you sure? You really don't sound too good."

"Really, I'm fine. All I need is a good sleep."

"Okay. Well, I just wanted to see how you were doing. I might call you tonight, depending on what time I get back."

"Okay. Have fun."

"Sure," Gloria said with a huff. "It'll be a blast."

After they hung up, Toby remained standing by the phone.

It would be so easy to dial the number of the Belford police. Tell them about Mr. Joseph. Let them deal with it.

Sure, like they'd believe me. A teenager rings up and tells them that their neighbor is a zombi? Sure, they wouldn't laugh me off the phone...

How can he talk? I didn't think zombis spoke? I thought they just shuffled around, wanting to eat people...

Jesus, I didn't even think zombis were real!

Toby wanted to scream. He hated Mr. Joseph for putting him in this position.

But then Toby reminded himself that he was the one who spied on Mr. Joseph that night. He was the one who, when he thought he heard a gunshot, went over to investigate instead of either minding his own business or waking up his parents.

Mr. Joseph was right—Toby wasn't meant to find out the truth, so who was he to go around telling the world about his secret? It was none of his business.

He just wished Frankie was still here. He could've talked it over with him, they could've gone through this together.

So what do you say, Frankie? We weren't far off. Drinking blood and eating chickens sounds about right for a zombi, don't you reckon?

With tears burning his eyes, Toby grabbed Mr. Joseph's letter and headed back upstairs. After placing the letter in the bottom drawer, at the bottom of a pile of comics, he climbed into bed, pulled the covers over his head and lay in the stuffy darkness.

He was still in bed under the covers when his mom arrived home from work.

Toby heard her banging around downstairs, then her footsteps clomping up the stairs. Soon his door opened and his mom whispered, "Toby? Are you awake?"

Toby considered playing possum, but knew that no matter how much he wanted to hide away from the world, he couldn't avoid his parents forever. So he pulled back the covers and said, "Yeah."

His mom stepped into the room. She had a mild look of concern on her face. "Are you okay? You haven't been in bed all day, have you? I tried calling a few times today, but all I got was the machine."

He had heard the phone ringing, but he hadn't wanted to leave his cocoon, so he remained in bed.

"Not the whole day. I'm just tired, that's all."

"Are you sure? Do you feel sick? Are your injuries acting up? Maybe it's about time we go to the doctors for a check-up."

"I'm okay."

"Well you don't sound okay."

Toby wanted to tell her all about Mr. Joseph, he wanted to unload all his fears, all the weight that was pressing on his mind. But he worried if he did, he would either be taken straight to a shrink, his mom frantic that he was delirious, spouting a whole lot of nonsense about no heartbeat and zombis, or, if she did happen to believe him, that either the cops or an angry mob would be at Mr. Joseph's door so fast not even Superman would be able to catch them. And he wasn't sure he wanted that, as scared and confused as he was.

Toby needed more time to think about things before he was ready for his world to change again so dramatically. "No, really, I'm okay."

"If you say so. You know you can talk to me if you need to. Dinner will be ready in about an hour."

Toby hadn't eaten all day, and though he still wasn't hungry, his stomach was empty, so he crawled out of bed and headed into the bathroom.

He used the toilet, showered, changed into jeans and a shirt.

At just before six, the doorbell rang.

Who could that be?

Toby knew it wouldn't be his dad—his dad wasn't due home for another ten minutes, and besides, why would he ring the doorbell?

So Toby wondered: Was it Suzie? Come over to apologize for the other day?

As Toby started down the stairs, another thought came to him, and he stopped, gazing at the front door below, head suddenly dizzy, heart pounding.

Surely not, he thought. *Would he risk coming over to my house?*

Toby remained on the staircase, sweaty hand clutching the banister. When the doorbell chimed again, and his mom called out from the kitchen, "Toby, would you get that?" Toby hesitantly continued down the stairs.

What am I going to say to him if it is Mr. Joseph?

Toby reached the door. He gripped the doorknob, took a deep breath, and when he opened the door, was relieved to see Gloria smiling at him, looking as radiant as ever.

"Gloria," he said.

"Surprise."

She had on a short denim skirt that ended a few inches above her knees, and a white blouse. Her hair was tied back in a ponytail, showing off her long, slender neck.

"My grandmother wasn't feeling well, so we came home early. Thought I'd pop around, see how you were doing. After how you sounded on the phone..."

"Yeah, sorry about that. You wanna come in?"

"Okay."

Gloria stepped inside. As Toby closed the door, he caught a whiff of her perfume—a fruity scent, like strawberry. He breathed it in and his head went swimmy.

"You look tired," Gloria said. "Still no luck in the sleep department?"

Toby shook his head. He was moments from leaning forward and kissing her, but before he got the chance, his mom strolled into the room, wiping her hands on her apron. "Oh, hello Gloria."

"Hello Mrs. Fairchild. I came over to see how Toby was doing."

"Well, he tells me he's fine, but I'm not so sure. Did you want to stay for dinner?"

"Oh, no, my mom's expecting me home."

"It's no hassle. I'm making chicken drumsticks and salad. There's plenty to go around."

Gloria looked at Toby.

Toby nodded. "If you want to."

Gloria smiled. Looked back at Toby's mother. "Sure, that'd be great. Thanks."

"Okay. Dinner will be ready in about twenty minutes." With a smile, his mom left.

"I hope you don't mind. I mean, if you'd rather be by yourself tonight..."

"No, I'm fine. Really. I'm glad you're staying for dinner."

And he was.

"Good. Maybe afterwards we could watch a DVD? You've got enough here to choose from. Something light and funny, like *There's Something About Mary*."

Toby nodded, trying to muster some enthusiasm. How cruel life was, Toby mused. Here he was, finally spending time with the girl of his dreams, and he had too much on his mind to fully enjoy it.

"So, is your mom a good cook?"

"She's okay. But it's not my mom's cooking you have to worry about—it's my dad's lame jokes."

Gloria smiled.

"You want a drink?"

Gloria nodded, and together they headed into the kitchen.

"So, what have you two crazy kids got planned for tonight?" Toby's dad said through a mouthful of chicken.

"David," his mom said. "That's disgusting."

"What? It was an innocent question."

Toby shook his head.

"Don't talk with your mouth full. We have a guest."

His dad looked over at Gloria. "You don't mind. Do ya, hon?"

"No," Gloria said.

"You see. She doesn't care."

His mom sighed.

They were sitting around the dining room table, which was unusual. Usually the Fairchilds ate in front of the TV, or in separate rooms. They only ever ate dinner at the dinner table on special occasions, like birthdays or Christmas. Or when they had a guest, which wasn't very often. Toby didn't consider Gloria to be a guest. She was a friend. They never used to sit around the table when Frankie came over for dinner.

"We're probably just going to watch a DVD," Toby said, answering his dad's question.

Swallowing the chicken, his dad said, "Which one?"

Toby sighed. "I dunno. Maybe *There's Something About Mary.*"

"Sounds like a porno," his dad said.

Gloria chuckled.

"Dad," Toby said, giving him a 'don't embarrass me' look.

"What? It just sounds like a movie I watched once in college."

"David," his mom said, trying hard not to let her own embarrassment show, but there was no hiding her red cheeks.

"Oh wait, that was *There's Something Up Mary*. Sorry, my mistake."

"You're not funny, Dad," Toby said, glancing at Gloria, who was smiling.

"Ease up, champ. You always used to laugh at my jokes."

"That must've been your other son. You know, the one who lives up in the attic."

"You've got someone living up in your attic?" Gloria said, grinning at Toby.

"Yeah, his name's Atticus."

"Is he named after the character or his place of residence?"

"Pretty and funny," his dad said. "You should hold onto this one, Toby."

Toby kicked at his dad's leg under the table.

"Hey!" His dad retaliated. The table shook and his parents' glasses of wine and Toby and Gloria's glasses of Coke almost toppled over.

"That's enough you two," his mom said. "Sometimes it's like having two kids in the house," she said to Gloria.

"Don't you mean three," Toby said.

Gloria laughed.

"Yeah, you forgot about Atticus," his dad said. "Atticus Atticus, holed up in the attic, named from a book, or perhaps a deformed addict."

"Isn't he talented?" his mom said, rolling her eyes.

"Wait, there's more—Nothing to eat, except bugs and spiders, but he doesn't mind, he takes what he finders."

"And you think I'm bad at English," Toby muttered.

"But if you think he's a monster, if you think he's a freak, well he ain't nothing compared to our neighbor down the street."

"David, that wasn't funny."

His dad apparently thought so. He was grinning. "What? It was just a joke."

Toby glared at his father. "Well it wasn't very funny. Have you forgotten what he did for me?"

"Of course not," his dad said, smile dropping from his face like a boulder through water.

"Well, then why did you say it?" Toby said.

His dad looked down at his plate of half-eaten chicken and salad. He looked old, the lines on his face deep, the hairs on his head turning gray seemingly by the day. "I don't know. You're right. It was a stupid thing to say. I'm sorry, Toby."

"That's the kind of thing the kids at school would say. I mean, if it wasn't for him..."

"Toby," his mom said. "That's enough."

"What? He's the one who said it, not me."

"And your father apologized. So let's drop it."

"You think I don't lie awake every night wondering what would've happened if Mr. Joseph hadn't found you?" His dad's eyes were dark, intense, but sad, even a little teary.

Toby shrugged. They were two peas, more alike than his dad probably realized.

"Can we please just drop it?" his mom said. "I don't think we're being very polite to Gloria."

Toby looked at Gloria. She looked uncomfortable and Toby felt bad for her. "Sorry," he said.

"It's okay."

"Yeah, I'm sorry, Gloria. I can be an insensitive jerk sometimes. I don't think before I speak."

Yeah, tell me about it, Toby thought.

The rest of the meal was eaten with an air of unease.

Toby didn't feel much like watching a movie, particularly a comedy, and especially not one that used to be a favorite of his and Frankie's.

But Toby agreed to please Gloria—it was one of her favorites too—and so, with a large bowl of hot buttered popcorn and two cans of Coke sitting on the table in front of them, they watched.

They talked sporadically throughout the first part of the movie, mostly about how much they loved this scene or that scene, but Toby's heart wasn't in it; he laughed at the appropriate places, but it was only for show. His mind drifted between Mr. Joseph and thoughts of the last time he had seen the movie; about a year ago, with Frankie.

About two thirds of the way through the movie, tears blurring the images on the screen, he stopped laughing altogether and when Gloria noticed, she said, softly, "Your dad was just kidding around. You know that. I don't think he meant to hurt you."

Toby wiped the tears away. "It's not that. It's... nothing, it's silly."

"You can tell me," Gloria said.

And so he had. At least, he told her about the last time he had watched the movie.

Afterwards, feeling better for getting his feelings off his chest, they watched the rest of the movie, though Toby was still too preoccupied to enjoy it.

A few times he came close to telling Gloria about Mr. Joseph. He desperately wanted some of the burden taken off him, wanted someone else to feel as confused and scared and angry as he was. But every time he opened his mouth to tell her, the words never made it past his throat.

After the movie finished, Toby's parents came in and said it was getting late and maybe it was time for Gloria to be getting home. He and Gloria reluctantly agreed and so Toby's dad drove Gloria home.

Later, lying on his bed, arms resting behind his head, there was a knock at Toby's door.

"Hey champ," his dad said, pushing open the door.

"Hi," Toby said, keeping his gaze locked onto the ceiling.

"Can I have a quick word?"

Before Toby could answer either yes or no, his dad had entered his room and was sitting on the end of Toby's bed.

With a sigh, Toby unclasped his hands and looked at his dad. "Gloria get home okay?"

His dad smiled, but it was a sad smile. "Sure. Your old man's not that bad of a driver." He sighed heavily. "So whatcha doing?"

"Nothing," Toby answered, not making it easy for his dad, even though, deep down, Toby felt sorry for him.

His dad tried to smile warmly at his son, but it just ended up as a tight line. His tired eyes looked like an old man's. "Listen, pal, I'm sorry about what I said earlier. It was a stupid thing to say. I know that. But you know your old man by now—always saying the wrong things. Most of the time I don't mean it, don't know why I say the things I do. But that's no excuse. It was just a silly song I made up on the spot, it didn't mean anything, just a little..."

"Dad, you're rambling," Toby said.

He nodded, offered a tired smile. "Yeah, I tend to do that, don't I? Anyway, I just wanted to tell you again that I'm sorry."

Toby yawned. It was a fake yawn. "Well that was pretty pathetic, Dad. But I accept. Only 'cos I'm tired and I want to go to sleep."

"Fair enough." His dad hopped off the bed, started for the door. He stopped, turned around. "So we still cool?"

Toby nodded. "Sure. Although I'm doubtful of you. Goodnight."

"Night Toby." His dad started closing the door.

"Dad?"

He peered back in. "Yeah champ?"

Toby gazed over at his father, a man who had aged ten years in the last month, a man, who, for all his faults, meant well and did truly love his family. Toby opened his mouth, drew in breath, and then exhaled. "Nothing. Goodnight."

His dad nodded. "Night." And then the door closed and Toby was again left alone with his thoughts.

He was in a room. It was white. So white it should've been blinding. Yet Toby found he didn't need to shut his eyes against the glare. He looked around. Couldn't see any doors, but there was a large window high above, like a viewing platform from which people can watch operations being performed. There was a solitary table, and lying on the table was something covered in a white sheet.

He started walking towards the table. As he neared, he noticed something sitting on top of the sheet. It stood out noticeably against the white. It was a gun.

At the table, Toby picked up the revolver. It was heavy. Suddenly the lump under the sheet stirred. Toby gasped and stepped back as the thing on the table started to rise. The sheet dropped away, revealing the monstrous form of Mr. Joseph—or what remained of him. Flaps of flesh hung from his cheeks and forehead. His lips were glistening strips of raw meat. He had no eyes. The sockets oozed black liquid, thick yellow worms slithered from the holes.

Mr. Joseph set his feet on the floor and stood up. He was naked. Globs of intestines slithered out of a hole in his gut, falling to the ground like thick, slimy snakes. Toby gazed into the old man's stomach and saw a chicken's head.

"Get away!" Toby screamed as the monster ambled closer.

Black blood sputtered from its mouth as it gargled, "I am not a monster, Monsieur Fairchild."

Toby stepped back until he hit a wall. He had nowhere to run to.

"Kill me," the Mr. Joseph thing pleaded. "Put me out of my misery."

"No, I won't kill you," Toby cried and he tried throwing the gun down, but it was stuck to his hand.

"Please, put me out of this hell I'm in," Mr. Joseph groaned. "You're the only one who can do it. But you have to remember."

"Remember? Remember what?"

A light clicked on in the window above and Toby saw his mom, his dad, Gloria and Frankie. They were all sitting by the window, wearing sunglasses.

"Hey!" he screamed. "Help!"

They didn't hear him; or maybe they did, but simply didn't care. Instead they were talking, laughing.

Laughing?!

Except for a person standing behind them—a dark person Toby couldn't see properly, a person also wearing dark sunglasses, as well as a black hat. This person seemed to be staring down at Toby, watching the events unfold.

You will remember... a strange voice intoned in his head.

"Frankie! Gloria! Mom, Dad! Hey! Help me!"

They continued to ignore him.

Mr. Joseph drew closer. Toby closed his eyes and waited.

"Here, chicken," Mr. Joseph sung. "Here, little chicken."

Toby wondered what it would feel like to have his head bitten off.

He decided he didn't want to wait to find out. So he raised his arm, stuck the barrel of the gun in his mouth, and pulled the trigger.

Toby woke with a start, sweating, panting heavily. He sat up, reached around to the back of his head. It was intact—of course it was. Only a dream. With a sigh he glanced at his clock. Two-fifteen in the morning.

"Damn it," he muttered.

He'd had enough trouble getting to sleep; was sure it was never going to happen as he lay in the darkness, thinking about Mr. Joseph, what he was, what that meant, and if he should tell someone. He didn't remember drifting into sleep. One moment he was wide awake, the next he was shocked out of his slumber.

Remember...

Remember what? Christ, what a fucked-up dream.

Toby reached over, switched on the bedside lamp and sat up in bed. He flung the sheet off and brought his knees up to his chest and hugged them. If this lack of sleep continued, come fall, he would look like he should be starting college, not high school. He had to do something, one way or another, about Mr. Joseph, or else he was either going to go nuts or die from lack of sleep.

Can you die from lack of sleep?

Toby closed his eyes.

Have to make a decision. Your sanity's on the line here.

He knew he only had two options—tell someone about Mr. Joseph, consequences be damned, or keep quiet. And if he decided to keep it to himself, then what? Pretend like nothing had happened and go back to the way things were before the attack, never speaking to the old man, seeing him only occasionally, mostly through a glass window? Or would he dare approach him, ask him about how he came to be a zombi; how such a thing was possible? Because, though he was frightened by everything Mr. Joseph stood for—death, shuffling monsters, strange, distant lands—Toby was also curious.

Opening his eyes, he hopped out of bed and sauntered over to the window. He pulled back the curtains. It was a cloudy, moonless night. The world was intensely dark, except for the solitary light in Mr. Joseph's house.

Toby swallowed. It was only last night he had stood at this very spot, fearing that Mr. Joseph had finally pulled the trigger. Unaware of the secret the old man had been carrying around with him for God knows how long.

Is that why he did it? Toby wondered. *Was he tired of being a zombi? Was the fear and pain too much?*

Toby stood at the window a while, watching the old man's house, thinking.

His reverie was broken when he noticed someone, it looked like a shadow, walking along the sidewalk. The person would've been too dark to recognize, except for the white band around his head.

Toby watched Mr. Joseph shuffle up the street and when he reached his house, he turned and walked up the porch steps and entered his house.

When the door closed, Toby released the curtains, letting them fall back into place.

Nice night for a stroll, he thought.

He turned to his desk. He opened the bottom drawer, lifted up the pile of comic books and took out the letter. He read portions of the letter again.

What I am now isn't who I always was. I was a normal human being, once.

My door is always open to you, Toby. If you ever want to come back, I will explain in greater detail about how I came to be the way I am. Maybe then, you will see that I'm not so scary after all.

Toby stared at the letter for a long time, thinking about how little he knew about Haiti and zombis. Placing the letter back in the drawer, he crept downstairs and into the study, where he switched on the computer and connected to the internet. He surfed for an hour, reading up about vodou, the gods that the Haitian people worshipped (spirits known as loa), and of course, zombis.

According to various websites, a zombi was traditionally a person who had been killed by an evil vodou priest—a bocor—and brought back from the dead for the sole purpose of working as a slave. They weren't the brain-munching, flesh-eating monsters portrayed in the movies, but rather sad, pathetic, soulless humans, trapped in their undead state for eternity, unless their brain ceased to function.

The websites disagreed on various points concerning zombis, but the one thing they all agreed on was that zombis were only a legend; that although most people in Haiti believed in the existence of the living dead, there had been no confirmed cases of zombiism. Only a lot of rumors and suspicion.

So in other words, Toby thought, *zombis don't officially exist. I wonder what Mr. Joseph would say about that...*

He also read about the poverty in Haiti, the crime, the constant fighting and changes of government. He read, briefly, about the history of Haiti, and of the black rebellion. He learnt that while most of the Haitian people practiced the vodou religion, the official religion of Haiti was Catholicism—a carryover from the slave era.

Reading about Haiti's religion made Toby think about Pastor Wakefield. If there was one person who might be able to help Toby, one person he could talk to—if not specifically about Mr. Joseph, then at least about Toby's fears and predicament—it was the Reverend Henry Wakefield.

He was no Frankie, but he was a good substitute.

And so, bleary-eyed, Toby snuck back upstairs and hopped into bed. He fell asleep almost straightaway and didn't wake until late morning.

CHAPTER ELEVEN

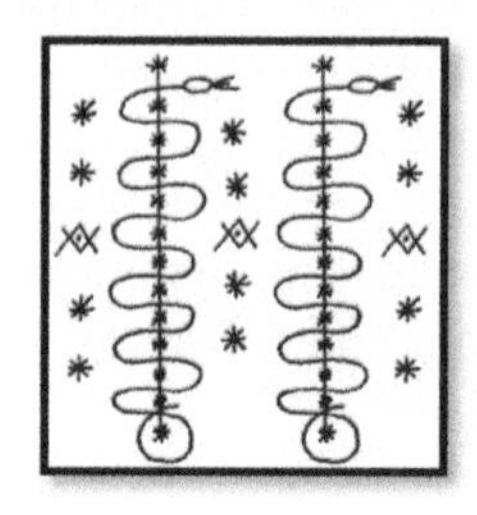

The following day, Toby headed off to Pastor Wakefield's house. Though it was another bright, sunny afternoon, he knew what would take ten minutes on foot would only take a few minutes by bike. But Toby hadn't so much as looked at his Schwinn since the attack. It was currently collecting dust in the shed and probably making a good home for a family of spiders.

His dad had brought the bike home from the police station a week after the attack, once it had been dusted for prints and checked for hair and fibers. His dad had placed the bike away in the shed and there it had remained, untouched, unseen for close to a month. He hadn't ridden it because he wasn't physically up to the task, but even if he had been, he doubted he would've gotten the bike out of the shed. It was another reminder of that night; but even worse than the scars or the hazy memories, the bike existed before the attack, when things were good. Toby wasn't sure if he could ever go back to his bike again. As much as he missed riding it, the pain associated with it was just too great. So Toby left the bike where it was and started walking to the Reverend's house.

As he walked, the sun pressing down, the smell of cut grass wafting through the air, he thought about what he was going to say to the Reverend, how he was going to discuss his predicament without actually telling him about Mr. Joseph.

Maybe I should tell him. He is a man of God. They're supposed to love everyone, regardless of who—or what—they are, right? If anyone would know the right thing to do, he would be the one.

But would even a man of God be prepared to hear such a tale?

No, Toby decided to keep quiet, unless he thought it absolutely necessary to tell the Reverend.

Ten minutes later, Toby arrived at the Reverend's house.

Pastor Henry Wakefield lived with his wife and two dogs in a cute lemon-painted single-story stucco right next to Belford United Methodist Church. It seemed too dainty for the Reverend, but then his wife, Alice, was into flowers and China cups and always smelled of lavender, so he guessed it suited her. Toby liked Alice Wakefield, but he hoped she was out today.

Toby strolled up the path, and at the door, rang the bell.

Toby heard yapping coming from the backyard.

Soon the door opened. Toby smiled and said, "Hey Rev."

Henry Wakefield smiled back, though his smile was skewed. "Toby, hi. This is a surprise. I know it's hard for you to keep track of the days, it being vacation and all, but church is not for another four days."

The Reverend was wearing a dark blue short-sleeved shirt, which showed off his strong, tanned arms, and light brown pants.

Toby nodded. "Yeah, I know that. It's just, I was wondering if I could talk to you for a moment?"

The Reverend nodded. "Sure." He stepped aside, and when Toby was inside the house, the Reverend closed the door. "Follow me."

Toby had only been inside the Reverend's residence once before, years ago when he was around nine or ten. His mom had asked Pastor Wakefield if Toby could use his bathroom (Toby had drank two big glasses of Coke before going to church that morning, and by the end of the service, had been bursting). The Reverend had kindly allowed Toby to use his facilities, for which Toby was eternally grateful.

The Reverend's house hadn't changed much in four years. The same religious pictures and framed sayings from the Bible still hung on the same walls and the house was as neat as it was back then, free from the usual clutter. There were lots of books, though. It felt more like a casual office than a house. The outside may have been the work of his wife, but the inside was most definitely the Reverend's doing.

Toby followed the Reverend into the living room, and was glad to see it empty, except for a TV, a radio, two small sofas and a desk in one corner.

"Alice is working today," the Reverend said, as if sensing Toby's relief. He sat in one of the sofas.

Toby took a seat in the other. "Oh, yeah, right."

"And the dogs are outside, so they won't annoy you. Would you like a drink?"

Toby shook his head. "No, thanks," he said, feeling uncomfortable. The pictures of Jesus and Mary and the other religious pictures that adorned the walls seemed to be staring down at him.

"Okay, so what's going on?"

Toby swallowed.

"You can relax," the Reverend said, laughing softly. "The pictures aren't going to come to life."

Toby nodded. "Sorry, I don't mean to be so nervy."

"It's okay, take your time. Remember, everything you say to me is in the utmost confidence. Nothing you tell me will leave this room. Unless, of course, someone bribes me with some whiskey." He winked.

Toby started to feel at ease—the Reverend had that way about him. He was like a cool uncle. He was also one of the few adults who came to visit him in hospital, aside from his parents. Even Mrs. Stein and Miss. Wilson waited until he was back home. "Okay." Toby took a deep breath. "What should you do when you find out that someone isn't who you thought they were? That this person is hiding a secret, a very dark secret?"

The Reverend frowned. He licked his lips. "Can you tell me what this secret is?"

Toby shook his head. "No. But to tell you the truth, I don't think you'd believe me even if I did tell you."

"Try me."

Toby gazed to the floor.

"No, it's okay," the Reverend said. "You don't have to tell me. It's not important."

Toby looked up; smiled thinly. "Okay."

"But let me ask you. This secret, is it... dangerous? Or illegal?"

Is being a zombi technically illegal?

Toby shook his head.

"Good.Okay. Go on."

"Well, I don't know what to do. Whether I should tell my parents about it, or even the police. I mean, I found out by accident, nobody knows except me. But the problem is, if I do tell someone, there's a chance this person with the secret may get, well, in a lot of trouble."

The Reverend's kind, blue eyes narrowed. "You say this secret isn't dangerous, or illegal, yet you're considering going to the police?"

Toby shrugged.

"And you're worried that if you do tell someone, this person will be in trouble?"

"Not trouble exactly. Danger."

"Well," the Reverend said. "I can see this is a serious matter for you. If you don't mind me saying, Toby, but you don't look too good. Are you still having trouble sleeping?"

Toby nodded.

"Because of this problem?"

"That, and other things. I only found out this secret the other night. I've hardly slept since."

"Are you sure you don't want a drink?"

"Maybe a glass of Coke, if you have it."

The Reverend smiled, then got to his feet. "Be right back."

While the Reverend was out of the room, Toby again glanced at the pictures on the wall. He was particularly drawn to the ones of Jesus. One picture depicted Jesus nailed to a cross. The second showed him deceased and buried in a cave. Lastly, there was a picture of Jesus standing by the cave entrance, a large boulder pushed to one side. In this one, Jesus was standing with arms outstretched, light glowing all around him, and people were kneeling before him.

(blinding white pain, screaming—Frankie?—a crowbar raised in the air)

The memory flash ended and when the Reverend came back, Toby flicked his eyes from the pictures and wiped his eyes. The Reverend handed Toby a glass of Coke.

"Is everything okay?" the Reverend asked.

"Sure," Toby said, taking a long drink.

The Reverend, carrying another glass, sat back down and sipped what looked like iced tea. "I'm curious, Toby. Is this person aware that you know their secret?"

"Yes."

"Did you promise not to tell anyone about it?"

"Well, not exactly. As I said, I found out by accident. This person told me I could tell my parents or the police if I wanted to. Of course they'd prefer it if I didn't—their life would be ruined if I did—but I never promised I wouldn't tell."

"So they didn't threaten you?"

"No," Toby said. "They didn't threaten me."

"Now it seems to me, Toby, that if this problem is keeping you awake, maybe it's too big for you to handle just on your own. Maybe you should tell your mom or dad."

"But I don't think they'd believe me," Toby said, taking a gulp of Coke. "They'd think I was making it up."

"You're not making this very easy for me," the Reverend said. "So this secret, it's not dangerous or illegal, yet if you told someone, you're worried that the person would get hurt. But you also think that you wouldn't be believed even if you did tell someone?"

Toby shrugged. "Sounds silly, I know."

"Not silly. Just... confusing."

"If I told my parents, they'd probably think I was telling stories. Or maybe even worry I was going crazy. And they're already worried enough. But if they did believe me, then the person in question would be in danger."

"Danger from who?"

"Everyone. The whole town, the police."

"The police?"

Toby nodded and finished the drink, set the glass on the floor.

"I think the bottom line is this—is this person any danger to you or anyone else?"

Toby paused. "No."

"Have they threatened you or anyone else?"

"No."

"So this secret, you're worried because it, what, scares you?"

Toby nodded.

"Why? If it poses no danger or threat, and it's not illegal, why does it scare you?"

Toby considered his answer. "I guess, because it's strange. I don't understand the person or their secret."

"Fear of the unknown?"

"Yeah, I guess."

"Toby, God made everyone in his own image. He taught us to love thy neighbor. As long as this person isn't dangerous, then you need to love and accept them for who they are. We're all different, that's what makes this world such an interesting place. Let me ask you something else: is it more dangerous to keep the secret to yourself, or is it more dangerous for the person if you were to tell someone about their secret?"

It didn't take Toby long to think of the answer. "It's a lot more dangerous to the person if I told," Toby said. "Keeping it a secret hurts nobody."

The Reverend nodded. "Well there's your answer."

Toby smiled. It felt like a great weight had been lifted from his shoulders. It all seemed so simple, so clear. "Thanks," Toby said. He got to his feet.

"I hope I was some help," the Reverend said as he stood up.

"A big help."

The Reverend led Toby to the front door. "You know you can come to me anytime. My door's always open."

"Not at the moment it isn't."

The Reverend grinned at Toby, gave him a gentle nudge. He pulled the door open. "Better?"

"Much."

Toby turned to say goodbye.

The Reverend placed a hand on his shoulder and looked at Toby with those kind, fatherly eyes.

"You're not a child anymore, Toby. You're an intelligent young adult, facing a whole new world of problems and obstacles. Ultimately it's your decision, but think very carefully about the choices you make, especially when they concern other people. It's not wrong to divulge other people's secrets, only if by doing so you're preventing other people from getting hurt."

Toby nodded, and the Reverend's hand dropped from his shoulder.

"Can I ask you one more thing?" Toby said.

"Shoot."

"You know how Jesus was crucified, and then rose from the dead three days later?"

"I think I may have heard about that, yes."

"Well, I was just wondering, wouldn't that make him, you know, a zombi?"

The Reverend first frowned, then he burst into a smile. Laughing, he said, "Well I guess, technically, it would've. Why on earth would you ask that?"

Toby shrugged. "Like I said, just wondered. Well, thanks again Rev. See you Sunday."

"I hope so. And Toby, good luck."

With a nod, Toby turned and left Pastor Wakefield's house.

Toby sat at Mr. Joseph's kitchen table, clutching a glass of water. His hands were trembling.

Mr. Joseph was sitting opposite, hands clasped around a cup of herbal tea. Bandages were wrapped around his head.

"I want to thank you, Toby."

"For what?"

"For not telling anyone about me. When I answered the door and saw it was you...well, I guess I was expecting the police. Your dad at the very least. But I'm glad it was you. I imagine it must have been a hard decision."

Toby nodded.

After leaving the Reverend's, Toby had thought a lot about what the Reverend had said. One thing in particular really struck a chord: that what scared him most about the whole Mr. Joseph situation wasn't the threat of violence, or the thought of some shambling, flesh-eating monster; it was fear of the unknown.

He recalled something his dad once said to him. One time when Toby was around six, he had woken up during the night, scared seemingly for no reason. When he turned on the light, there, perched on the wall near his bed, had been a great big hairy spider. He had screamed and his parents raced in and upon seeing the reason for their son's outburst, his dad had smiled, put his arm around Toby and told him there was nothing to worry about. While his mom went about capturing the spider, using only a jar and a sheet of paper, his dad had told Toby that though it may look scary, really, the spider was a lot more afraid of him than Toby was of it. Toby had seriously doubted his dad's logic, and up until now, had always thought his dad was wrong—after all, how could something so ugly, so terrifying be afraid of a harmless human such as himself?

Toby now understood what his dad had meant.

You had to look at things from the other person's (or, in that case, spider's) point of view—see it from their side. To a spider, even a six-year-old would look like a giant.

He thought about Mr. Joseph cooped up inside that house for the past twenty years, hardly ever venturing outside except to work at Barb's, constantly being laughed at, always the recipient of mean-spirited pranks, all the while worrying about the truth being discovered.

And so, he realized on the long walk home, that the only way to face ones fear was to meet them head on. And the only way to face the unknown was to get familiar with it. So, instead of heading home, he decided to keep going to Mr. Joseph's house. He figured he at least owed the man a chance to explain—he had, after all, saved Toby's life.

"I haven't slept since I found out," Toby said. "It was all I could think about."

"I know the feeling."

"You have trouble sleeping?"

"No, I don't sleep, period. I haven't slept in over ninety years."

Toby's eyes widened. "You don't sleep at all? Never?"

Mr. Joseph shook his head. "One of the unfortunate side effects of my condition. I pass the time by watching TV or reading. And I don't watch much TV, so I do a lot of reading. I buy most of my books from second-hand shops, and I also borrow a lot from the library. But, I guess you'd know that."

"Yeah. So, what do you read?"

"Oh, just about everything. I love history the most. But I've read just about every type of book there is. It's a great way to pass the time." Mr. Joseph's face grew sad. He sipped some tea, then said, "Well you must have a million questions you want to ask me."

Toby, gazing down at the old wooden table, nodded.

"I'm just as scared as you are, Monsieur Fairchild," Mr. Joseph said. "Even after all these years, the idea of what I am still scares me. I can only imagine what you must think of me."

"I... I don't know what to think."

Mr. Joseph took another sip of tea. "I'm curious, why did you come over the other night? How did you know the gunshot had come from my house?"

Toby sighed. He hoped this wouldn't come up, but then he figured, compared with everything else, Mr. Joseph knowing the truth seemed slight. "About a month ago, some friends and I sneaked over to your place to, you know, play a prank. While my friends went into your backyard, I stayed and watched you at the window. I saw you... you know, with the gun."

Mr. Joseph nodded. Then he said, "So that was you and your friends who tipped over my garbage can?" He smiled thinly. "Funny how things work out."

Toby gazed at the old man with the bent neck, jagged scar and thick wad of bandage wound tightly around his head. "What do you mean?"

"Well, hearing that noise stopped me from going through with it that night. And if that hadn't happened, well, I may not have been around to find you a few days later, wandering up the street."

Toby looked at the glass in front of him. "Oh," he said. "Right. So anyway, I was awake the other night, unable to sleep, when I heard what sounded like a gunshot. And I figured, you know, after what I saw that night, that you might have... finally gone through with it. So I came out to investigate." Toby looked back up at Mr. Joseph. "I don't understand. I don't understand any of it. How can you be sitting here, talking to me, if you're...?"

"Dead?" Mr. Joseph sipped more tea. "It's a long, sad story Toby."

"Will you help me to understand?"

"Sorry?"

"I want to know about your past. I want to hear about how you became a zombi. I'm scared. But I don't want to be. In order to face your fears, you have to meet them head on, right? Well, here I am. I want to know about your life. I want to understand."

"I haven't spoken about my past to anyone. I think about it every day, but..." Mr. Joseph's voice trailed away, and his blank, glassy eyes fixated on the cup he was holding. He stayed that way for a long time. Finally he blinked, and snapped out of his daze. "First, you must understand something. I'm what is known as a *zombi savane*—basically, that means someone who has died, been brought back as a zombi, but has then awakened and returned to the state of the living. That doesn't mean I'm alive, like you are, I'm still a zombi, I'm still without life, but I can think and act and feel. You see, if you give a zombi salt, whether it's a piece of meat or a salted cracker, it awakens them from their trance-like state. They can think and talk, even feel, again. Salt equates with blood, which is the life force, so the moment a zombi tastes salt, he or she is suddenly aware of what they are."

"Is that what happened to you?"

Mr. Joseph nodded. "Zombis—real zombis—aren't flesh-eating ghouls; they're simply people who have been cursed, who have had their souls taken from them by an evil vodou priest, have died as a result, and then been brought back to do slave work, or other menial tasks. I'm not dangerous. Zombis aren't dangerous. We're simply soulless beings."

Toby took a moment before asking, "So, you left Haiti because of what happened to you?"

Mr. Joseph nodded. "Yes."

"Is that why you left your wife and daughter behind?"

Mr. Joseph finished off his tea. "You know, I never used to drink tea before I came to America. All I drank was coffee. But after I became a zombi, my taste for coffee went away. I guess it reminded me too much of my past. And God knows, I've got enough reminders." He touched his scar, but quickly took his hand away. "Okay, I'll tell you, if you really want to know. But it won't be easy for me, Toby."

"I understand," Toby said.

Mr. Joseph poured another cup of tea from the pot. He took a sip. "Right, let's begin."

"It was late 1918. I was a farmer in the northern central plateau region, living on a small plot of land at the foothills of Morne Savanette, near the town of Pignon. I lived with my wife, Mangela, our daughter Felicia and her daughter, Rachel, who was six years old. We farmed mostly vegetables, but we also had some cattle. There were two huts—*cailles*, as they are called in Haiti—on our tiny habitation; one where Mangela and I lived, the other housed Felicia and Rachel. Our nearest neighbors were about a mile away, so we were fairly isolated, the area of the plateau where we lived being sparsely populated. We had part of the great mountain range, the Massif du Nord, behind us, but the view out our front door was flat and relatively treeless—not particularly scenic by Haitian standards. It was dry and dusty in the summer, constantly muddy during the rainy season. Like the vast majority of Haitians eking out a living in the mountains or on the plains, we were poor. We barely made a living selling our produce and occasionally meat at the Pignon market. It was a simple life, but we were healthy enough and, until recently, happy. Even though we were far from the cities where all the business with the marines was happening, recently, with the fighting between the rebels and the Gendarmerie igniting once again, the interior was becoming an increasingly dangerous place to be, especially if you lived in the northern regions—and we, like so many peasants, had been affected by this violence.

You see, almost four years earlier, America had sent its military to occupy Haiti. According to their government, it was on 'humanitarian grounds'. They were coming over to help stabilize the country, and to look after the American citizens living in Haiti. At the time of the U.S. occupation, Haiti was in a state of disarray and continual bloodshed. Presidents were being overthrown by violent coups at an alarming rate, so the U.S. government sent marines over. But in truth, President Wilson sent marines over to protect his country's financial interests, and because of his government's concern over foreign parties gaining control over

Haiti and her waters—America had recently completed the Panama Canal, and the war in Europe had begun.

While the Americans were in Haiti—they occupied the country for almost twenty years—they brought Haiti up to date with the rest of the so-called civilized world, Haiti being such a poor country and all. They constructed new roads and improved the old ones, built schools, hospitals, and set up irrigation and telephone systems. From afar it looked like they were doing good things for my country. Well, let me tell you, things often look good from a distance. It's not until you get up close and see what's really happening that you see how horrible and ugly the truth really is.

Along with their modern ways, the marines also brought with them their racist ideals. They saw our way of life—the peasant way of life—as backward, and the peasants themselves as ignorant, primitive apes, nothing but "niggers" and "gooks". But even worse than their attitudes and racial slurs was when they introduced the *corvée*. This was an old mid-nineteenth century law, dusted off by the Americans for modern-day use. Essentially the corvée meant that peasants were required to perform manual labor on local roads in lieu of paying a road tax. So, in effect, forced labor was re-introduced to Haiti.

I was too old to be of any use to the marines, but the younger men were made to work hard for no pay. The corvée gangs were kept under the armed guard of the Gendarmerie—the local Haitian constabulary, organized and officered by the marines—and soon abuse was rife: marching the peasants to and from work bound together by ropes, violence against those workers deemed lazy, even shooting peasants attempting to flee from these road gangs.

Of course, it would be an understatement to say that this system of mass forced labor didn't sit well with the people. The corvée stirred up the past, of when their ancestors were made to live and work as slaves under French rule. People feared the return of slavery and torture. With rumblings of Gendarmerie torture, and the rising tide of unrest against the corvée, the forced labor program was finally abolished in October of 1918. But the corvée still continued illegally in some parts of the country, particularly in the northern and central regions, and this led to an uprising of a rebel guerilla army—*cacos*. These cacos hid in the rugged mountains of the north, attacking Gendarmerie detachments to procure guns and ammunition, ambushing gendarme patrols. Finally, with the marines bringing in extra reinforcements, including the air squadron, and with the superior firepower of the marines compared with the ancient rifles and machetes of the cacos, the uprising was quashed. Their leader, Charlemagne Peralte, was eventually captured late 1919 and killed. His body was nailed to a door to serve as a warning to the cacos rebels. The rebel uprising quickly died after that. But that all happened after I had left Haiti. All of this brief history I've just told you, I read about in books long after they happened.

The war between the marines and the cacos was still very much in full swing and I was just a simple peasant farmer when my story begins.

It was a typically humid day in December. Mangela was inside our tiny two-room caille with Rachel, Felicia was in hers, resting. She hadn't been well since her husband had died a month ago. I was in the field behind our tiny habitation, plowing, when I saw three men walking towards me. Though I had never seen them before, it didn't take me long to figure out who they were—or, more appropriately, what they were. If the old rifles two of the men were carrying didn't give them away, the red patches on their clothes did.

Two of the men were holding up a third between them; blood spattered all their clothing.

"You have to help us," one of the cacos said. He was a small man with a bushy beard.

I put down the hoe, took off my straw hat, wiped an arm across my forehead and prayed that all they wanted was a glass of water or something to eat.

"Hello," I said, nodding my head. I put my hat back on.

"This man's hurt. Can we take him into your house?" He wasn't being rude, just blunt.

I glanced from the wounded man—a makeshift bandage made from someone's shirt was tied around his left shoulder and was soaked in blood—to the small man. I swallowed and said, "What's the problem?"

"Can't you see? He's been shot." Now the small man was getting impatient.

I couldn't refuse. These men meant me no harm, but they were asking for my help, and would turn nasty in a heartbeat if I didn't give it to them. Also, they had guns.

"Okay," I said and led them around to the front of my hut. I stopped at the door and turned around. "My six-year-old granddaughter is in there. Can I go in and prepare her first?"

The small man nodded. "Hurry."

So far the other man, a taller, stronger looking man in a cap hadn't said a word. The wounded man just groaned.

I hurried into the hut. It was slightly cooler inside our wattle-and-mud-walled, thatch-roofed house than it was outside. Mangela and Rachel were sitting mending clothes—Mangela had a dress across her lap, Rachel was holding a ball of cotton.

They looked up at me and smiled when I entered.

"There are some men here," I said, taking off my hat and tossing it to the earthen floor.

Mangela's smile dropped. "What men?"

"Three cacos. One of them is hurt. They want to bring him inside."

"What for?" Mangela said, frowning.

"I don't know. Food, water, perhaps. But I have to warn you, one of the men has been shot." I crouched down and looked at Rachel, who was wearing only a loose fitting hand-made dress, but looking pretty with her braided hair and wide, bright eyes. "Now little one," I started, but stopped when Rachel gasped. Her eyes were now even wider and she was looking over my shoulder.

I stood and turned around.

"We couldn't wait any longer," the small caco said. "Who lives in that other hut?"

I heard Rachel behind me whispering to Mangela. My wife said, "It's okay, darling. Go outside and play."

Bare footsteps pattered across the floor as Rachel headed outside.

"My daughter lives there, but she's resting, she'll cause you no trouble," I told the man.

That was a lie, but I couldn't tell them the truth, the reason why she hadn't been well for the past month. If she knew there were cacos here, she would have a fit.

"Get my man something to lie on," the small caco demanded. "And some rum."

I rushed outside to where our straw mats were lying under the hot sun. I dragged one of the thick mats inside, over to one corner. Mangela was pouring some of our clairin into a tin cup.

The two cacos dragged the wounded man over to the mat and laid him down.

I looked over at Mangela. With a displeasing look, she walked over and handed the smaller caco the tin of raw white rum.

I saw him eye Mangela as he took the cup from her.

My wife may have been four years off sixty, but she was still a remarkably good-looking woman with high cheekbones, smooth chocolate skin and a trim figure.

"What happened?" I asked, trying to divert the small man's attention away from my wife.

"Americans," the small caco spat as he bent down and muttered to the injured man.

"Oh," I said. I had figured as much. "I am Jacques Joseph, by the way."

The two cacos ignored my friendly gesture. The injured man fumbled for the cup and once he had a hold of it, drew the cup to his mouth and took a long drink.

"Is he badly injured?" I asked.

"No," the smaller caco said. "It's not severe. But it's bad enough that he needs rest and someone to tend to him. And to keep him safe from the Gendarmerie. He will stay here."

"Excuse me?"

The small man with the bushy beard looked at me with hard eyes. "We can't take him with us until he is better. You will take care of him until we come back for him."

I glanced at Mangela. She had a look that could burn steel.

"Isn't there a camp you can take him to?" Mangela said.

"The Americans ambushed our nearest camp. Most of our brothers were killed. We only got away by pure luck. It's a long way to the next camp. We can't drag him through the mountains in his condition."

"How about we take him to Papa Louis? He's the local houngan. He would be able to help your friend."

"No. No priests. Besides, the Americans have been trying to rid our country of vodou, so taking him to a hounfor is too risky."

"But we can't..." Mangela started.

I reached out and gripped Mangela by her shoulder.

Mangela looked at me, saw the pleading in my eyes. She closed her mouth, then looked down to the floor.

Maybe I should've spoken up and told these men no, but I didn't. I didn't want to endanger my family. Even though harboring a caco was danger enough.

"Okay, we'll look after him," I said through clenched teeth. I knew better than to argue with cacos. These were strong, fearless men.

Plus, they had connections with powerful bocors—evil priests.

"If any Americans or gendarme come snooping around, you haven't seen anything, and this man is your nephew," the smaller man said. "Don't tell anyone about him being here. And make sure he stays inside."

I nodded and began to wonder if the taller man could speak at all.

The smaller man reached down, ripped off the injured man's red caco patch, stuffed it into his pocket and then motioned to the taller man to leave. "We thank you for your help," he said.

"When will you be back?" Mangela asked.

"That, we cannot say. Hopefully in a week, but it could be longer."

The two cacos left.

"Why didn't you tell those men no?" Mangela sighed. "Why didn't you stand up to them, Jacques?"

"And what? Have them shoot us? And what of Rachel and Felicia?"

"Well did you see the way that small man was looking at me?"

"Of course I did."

"And still you did nothing!"

"They are fighting for the cause. I have to respect them."

Mangela huffed. She put her hands on her hips. "You couldn't care less about 'the cause'. It doesn't affect us. You've said so yourself."

"That may well be, but he's still a wounded man. How can we turn away a wounded man?"

"He's not that hurt."

I turned and looked at the man lying on the mat. He appeared to be sleeping and didn't look to be in much pain.

"Well, what's done is done," I told Mangela.

"When Felicia finds out we have a caco..."

Rachel stepped into the hut.

"Who were those men, gran?" she asked, looking scared.

Mangela turned to Rachel. "Just some men who needed our help, darling." She went over and took Rachel into her arms.

"Is the man dead?"

"No," I answered, trying to smile. "He's not dead. Just sleeping."

I turned and gazed down at the man. At least a week. Possibly longer. And I didn't even know his name.

The wounded caco woke up a couple of hours later. I was inside resting while Mangela and Rachel were down at the river doing some washing.

"Who are you? Where am I?"

I jumped. I wasn't asleep, just dozing in the chair, but hearing the man's voice had startled me. "You're awake," I said.

The man sat up. He winced, then looked at his shoulder. "What happened? How'd I get here?"

"You were shot by some Americans. Two of your friends brought you here. You are in my house, about half an hour's walk from Pignon. I am Jacques Joseph."

"You say two men brought me here?"

"Yes. A small man with a bushy beard and a strong looking tall man."

He nodded and muttered to himself. "Can I get something to drink?"

"Of course." I hopped up from my chair and went over to the bucket which held the water—it was nearing empty; I hoped Mangela remembered to bring some more back from the river. I filled a tin cup with water and then handed the cup to the man.

He snatched it off me, sniffed the contents and threw the cup down. Cloudy water spilled over the floor as the tin cup clanged on the ground.

"I meant a real drink, old man. Rum."

"Of course, my apologies."

Grimacing as he shifted, the man huffed.

I had already taken a disliking to this man. Here we were, taking him in, a stranger, a member of the rebel cacos army no less, and he was being rude.

I picked the tin cup from off the floor and headed over to the table, where the bottle of clairin sat. I was just about to pour some rum into the cup, when the caco called out:

"Just bring the bottle, old man."

Rum, even raw clairin, was expensive for peasants like me, so I didn't want to give him the whole bottle.

So I poured him a cup, put the bottle under the table, and took the cup over to him. "This is all that was left in the bottle, I'm afraid." I handed him the cup.

Again he snatched the cup from me. He finished the rum in one gulp. "Cheap, but it does the job," he said. "You will need to buy some more, soon."

I nodded. Though we still had half a bottle left, with this man staying with us, it seemed we would indeed have to buy some more. Lucky tomorrow was Saturday, market day; Felicia or Mangela would have to get some more tomorrow.

"So what's your name, stranger?" I asked, trying my best to be friendly. I figured if he was going to be with us a while, I should at least try and be pleasant to him.

The man threw down the empty cup and laid back down. "Just call me Marcel." He closed his eyes and soon began snoring.

I picked the cup off the floor, poured myself some clairin, had just finished when Felicia stepped into the hut. "Papa, who is that man?"

I flinched at her voice, turned and said, "Felicia, you startled me."

"Sorry papa."

She stepped further into the hut, up to the sleeping caco. She looked tired, her face had an unhealthy pallor. Her dress was crinkled, her hair more so. "He's been shot," she said. "What's going on?" She turned and faced me.

I swallowed. Took some deep breaths. "Come outside," I said, and I walked out into the bright sunshine.

"He is a caco," I said when my daughter joined me out the front of my hut. There was no point in lying to her.

She drew in breath. "What's a filthy caco doing here?" Her eyes were suddenly hard.

"Two other cacos brought him here. They were attacked by Americans, but they couldn't take him with them, so they left him here. We're to look after him, see that he's not captured by the Gendarmerie."

"I'm going into Pignon now and informing the police," Felicia said, turning around.

I put out my hands and grabbed her shoulders. "No, darling, please. I'm not happy about this either, but telling the police won't help. It'll just get us into more trouble."

When Felicia turned back around, she was crying, her mouth a tight line. "I can't stay here with a caco. They killed my husband!"

Technically the Gendarmerie had killed her husband, but because he went off to join the rebels in their fight against the marines, against Felicia's wishes, she blamed the cacos for her husband's death. In her mind, they brainwashed Henri into joining. He was a farmer, not a fighter, but all the talk about nationalism and the pride of the black folk roused something in him and so, a little over a month ago, he left our tiny habitation to join the 'good fight'.

"I know, darling, but please, for your daughter's sake, just leave it be for now. Just stay away from him as much as you can, be pleasant to him whenever you see him, and soon he will be gone."

Felicia sighed. "Okay papa. Where is mama and Rachel?"

"At the river, washing."

"I think I'll join them."

"Good idea."

With an angry glance back at my hut, Felicia started off towards the river.

I went back to work, digging out weeds in the small cornfield.

The three girls came back an hour later, Mangela and Felicia carrying baskets of clean washing on their heads, Rachel leading the way, a bucket swinging by her side.

"How's our guest doing?" Mangela asked.

"He woke up earlier. Briefly. He had a drink and then fell straight back to sleep."

"Did he say anything?"

"Told me his name is Marcel."

Mangela sighed. "I don't like this, Jacques. Not one bit."

Felicia took the basket off her head and placed it down on the ground. "Come on Rachel, nap time."

"But mama..."

"Come." Taking Rachel by the hand, Felicia pulled her daughter over to their hut and vanished inside.

Mangela looked at me and shook her head. "Your granddaughter's been asking all about the man. Who he is and why he is wounded."

"That's natural. She's just inquisitive."

"Felica's not happy about this," she said, "not happy at all," and then she turned and walked inside our hut, leaving the second bundle of washing by my feet.

Marcel slept for the rest of the day. He woke again while the three of us were having dinner—Felicia was again resting in her house, begrudgingly agreeing to let Rachel sit with us for dinner, but making it clear that afterwards, she was to come straight back home.

"My shoulder hurts," the caco said, sitting up. "Give me some more rum."

I considered not giving him any, but I figured it'd be best for all of us if I did. I just hoped he didn't remember what I had said earlier about the bottle being empty—which, with the two cups

Mangela and I were having with our dinner, it almost was. I hopped up from the table and poured him a cup.

"Well hello," Mangela said, putting on her most pleasant face. "Nice to finally meet you. I'm Mangela."

Rachel was gazing at him, her round eyes wide.

I handed Marcel the drink. He downed it in one mouthful.

When he was done, he placed the cup on the floor and gazed up at Rachel. "And what's your name, little girl?"

"Rachel," she said in a small, shy voice. She started giggling.

"Rachel, huh? Pretty name for a pretty girl."

Rachel giggled some more.

I sat back down.

"I think you're gonna grow up to be as beautiful as your mother." He looked over at Mangela and winked.

Immediately my wife gave me a look.

"She's not my mama, she's my gran," Rachel said.

"Oh, well, apologies miss. Your mama must be something special, then." His gaze turned cold as he looked at me. "I'm hungry."

Mangela grabbed another plate and on it put some chicken, millet and beans.

"You forgot to say please," Rachel said.

"Did I?" Marcel said, rubbing his shoulder. "Well I'm sorry, little one. I'll remember for next time."

Rachel laughed.

"Eat your dinner," Mangela said to Rachel.

Pouting, Rachel turned back around and picked at her food.

Mangela walked over and handed Marcel the plate.

"Thank you." He looked up at Mangela with hungry eyes. I knew what was on his mind. It made me furious.

"Mmmm," Marcel said, stuffing his face with the chicken. "I haven't had food this good in a long time."

I could only imagine what he had been living off up in the mountains.

Mangela sat back down.

We ate the rest of the meal in silence.

Marcel slept for most of the first week. He only ever woke to eat, drink, go to the bathroom, or when Mangela tended to his gunshot wound.

Sometimes he would wake in the middle of the night, screaming. I don't know whether that was due to the injury, or some bad dream, memories of what he had seen and done up in those mountains.

But the wound got better. Mangela continually cleaned and dressed it, using her basic knowledge of medicinal plants and herbs to stave off infection—her knowledge of such things was nothing compared with Papa Louis, but we had been given strict orders by the cacos not to involve any houngans. By the end of the second week he was up and walking around. He never helped out, mind you. He ate our food and drank our clairin and coffee, but he never once helped out with any chores.

Felicia, as requested, stayed away from him as much as possible, but she couldn't avoid him completely, and the times their paths crossed, I noticed the lust in the caco's eyes, and the hatred in Felicia's.

It was a Saturday when it happened. I had planned on doing some general clean-up around the house that morning—the three girls had left early to walk to Pignon for market day—but I was tired, and the thought of working on a Saturday didn't particularly appeal, so I decided to walk over to one of my neighbors and play cards, something I often did, and enjoyed very much. Marcel was up, drinking our coffee, and since the girls were out and would be gone for the whole day, I thought it would be okay leaving him by himself. I told him where I was going, suggested it would be wise to keep indoors—he half-heartedly agreed, I think he was growing bored sitting around, not being able to do anything—and then left. It was a hot, humid day. The path to the nearest village was muddy due to some recent rain, but I enjoyed walking. It was work I loathed.

I must've been gone a few hours. I lost most of the card games; Pierre, an old friend, was in fine form. It didn't rain on the way back, so the walk was just as pleasurable as the one earlier. When I arrived home, I headed for my hut.

I entered, and noticed there was no sign of Marcel. He had been sitting at the table, slurping his coffee when I left earlier. I checked the small room usually reserved for vodou worship, currently mine and Mangela's sleeping quarters, but that was empty.

Strange, I thought. I hadn't seen him in the fields on my way back from Pierre's. Had his caco brothers come and retrieved him while I was gone? In many ways, I hoped so. I knew that Mangela and in particular Felicia would be happy if that was the case.

I headed back outside. Standing by the hut door, I scanned the farmland. Around me chickens squawked, cows mooed, but there was something else, another sound.

I listened closely. It sounded to me like crying. But not a gentle weeping; more like a pained sobbing.

I started towards the sound. My heart started beating harder when I realized I was walking towards Felicia's house—which I thought was strange, considering Felicia went with Mangela and Rachel to Pignon.

The crying grew louder; my footsteps grew faster.

By the time I arrived at my daughter's hut, I could hear a second voice, a man's, grunting.

I flung open the door and charged inside. And there was Felicia on her back, dress crumpled around her waist, face squeezed shut and sobbing. Marcel was on top of her.

I raced over and grabbed him around the throat.

I threw Marcel off my daughter. He fell hard to the earthen floor. He cried out when his wounded shoulder hit.

I may have been an old man, but I was strong, owing to many years of hard labor.

I rushed over to Felicia, now curled up against the wall. Her face was streaked with tears. I put an arm around her. "Are you okay?"

"No," she whispered.

I kissed her on the top of her sweaty head and held her. She cried some more into my chest.

Marcel was still on the ground, breathing hard.

When Felicia's crying eased some, I let go of her, stood, strode over to Marcel and kicked him in the stomach. "You bastard," I growled. "How dare you." I kept on kicking until a voice in my head screamed: "Stop it, Jacques or else you'll kill him!"

Though I desperately wanted to, I knew what it would mean to kill a caco, so I stopped.

Sweating and breathing harshly, I went back and helped Felicia to her feet. Once standing, she fell into my arms and cried some more. I tried to comfort her. But I knew that was impossible.

I was stroking her hair when my head was pulled back and I felt a cold, hard object press against my throat.

Felicia pulled back. "Oh god," she cried.

"I ought to kill you, old man," Marcel said, his breath tickling my left ear. "Nobody attacks a caco and lives. Nobody."

I stood still, hardly daring to breathe for fear of the blade slicing my throat.

"You were raping my daughter," I said, speaking gently. "We fed you, kept you warm, gave you a bed to sleep in. And this is how you repay us? What else was I supposed to do?" If I was going to die, I wanted to die with respect. Like a man.

"I was only taking what I wanted. I am fighting for you, you stupid old man. For our country. I deserve to be compensated for that. You're just lucky that little girl wasn't here."

"You bastard!" Felicia screamed and stepped forward.

I felt the blade press harder against my skin. Blood trickled down my throat.

"I wouldn't, unless you want that pretty dress sprayed with your papa's blood."

Felicia halted. Though her face was dirty and tear-streaked, her eyes held fire, a burning hatred. Her nostrils flared.

Finally, Marcel took the knife from around my throat. He pushed me forward. I stumbled, fell to the floor. Felicia crouched down, helping me to sit up.

I sat and glared up at Marcel. Blood was running down his face. There was a cut on his forehead. Blood was seeping through the palm fronds on his shoulder. As much as I wanted to do something, I knew he would just as soon slit my throat if I tried. And then he would be left alone with the three girls. I felt sick at the thought.

So what was stopping him from killing me? Believe it or not, it was respect. He couldn't kill another black man that had housed and fed and looked after him. Not unless the other man was directly threatening to kill him.

"Just get out of here," I said to him. "Leave."

Marcel shook his head. "Have to wait for my brothers. Besides, I like it here." He winked at Felicia. Then he slipped his knife down the back of his pants and left the hut.

"I want to kill him," Felicia said after he was gone.

"Don't you touch him," I said, getting to my feet. I touched a finger to my throat; it came away bloody. "Don't worry, he won't hurt you again."

"I just wish he was gone," Felicia muttered, choking back a few gentle sobs.

"I'm sure he won't be here for much longer. His caco brothers will come and get him soon."

"But what if they don't? What if they're dead?"

I opened my mouth to answer, but nothing came out. Instead, I said, "I thought you were going into Pignon with Mangela and Rachel?"

"I was going to, but at the last minute I decided I wasn't up to it."

I nodded.

"But I think I'll head there now. I don't want to be around him."

I nodded again, and just before Felicia left, I grabbed her and hugged her. "Are you sure you're all right?"

"I'll live," she said, and then sauntered outside.

When I arrived back at my hut, I saw Marcel asleep on his mat.

I looked down at him, snoring, a stupid grin on his face, and thought about grabbing a knife and sticking it into his throat.

I wanted to so badly. It would have been so easy.

But I left him be. I wasn't a murderer. Besides, I knew what would happen to me if the other cacos ever found out I had killed one of their brothers. I would just have to keep an eye on him at all times until his friends came and took him away. Never would I leave my girls alone with him.

"Bastard," I said and then walked over to the bottle of clairin.

It was a few days later. Marcel was sleeping, Felicia resting in her hut, and Mangela had taken Rachel over to one of the neighboring villages to play with the kids who lived there. I was sitting in a rickety old chair outside my hut, casually feeding the chickens, when I saw a group of six men walking in my direction. I stood, and even from a distance I could tell they were Gendarmerie.

At about forty feet away, the group speared off into three pairs; two of the groups started searching nearby bushes, the third pair kept on coming towards me.

I noticed, as the two men grew closer, they were blancs, I guessed American soldiers, the leaders of this rag-tag army. They were wearing khaki uniform, wide-brimmed hats and thick boots that were caked in mud. They were carrying modern rifles and walked extremely tall and straight. Typically proud marines.

"Bonswa," one of the marines said, giving a small nod.

"Bonswa," I replied, wiping my neck with a handkerchief.

"Pale...ah...?" The marine sighed. "Pale...um...pale...?"

"Angle," the other marine said, and then looked a touch sheepish.

The first marine nodded, then asked me, "Pale Angle?"

I shook my head. I would've thought it obvious by then I couldn't speak English.

The first marine muttered and looked annoyed. He turned to the other marine and pointed to one of the groups of Haitian gendarme searching clumps of bushes.

The second marine spoke in English to the first—the only word I recognized was "Creole"—and the first, and I presumed senior, officer nodded.

They turned back to me. "We look at cacos," the second marine said in rough Creole. "You know anyone?"

His grasp of Haitian Creole may have been rudimentary, but I understood what he was asking.

I started sweating greatly. I didn't know what to do. This could be my chance to be rid of Marcel, but I struggled with my decision: betray my country, or betray my family? "I haven't seen any cacos," I told him reluctantly. "Sorry."

Just as the second marine started relaying my answer to the first in English, a voice shrieked: "No, no, there is a caco here. He's inside that hut."

It was Felicia.

The marines eyed me long and hard. "Is true?" the second marine asked.

I sighed. Glanced back at Felicia, standing by the door of her hut, a look of expectation on her pale face.

"Yes, it's true," I said. "I took in a man a few weeks ago. Two men brought him, he was injured, had a gunshot wound on one shoulder. They were cacos."

The second marine told the first what I had said.

They both eyed my hut.

"So he still inside house?" the second marine said.

"Yes. He's currently sleeping. And he's unarmed, except for a knife."

The marines looked at each other, and when the first was up to speed, they nodded and raised their rifles. "You stay here, sir, you too ma'am," the second marine said in Creole.

I nodded. I watched them advance towards my hut.

I was scared. We were turning over one of our own to foreigners.

With guns ready, the marines entered my house.

Soon I heard shouting, a struggle, then the marines came out with Marcel, hands clasped around the back of his head, the rifle of the first marine pointed directly at his thumbs.

"Jacques!" Marcel cried. "Tell them they've made a mistake. I'm your nephew who was wounded in an accident."

"Is he my nephew?" the second marine asked.

Marcel looked shocked at this blanc speaking Creole.

"No!" Felicia cried, standing just inside her hut. "He's a dirty caco!"

The marines looked at me.

"No," I told them. "He's not my nephew. I hadn't seen him before last week."

"You fools!" Marcel screamed. "Do you know what you've done?"

"We thank you," the second marine said. "You have done your land a great service in identify this man. He is animal and killer, and will be dealt with approvingly."

The marines led him away from my hut.

"You will pay!" Marcel yelled. "And your daughter has a big smelly cunt!"

The second marine thumped Marcel in the gut with the butt of his rifle, putting an end to his ranting.

I watched the marines round up the rest of their gendarme patrol and soon they were gone. I wondered what Marcel's fate would be—based on the stories I had heard, I shuddered to think.

Felicia came up to me. "We did the right thing. Don't worry, papa. Everything will be okay. We did a good thing, an honorable deed. Le Bon Dieu will be happy."

I didn't feel like I had done an honorable thing. I felt rotten. Why, I wasn't sure. I was glad to be rid of the man. Maybe I was just scared.

Scared of what was to come.

Mangela and Rachel arrived home just before dusk. I was clearing away some of the junk that had piled up around the house.

"Hey papa," Rachel said, chewing on a sugarcane. "What ya doing?"

"Just clearing away some of this old junk. Did you have fun?"

"Yeah," she said, grinning.

I looked from Rachel to Mangela. "I've got some good news."

"What?" Mangela said.

"Marcel is gone."

A big smile bloomed across her face. "He's gone?"

"Yes. For good."

"That's fantastic!" Mangela said, clapping her hands together. "Did the other cacos finally come and get him?"

"Uh, no. A gendarme patrol came by."

Her smile dropped. She looked down at Rachel. "Go to your house darling and tell your mama all about your day."

"Okay," Rachel said, and, still chewing on the cane, skipped away.

"What do you mean?" Mangela said when Rachel was gone.

"Two marines came to our house looking for cacos. I hesitated to tell them, but Felicia must've heard us talking and she spoke up. I had to tell the marines the truth after that."

Mangela looked worried. Her normally beautiful face was crowded with lines.

"I thought you'd be happy," I said. "That animal is gone. You'll never have to see him again."

"I know," Mangela said. "But what will we tell those other men?"

I sighed. "Hopefully they won't come back," I said. "Hopefully they're dead, or in jail."

"That would be a blessing," Mangela said. "But what if they do come back, Jacques? What will we tell them?"

I took a hold of Mangela and kissed her. "Don't you worry about it. Marcel is gone, that's the main thing. You and Felicia and Rachel are safe, now. I'll deal with them when they come. If they come. But I'm sure everything will be fine."

"Okay," Mangela said. She smiled, but it had lost all happiness.

And standing there holding Mangela, I honestly thought everything would be okay..."

Mr. Joseph sipped the last of the tea. "My throat's a little sore," he said. "I haven't talked this much in a long time. Mind if we stop for today?"

Toby shook his head. "Sure, that's fine. But listen, if you don't want to tell me, if it's too hard for you..."

"No, I want to. I think about my past nearly every moment of every day, but understand, I haven't spoken about it to anyone. The only person who knew was Jean-Philippe, and he's dead."

Toby frowned. "Jean-Philippe? Who's he?"

"An old friend. We'll get to him later."

"Oh. Well, I guess I'd better get going." Toby got to his feet.

There was still so much Toby wanted to know about Mr. Joseph, but he knew he just had to be patient, and hopefully, in time, he would get his answers. "See you later," Toby said and started for the back door.

"Toby, wait."

Toby turned back. Mr. Joseph was looking up at him, face serious. "There's something I should tell you. It's only fair. If I'm to tell you my story truthfully, then you'll learn about it eventually. That old friend I just mentioned, Jean-Philippe, he was that stranger who came to town. The one who killed himself last month."

Toby's ears started ringing. "Oh my god," he breathed. "You knew him? But... but everyone thinks he's the one who attacked me and Frankie."

"I know that, but it's not true. Please, sit down. I can explain."

This was all too much. First finding out about Mr. Joseph, and now learning that he knew the main suspect in the attack? "Why didn't you tell me sooner? Do the cops know?"

"No. Please, Toby, sit down and hear me out. I know for a fact that Jean-Philippe didn't attack you and Monsieur Wilmont. You have to trust me."

Trust him? How can he expect me to trust him? I hardly know him!

Toby remained standing. "How do you know he had nothing to do with the attack?"

Mr. Joseph paused, then answered, "Because he was already dead when it happened."

"But the newspapers said he died a few days after the attack; that the cops found him a week later, and said he had been dead only a few days. They said he had a motive..."

"You believe everything you read in the papers? Jean-Philippe wasn't some vagrant who happened to wander into town; he came to Belford to find me. And when he found me, and told me what he came to tell me, he left. That was the Saturday of your campout. It was a shock when I opened the door to see him standing there that morning. Apparently he had followed me from Barb's. I was shocked not only by his appearance, like he had been in a fight, but also because it had been so long and seeing him brought back a flood of memories. But I wasn't surprised by his arrival; I had a feeling I would be seeing him soon."

"But he was a pervert. He spied on some kids making out. You heard what happened at Jinks Field?"

Mr. Joseph nodded. "Again, all lies. He didn't spy into that car. He wouldn't do that. He wasn't that sort of person, and besides, he wouldn't want to draw attention to himself like that. No, I'm afraid the truth was, he saw the car pull up at Jinks Field, and figuring it might not be such a good place to hideout—he worried that more cars, more people would come—he started to leave. Well, I guess either the girl or the boy saw him walking nearby, and thought he was coming to spy on them, or had spied on them and was leaving—either way, the guy jumped out of his car and, calling Jean-Philippe names, started beating him when Jean-Philippe tried to run away. And soon more cars came, with more kids." Mr. Joseph shook his head. "And even after all that, he still stayed, until he found me."

"But that doesn't prove he wasn't the attacker," Toby said. "And how can you know he was already dead at the time of the attack? He might've left town, attacked us a few days later, and then killed himself."

"Jean-Philippe and I go a long way back together, all the way back to Haiti. We had a kind of connection. I hadn't seen him in over ninety years, yet, like I said, I knew he was coming even before he arrived, and I know he died that night. I felt his presence vanish from this earth, I felt his pain lift. He was able to do it right the first time, unlike me." Mr. Joseph cast his gaze downwards; his chin started to tremble.

Toby thought back to what he had read about the stranger. The newspaper hadn't said much, other than he seemed to be an immigrant drifter, whose worldly belongings included a bag full of clothes, a bottle of rum, a bunch of old, crinkled maps and a...

A gun! He killed himself using a...

"Holy shit," Toby breathed. "He was a zombi too, wasn't he?"

Mr. Joseph nodded. "He ended his pain that Saturday night. I know he did."

"And you're sure about that?"

"Yes," Mr. Joseph answered, voice barely a whisper.

"Well if he didn't attack me and Frankie, then why did he kill himself?"

"Because his job was done. His mission in life was over; he had found me and delivered his message. There was nothing left for him to do."

"What message?"

"Please, have a seat, Toby."

Though he felt numb, his mind a whirlwind of confusion, Toby found himself walking back to the table and taking a seat.

"Toby, you need to understand something. Being a zombi is a curse. It's not simply a corpse who has risen from the dead. It's when a bocor—that's a vodou priest who works with both hands, one who works in black magic—captures a person's soul, thus controlling his body. He can do this by either waiting until a person has died, and then capturing the soul, or by placing his lips against the crack of the person's door and sucking out their soul. The person becomes ill and soon dies. Once the zombi has risen, he's under the command of the bocor, or the master, if the bocor hands over that power. What I'm trying to say is, a zombi is an empty vessel, just a body without its essence. It can't die, not unless the brain is destroyed. You understand what I'm saying?"

Toby swallowed. "I think so. You're saying that a zombi lives forever? Unless...?"

Mr. Joseph nodded. "That's a mighty horrible curse, Toby. To live forever, not really being alive, while all those you care about die. That's why I've had to move from place to place. Every twenty years or so I move. I have to, or else people would get suspicious that I haven't aged or died. But anyway, that's getting ahead of myself. What I'm trying to say, Toby, is that being a zombi is like being a slave, a slave to the curse, and the idea of living forever is too terrifying to contemplate. There's only one way out, and most zombis, sooner or later, end up taking that path. So, once Jean-Philippe's job was over, he had nothing else to live for. He wanted his pain to be over. You understand?"

Toby nodded. "But what was his job? Why did he come to Belford to see you?"

Mr. Joseph closed his eyes. He didn't speak for a long time.

"When I left Haiti all those years ago, Jean-Philippe made a promise to me. He didn't have any family of his own, so he promised to look out for Mangela and Felicia and Rachel. He wasn't to interact with them, just be near them, make sure no harm came to them." Mr. Joseph paused. "You see Toby, being a zombi means great shame in my country, the ultimate shame. My family thought I was dead, so when I became a savane, and escaped from my master, I knew I couldn't go back to them. So I left Haiti, but Jean-Philippe promised me two things before I left. One was to look out for my family. The other was to come and get me when they were all dead. Only then would I return to Haiti."

"Is that why Jean-Philippe came to Belford?"

Mr. Joseph nodded. "I knew Mangela and Felicia would be dead by now, and I suspected Rachel, but there was no way of knowing for sure. It took Jean-Philippe almost five years to find me. But he eventually did."

"So you're going back to Haiti now?"

"No," Mr. Joseph said. "Jean-Philippe came to me with other news. Yes, both my wife, child and grandchild were dead, but Rachel got married a long time ago, and had children of her own. And they in turn had children. I never thought...well, I had always thought that when my three girls were gone, then it would be over. That I could go back to Haiti and be with my family again. But now I find I have more family. I have great-grand-children, and great-great-grand-children. So I can't go back, not now, not ever."

Mr. Joseph paused before continuing.

"So that's why I did what I did the other night. Or at least, attempted to. And why Jean-Philippe came to Belford. He wasn't a violent person. He was just the opposite. He spent the last five years tracking me all over this country, and had spent the last eighty-five before that looking out for my family back in Haiti. You have to trust me, Toby. He wasn't the one who attacked you and Frankie."

Toby took a deep breath. "If you're so sure, why didn't you go to the cops?"

"And tell them what? That I know Jean-Philippe wasn't the attacker because he was a zombi and he killed himself a few days before the attack because his job was over and he wanted his pain to be over?"

"But then whoever attacked me and Frankie is still out there. If the cops knew Jean-Philippe wasn't the one, they would be looking harder for the real murderer."

"Toby, Toby, Toby," Mr. Joseph sighed. "One day you'll come to learn that not everything in this world is fair or just. Jean-Philippe was simply in the wrong place at the wrong time, with the right colored skin. He was a policeman's dream suspect—a dead black drifter who couldn't plead his innocence."

"But... but that's unfair."

"Oh sure, it's not on record that he was the person responsible for the attack. There's no hard evidence linking him to the crime. But he's guilty in the eyes of the law, and he's guilty in the eyes of the town. To them, him killing himself was just further proof of his guilt. If only people knew the real reason."

"This is all too much," Toby said. "I mean, I was never one hundred percent certain Jean-Philippe was guilty, but at the same time..."

"You hoped he was? That's understandable. I'm sorry Toby, I wish I could tell you it was him. But I can't give you that closure. You do believe me though, don't you?"

Reluctantly, Toby nodded.

"And you understand why I couldn't go the police?"

Again, he nodded.

"Even if I neglected to mention Jean-Philippe was a zombi and told them that he was simply a friend and was with me at the time of the attack, they would have no choice but to investigate, which means investigating me, which means they might discover my secrets. Besides, it wouldn't make one bit of difference. Whoever attacked you would still be free, and the police would still be working as hard, or should I say not as hard, as before in finding the real person responsible. In their eyes, that person is already dead."

"But they're not. Whoever attacked me and Frankie is still out there. I even told the cops it could've been more than one attacker —my memory of that night is a little fuzzy—but they just nodded, said thanks for my help, and that was it."

"So who do you think it was?"

Toby shrugged. "I don't know. I don't know of anyone that violent living in town. Dwayne Marcos has crossed my mind, but then he and his gang have alibis, so it can't have been them. So I really don't know."

"You want to know what I think? Honestly, I think whoever attacked you and Frankie left town a long time ago."

"But why attack us? We were just kids. We didn't have any money."

"That, I cannot tell you."

Toby nodded. Then he frowned. "You said secrets just before. What else is there?"

"Sorry?"

"Just before, you said the police might find out about your secrets, plural, if they investigated any link between you and Jean-Philippe. What else, besides finding out that you're a zombi, could they uncover?"

"Well..." Mr. Joseph said.

"I know about you being a zombi, and I didn't tell anyone. You can trust me."

Mr. Joseph nodded. "You're right. But please, keep this to yourself."

"Okay."

"I'm an illegal immigrant. Like Jean-Philippe, I have fake papers. I came over on a cargo ship—paid my way, which was easy to do back then. I shouldn't be in your country, Toby, and if anyone ever found this out, I'd be thrown in jail or deported. Either way, once they found out I was an illegal alien, they would surely find out my other secret."

"It's okay," Toby said, "your secrets are safe with me."

"Thank you."

Toby got to his feet once again. "I really should get going. I'm tired."

"Yes, you've spent far too long with an old fart like me."

Toby's face dropped. Mr. Joseph frowned and said, "What's wrong Monsieur Fairchild?"

Toby shrugged. "Nothing. It's just... well, that's something Suzie used to say."

"Frankie's mom?"

"Yeah. We used to get along great, but since Frankie's death, she's changed. Hearing you say that brought back memories. I miss the old Suzie."

Toby left Mr. Joseph's and sauntered home, head down.

Later that night, seeing that his dad was alone in the kitchen, stacking dishes in the dishwasher (his mom was relaxing in the family room, watching re-runs of *Everybody Loves Raymond*), Toby asked, "Dad, do you believe that the stranger attacked me and Frankie?"

His dad stopped what he was doing, straightened and looked at Toby. "Why do you ask?"

"I'm curious. I mean, there was no evidence, right? The man wasn't found with a bloody baseball bat or anything."

"That we know of."

"Huh?"

"We don't know everything about the case, Toby. The police probably know more than they're allowed to tell. They seem pretty sure it was that stranger, so they must have good reason to suspect him."

"So you do think it was him?"

His dad swallowed, ruffling the prominent veins that had only recently popped up along his neck. "He's the most likely suspect, yeah."

"But why? I mean, the police only suspect that stranger of attacking me and Frankie because he was black."

His dad frowned. "What on earth gave you that idea?"

"There's no proof that man attacked us. So why does everyone seem to think it was him?"

"It has nothing to do with race, Toby. It's just simple logic. Nothing like it had ever happened in Belford, then, a few days before you and Frankie were attacked, this strange man drifts into town, is himself attacked by youths—at Jinks Field—the attack happens, and then, a week later, he's found dead and nothing like it has happened in the month since. And you have to remember, this man isn't the only suspect, he's just the main suspect. The police are still investigating."

"Are they?"

His dad shrugged and when he spoke, he didn't sound too confident. "I guess they still are. Anyway, if it wasn't that stranger, I'm sure whoever did attack you and Frankie..."

"I know, I know, is probably long gone by now."

"Right." His dad reached out and placed a hand on Toby's shoulder. "Toby, is there anything you want to tell me? You look... distracted. Like there's something else on your mind."

Toby shrugged. "Well, I guess I was wondering, what would happen if the police discovered that the stranger couldn't have done it? You know, like he had an alibi for that night... or that he was already dead when the attack occurred."

His dad's arm fell away. He continued stacking the dishes. "Why do you ask?"

"Like I said, just wondering."

"Well, he'd simply be ruled out as a suspect, and the police would continue to look for the guilty party. Like they're doing now," his father added. "But you don't have to worry about this, Toby. The man who attacked you and Frankie is dead. The police wouldn't be so sure he was their man if they didn't have good reason to suspect him."

Toby watched his dad rinse some plates before carefully stacking them in the appropriate racks. "Yeah, I'm sure they have good reason," he said, and then walked out of the kitchen.

CHAPTER TWELVE

Two days later, Toby headed back over to Mr. Joseph's.

He had spent the past few days mostly sitting in front of the TV, thinking about Mr. Joseph and what he had told him so far about his past. And though Toby was still coming to grips with the truth of Mr. Joseph, that zombis were real and did in fact exist, his fear was slowly easing. He also had thought a lot about Jean-Philippe. It seemed unbelievable to Toby that an innocent man could be judged guilty in the eyes of the law and the town—especially considering there was no evidence. But what could he do about it? He was sure there was something about the night of the attack that would help clear Jean-Philippe—if only he could remember.

Remember...

Standing at Mr. Joseph's front door, Toby knocked. After a minute ticked by without an answer, Toby headed around to the back of the house.

He wondered if perhaps the old man was working at Barb's, but in the backyard, he saw the door to Mr. Joseph's shed was open.

A flash of nerves tingled through Toby's gut.

Relax. It's just a shed. Nothing to be afraid of.

But still, Toby wondered, *after all these years, what was actually inside Mr. Joseph's shed?*

He walked around piles of old bricks, dirt, empty bottles, pieces of corrugated iron and old cans of paint, finally stopping at the shed. Mr. Joseph ceased sweeping, looked up and said, "Bonjou, Monsieur Fairchild." The old man was wearing a black shirt and dark-colored shorts, which showed off his rich chocolate skin and long, thin legs.

"Welcome to my *hounfor*," Mr. Joseph said. "I was just doing some cleaning. Gets a bit dusty. Come in, I'll show you." Mr. Joseph set aside the straw broom and motioned for Toby to venture inside.

With some hesitation, Toby stepped over the slightly raised threshold and entered the shed.

He was first struck by the bright colors and the overall strangeness of the interior. Most striking was a tall wooden pole in the middle of the shed, painted in bright red and blue spiral bands. The walls were also splashed with color—one wall was painted blue, one red and the other orange. All had strange drawings on them. There was a wooden cross over to one side, painted black, and sitting atop one arm was empty rum bottles, small drums and a pair of dark sunglasses. On the other side of the cross rested a shovel, a hoe and a pickaxe.

After the initial awe of the shed, Toby felt a sudden sense of déjà vu—like he'd dreamt about this place. But that was ridiculous. He'd never been inside Mr. Joseph's shed before. Nobody had.

"Wow," Toby said, turning to Mr. Joseph. "This is amazing."

"Mèsi. This is my temple, my religious sanctuary, if you like. Well, a modified version of one, but it serves me well enough. Vodou isn't some scary black magic, like most people think it is. It's a religion, like any other, except it deals more directly with the spirits, sees them as guides who can help us, not just something to pray to. It's a very organic religion, which merges African tribal rituals, with some Christian myths and rites. You see these pictures on the wall?"

Toby looked again at the various crude paintings. On the blue wall was a red drawing, an X with a round face in the top V, and a small v on the bottom, with the letter G inside. Looming over this painting was a cross. On the red wall was a more elaborate painting of a person with no legs, looking slightly angry, with both hands facing downwards, fists balled, and what appeared to be a branch with leaves sprouting from his head. And on the orange wall was what looked like a cake with a cross on top. Two coffins sat to either side of this coffin-cake.

"They are what are known as vèvè, ritual drawings of whatever loa a particular vodou hounfor is dedicated to. Usually they're drawn on the ground using flour or maize, as part of the ritual to invoke a loa during a vodou ceremony. Back home, I used to honor Azaka, loa of agriculture. These vèvè are of Guédé, the spirits of the dead, masters of the cemetery, and guardian of the children. I honor specifically Guédé Nimbo, a loa close to my heart."

"Why is that?"

"Nimbo is a special protector of the children." Mr. Joseph closed his eyes and started singing, gently, and in a surprisingly harmonious and pleasant voice, "Guédé, take the money, I will give you money, money, I will give you money to guard the children. I will give you money to guard the children." He opened his eyes. "Song of Nimbo." Then he turned to the pole in the middle of the shed. "This is a *poteau-mitan*—a center-post. Well, a rough replication of one. Usually it's found in the peristyle—that's where most of the vodou ceremonies take place. The poteau-mitan is where the people dance around to honor the loa, and sometimes get mounted."

"Mounted?"

"It's when a person is taken over by a loa, so the loa can speak, give advice or grant favors."

Toby stared wide-eyed at Mr. Joseph. "You mean a person can be taken over by a god?"

Mr. Joseph nodded. "But vodou gods are not the same as Christian gods. The loa are more akin to spirits, and there are many, many loa, some good, some not so good. All are different, and require different rituals in order to invoke them." Mr. Joseph shook his head. "But it's much too complex and involved to get into." He turned to the wooden cross. "This altar is where I pay my respect to Guédé Nimbo. You place items favored by whichever loa you worship at your altar. But like I said, this is only a make-shift hounfor, the ones back in Haiti are much more elaborate. It's silly, really. I don't know why I bother. I guess it just... makes me feel closer to my country."

"So you make a ho... houn..."

"Hounfor."

"Right, one of those at every place you've lived?"

"In one way or another. If I live in a house, I will either construct a hounfor in one of the rooms, or in a shed or garage, if it has one. The times I've lived in apartments, I've just allocated one corner for my altar."

"So you've moved around a lot?"

"Come, let's go inside. I need a drink. We can talk more then." Mr. Joseph stepped out of the shed.

Toby aimed to follow, but he remained in the make-shift vodou temple, wondering why it seemed familiar.

"Is everything okay?" Mr. Joseph asked.

"This may sound strange, but I can't help feeling that I've dreamt about this place."

Mr. Joseph laughed, softly. "You don't say?"

"Silly, I know." With a shrug, Toby stepped out of the shed. Once outside, he watched the old man chain then padlock the shed door. Then he followed Mr. Joseph into the kitchen.

"Water?" Mr. Joseph asked.

"Please."

Mr. Joseph filled a glass and placed it down in front of Toby, seated at the table. "I'm sorry I don't have anything else to offer," he said.

"That's okay. Mom says I should drink more water anyway."

"I wasn't sure you would be back," Mr. Joseph said as he went about making some tea. Once the kettle was on the stove, he wandered back over and sat down. "I thought maybe you had changed your mind. Maybe gone to the police about Jean-Philippe—or me."

"No," Toby said.

Mr. Joseph nodded. "You looked tired," he said. "Still having trouble sleeping?"

"Yeah."

"Your injuries?"

"That's partly the reason, but they're not so bad anymore. I went to see Doctor Hampton yesterday. He said I was healing fine and should be ready for high school come September."

"Are you ready for high school?"

Toby shrugged. "Is anyone ever ready for high school?"

"I wouldn't know. I never even went to elementary school."

"You didn't?"

"Most kids in Haiti don't, especially those from the country. So is that what's keeping you awake?"

"Hmm?"

"You said you were having trouble sleeping. And since your wounds don't seem to be much of a problem, I thought maybe it was the idea of starting high school."

"That, plus other things."

"Care to talk about it?"

Toby shrugged. "Well, remember how I said my memory of the night of the attack is a little fuzzy? It's more than a little fuzzy. The attack itself, until I awoke in the hospital, is a blank. I have brief flashes from that night, but they're just that—flashes that don't mean anything. Basically I have no recollection. But I can't help but feel that if I could remember the attack, I would be able to tell the police who it was that attacked me and Frankie."

"I see," Mr. Joseph said. "And you feel...guilty for not being able to remember?"

"I guess. A little. Also I've been having these weird dreams, it's almost as if they're trying to tell me something, trying to get me to remember that night." Toby huffed. "Sounds silly."

"No, it doesn't." When the kettle started whistling, Mr. Joseph hopped up, shuffled over to the stove and soon came back to the table with a teapot and cup. He waited a few minutes before pouring the tea.

Toby wrinkled his nose. "What is that? It's green."

"It's peppermint. I like herbal teas. Green teas. They sit well in my stomach."

Toby took a sip of water. "What about food? Can you eat?"

"Sure. Though I don't eat a lot, usually one meal per day, and only the most basic of foods, such as fruit, oatmeal or corn."

"Sounds tasty," Toby said, making a face.

"It keeps me going. I can't stomach rich foods." Mr. Joseph sipped his tea, careful not to spill a drop. "So, you were asking about all the places I have lived. Well, I couldn't name them all, but some of the places I've lived are: Miami, New York, Atlanta, and lots of smaller towns in between. I was living in Cleveland before I moved here."

"Why did you move here? I mean, it's such a small town and all."

"Well, we'll get up to that part later. How about I continue telling you about my life in Haiti? Unless you have somewhere else to be, I don't want to hold you up."

"I'm meeting Gloria later, but that's not for a few hours."

"Well okay then."

"So Marcel was gone. We were all happy about that. But there was an underlying nervousness about the situation, too. We just hoped his friends wouldn't return.

Three days after the marines had taken Marcel away, they came for him.

We were inside the main hut, eating breakfast, when they stepped into the house. Looking filthier, angrier than when we had last seen them, over two weeks ago.

"We're here for Marcel," the small caco demanded. "Where is he?"

"Go outside and play," Felicia whispered to Rachel.

Rachel did as she was told.

I stood up from the table and walked towards them.

I took a deep breath. I was shaking. "He's not here," I told them.

"Where is he? He was not supposed to go outside for any reason."

I tried to remain calm, but it was hard to do when two mean, dirty looking men with guns were glaring at you. "He's gone. The marines took him away."

The small man's eyes widened in manic rage. "What!" he roared.

They both pointed their guns at me. Mangela and Felicia gasped behind me.

"He was captured?" the taller man said. It was the first time I had heard him speak. He had a deep, hoarse voice.

I nodded.

The smaller man struck my cheek hard with the butt of his old rifle. It hurt like hell and I collapsed to the ground. I was dazed for a moment, and when I opened my eyes, I was staring down two barrels.

"You're dead," the small man said, snarling.

"Don't shoot him," Mangela cried.

"Yes, it wasn't his fault," Felicia cried. "It was..."

"Felicia," I warned, cutting her off.

The larger man shifted his gun to the table. "Shut up the both of you!"

"You're a traitor to your people," the smaller man said to me. "I spit on you." He did just that. Got me right in the face. It stunk, but I was too afraid to wipe it off.

"But you don't understand," I said, my voice shaking. "I can explain." I needed to go to the toilet and I was sweating profusely.

"You pitiful fool. Hurry up before I blow your brains out."

And he wasn't kidding. I could see his finger resting on the trigger. "I saw the marines approaching from the window one day. Marcel was in the altar room, resting. I told my wife to go and tell Marcel to stay out of sight, then I went out to see them. They asked me a bunch of questions, like if I had seen any cacos in the area. I told them I hadn't. They didn't believe me. They asked if they could search my house. I told them no, that I was telling the truth, so there was no reason to search my house. But they barged in anyway and found Marcel. I couldn't do anything about it."

I prayed they believed my story. I didn't want to think about what would happen to the girls if they killed me.

"If you're telling the truth then you are a pitiful man. Weak. The Americans must've seen through you."

I lowered my head. "I know. I am sorry. But I did all I could to help my brother."

Though I suspected they believed my story, I was still expecting them to shoot me. When some time passed without a gun going off, I looked up. Both men had their guns lowered. I wanted to cry I was so happy.

"Don't worry, old man," the smaller man said with an evil smirk. "We're not going to shoot you."

I nodded. Behind me Mangela was crying softly.

"After all, it wasn't your fault those filthy Americans stormed your house."

"I'm sorry," I said again.

The smaller man whispered something to the other caco. They both laughed.

"Goodbye," the smaller man said.

Then they left. Just like that. I stood up.

Mangela came over and put her arms around me. "I was so scared. I thought they were going to kill you for sure. Thank God it's over."

I kissed her.

Mangela smiled. She still had tears in her eyes.

"Thank you, papa," Felicia said. "I'll go and check on Rachel." She hurried outside.

Mangela and I hugged each other for a long time. Perhaps I knew it then, but everything wasn't going to be okay. It wasn't over. Far from it.

A few days later I decided to finish clearing away all the junk that was piled around our house. I had already dug a large hole in the ground, and was throwing in old mats and bottles. Mangela and Rachel were in the field, picking plantains, Felicia was doing some washing down at the river.

Just before lunch Mangela and Rachel came over with two baskets filled with plantains.

"How are you going?" Mangela asked.

"Getting there. Should be finished by lunch."

"Well don't strain yourself too hard, darling."

I threw a broken chair into the pit then turned to my wife and granddaughter. "Did you pick all those by yourself?" I said to Rachel, nodding at her basket.

"Yep," she said, grinning.

"Wow. What a good girl." I took her basket, placed it on the ground, then picked her up in my arms and swung her around. She always loved it when I did that, and she screamed with delight. When I began to feel dizzy, I stopped and put her down.

"Do it again," she said.

"Maybe later." I kissed her on the cheek. "Go on. You'd better get going. You have to make lunch for your papa."

I watched as Mangela and Rachel headed inside the hut. Then I went back to work.

Close to an hour later I was hot and thirsty and ready to go inside for something to eat and drink. I had my shirt off and was letting the sun beat its fiery rays against my body. I bent down to retrieve my shirt from a box I had lain it on. When I straightened, I caught movement in the distance, over in the hills. I looked and saw two men sitting atop two mules. I wouldn't have thought much of the sight but for two things. One, they seemed to have stopped on the ridge overlooking my habitation, and appeared to be looking right at me; and two, though my eyesight may not have been the greatest, I could've sworn one of the men was the smaller caco. The other looked to be an old man, with a thick beaded necklace looped around his neck. I saw the smaller man point, and a shiver of icy chills passed through my body. Then the mules were turned around and the two men disappeared into the mountains.

I stood gazing up at the hill for a long time, wondering if it was in fact the caco, and if so, who was the old man with him. I knew only houngans wore thick beads around their neck, but why would the caco bring a vodou priest to my habitation?

Maybe it wasn't just any houngan, I thought to myself. Maybe it was one who serves with both hands.

The thought scared me.

No, it wasn't the caco, I reassured myself. They were too far away; I was clearly mistaken.

Or so I hoped.

My daughter's voice broke my daze.

"Papa, are you okay?"

I turned around to see Felicia strolling towards me, wrapped bundle of washing in a basket atop her head.

"You were staring up at the mountains like you were in a trance or something."

"Oh, well, I guess you just caught me having one of my moments—I'm going senile, you know."

"Oh papa, you are not."

Mangela popped her head out. “I thought I heard voices. Good, Felicia, just in time. Lunch is ready.”

“Okay mama, I’ll be in shortly.”

Mangela turned to me, and her smile dropped a little. “Jacques, is anything the matter?”

I shook my head, rubbed my clammy hands on my overalls. “No, everything is fine. Just hungry.”

“Well, that’s no surprise.” She ducked back into the hut.

I glanced again up at the hills, felt a shiver wash over me once more, and then headed inside.

That night, back sleeping in the main room of the hut, I had a dream. I dreamt of a strange old man wearing colorful dress, a red hat and scarf tied around his neck, and heavy beads looped around his thin neck. His eyes were closed, he was chanting and shaking an *asson*—a sacred rattle—but I couldn’t understand what he was saying. Whatever it was, it filled me with terror.

Then he started dancing, shaking the rattle even more vigorously, and from his pocket he drew out some kind of white powder and began tossing it on the ground, over a vèvè for Guédé.

I noticed black candles all around the hut, but their scent was of blood, not melting wax, and then I heard someone laughing; it was a cruel laugh, and then a voice filled my head. “You will pay, old man. Shooting you would’ve been too quick.”

Then I was sucked back, out of the small, colorful hut the old man was dancing in, through the night, over rugged mountains and flat plains. I started falling, I feared I would crash into trees, or land in a deep, rocky ravine, but I just kept on falling. Darkness swooped down on me. On and on I fell.

I started having trouble breathing. It felt like I had inhaled a mouthful of dirt. A burning sensation tore through my chest, up my throat and out my mouth. I was left with a sick feeling and my head feeling light. And through it all I could still hear the old man chanting softly, and the sound of the small caco’s laughter echoed around in my dizzy head.

When I awoke, it was night. I sat up and thought I heard the sound of hooves galloping away, but it might've just been my heart thumping.

I was having trouble drawing breath, like I couldn't get enough air into my lungs. But that feeling soon went away and I was able to breathe normally again.

I could just make out the dim shape of Mangela sleeping nearby. She hadn't woken. Good, I thought. I lay back down, musing on the dream.

As I drifted back to sleep, I felt the beginnings of a headache, but I was too tired to worry about it. I soon fell asleep.

The next time I woke it was still dim outside, but not quite the pitch-blackness of earlier. I guessed the time to be around three or four in the morning.

I usually didn't wake so early. I usually woke at six on the dot, but it seemed the headache had grown progressively worse in my sleep, enough to wake me. I sat up, tired, lethargic, but my head pounding. I rubbed my temples, but that only made things worse. Not wanting to wake Mangela, I lay back down, closed my eyes and tried to sleep. But sleep was impossible. The throbbing in my head wouldn't cease—it was like a large maman drum at a rada ceremony—*thump thump thump*. An hour passed, the headache remained, squeezing my head like it was trapped in a vice. I began to feel ill.

As the roosters crowed, I staggered outside and vomited. Unfortunately, doing so didn't ease the pain in my head. When I staggered back inside, Mangela was up, a look of worry across her face. "Jacques, what's wrong? You sick?"

"I have a bad headache," I said and flopped back down on my mat. "It's nothing."

Mangela walked over, crouched and placed a hand across my forehead. "My God, you're burning up."

I hadn't noticed. If anything, I felt cold.

"You're shivering," Mangela said, concern growing in her voice. She drew the blanket over me. "When did you start feeling ill?"

"I woke up with a bad headache," I murmured, suddenly feeling overwhelmingly tired. "I think it started during the..." I fell asleep.

The next time I awoke it was daytime. I lifted my head with difficulty and saw that I was alone. The door was open and there was a warm breeze blowing in.

I laid my head back down on the mat. I still felt sick. But instead of feeling bitterly cold, my skin felt like it was on fire. I was sweating, my muscles ached, and I had a foul taste in my mouth—like I had just eaten some rotten food. I threw off the blanket.

I admit, I was scared. I knew I was terribly ill and last night's dream still haunted me.

Someone entered the hut.

"You're awake," Mangela said. She came over to me. Her luminous face appeared over me. "Are you feeling any better?"

I think I shook my head, but I couldn't be sure.

Mangela frowned.

As she bent down to feel my forehead, someone else walked in.

"How's papa?"

"He's..." Mangela swallowed, straightened. I could tell by the look in her eyes she was scared. I don't ever remember seeing fear so deep in her big brown eyes.

"Want me to get some water? Rum?" Felicia said.

"No," Mangela said. She turned around. "No, I want you to go and fetch Papa Louis."

Felicia was silent for a bit. "You think it's that serious?"

"I don't know what to think, but I know he's the only one who can help my Jacques. Go, I'll look after Rachel."

Quick footsteps pattered away.

I swallowed, felt fire run down my throat. I opened my mouth. "Rachel," I breathed. It hurt to speak. "Bring Rachel."

Mangela nodded. "Okay darling."

Mangela left and all of a sudden I began to feel icy cold. I started shivering uncontrollably. I was dying. I knew it. And there wasn't anything I could do about it.

I couldn't tell them about seeing the men in the hills yesterday, nor the dream that I suspected wasn't a dream, nor that I was sure a bocor's curse was behind my sudden illness. I didn't have the strength to tell anyone these things, and I was afraid. Afraid of dying, but more than that I was afraid of what waited for me beyond death. For what purpose had the bocor cursed me?

I had my suspicions, but they were too terrifying to contemplate.

Soon Mangela came back with Rachel. My darling granddaughter knelt down beside me and took my hand. She looked worried, tears were trickling down her cheeks. "Little one," I muttered. I could feel my throat starting to constrict. Soon I wouldn't physically be able to talk.

"Papa, you'll get better," Rachel whispered. "I prayed to Loco and Ayizan to protect you and make you better."

I squeezed her hand ever so gently. I loved her for wanting to help, but no loa would be able to help me now, nor Papa Louis; not even God Himself could help me now.

I closed my eyes.

Over the next couple of hours—I say hours because that's how long it felt, though I don't really know how long it was—I slipped in and out of consciousness. One moment I would be lying in the hut shivering, the next I would startle awake to find myself burning up.

The pain became almost unbearable. Every fiber of my body seemed to be alive with fire—even my tongue hurt.

Soon I began hallucinating. There were times I thought I was home, with my long-dead mama by my side stroking my head and smiling. Other times I thought I could see pointy-headed monsters with little wings and horns flapping around the hut, grinning.

One time—and I was sure this was real, not some delusion—I awoke to see two people standing over me. One was Papa Louis, the houngan, the other a young woman, probably his hounsis, his assistant.

I didn't stay awake long enough to hear what they were saying.

I slipped into darkness.

This time I stayed there."

Mr. Joseph stood up from the table. "You want another glass of water, Toby?"

"No thanks." Toby watched Mr. Joseph walk over to the cupboard under the sink, open the door and pull out a bottle of rum.

He filled a glass with the clear liquid, downed it in one shot, then bringing the bottle and glass with him, sat back down.

"This must be hard for you?" Toby said.

Mr. Joseph nodded. "But you know, in some strange way, it feels good to tell someone about my past."

"Facing your fears?"

Mr. Joseph chuckled softly. "Yeah, maybe." He poured another glass, took a quick nip. "I think Mangela would've liked you. Rachel too."

"Really?"

"Sure. You're honest, kind. Not many people would have kept my secret to themselves. Most would have gone straight to the police, or stayed as far away from me as possible."

"Do you have any pictures?"

"Of Mangela and Rachel? No. Nor of Felicia. We couldn't afford things such as cameras."

"Didn't Jean-Philippe bring any when he came?"

"No. Like I said, he never spoke with them. Just looked out for them."

Toby drew in a solemn breath. "Would it really have been so bad if they had known? Maybe they would have understood. It wasn't your fault, right?"

Mr. Joseph gazed into the glass of rum. "They would have turned away in horror if they had seen me, Toby. To see your loved one turned into a zombi is the worst possible thing imaginable. Worse than death. Some people in Haiti take measures to assure their departed loved one isn't brought back as a zombi."

"Like what?"

"Well, for example, cutting off the head, or dismembering a part of the body, so it won't be of any use as a slave. Or they might lay heavy stones on the coffin so the soulless creature can't leave the grave. I've even heard of family members throwing handfuls of rice into the coffin."

Toby frowned. “Rice?”

“So when the zombi is called forth by the bocor, the zombi will see the rice and instead of answering the call, thus being enslaved forever, will instead see the hundreds of grains and want to count them, forgetting about the bocor’s instructions.”

“And that works?”

“Well, I’ve never actually seen it myself, but I’ve heard from people that it does. So as you can see Toby, the idea of a loved one becoming a zombi is a fate worse than death. At least in death, the soul is free to return back home; which in Haitians’ case, is Guinée, or Africa, if you like. But a zombi’s soul is trapped forever, controlled by his master, and not only is that a frightening concept in of itself, but it also brings back bad memories of our ancestors. They were brought over to Haiti by the French to work as slaves, similar to what happened in this country. They weren’t zombis, but they were just as enslaved. Being turned into a zombi reminds Haitians of those dark days, and so the idea of being without thought or will or freedom for eternity, well, that’s too awful to contemplate. I couldn’t put Mangela and Felicia and Rachel through that. It was best they thought I was dead, my soul free. You understand?”

“But you’re not a zombi. Well, not really. Couldn’t you have gone back to them after...?”

“My awakening?”

“Yeah.”

“I am a zombi savane, that is true, but I’m still a zombi. My soul is still trapped, I’m still trapped. That fact doesn’t change. I couldn’t imagine going back to my wife and children, even as a savane, and living with them, knowing I wasn’t really alive, that I would live long after they had gone from this world. It would’ve been too hard for all of us.”

“But at least you would’ve spent time with them.”

Mr. Joseph smiled at Toby. It was a sad smile. “That’s what I love about youth. They always see the world in the simplest, purest way. You’re right, I could’ve spent time with them, but it would’ve been too hard for them, knowing what I had become, imagining the pain I was going through. No, it was best that I left Haiti altogether. That way, there was no chance of them finding out about me. Also, it was less dangerous. There were people constantly on the look-out for stray zombis, like dog-catchers, but for the undead. If they caught a zombi, they would put it in an asylum, or, if it was in good enough condition, sell it to another master. But a stray zombi savane was considered most undesirable. They were rarer, so not many were captured, but nobody wanted a savane on the loose."

"Why not?"

"They're aware of what they are. At least a zombi is essentially brain-dead, unaware of what they are, just blindly obeying orders. A savane is a thinking zombi, a talking zombi, and that's incredibly dangerous to the establishment. If I had been captured, I would have been sent to jail, my family would've been in danger. Jean-Philippe stayed, knowing the risks, but he laid low, kept to himself, and fortunately, he was never captured."

"What about your grandchildren and great-grandchildren? Don't you want to see them? Maybe things have changed since you were there, maybe they won't care that you're a savane."

"Ridiculous," Mr. Joseph huffed. "Of course they'd care. Besides, I can't go back after ninety years, and suddenly show up, a grandfather they thought died a long, long time ago. Imagine their horror and shock at finding out what I was. No, there's no way I could go back to Haiti and see them. Not now, not ever."

"I'm sorry," Toby said. "I shouldn't have brought it up."

"Then let's drop it, okay?" Mr. Joseph finished off the glass of rum, poured himself another. He downed that in one gulp. "So," he said, wiping his mouth. "You want to hear some more of my story?"

"Only if you're up to it," Toby said.

"What time do you have to go?"

"Well, I'm meeting Gloria at her house at around four." Toby glanced at his watch. It was just after three. "We've got time."

"Okay, so where were we? Right..."

"I of course don't remember dying, but I must have. The funeral would have been a small affair, carried out either the day of my death or the next day—bodies don't stay fresh for long in the tropical heat, and peasants can't afford things like a mortician and embalming.

I knew Mangela, Felicia and Rachel would've been there, as would Papa Louis, his hounsis and friends from neighboring villages. I can only imagine what would've been said, the prayers spoken, but one thing I can be sure of was that my family didn't take precautions against my coming back as a zombi. Either they thought my death was natural, simply old age running its course, or they knew it came about due to an evil bocor's spell, but Mangela couldn't bear to cut off my head or put a knife through my cold dead heart.

Whatever occurred in the days following my demise, the result was the same. There was only darkness, a deep black nothing, and then someone spoke my name.

The voice was as loud and clear as if the person was lying next to me.

The first time he called my name I felt the sensation of being awakened, like I had been asleep and was slowly waking up.

He called my name a second time, and it was like the gears in my body had been switched on. My mind began swirling about and I could start to feel sensation in my limbs. I didn't know what was happening to me, nor did I care. I couldn't think at all.

He called my name a third time.

I opened my eyes, sat up and answered, "Yes." Then I waited for instruction.

I saw a face appear above me amid the nighttime sky, though I was looking at him at a strange angle. An old man wearing thick heavy beads around his neck. In some distant past he seemed vaguely familiar, like I had met him in a dream, but I couldn't think where I had seen him—and I didn't particularly care. The old man had in his hand a small clay pot, its lid off, and this he passed under my nose.

It was as if somebody had replaced my mind, my awareness, my soul with dead air. My movement had been revitalized, but that was about it.

I was suddenly aware of my surroundings, that I was in a shallow hole in a wooden box with dirt all around me; aware that I was present in whatever reality I was in, but other than that, I did not think of where I was, why I was there, or who I was.

"Rise," the old man said.

I did as I was told.

I crawled out of the shallow grave. When I was out, the old man with the beads tied a piece of rope around my neck, leaving a piece dangling down my back.

"That's what you are," another man said to me. "An animal. Worse than an animal, a zombi." He laughed. "And a deformed one at that. Hell, look at you."

This small man, a rifle slung over one shoulder, was more familiar to me than the old man, but the thought stopped there.

Also familiar was the small graveyard I was in. I didn't have the capacity to think about it, but if I did, I would have known that I was in a local cemetery about two miles from my habitation; a small country graveyard near the base of a hill, full of cheap wooden crosses.

"What's the matter with him?" another man cried. This man, a man somewhere in age between the other two, looked upset. I had never seen him before. "What happened?"

"Don't worry," the old man said. "He will be fine. The coffin was a little small for him, that's all. They had to fit him in somehow. He will still be able to work, that I can guarantee."

"Yeah, those imbecile peasants made the coffin too small," the younger man said. "We saw it all from where we stood on the hill. They were panicked, but eventually they had no choice—either bury him in the dirt, or break his neck to fit him in the coffin. I just wish I could've been the one to snap it. I would've enjoyed doing that."

"And he's also bleeding," the man continued. "Look, there on his cheek. What are you two trying to pull on me?"

"Must've happened when those imbeciles nailed down the coffin lid," the small man said with a chuckle.

"Don't worry," the old man said. "It won't get infected. It will leave a nasty scar, but it won't get infected."

"It better not," the man said. He sighed. "Well, I guess he looks good and strong, despite his age and the broken neck. He will be useful."

"He was hauling rubbish the day Emmanuel took me to him. He was a strong human."

The man looked at me. "Okay. I will take him and see how he goes. I didn't come all the way down here for nothing."

The old man turned to me. "Close the coffin lid, then pick up that shovel and fill in the hole with dirt."

I followed the old man's instructions. I may have been a zombi, but I could still process basic information. I still retained innate mental and physical capabilities. I could understand instruction on a basic primitive level, even if I didn't consciously think about what it was I was doing, or why I was doing it.

While I busied completing the job, the three men sat on the ground, smoking cigarettes, the smaller man laughing every so often, muttering things like, "Look at the animal work," and, "This is for Marcel."

When I had finished filling in the hole, the old man collected the shovel, as well as a few other tools and candles, placed them in a sack that was slung over one of the mules, then said, "Okay, come on. We'd better get going while it's still dark."

The old man grabbed the rope around my neck and pulled me towards the old brown mule. I followed blindly, like I was in some kind of a trance.

"Not me," the small man said. "I saw what I came to see. Make sure you work him hard, Silva." Stopped by the mule, the small but mean looking man with the rifle walked over and whispered to me, "Oh, and I just want you to know that your wife and daughter are being taken care of real good, zombi." He chuckled, then hopped on his gray mule and trotted away.

The old man climbed onto the brown mule and, looking down at me, said, "Get up."

I clumsily swung my leg over and sat behind the old man. Nearby the other man was mounted on his mule.

"Follow me, and if we encounter any gendarme, just let me do the talking."

The three of us rode the few miles in the moonlit night across endless fields, until finally we arrived at my house. At the time I wasn't sure where we were or why we had come here. The small hut meant nothing to me, other than it was familiar, and that I felt fear being there. To me, it was an evil place, one that I never wanted to see again.

When I started whimpering and struggling, I heard the old man say, “Good, he won’t ever return here,” and then, much to my relief, we left.

“We head to the mountain path,” the old man said. “The one near Saint-Raphael. Be careful.”

We rode down narrow paths between plots of land, the scattered huts around us bathed in darkness. The moonlight was our only guide, and the clip-clopping of the mules seemed to blend in with the night sounds of dogs barking and the occasional baby crying. We crossed over a river, which due to the meager rain of late wasn’t too deep, and continued through fields, towards the massive mountains ahead.

At the base of the mountain, the old man spoke. “Get down, zombi.”

I hopped down from the mule. Then stood there in the darkness, not thinking, not feeling, just waiting.

“I have done my part, now for the payment.”

The other man nodded, reached into a sack and pulled out some money. He handed the old man some notes, I couldn’t see how many. The old man placed the money in his pocket, then handed the man the clay pot that had been passed under my nose earlier, except now a cork was wedged into its top. “Here. He is now yours. Don’t be afraid to use the rope if you have to.”

At that the old man steered his mule around and soon vanished across the fields.

“Okay slave,” the man, now my master, said. “Get up here.”

I hopped up onto my master’s mule, sitting behind him.

“Now don’t get used to this kind of luxury. You’re only up here because you can’t be expected to ride a mule by yourself, and it’s a long journey on foot to my plantation, and most of it’s through the mountains. So hang on, don’t fall off and don’t whine. And try not to look so... zombi-like. We’ll probably run into a gendarme patrol at some point.”

The master sighed.

“It’s risky enough transporting a zombi, they had to give me one with a broken neck and a nasty cut on its face,” he muttered.

"Christ, I'll be lucky to make it back without getting shot by a marine. I'm getting too old to be doing this."

We started up the winding path leading up into the mountains, and so began our long journey."

Mr. Joseph finished off his fourth glass of rum. "This all feels like it happened yesterday," he said, shaking his head, obviously affected by the memories.

"I can't imagine what it must've been like, going through all that," Toby said.

"And you should be grateful for that," Mr. Joseph said. "Nobody should have to go through what I did. It's just a pity there are so many people who don't appreciate being alive and free." Mr. Joseph pushed away the empty glass. "If they knew what it felt like to be enslaved, truly enslaved, both in body and mind, they would appreciate every breath, every moment they were alive."

"Yeah, I kinda know what you mean," Toby said.

Mr. Joseph looked at him, eyebrows raised. "You do?"

"Well, if you hadn't found me when you did..." Toby sighed. "I guess it made me see things differently. I think back on what it used to be like, you know, before the attack, and I wish I could go back to those times. It's funny, but only a month ago I couldn't wait to grow up, be treated as an adult, not like a kid and all that. Now, I wish I could be a kid again and have Frankie back."

Mr. Joseph nodded. "Freedom," he said. "Something most people take for granted. But without freedom, there is only misery. That's what you're missing, I'm guessing."

"Yeah, maybe," Toby said.

"That's why I sit by the window and watch you kids go by." Mr. Joseph smiled. "I know it must seem weird to you and your friends. I see the way you look at me as you go past. And I do understand. If I was your age and saw a strange old man sitting watching me, I would've thought it weird, too. But it's simply about freedom. Watching freedom in its purest form."

Toby shifted in the chair, feeling bad for all the times he had hurried past Mr. Joseph's house, all the jokes he had made about the "freak by the window".

"That's also why I walk around town at night. I feel safest at night, under the cover of darkness. There are no accusing eyes or whispering mouths. It's when I feel the most free. I wish I could walk around during the day, but it's too unpleasant. Still, I've gotten used to the night, its sounds, smells, its quiet. It helps pass the time. Sometimes I walk for hours."

"Where do you go?"

"Wherever I feel like. I suspect I know this town as well as anyone."

"So you don't go anywhere in particular? You don't do anything...?"

"Untoward?"

Toby frowned.

Mr. Joseph chuckled. "Suspicious."

"Oh."

"No, I'm afraid not. I just walk around. It's all rather boring."

Well there's another rumor dispelled, Toby thought, and found it strange he would feel disappointment. He should be happy that Mr. Joseph wasn't some Peeping Tom.

He checked his watch. It was 3:40.

"Well, I'd better get going," Toby said. He stood up, pushed the chair into the table.

"Take care, Monsieur Fairchild."

"You too." Toby started for the back door. But he stopped when a thought entered his mind. With all the talk about vodou, zombi spells and him missing Frankie, something occurred to Toby that was frightening in its possibilities. He considered walking out the back door, not bothering to ask Mr. Joseph such a question, but he had to ask. He had to know. He turned around and looked at the slightly hunched man sitting at the table. "Mr. Joseph?"

Mr. Joseph gradually eased his body around. "Yes?"

Toby took a deep breath. "I was wondering. Is it possible to... do you have the power to... could you bring Frankie back if you wanted to?"

Mr. Joseph stared at Toby for a long time.

"I mean, he wouldn't have to be a regular zombi. He could be a savane, like you." Tears stung Toby's eyes. He wiped them away.

"Toby," Mr. Joseph said with a sigh. "Why would you ask such a thing?"

"Because I miss him. I want him back. I could be talking to him like I'm talking to you."

Mr. Joseph shook his head, and Toby didn't know if that was his answer, or just a sign of his disapproval at the question. "If I said yes, I could bring Frankie back, would you really want him to live this way? After what I've told you about me, what it's like to be a savane, would you really want Frankie to be put through that?"

Toby knew it wasn't fair to ask Mr. Joseph such a question. But damn it, he missed Frankie so much it was a palpable pain that was constantly gnawing away at his body. Still, as he brushed more tears away, he said, quietly, "No." He looked to the floor. "No, I wouldn't want him to be like you."

"He would hate you for it. He wouldn't be able to live a normal life. He'd be living in constant pain and fear. He wouldn't be the Frankie you knew. That Frankie is dead. You can never get that back."

Toby nodded. He turned around and opened the back door.

"But Toby, to answer your question... no. It's not possible. I don't have the knowledge or the power to bring Frankie back. I'm not a bocor. I was a simple peasant farmer."

"Okay," Toby said, and then he stepped outside.

The afternoon was warm and there was the smell of perfumed flowers in the air. Toby breathed in deeply as he closed the back door. He wiped his eyes dry and left Mr. Joseph's house.

Stupid question. What did you think Mr. Joseph was going to say? Sure, of course I could do that, let's go over to the cemetery now and bring Frankie back from the dead.

Feeling foolish, Toby started along Pineview.

He walked with heavy steps, his mind drifting like pollen in the wind, had turned from Pineview into Bracher, when he heard a voice whisper, "Toby."

Toby stopped, looked around, but couldn't see anyone.

"Psst... Toby."

"Who's there?" he said, suddenly nervous.

A figure stepped out from behind an oak tree.

"Warrick?" Toby said.

"Sssh, not so loud."

Warrick remained half-hidden behind the oak's thick trunk, head darting this way and that as if he was worried about being seen.

"What the hell are you doing?" Toby said. "Why are you hiding behind that tree?"

"I... I just wanted to speak to you," Warrick said, his voice barely louder than a whisper.

"Then why didn't you just come and see me at my house like any normal person? Oh, that's right, that's because you're not normal."

Toby remained tense, cagey; Warrick hadn't so much as said boo to him this past month, and now here he was hiding behind a tree, acting stranger than usual.

"What do you want, Warrick?"

With eyes still searching, head shifting from side-to-side, Warrick said, "I don't know."

He was acting different, not like the usual Warrick Coleman, all cocky. He sounded sad, his voice flat and if Toby didn't know any better, he would've sworn he was scared.

What has Warrick got to be scared about? Toby wondered.

There was silence. The wind blew gently, leaves skipped along the pavement.

This was the first time he had seen Warrick since that horrible night. He didn't know what to say to him, how to act around him; and by the way Warrick was standing there nervously, as quiet as Toby had ever seen him, it looked like Warrick felt the same way.

"I... I'm sorry," Warrick said, softly. The words sounded strained, foreign to his tongue.

"Sorry about what?" Toby said.

Warrick shrugged. "For what happened. To Frankie. I bet you miss him."

Toby swallowed, found it difficult to get the words past the golf-ball sized lump in his throat. "Yeah, I do," he said. "Every day."

"They reckon it was that hobo that did it, huh?"

"Yeah, that's what most people think."

"Huh," Warrick said. "Look, Toby..." Warrick drew in breath, jerked his head towards a car cruising towards them. He watched it sail past, and then turn into Pineview.

When Warrick turned back, his eyes were wide, and he had beads of sweat on his top lip. "I gotta go, Toby," he said, and started walking away, fast.

"Warrick, is there something you want to tell me?" Toby called, standing on the sidewalk, baffled. "Warrick?"

"I have to go," Warrick called back, his high voice wavering. "I have to go."

Warrick jogged off down Bracher and was soon out of sight.

What the hell was that all about? Toby wondered, and he stewed on the strange encounter the rest of the way to Gloria's.

Toby pressed the doorbell. Chimes ding-donged inside the Mayfour house and when the door opened, Helen Mayfour—local florist, church-going Christian, member of the PTA—smiled out at him.

"Hi Toby. Please, come in."

Toby stepped inside.

As the door closed behind him, Toby felt a surge of paranoia and a fluttering of nerves. He had never been inside the Mayfour house—never been inside any girl's house. Stepping into the home of the two hottest girls in town was kind of like being given permission to enter the girls' locker room at school; it was unfamiliar territory, a little scary, a lot exciting.

"Gloria's in the family room watching a movie," Helen Mayfour said. "Follow me."

Toby followed her down the cream-tiled hallway, past framed picture after framed picture of the Mayfour family. In the early photos young Gloria was all smiles, pigtails and pretty dresses. Debbie seemed colder. She was still smiling, but Toby wouldn't have been surprised to learn she had been a brat. In all the photos of Helen and Rudy, both were immaculately dressed and groomed, complete with designer smiles.

The house itself was as white and sparkling as their teeth. And big. It was the kind of house usually featured in those glossy lifestyle magazines, and was easily the most luxuriant house Toby had ever been in—but then Gloria's dad probably made double what Toby's dad did.

Toby had never spoken much with Rudy Mayfour, only the occasional 'how d'ya do' at town festivals, or bank picnics, but he had already long ago formed an opinion of Gloria and Debbie's father, thanks mostly to his dad's grumblings. But, Toby figured anyone who could produce and raise a girl like Gloria couldn't be all that bad.

Mrs. Mayfour led Toby into the dining room. The room was bigger than Toby's, the furniture looked more expensive, and there were lots of large paintings hanging on the walls. Down the opposite end were two doors, presently closed, behind which Toby could hear the sounds of a movie playing.

When they reached the doors, they stopped. Mrs. Mayfour pulled them open and the gun blasts and screaming grew louder. Toby followed Mrs. Mayfour into the dimly-lit room. Aside from the glare of the TV, the room was in darkness. Mrs. Mayfour flicked on the light switch. Gloria, lounging on the sofa, jumped. She turned around and at the sight of her mom and Toby, she paused the DVD. She smiled shyly. "Oh, hey Toby."

Toby smiled shyly back. An awkward silence filled the room. Finally, Mrs. Mayfour said, "Would you like a drink, Toby?"

Toby swallowed, throat dry. "Thanks."

"Gloria?"

"I'm fine."

"Well, I'll leave you two kids alone." Mrs. Mayfour left, leaving the doors wide open.

Gloria's family room was bigger than Toby's and was populated with a pool table, a couple of beanbags, a stereo system, the large flat-screen TV, and two sofas—the one Gloria was sitting on facing the TV, and another sitting adjacent. Both were cream-colored and looked expensive. A well-stocked bar took up the entire far wall, and behind it a row of trophies sat proudly on shelves.

Gloria hopped up and walked over to Toby.

"Hey," Gloria said, still smiling.

"Hey," Toby answered. "What were you watching?"

"Huh? Oh, *Heat*. It's one of my dad's favorite movies. It's pretty good, actually."

Toby nodded.

"Are you okay? You seem... nervy."

Toby shrugged. "I guess it's... you have a really nice house."

Gloria frowned, then laughed. "It's okay, I feel strange, too. I've never had a boy come over before. Mom's acting strange, too. Doesn't know how to behave. I mean, Deb's had boys come over since she was in elementary school, but me..."

A door near the bar opened and Mrs. Mayfour came in. "Here you go, Toby." She wandered over to the table in front of the sofa facing the TV and placed a can and a glass on top. She straightened and then stood there for a few beats. "Well, I guess that's it. If you need anything..."

"I know where the kitchen is, Mom. Straight through that door. I do live here, remember?"

Mrs. Mayfour nodded. She looked embarrassed. "Don't have the TV up too loud, okay?" Then, reluctantly, she turned and headed back through the door leading into the kitchen, leaving it hanging open.

Gloria expelled a long sigh and striding over to the door, eased it shut. "Sorry," she said, moving back to the sofa. "She's not usually this uptight. Come, have a seat."

Toby looked behind, to the open double doors, then turned around and made his way to the sofa.

"We'd better leave the dining room doors open," Gloria said. "Mom would have a conniption if she saw those closed. But don't worry, I don't think she'll spy on us. Deb on the other hand..."

Toby sat in the sofa beside Gloria. The material was soft and smelled of leather, and the cushions felt like marshmallows. As he had expected, it was the comfiest sofa he had ever sat on.

Gloria leaned forward and kissed Toby on the lips.

It was a short, but tender kiss. "I missed you," she said, pulling back. "I know it's only been a couple of days, but I have."

"I... I've missed you, too." Toby reached over and picked up the can of Diet Coke. He cracked the can open, was about to take a drink, but then eyed the empty glass sitting on the table. He filled the glass, set the can down and then took a drink. He must've made a face, because Gloria chuckled.

"Sorry, Mom only buys diet drinks. Want something else? Juice? Water?"

"No, it's okay." He set the tasteless drink down.

Gloria picked up her drink, Toby guessed apple cider, took a few sips, and then said, "Are you sure everything's all right?"

Toby sighed. "It's just... well, I ran into Warrick on the way over here. And he was acting really strange."

"You mean stranger than usual?"

"He was hiding behind a tree, acting like he didn't want anyone to see us talking. He was really jumpy, too."

"Yeah, that is weird. Maybe he just doesn't know how to act around you. You know, because of everything that's happened. You said so yourself he hasn't been around to see you. Maybe he just doesn't know how to deal with his emotions."

Toby took another sip of the Diet Coke—his mouth was exceptionally dry. "Yeah, I guess that could be it."

"You don't sound convinced."

"He apologized. For what happened to Frankie. And then it looked like he was about to say something else, but then he got spooked and ran off."

Gloria was silent for a moment. "What do you think he was going to say?"

"I dunno. It was probably nothing. You're right, he probably just feels weird around me. So anyway, I've got some news to tell you."

Gloria sat up. A smile threatened to burst across her face. "This better be good news."

"I guess it is. I finally went over and thanked Mr. Joseph."

The smile exploded. She leaned over and hugged him. Toby's heart-rate quickened at the feel of her slender body against his and her smell washed over him. All too soon she pulled away. "That's great news. I'm proud of you, Toby. So when did this happen?"

"A few days ago."

"Why didn't you tell me earlier?"

"Slipped my mind, I guess."

"So, what was he like?"

Toby took some deep breaths. "Not like what I expected."

"How do you mean?"

"Well, I've been spending some time with him these past few days, so I've sort of gotten to know him a little."

He didn't mind telling Gloria. He knew she would understand.

Still, she looked taken aback. "You have?"

"He's been telling me all about his life back in Haiti. It's really very interesting. He's a nice guy, Gloria. I think you'd like him. He's smart, funny..."

...a zombi.

"Sounds like you don't need me anymore."

Toby smiled. "Nah, he's not as good a kisser as you."

Gloria laughed.

Toby relaxed. He knew she'd understand.

"Well I'm happy for you. I guess he's not the big bad boogeyman everyone thinks he is."

"No, I guess not. He even has this cool vodou temple in his shed—it's called a hou...hounfor. And did you know he used to be married, and that he had a kid and a grandchild?"

Gloria shook her head.

"Yeah, they're all dead now. The old man's been through a lot. I feel sorry for him. All those times I played pranks on him, laughed about him at school. And then the guy goes and saves my life..." Toby looked to the coffee table.

Gloria took hold of his hand. She gave it a gentle squeeze. "Say, you mind if we watch the rest of *Heat*?"

Toby shook his head. "That's fine."

"You seen it?

"Nope."

"I haven't watched too much of it, so I'll fill you in as we go. Want something to eat? Some popcorn?"

"You got butter-flavored?"

"Of course."

Toby smiled and Gloria hopped up from the sofa and walked towards the door leading into the kitchen. Before she reached it, she stopped, turned around. "You sure you don't want another drink? We could go down to Barb's and get some real Coke if you'd like."

"I'm fine," Toby said and then Gloria headed into the kitchen.

While she was gone, Toby heard the murmur of people talking. A few minutes later Gloria came back carrying a large bowl overflowing with yellow popcorn.

She sat back down, offered the mountain of popcorn to Toby.

"I hope your mom was okay with us staying in here and watching a movie?" Toby mumbled through a mouthful of popcorn.

"Huh?" Gloria said, scooping a handful for herself.

"Isn't that who you were talking to in the kitchen? Your mom?"

"Oh, no, that was just Deb. When she's fighting with Dwayne, she hangs around here like a bad smell."

"Oh," Toby said, and settling back to enjoy the movie (as well as the company), shoveled another mouthful of butter-flavored popcorn into his mouth.

CHAPTER THIRTEEN

"You're up early," his mom said as Toby shuffled over to the cupboard and took out the box of Cheerios. He'd had a decent night's sleep, his first since the attack, and it was nice to be up before noon for a change. Toby plucked the milk from the fridge and taking both the milk and the Cheerios over to the table, prepared his bowl of cereal.

"So what's on for today? Seeing Gloria?" His mom was dressed and ready for work.

"Uh-huh," Toby said.

"Your vocabulary astounds me sometimes."

Toby started munching on his Cheerios.

"Well I'm off. Have fun today, but take it easy, okay?" She kissed him on the cheek as she walked past.

"Bye," Toby said.

"See you tonight."

His mom left, and Toby sat eating his cereal, thinking how to kill time before seeing Gloria.

He was meeting her for lunch at Patterson's at around one. Just a little over four hours until he saw Gloria again—this time without the burden of being watched by Ma Mayfour.

He guessed he could always hang around at home, watching bland day-time TV; or he could kill time walking around town, enjoying the sunshine.

But he didn't want to do either of those things.

He wanted to hear more about Mr. Joseph's life back in Haiti—the old man's story was as good as any book he'd read, just as exciting and scary as any movie.

He'd spent most of the weekend thinking about what he'd heard so far, and imagining what else was to come. He found he was getting used to the old man, with his odd features and high, nasally voice. Unable to visit due to his parents being home, he found he even missed his company. But a few times he caught himself wondering whether he was doing the right thing in not telling anyone about Mr. Joseph.

He had told Mr. Joseph he wouldn't tell anybody about his secret; he felt in his heart he was doing the right thing—but what if he wasn't? What if he was letting his emotions get the better of him and cloud his judgment? After all, behind the pale yellow curtains of that bland house lived an actual zombi.

How can I not let my emotions play a part in this? he had thought. *He saved my life. I owe him.*

Besides, zombi or not, he seemed like a perfectly harmless old man.

And how much does anyone know about zombis, anyway? Toby had wondered. *For all we know, there could be thousands of zombis like Mr. Joseph living in this country. All over the world. Living seemingly normal lives, nobody the wiser.*

The thought had intrigued Toby.

And it continued to intrigue him as he ate his breakfast.

"Drink?"

"No thanks. Maybe later."

The old man eased himself into the chair.

"I didn't think you grew older?" Toby said.

Mr. Joseph frowned. "What do you mean?"

"Well you seem to have trouble getting in and out of chairs, like my grandparents."

He smiled. "I was old when I died, remember? Considering that was over ninety years ago, I think I'm holding up pretty well, don't you think?"

Toby nodded.

"But to answer your question, no, I'm not getting older. My body is not deteriorating like a living person's. I'm pretty much the same now as when I died. Perhaps a little stiffer, and of course... this." He pointed to his head. "But that wasn't my fault, as you know."

"So, how old are you?"

"Well, I was in my early seventies when I died, so if you count the time I've been a zombi, I guess you could say I've been alive—so to speak—for around one hundred and sixty years."

"My God," Toby breathed.

"And I don't feel a day over a hundred and twenty." Mr. Joseph smiled.

"One hundred and sixty," Toby repeated.

"Are you sure you don't want anything to drink?"

Toby shook his head. "I'm fine, really."

"Okay. So, where was I?"

"Sorry?" Toby said.

"Had I just been buried?"

It took Toby a moment to understand what Mr. Joseph was talking about. "You had been brought back and were just about to start the long journey."

"That's right. Say, you don't mind if I help to calm myself before we continue, do you?"

"No," Toby said.

Mr. Joseph got up from the table and grabbed the bottle of rum from off the kitchen bench.

Toby wondered—did Mr. Joseph always drink in the mornings?

Toby thought about Suzie. She certainly drank in the mornings.

Mr. Joseph's not like that. He's different. He's not a drunk—at least, I don't think he is.

Maybe stirring up all these memories wasn't such a good idea, Toby thought. He hadn't considered how reliving the past would affect Mr. Joseph.

Mr. Joseph sat back down with a glass and the bottle of Barbancourt rum. He poured half a glass and downed it in one go. "Better," he said. "Okay, I'm ready."

"I won't bore you with the details of that journey to the plantation. Other than it was long, it seemed like weeks, but was probably really only days, and nothing much of interest occurred. Besides, to me, it was all one long dream. Hazy, almost surreal when I look back on it. I was conscious, but not aware. Mostly I remember lots of trees, miles of narrow winding paths, and me having to constantly hop down from the mule to lead the animal through streams and up and down deep ravines—I guess luxury for a zombi only extended so far. We stopped during the day to rest, in out of the way places where there were no huts or small villages around. Nights were spent traveling and when we passed villages or lonely mountain huts, it was either too late at night for the inhabitants to be of any concern, or, if we did see peasants, they paid us no mind. If they were aware of what was sitting blankly behind the plantation owner, Silva, they knew not to ask questions or even say hello to the passing strangers. I remember hearing lots of drumming, too, but I couldn't tell you if it was a vodou ceremony, a Congo celebration or even the call of a secret society. To me, it was simply drumming.

As I recall, we only passed one gendarme patrol. They were on horses, but they must've thought we were no threat, because they passed right on by. It was nighttime, so they mustn't have been able to see my face clearly. For I think if they had, their suspicions would surely have been aroused.

Finally, we came out of the mountains. We had been following a river for a long while, later I was to realize it was the Limbé. The mountains grew gradually smaller, we seemed to be going downhill for a long time, and eventually the mountains thinned out completely and the world leveled out—well, not completely for me, but for Silva and his mule.

It was dark, and I had seen distant lights as we were coming down the mountain. I had also seen the ocean further in the distance, moonlight glinting off the water, but that soon vanished when we reached the flatland of some northern plain.

"Almost there," the master said, though I wasn't sure who he was talking to—me or his mule.

The master left the river and we headed away from the scattered lights of some nearby town. We edged slowly along, passing the town over on our left. I felt the master's muscles tighten as we crossed over a road, one of those newly built ones. I guess he was worried about marines or the Gendarmerie stopping us.

But they didn't. We didn't see any patrols, and the master's body relaxed when we were back on farmland, leaving the town behind us.

We soon joined up with a river—whether it was the same one we had followed through the mountains I didn't know at the time. We followed its banks, passing dark huts and silent villages along the way.

We crossed the river at a particularly narrow bend, the water was a little deeper than the river near Saint-Raphael, but the mule made it through.

We rode some more, through more lush fields, finally coming to a stop at a group of huts. There were half a dozen mud and straw-thatched cailles, all plunged in darkness. Stretching before them was a large field of sugarcane.

"We're here, slave. Welcome to your new home."

Silva hopped down off the mule and ordered me to do the same.

"Okay, follow me."

I was led over to one of the huts. He opened the door. He drew a knife from his belt, slipped the blade under the rope around my neck and sawed. The rope dropped away.

"We won't be needing that anymore," he said with a sly grin and then ordered me inside. I stepped into the hut, the door closed, and soon I heard Silva's mule trotting away.

The only sound I now heard was groaning, but I gave no thought as to who was in there with me. I sat down and stared at the door until, hours later, the sun allowed enough light in for me to see my surroundings.

I saw two zombis, one young and strong looking, the other old; about the same age as me, hair turning white, body leathery. Both wore soiled, ratty clothing. I only looked at them out of some innate curiosity. But beyond that, they didn't interest me.

It seemed the feeling was mutual.

The young one was sitting with his back against a wall, picking at a nasty looking wound on his left arm. Gore and skin dropped onto the earthen floor and onto a machete lying beside him.

The older one was sitting closer to me. His eyes were glassy and his skin was tinged gray and looked paper thin. He was staring at nothing in particular, face expressionless, and he was moaning. A hoe was resting next to him.

Bored with looking at them, I continued watching the door. It seemed the right thing to do. I was hungry, but I wasn't tired and since I had no real conscious thought, I knew no better.

It was sometime early morning when the door of the hut opened and a man came in. He was young, probably early twenties and was thin. He had the same features as the master, except they were less obvious and less defined.

"Okay get up," he said. He remained at the doorway. "Time for work."

The other two got to their feet. I remained on the floor. For some reason I didn't feel compelled to follow his orders.

The young man sighed and entered the hut. "Always happens with the new ones," he muttered. "I said get up. On your feet."

I didn't obey.

The man turned his attention from me to the young zombi clawing at his wound. "Stop that! You stop that right now!"

He didn't.

"Hell!" the young man said. "I'm sick of you. You're causing us nothing but trouble. Stop it!"

The young zombi growled. A deep, animal-like growl.

The man shook his head. "I'll get the master if you two don't obey me. Now, you stand up and you stop scratching yourself."

When neither of us complied, the young man huffed, said, "Stupid zombis," then stormed out of the hut.

I gazed around, unsure of what to do. The young zombi continued to pick at his open wound, while the older zombi just stood still, doing nothing.

Soon the young man came back with our master. He was holding a long whip and looked angry.

"I'm in no mood for trouble," he said. "I'm tired and want to sleep." He turned to me. "You are to obey this man as well as me.

He is your second master. If you don't obey him, you'll be punished. Now, stand up." He raised the whip and brought it down across my back.

I was shocked to find that it hurt. A sharp, stinging sensation cut across my skin and I let out a small cry. I stood.

"That's more like it," the master said, and then turned to the young zombi. "Look at you," he said. "You keep picking at your arm and there'll be nothing left and you won't be able to work." The zombi stopped picking at his wound and looked up at the master.

"He's been nothing but trouble," the young man said from the door. "I told you he'd be a problem. The moment he arrived last week I told you."

"Be quiet, Marc," the master said. "He just needs some discipline. I've been dealing with these things for thirty years. I've seen all kinds. Ones that act up, ones that sit in the corner and shiver like a baby. I've even seen ones that like to eat their own shit. Hell, this one ain't much better, but with each and every one I've made them obey me. They all obey, eventually." The master lifted the whip and cracked it across the young zombi's face. The zombi screeched and cowered against the wall. The master whipped him again, this time across his back. "You'll obey us at all times." He brought the leather strap down a few more times; each time the zombi cried out.

Sweating and puffing, the master lowered the whip. He turned to Marc. "You need to be more firm with them, like Raoul. You're too soft, that's your problem."

"Yes papa," Marc said, lowering his head.

"This slave gets no food for a few days," the master said, pointing the whip at the younger zombi. "He must learn there are consequences for disobeying." The master turned and looked at us. "I want no more problems from either of you. Now get to work!" He left.

Marc entered the hut. He was holding a stick. It was long and broad. "Okay, out," he said and started hitting me on the backside. I would've obeyed him without the stick, since the master told me I had to. But the small, sharp pain that accompanied each whack served as a reminder to do whatever the young master said.

It was sunny outside. If I was still in the land of the living, I'm sure I would've thought how lovely the sun beating down on my face was. But other than simply being aware it was sunny, I didn't think much beyond that. It was like being in a dream, one in which I couldn't think for myself, only act. Nothing seemed or felt real, yet at the same time I knew it was. In some strange way I knew what was happening to me, but I had neither the intelligence nor the will to do anything about it.

Me and the other two zombis were led to the large sugarcane field, where the tall reeds seemed to stretch to the horizon and beyond, all the way to the mountains in the distance.

As we got closer I could see other zombis already at work in the field.

"You, stop here," Marc told me.

I stopped just short of where the cane field began. The reeds were over twice my height.

My two roommates ambled off into the field. Soon they blended in with the other workers, methodically chopping down the cane and plowing the soil.

A young zombi walked past me carrying a bundle of thick cane stalks. He walked towards a cart already half filled with bundles of cane and heaped his bundle on.

"Wait here," Marc told me.

I stood staring at the cane stalk. Marc wasn't gone long. When he came back, he was holding a machete.

"Now, watch and learn." He strolled over to one of the towering cane stalks. "With each stalk of cane, you have to chop the top off and chop it at the bottom. First you chop the cane down, like so." Marc hacked the cane stalk a few times. The stalk fell to the ground. "Then you chop off the leaves." Marc proceeded to slice off the leaves. "Got it?" he said, turning to me.

I nodded. Somehow, I understood.

Marc walked over to me and handed me the machete. It was heavy, strong and lethal.

"Okay, get to work."

I walked into the towering sea of cane stalks. Stopping at one of the reeds, I lifted the machete and hacked into the bottom of the cane. It made a small nick, but that was about it.

"Tough son-of-a-bitch that cane," Marc laughed.

I tried again, harder. I made a sizeable cut, but still the cane didn't fall. With the third chop it came down.

"That's it," Marc said.

Next I lopped off the top. What was left on the ground resembled a thick cylindrical stick.

"Now, after you've got enough canes, pack 'em up in a bundle and put them in the back of one of the carts."

Marc left and I continued cutting down the sugar cane. I worked all day, one cane after another.

But I didn't complain. I didn't care. All I knew was that I had a job to do. At some point, another man arrived at the field and this man, tall, strong looking, about the same age as Marc, started shouting at the slaves and hitting us with a thick, broad stick, yelling at us to work harder, faster.

The sun was beginning to sink when a shrill whistle blew. I stopped what I was doing and stood there. I watched as the other zombis shuffled out of the field, machetes and hoes resting on their shoulders, blank faces unaware of their own existence. But I had no instruction. So I continued working.

The angry man with the painful stick had already left, so it was a little while before Marc came striding down into the field. "That whistle means work is over for the day and you can go back to your hut."

I stopped cutting cane and started walking.

"Keep your machete with you and bring it with you tomorrow for work."

In my white cloudy haze, I ambled back to the small hut. Inside, the young zombi was still picking at his wounds—including fresh ones that were on his face; the old zombi sat staring at the floor.

I sat down on the hard earthen floor and stared at the flimsy wooden door.

I don't know why that door held so much fascination for me. Maybe, deep down, I knew it meant escape. That if I wanted to, I could just open the door and walk out.

But I had no desire to escape.

Soon after I arrived back, a zombi came into our hut. He was probably ten years younger than me, and was carrying two bowls.

The zombi placed one down in front of me and the other in front of the old zombi. Then he turned to leave.

The young zombi leaped up and tackled the zombi. They landed on the ground, the younger zombi landing on top of the older one. I glanced over, saw the zombi trying to bite its brethren on the neck, but disinterested, turned back to see what food I had been given.

As the zombis continued to struggle, making ugly, throaty grunting noises, I stuck my hand into the bowl and scooped the cold mush of plantains into my mouth. It was bland, but it was good to finally have something to eat.

It seemed the fighting was loud enough to attract attention and soon Marc came in and upon seeing the tussle, drew his stick out and started hitting the younger zombi. It took a lot of hitting before the snarling, drooling zombi stopped fighting the older one. He scampered back to his corner, a mean look on his face.

"That's it, you've had it," Marc said.

The young zombi bared his teeth and growled.

"Come on," Marc ordered the older zombi and then stormed out. The older zombi, dazed and covered in dust, got up off the floor and followed Marc.

I concentrated on eating my meal. Finished the whole bowl, which wasn't much, in a few hungry mouthfuls.

The old zombi was taking his time.

Soon night came and the hut was plunged into darkness. The old zombi had stopped munching on his meal, the only sound now coming from the young zombi softly growling under his breath.

Suddenly the door burst open and light flooded our tiny abode. Marc and Raoul came in holding pine torches. Our master followed.

"Get him," he ordered.

The two younger men ventured towards the troublesome zombi. He started to snarl, but soon stopped when the two men drew out whips and started hitting him.

The zombi cowered, trying to shield himself from the blows. Finally the two men stopped whipping, then bending down, tied rope around the young zombi's feet and hands. The zombi didn't put up any fight. With his face, chest and back now one big open wound he just lay down and let them restrain him.

Then the two men dragged the zombi out of the hut.

When they were gone, the master said to us, "Let this be a warning to you both. Obey us and don't cause any trouble and you won't be punished."

The master left, slamming the old wooden door.

Now it was just me and the old zombi. Without the younger zombi picking at his wounds, it was deathly quiet. We didn't speak, nor breathe. Aside from some occasional gas passing through our bodies, neither of us made a sound nor moved for the entire night.

I didn't sleep.

I wasn't tired and I had no desire to rest. From the time I shuffled into the hut after work, until the sun rose the next morning, I simply sat on the floor, doing nothing.

Sounds incredibly boring, I know, but it wasn't. I didn't have the capacity to feel boredom. I was like a faithful dog waiting for my master to return.

Being it was so quiet inside the hut, I heard other noises, some faint, like dogs barking and roosters calling; others close by, like groaning, or gentle whimpering. One time I heard snarling and what sounded like a fight.

That first day cutting sugarcane and that first long night in the hut was prototypical of all my days and nights on the plantation. Every day and every night were the same—work all day in the cane fields, then at dusk head back into my hut where I'd get fed a bowl of cold, unsalted plantains and then be left in utter darkness until morning came.

There were only two events that offered any variance—before the uprising that is. The first happened the following day after the young zombi was taken out of our hut.

The door opened, sunlight poured in, but instead of the usual, "Time for work," Marc said, "Outside, and stand in front of your huts."

Diligently, the old zombi and I got up and walked outside. The cane looked like columns of yellow candy in the sun, the mountains were gold-capped monsters that seemed to box the plantation in like the walls of a castle.

As Marc had ordered, when I stepped outside I stopped in front of my hut and didn't move. The old zombi stood beside me.

All around, zombis stood in front of their huts. Some had two to a hut, like us; most had three, a few even four.

There must've been around twenty zombis, of all different shapes, sizes and age, some wearing barely a stitch of clothing, standing outside the collection of huts that sat on the edge of the cane field. While most were in fairly good condition, I did notice one zombi had half his face missing, like he had been shot in the side of the head. His right eye, cheek and half his jaw was missing; what was left was a gaping hole where his teeth, jagged and discolored, could be seen. Another had marks all over his face and arms, red welts and burn marks. I wonder, now, how I would've looked to the other zombis, the way my neck was crooked and the raw scrape down the side of my face.

But it didn't matter that you had half your face missing, or that your head was more horizontal than it was vertical; as long as you could swing a machete and carry loads of cane, you were perfectly fit to be a slave.

Which, as I saw once my lazy brain and eyes finally settled on it, the young zombi that had been taken from my hut last night was now most certainly not.

He was hanging from a tree. There was a thick rope noosed around his neck, the other end was strung to a thick branch above. His hands were tied behind him and his legs were bound together.

His face, now a bluish-black tinge from lack of blood in his head, was puffy. His torn clothes were filthy with blood.

It looked like he had been beaten and whipped even more after being taken away, but he was still alive.

One eye, the one that wasn't puffed over like he had just gone twelve rounds, twitched and flickered open, gazing emptily out at the gawking masses.

A living human would've been dead long ago. If not from the beating, then the rope around their neck would have already strangled them, if not broken their neck outright.

But this was no ordinary living person. This was a zombi, one of the undead. He couldn't be killed, not unless the bocor that had turned him into a zombi broke the spell, or if the zombi was hit in the brain.

But it looked like the young zombi who had acquired a nasty itch would be left hanging for however long the master wished; unable to work, unable to scratch his wounds, unable to eat, unable to die.

From the main house came the master. He stopped before the huts and surveyed the zombis with a satisfied grin. "This," he said, his deep voice booming, "is the price you pay for misbehaving. If you continue to obey me, work hard and cause no trouble, you will be fed and housed. Look upon this fellow slave each time you leave for work in the morning, and whenever you come home at night. Fear him, fear me." He turned to Marc. "They're yours now. Try and keep them under control, son. You are, after all, the head foreman." The master left.

I saw Marc scowl at his father after he was gone. "Crazy old fool," he muttered. Turning to us, he said, "Okay, everyone go to work. Move!"

So that's what we did. I cut the cane, just as I was told to do. Day in, day out. And each day as I passed by the tree, I glanced up at the zombi dangling, and I felt fear ball up inside me, but it went away as soon as the tree was out of sight.

As the days became weeks, the young zombi's face became grotesquely bloated, and both his eyes started bulging out of his head. His clothes started to hang off his bones, until finally, his body wasting to nothing, they dropped off. He was a pitiful sight. Body as skinny as a twig, face like a round black balloon. It would only be a matter of time before his head popped clean off.

He no longer thrashed around, or even jerked. He hardly made any noises, other than the occasional whispery groan, which I heard at nights when all was quiet.

I didn't feel sorry for him. No, he was simply a symbol of fear. A visible reminder of what would happen if we disobeyed either of our masters.

Then one night, Marc came into my hut. It was not long after dinner. Whip in one hand, flaming pine torch in the other, he looked like a ghost the way the torch sprayed his face with firelight. "Both of you, get up," he said.

Me and the old zombi got to our feet.

He pointed to me. "You, leave the machete." He pointed to the other zombi. "You, bring your hoe. Both of you, follow me."

We followed Marc outside.

The moon was a round hole in the sky. The zombi hanging from the tree was barely visible as a dark shape seemingly hanging in mid-air.

Marc walked over to another hut, stopped in front of it and opened the door. "You, go inside. It's your new home."

The old zombi shuffled in and the door was closed.

"You, come with me."

I limped behind the young master. We walked past the huts, up a path leading to the main house.

The master's house was big, a solid-looking wooden house with a wide veranda and a nice garden. We stepped through the door. Inside was lit by kerosene lamps, and it smelled different than the hut—cleaner.

"You have a new job," Marc said, facing me. He had doused the torch and placed the club on a side table. "You are to be the master's personal slave. Bring him whatever he wants, clean whatever he asks, any time, day or night. You're also to prepare the food for the slaves and bring them their dinner, as well as clean the huts and the mule and horse pens. Our last personal slave was, well, let's say severely injured tonight, so he's incapable of performing his duties any longer. You're the oldest zombi here, apart from that other one you were roommates with, but he's too old and slow. So you've got the job. It's a good job, it's less work than being out in the fields, so don't mess around or cause any trouble or else you'll be swinging next to your other roommate, understand?"

I nodded.

"Good. Okay, wait here."

I waited and soon Marc came back into the room. He was holding a bell. "Whenever you hear this noise..." He rattled the bell and it jingled with a high-pitched sound. "...that's the master calling. Come, I'll show you around the house and your living quarters."

The house, although much bigger than the huts, was still basic, consisting of six rooms altogether—a kitchen, a toilet, a dining area, the master's bedroom, Marc's room near the back of the house, and a room Marc called the 'forbidden room', its door always locked. As I was shown these rooms (except for the master's, as he was sleeping, and the forbidden room; which, I was told, I was never to enter), Marc explained to me what I was to clean, and, in the kitchen, where the food was kept. The kitchen was cramped, full of dishes, alcohol and spices. There was a fridge, which housed mostly meat, eggs and milk, but I was forbidden to eat any of the food, especially the meat, or else I'd be punished worse than the zombi hanging from the tree.

He asked if I understood, I nodded and then he showed me to a small room off the kitchen, barely bigger than a broom closet. Aside from a few boxes and other assorted junk, there was a blanket on the ground.

"This is where you stay," Marc said. "It's a little smaller than the hut, but it's all yours and it is warmer and comfier. So be thankful you have this job. Okay, I have to go and get some sleep. Wait here until you hear the bell. That means the master has woken. Then go to him and see to his needs."

Marc left.

I stayed in that storage closet-cum-home until I heard the jingle of the bell.

I walked out of the closet to the master's bedroom, opened the door and stepped inside. The master was sitting up in bed. When I came in he placed the bell on a side-table. "So you're my new personal slave. Okay, get me some coffee, black, no sugar, and a plate of fried eggs. Hurry."

I left the bedroom and hurried back into the kitchen.

That first attempt at making breakfast for the master was a bit of a disaster. The part of my brain that dealt with instinct and memory was intact enough so I knew basically what I had to do, but with my muscles stiff and my head the way it was, it took me some practice to get something as simple as eggs and coffee right. I broke a few eggs and spilled a lot of coffee over the counter, but finally—and after a few scratchy "Hurry ups" and "What the hell are you doing in there?"—I brought the master his breakfast.

I waited patiently as he forked some egg into his mouth, then took a sip of coffee. He nodded, took another bite of the eggs and mumbled, "Not bad. Not bad at all. You're a better cook than the last one. Okay, go outside and clean up the dog shit, then come back inside and see me and I'll give you some more chores. There should be a shovel outside in the shed, that's if that no-good zombi you replaced put it back as he should have."

I left the master to his eggs and coffee and headed outside.

The backyard wasn't huge, but it was big enough. A mangy wooden fence encircled the yard and an even mangier dog was over near the shed in one corner. The mongrel was playing with a bunch of rags, biting and throwing its head from side to side. It was growling with happiness, but the moment I stepped outside, it stopped, looked up at me and began growling with suspicion. It started barking and leaving its plaything, bounded towards me.

Bile and blood flicked from its teeth-baring mouth. The area around its mouth and nose was matted with dark blood.

I began mewling, not understanding why this creature wanted to attack me, yet knowing, deep down, that it was probably more scared of me than I was of it.

I took a step forward—I had to get to the shed and get the shovel—and the moment I did, the dog stopped barking and backed away.

I took another step, and the dog high-tailed it back to the thing it had been gnawing at when I first came out.

The dog dragged it away from the shed, to another part of the yard. Suddenly the lump moved, groaned, and sat up.

The dog jumped back, like it had been scorched by fire, but then, seeing the zombi posed no threat, went back and continued feeding off of it.

I found the shovel in the shed—which was dark and smelled of dust and mold and housed a lot of other tools and farming equipment—and went about scooping up all the bits of dog shit I could find.

Whenever I got near the dog and his play-thing the dog snarled and eyed me with fear and uncertainty. Unlike the poor zombi who could no longer walk or defend itself I was something to be feared. I guess, thinking back, the dog knew I was an abomination, not of this world. It probably sensed death on me.

After I had cleared the backyard of the dog's waste, I went back inside and the master told me to first clean the dishes—which included yesterday's lunch and dinner as well as that morning's breakfast—and then to clean all the zombis' waste from the huts. After I had finished all that, I was to prepare lunch.

So I got to work and began my first full day as the master's personal slave."

Mr. Joseph downed another half-glass of rum. The bottle of Barbancourt was nearly empty.

"So," Toby said. "That old zombi you stayed with, in the hut, was that...?"

"Jean-Philippe? Yes."

Toby pulled his clinging shirt from his sticky body, fanning the fabric against his body.

"Sorry about the heat," Mr. Joseph said. "I don't feel temperature, so I have no use for air conditioners or heaters. And I've never had any visitors, so..."

"That's okay," Toby said. Outside, cicadas buzzed—it was shaping up to be a scorcher of a day.

"You look hot, are you sure you don't want anything to drink?"

Toby eyed the bottle of rum. He wiped sweat from his forehead and ventured to ask, "Don't suppose you'd let me have a sip of rum?"

"Well now, I wouldn't want to get you in trouble with your parents—or the law."

"No one would have to know. Just a small taste."

"It packs quite a kick for those who aren't used to it."

"Like whiskey?"

Mr. Joseph nodded. "Yeah." He frowned. "You've had whiskey?"

Toby nodded. "Can't say I liked it very much. Although it did taste much better with Coke."

After a short deliberation, Mr. Joseph said, "Okay, just a taste. But don't tell your parents." He hopped up and went to the cupboard. "I'm sorry, I don't have any Coke," he said. "Maybe I should think about stocking up the fridge with some, now that you're a regular visitor."

Toby smiled politely, but he couldn't lie—it was strange hearing Mr. Joseph say such a thing.

Toby Fairchild, a regular visitor of old Mr. Joseph. What would've Frankie thought about that? Toby wondered and the thin smile turned sad.

"What's the matter?" Mr. Joseph asked as he sat down, placing an empty glass in front of Toby.

"Hmm? Oh, nothing." Toby thought about how Mr. Joseph had been trusting enough to reveal secrets he hadn't told anyone. It seemed only fair to reciprocate. "Well, I guess I was just thinking what my friends would think if they knew I was here, talking to you."

Mr. Joseph nodded. "They don't like me much, do they?"

"They just don't know you," Toby said.

"And they never will," Mr. Joseph answered. He tipped a splash of the white rum into Toby's glass. "There, see how you like it."

Toby picked up the glass and sniffed. The smell reminded him of whiskey. He threw the small amount down his parched throat. Like whiskey, the drink was sweet at first, but with an undercurrent of fire that lit his throat and burned his gut. "Wow," Toby said, coughing.

Mr. Joseph smiled. "Want some water?"

"Please."

Mr. Joseph hopped up again, taking with him Toby's glass. After rinsing it out, he filled the glass with tap water, then came back and handed it to Toby.

Toby gulped down the water. "It's worse than whiskey," he said afterwards.

"Perhaps. But I prefer it over whiskey. It's the only rum I drink. I've tried other brands, American brands, even Jamaican, but they don't sit well with me. Mrs. Stein stocks bottles of Barbancourt in her store, though I don't think anyone else buys the brand but me. She's a kind, considerate lady."

"Why do you like drinking only this brand?"

Mr. Joseph shrugged. "I guess it reminds me of home, one of the few good reminders I have of the place. Not that I could ever afford to buy Barbancourt back then. Only on rare occasions. But I like the taste; it's good strong Haitian rum. Also, and I'm ashamed to admit this, but drinking it helps me cope with the memories. The fear hasn't diminished in all the years."

"Why don't you face your fears instead? Why don't you go back home?"

"Back to Haiti?"

Toby nodded.

"I already told you. I can't. I have grand-children and great-grand-children. Nephews, nieces; I made a vow to myself that I wouldn't go back to Haiti until my family were gone. All gone."

"I know, but why? Have you thought that maybe they won't be as scared and ashamed of you as you think they would be? A lot of time has gone by since you left, maybe things have changed?"

"You think zombis are in fashion? That we're walking the streets like regular folk? No, my country has a long history of superstition, and though some things may have changed, my people's fear of zombis hasn't—of that I'm sure."

"Maybe not regular zombis, but what about savanes? Maybe they've been accepted into society? I mean, you're practically huma..."

"Don't," Mr. Joseph said, raising a hand. "Please, Toby, don't say it. It's not true, it's never been true, and it'll never be true. Just accept it, like I have, that I can't go back and face my family, not like this. They'd be too afraid, too ashamed."

"But... but what about me?" Toby said, voice soft. "I'm here, listening to you. I don't think you're a... a... freak." Toby gulped down the rest of his water.

Mr. Joseph stared long and hard at Toby. Finally, a thin smile curled on the old man's dark, wrinkled face. He reached out and patted Toby on the hand.

His touch was cold, but Toby didn't pull away.

"I appreciate that, Monsieur Fairchild. I do." Mr. Joseph flicked his eyes to the cheap-looking watch on his wrist. "What time are you meeting your lady-friend?"

Toby glanced at his own watch. It was almost one o'clock. "Shit, I'm gonna be late." He hopped up. "Sorry to leave so suddenly."

Mr. Joseph waved a hand. "Nonsense," he said. "Go, have fun."

"I'll see you tomorrow, maybe?"

"I'm working tomorrow. But I finish at two, if you feel like dropping by in the afternoon."

Toby turned and started for the back door.

"Toby?"

He stopped, turned around.

"Thank you."

Toby nodded. Then he left Mr. Joseph's house.

Standing outside Patterson's, Toby felt a wave of sadness sweep over him. The last time he was here he had been happy and free, and neither he nor Frankie had any idea what was to come.

Taking a deep breath, Toby opened the glass door and stepped inside. It was deliciously cool inside the diner. He stood by the entrance taking in the familiar din of the crowd and the smells of burgers and onion rings. He spotted Gloria in one of the side booths over on his left. She was sitting with some friends, including Danielle and Emma.

He started forward, trying to put on a brave face. As he got closer, Gloria stood and he noticed her pained expression, like she had just gotten some bad news.

Toby's gut went squirmy and he wondered why she looked so sad.

Maybe she feels bad about suggesting we meet up here? But I agreed, I didn't think it'd be a problem, not until I actually saw the place again.

He started to notice eyes on him; kids and teens grinned at him, then turned to one another, giggling, whispering.

Toby itched to check his fly—had he left it open and was his member poking out?

Oh God, what is it—what the hell's going on?

By the time he arrived at Gloria's table, he was sweating, despite the cool air circulating inside the diner.

Gloria, wearing a short plaid skirt and white shirt, smiled thinly, briefly, and then she said, "Hey Toby."

Toby nodded. Swallowed. Glanced at Gloria's friends, who were looking at him like he had just sprouted another head.

Someone squawked like a chicken and a titter swept through the diner.

"Toby, come outside," Gloria said and took Toby by the hand.

As she led him towards the door, he felt the stares, like knives jabbing into him. When they were out in the glaring sunlight and suffocating heat, Toby gasped, "What the hell's going on?"

"I tried calling your cell, but you didn't answer."

Toby absently patted his shorts. "Oh yeah, I must've left it at home."

Gloria sighed. "Come on, let's get away from here."

"But..."

"Please." Gloria started down Main Street. Toby followed, and when they reached the corner, they turned right onto Longview Road.

"Where are we going?"

"People know."

Toby stopped, looked at Gloria. "Know what?"

"It's all over town—well, probably not all over, but most people I've run into today know."

"Know what!" Toby cried.

Gloria sighed again, and Toby smelled vanilla on her breath. "About you and Mr. Joseph. That you've been spending time with him. That's all the people in the diner have been talking about. Well, that and Warrick."

Toby suddenly felt sick. The glaring sunlight and the heat didn't help matters. And what was that about Warrick?

"What about Warrick?"

"You mean you haven't heard?"

Toby shook his head. How could so much have happened in just a few days? And how come it seemed everyone in town knew about these things except for him? Had he been asleep for a week without realizing?

"...vanished."

"What was that?" Toby said.

"I said Warrick didn't come home over the weekend. Nobody knows where he is. He's just... vanished."

Toby felt like he had been sucker punched—twice. "I need to sit down," he said. He planted his butt on the curb, put his head in his sweaty hands and breathed a shaky sigh.

Gloria sat beside him. "You haven't heard any of this?"

"No," he sighed. Raising his head, he turned to Gloria, who was looking at him with an almost parental concern. "How do people know about me and Mr. Joseph? Did someone see me go into his house?"

Gloria shrugged. "I don't know for sure. But I think it was Deb."

"Deb?"

"She must've overheard you telling me about Mr. Joseph on Friday. Bitch likes to eavesdrop and then spread gossip."

"Man," Toby said. "I don't believe this. What have people been saying?"

"Just the usual stuff."

"Tell me."

Gloria winced. "You really want to know?"

Toby thought about it for a moment. He looked to the other side of the street, to some kids zooming by on their scooters. He turned back to Gloria. "No, I don't." He could use his imagination.

"I'm sorry Toby."

"Why? Why the hell should you be sorry? You haven't done anything wrong."

"I know but..."

"And neither have I. So I've been spending time with an old man. Jesus, do people in this town really have nothing better to do with their time than spread stupid rumors? Anyway, it doesn't matter. I don't care, let people think what they want." Toby swiped an arm across his forehead, wetting the fine layer of hair on his forearm. The truth was, he did care. People were going to laugh at him, point their fingers at him, all the while wondering why a fourteen-year-old boy would want to spend time with a strange old man.

Gloria reached out and gripped Toby's right hand. "I'm sorry," she said again.

"I mean, poor Mr. Joseph. He'll get it from this, too. He's got enough to worry about. I wish people would just leave him alone."

"People can be cruel."

"Some summer this has turned out to be."

"I'm sure this will all go away soon enough. Give it a few days, maybe a week, and then the kids in town will find something else to laugh about."

Toby shrugged. "Yeah, I guess. Still, I think I might just stay home for the next week or so. It's not like I was doing much anyway."

"Then they'll win," Gloria said.

"Let them win. I can't be bothered with all these people staring at me, giggling." Toby got to his feet.

Gloria did the same. "So, where do you wanna go?"

"Home," Toby said, the word spilling from his mouth. "I just want to go home."

The first thing Toby did when they arrived back at his place was put on the air-conditioning. He used the remote to amp up the cold and, while Gloria was taking care of business in the bathroom, he stood in front of the cold air, eyes closed, hair blowing. He thought of Mr. Joseph, sitting in his oven-like house.

Could he really not feel the heat? Toby wondered.

Everyone knows. Christ.

On the walk back home, Toby was certain everyone they passed was staring at him. He was positive he saw them grin, and he knew what they were thinking—"There goes that kid who likes hanging out with that old pervert"; "You think Toby bites the heads off chickens too?"; "I wonder why an old man would want to spend time with a fourteen...?"

"Better?"

Toby flinched, opened his eyes and turned to see Gloria standing in front of him. He nodded. "Want a drink?"

"That'd be nice."

Toby led Gloria out of the family room and as they headed down the hall, Toby noticed the answering machine was blinking, letting him know there were five messages. He figured most would be his mom, so he was tempted to keep on going, but he stopped. "Mom rings me about three times a day, just to make sure I haven't fallen into a coma."

Gloria chuckled. "What are you gonna do? Moms, they can't help but worry."

Toby smiled as he pressed the 'play' button.

The first message was from his mom, wondering how he was doing, telling him to just take it easy, that she'd call again later.

The second message was from Suzie, asking Toby if he wouldn't mind giving her a call.

"I bet she wants to finally apologize," Toby said.

The third message was from Warrick's mom, and her message sent a cold wave of unease through Toby.

"It's Mrs. Coleman here, Warrick's mom. I'm calling all of Warrick's friends, seeing if anyone has seen or heard from him. I haven't heard from him for days and I'm worried. So please, if you know or hear anything, call me at home. My number is..."

She sounded tired, her voice dry and crackly.

The fourth message was his mom again ("Just seeing how you're doing, guess you must be asleep, or have the TV up too loud. I'll see you soon. Bye, darling.").

The last message sent a spike of fear and anger through Toby's gut.

There was a long period of silence and then a voice, deep and obviously distorted: "We know." Another pause. "Nigger fucker." Then the phone went dead.

"Assholes," Gloria muttered.

Toby went to press the 'delete' button, but Gloria reached out and stopped him. "No, could be evidence."

Toby frowned. "Huh?"

Gloria shrugged. "I mean, it can't hurt to keep it, just in case. Maybe the police will want to hear it."

"It's just a stupid prank call," Toby said. Still, he took back his hand, Gloria let go and they headed into the kitchen.

"Coke?" Toby asked. Gloria nodded.

As Toby grabbed two cans from the fridge, Gloria said, "You know, thinking about the police and all, maybe they'll want to speak to you."

"Glass?"

"No."

Toby handed Gloria the frosty can and led her back into the family room. "But it's only a prank call," Toby reiterated. "I doubt the cops..."

"No, I mean about Warrick. You did talk to him a few days ago. And the way you said he was acting... maybe the cops will want to talk to you about him."

Toby's gut, already tight and feeling queasy, went into overdrive. As he sat down on the couch, Gloria sitting next to him, he nodded, cracked open the can, and said, "Yeah, you're right. What if I was the last person to see him...?"

"He's not... dead," Gloria said with uncertainty. She popped open the can and took a long drink. "He probably just ran away from home, or is off with Dwayne and those guys, drunk."

Toby nodded. "Yeah, that's probably it." He sipped his Coke. "Still, it is kinda strange. I mean, he was acting weird. He could be a pain in the ass sometimes—hell, most of the time—but I hope nothing bad has happened to him."

After that, they sat in silence. Toby switched on the TV, just for some background noise. After much slurping and a few furtive burps from both parties, Gloria said, "So, what were you doing this morning?"

Toby almost lied—but then he remembered who he was with. "I was over at Mr. Joseph's. He was telling me more about his life back in Haiti."

"So he's really a nice guy? He's not a little bit weird?"

Toby chose his words carefully. "Well, he spends most of his days inside, reading. He hasn't got any friends. I think he's very lonely."

"Yeah, but I can't imagine being in his house, talking to him," Gloria said. "After all the years of hearing the rumors and stories, and, well, being kinda scared of him..."

"Yeah, I know what you mean."

"Not that I believed those rumors. Well, not really. I guess a small part of me wondered if some of the stories were true. I guess not, huh?"

Toby finished off his drink and turned to Gloria. His closest friend, the only person he could truly trust. He gazed at her soft, lightly tanned skin and warm eyes. He leaned over and kissed her. Gloria was initially stunned; her cold, Coke-riddled lips remained tight, but they soon loosened and she let Toby in.

They kissed long and passionate, their tongues exploring each other's mouths. Toby's head swam, his shorts were suddenly much too tight, and his heart pounded.

As they kissed, Gloria reached down and grabbed Toby's left hand, which was resting on the couch. Her touch was cold, but nice, and Toby was only vaguely aware of her raising his arm—until it landed on her right breast. Her hand went away, and Toby, tongue still swirling, could hardly believe where his hand now lay.

His mind, clouded with pleasure and excitement, wondered—what was he to do now? What did she want him to do?

As they continued to kiss, Gloria's hand snaked towards his bulging crotch and when she tentatively started caressing the hardness through the fabric of his shorts, he let out a groan. He felt self-conscious for doing so, but Gloria didn't seem to mind.

Toby cupped his hand around her breast; felt the slightly stiff material of her bra under her shirt, but underneath was soft and springy.

Abruptly, Gloria pulled back. She took her hand away from his crotch—and not a moment too soon; Toby was close to turning his dry boxers into very sticky ones.

She stared at Toby, her breathing harsh. She offered a brief, timid smile, which Toby replied to with his wet lips and aching jaw—who knew kissing could be so strenuous?—and then, in the relative darkness of the family room, she reached behind and slipped her hands under her shirt. Toby watched with nervous anticipation as Gloria first unhooked her bra and then, in a trick to rival any of the great magicians, she somehow got her bra off and out through one sleeve, all without taking off her shirt. Then she dropped the white bra on the couch.

Toby swallowed. Under the shirt, she was now naked.

Gloria hesitated and then she reached out and gripped Toby's hands. She raised them to the bottom of her shirt and then slipped them under. She let go and Toby continued up, hands shaking, until he reached her bare breasts.

Toby's breath was sucked from his chest as he touched the smooth skin. And when he brushed the stiff nipples, Toby knew he had died and gone to heaven.

He explored her breasts like a blind man exploring a person's face; softly, gently, but with all the intent to know every inch of this new and wondrous place.

Gloria reached over and unzipped Toby's shorts.

Toby noticed Gloria's hands were also trembling.

She pulled the zipper down and then slid a hand into his shorts.

Toby flinched when she touched his cock.

With his hands still on Gloria's breasts, Toby closed his eyes and listened to Gloria breathing hard and deep—like Toby, it was probably a combination of nerves and excitement; of discovering things and places hitherto unknown.

She started stroking Toby gently, cautiously, bordering on clinical.

Toby felt the sensation rising and he pulled his hands out from under Gloria's shirt and tried to pull away, but Gloria wouldn't let him.

"It's okay," she breathed.

Toby, as mortified as he was consumed by pleasure, couldn't stop the rising tide and as Gloria continued to stroke him, faster now, he erupted. He squeezed his eyes shut, balled up his fists as he pumped.

When he was done, he opened his eyes.

His breathing was deep, his head swimmy, and he couldn't bear to look at Gloria.

She took her hand away. "Was... was that okay?"

Staring at the cushions on the couch, Toby nodded. "Great," he said, and at that moment he wasn't sure he was capable of saying anything else.

"I didn't realize it'd be so... hot," Gloria said. "And it kinda smells."

Toby nodded, risked a glance at Gloria. She looked awkward, unsure of what to do or say. "I'll, ah, go and get cleaned up."

Gloria got to her feet and hurried out of the room.

The moment she was gone, Toby grabbed some tissues from the box on the coffee table, cleaned himself up, zipped, and then blew out a long, quivering breath.

I can't believe that just happened!

Toby remembered how Gloria felt under her shirt. How soft and smooth her skin was.

He shook his head, a goofy grin cutting across his flushed face.

Come on Warrick—now ask me how far I've gotten with a girl...

A wave of despondency came over him. Not just at the memory of the night up in the tree house, when Frankie was still alive, but at the thought of Warrick missing.

Jesus, what if something serious has happened to him?

Soon Gloria came back. She snatched her bra from off the couch and said, "I'll be back in a sec." She left the room again and when she returned this time, Toby gazed up at her, wondering what the protocol was. Were they supposed to talk about what amounted to Toby's—and, he was pretty sure, Gloria's—first real sexual experience? Did she want to discuss mushy stuff like how it felt emotionally as well as physically? Or were they to not mention it at all?

When Gloria didn't speak, Toby took it upon himself to break the awkwardness. "Are we still okay? You don't feel weird or anything?"

Gloria, head down, shrugged. "Do you?"

"No," Toby said. "It was great."

Gloria looked up and smiled. "Yeah, but kinda weird."

"I guess." Weirder for her, Toby knew.

Gloria sat down next to Toby. "Let's not let this spoil anything. I mean, it was fun, right?" She leaned over and pecked him on the lips.

Toby smiled as relief swept through him.

It was more than fun, Toby thought, *but decided to keep that thought to himself.*

They watched TV for the rest of the afternoon. Gloria left just after four, so Toby decided to go around and see Mr. Joseph, before his mom came home from work.

"Monsieur Fairchild," Mr. Joseph said, standing inside the doorway. "What brings you back so soon? Is everything okay?"

"No, not really."

Mr. Joseph frowned. "Do you want to come inside?"

"I guess. But I can't stay long."

Mr. Joseph stepped aside. Toby entered the exhaustively hot house.

"Come into the kitchen," Mr. Joseph said.

Toby followed the old man to the back of the house.

The kitchen was mercifully cooler, with the blinds drawn and the linoleum on the floor. Toby took a seat at the table

"Water?"

"No thanks."

Mr. Joseph sat down. "So, what seems to be the problem?"

Toby sighed. "People know about me coming here."

For a while, the only sound was the buzzing of cicadas.

"People like your parents?"

"No. At least, I don't think they know yet. But the kids in town have been talking about it. I was over at Patterson's earlier, and they were all laughing about it."

"I see," Mr. Joseph said.

"I've already had one prank call. It'll get worse before it gets better. I know the kids in this town. They won't let it rest. You'll cop it, too."

Mr. Joseph smiled ever so slightly. "Don't worry about me; I'm used to it. The important thing is, how do you feel about it?"

"Annoyed. Angry."

"About?"

"How immature and cruel people can be."

"But also that they found out at all, right?"

Toby knew there was no point in lying to Mr. Joseph. "Yeah, I guess so."

"It's okay, I understand. I would've been worried if you weren't a little embarrassed that people know you've been spending time here. I was worried people would find out; hoped they wouldn't, but I guess that's the price of living in a small town."

"But mostly I'm angry at how the kids looked at me, like I've done something wrong."

Mr. Joseph nodded. "So, what do you want to do Monsieur Fairchild? It's your call. Me, I'm more than happy to have you keep coming around. But I'm used to people looking at me strangely, laughing behind my back."

"Screw 'em," Toby said. "Let them point and laugh. I don't care."

"Good for you."

Toby smiled, though it wasn't filled with joy. He was proud of himself for making a stand against the pettiness of the townsfolk, but truth was, he did care. And he was scared. Sitting in front of Mr. Joseph and saying he didn't care if people laughed was one thing; not letting it affect him out there, in the real world, was another. Like he told Mr. Joseph, things were bound to get worse before they got better—if they ever got better. Was he strong enough to withstand all that teasing and finger-pointing? He wasn't the most popular kid to begin with; being associated with the likes of Mr. Joseph would only make him more of an outcast.

At least I've still got Gloria. But for how long?

"Well, I'd better get back home. I just thought you should know."

"I appreciate it."

Toby stood and made his way to the front door, Mr. Joseph shuffling behind.

As Toby stepped outside, the old man said, "If you want to call this quits and go back to being strangers, I'll understand. No hard feelings."

Though Toby was tempted to take the easy way out and answer, "Okay, sounds like a plan. Have a nice life," he shook his head. "Thanks, but no, I won't let them win."

Mr. Joseph nodded.

The door closed behind him, and before leaving Mr. Joseph's house, Toby instinctively looked both ways down the street.

When he realized what he had done—and more importantly, why—he felt angry and disappointed with himself.

He crossed the street and headed home.

"Toby, can I have a word with you?"

Toby, who was watching television, his mind drifting between Mr. Joseph, and what had taken place with Gloria on the very couch he was slumped in, turned from the TV to his mom. When he saw the look on her face, he knew straightaway she had heard about him and Mr. Joseph. "Hey Mom, have a good day at work?"

His mom stepped into the room and sat in one of the chairs near the couch. "I heard some talk today. I want to hear it from you if it's true."

Toby turned back to the TV. "If what's true?"

"Toby, can you please turn down the TV and look at me."

Toby sighed. Reluctantly, he picked up the remote, pressed the 'mute' button, then he sat up and faced his mother.

"Thank you," she said. "Now, you're not in trouble or anything, but I heard some kids talking in the library today. They said that you have been going over and spending time with Mr. Joseph. Is this true?"

Though his mom was trying her hardest to speak in a kind, even tone, Toby could read her face—and it was tense. "Yeah, it's true."

"I see." Her kind expression faltered. "I didn't realize you were spending your days over there. Why didn't you say anything to either your dad or me?"

"I haven't been spending all my time over there. Just a few hours here and there. Why, is there a problem?"

"No," she answered too quickly. "No, it's just... well, what do you do there?"

Toby was tempted to answer with something snide, even crude, but he wasn't that sort of person. "We talk, what else? He's been telling me about his past, back in Haiti."

"I see," his mom said again—her code word for 'I don't really like what I'm hearing, but I'll pretend to be civil'. "I won't repeat what the kids at the library were saying, but Toby, I don't think people are going to take too kindly to you going over to Mr. Joseph's place."

Toby frowned. "What are you saying?"

His mom stared at her hands, wringing them like she was trying to rid them of dirt. "I'm just saying be careful. A lot of kids are scared of Mr. Joseph. Now I'm not condoning their behavior, but that's just how it is. I just don't want to see you get hurt, that's all. So maybe, for the moment, it's best if you refrain from seeing Mr. Joseph."

Toby didn't know what to say. He turned and glared at the TV.

"And your father agrees."

Toby turned back to his mom. "You've already spoken to Dad about this? What, did you call him at work?"

His mom nodded.

"I don't believe this," Toby muttered.

"Sorry Toby. But you do understand?"

"No," he said. "I don't. But you can't stop me."

His mom looked shocked. With a slightly fearful frown she said, "Excuse me?"

"What are you going to do, chain me up in my bedroom? You can't stop me from going over to Mr. Joseph's. I'm not a kid!"

"Toby..."

Toby hopped up from the couch, fire running through his veins. He stormed out of the family room and stomped up the stairs.

In his room, he lay on his bed staring at the ceiling, feeling neither his usual embarrassment nor confusion towards his parents, but anger and, for the first time in his life, disappointment.

Half an hour later, there was a gentle rapping at his door. "Toby?"

Toby ignored his mother; he didn't feel like talking to her. But she entered his room anyway.

"Toby? Please, don't be angry."

Toby didn't answer—he feared if he spoke, he'd say something he'd regret.

"Well anyway, I didn't come up here to fight, or to talk about Mr. Joseph. I heard the message from Mrs. Coleman."

Despite Gloria's insistence, Toby had deleted the prank call, but left the one from Warrick's mother. He figured his mom would want to listen to it.

"Toby, have you seen or heard from Warrick?"

Toby didn't answer her straightaway, but then the thought of Warrick missing made the Mr. Joseph situation seem trivial by comparison, so he sat up and muttered, "Not since Friday afternoon, on my way to Gloria's house."

"Well, apparently he hasn't been seen since Friday evening," his mom said. "Sally is beside herself. I'm sure he's fine but... Toby, I think I should take you down to the police station. They might want to talk to you."

"What about? I don't know anything. He's probably just lying drunk somewhere with Dwayne. Or run away from home. You know what Warrick's like." And his parents, Toby wanted to add. Because if the rumors were true, Warrick's parents, particularly his old man, weren't exactly saints. Those bruises that appeared every so often on Warrick's face and arms didn't get there by themselves and really, how many doorknobs could one person run into?

"Still, you saw him on the day he disappeared. Come on, get ready. I'll call your father and let him know we're going over to the police station." As she turned and walked out of the room, Toby heard her mutter, "First you get attacked and now a boy is missing. What's happening to this town?"

Toby wondered the same thing—though not for the same reasons as his mom.

When Mrs. Mayfour picked up the phone after three rings, Toby said, in his politest voice, "Hi Mrs. Mayfour. It's Toby. Would I be able to speak to Gloria?"

There was a moment's silence. Toby started getting antsy, thinking she must have heard about him and Mr. Joseph. But when she said, "Hold on, Toby, I'll get her," he sighed with relief.

It was just after eight, and Toby and his parents had only just finished eating dinner—which for them was late. The police station had taken longer than expected. Toby had told Chief Willard of his encounter with Warrick (the Chief said that Toby was probably one of the last to see Warrick, which unnerved Toby) and of his suspicion that Warrick seemed anxious and scared, like he was worried someone would see him talking to Toby.

Apparently there was still no word from Warrick, so the police were officially treating him as a missing person, even though Chief Willard said, with a forced smile, that he was sure it was a simple case of Warrick having run away—most of these cases were.

Chief Daniel Willard's parting words were: "Don't worry, I'm sure Warrick will turn up".

Toby could always tell when adults were lying.

"Toby? Hey."

Gloria didn't sound like her usual cheerful self.

"Hey. I've just come back from the police station."

"The police? Is anything wrong?"

"No, my mom thought I'd better go down and tell them of my little chat with Warrick. Just like you said."

"Oh. So what did they say? Still no word?"

"No. Warrick's officially a missing person, but they reckon he's probably just run away from home."

"Did you also tell them about that awful message that was left on your machine?"

There was a definite sadness in Gloria's voice. "No. I didn't see the point. Anyway, get this, my mom had a chat with me earlier, said she thinks it best if I don't go around to see Mr. Joseph. Can you believe that? Bitch. Telling me what I can and can't do."

Dead air filled Toby's ear and he thought for a second they had been cut off. "Gloria? You still there?"

"I'm here," Gloria said with a sigh. "Toby, my parents sort of said the same thing. Only about you."

Toby felt like he had been kicked in the balls. "What?"

"They said they thought I had been spending too much time with you, and not enough with my other friends—my girlfriends. They said they like you and all, but that I'm not to see you as much as I have been."

Toby closed his eyes; he felt like screaming.

"It's all bull. I think the real reason is they don't want me associating with anyone who is friends with Mr. Joseph, but they're using the 'seeing too much of you' thing as a cover, so they're not seen as racist."

"But they can't stop us from seeing each other. We're friends. It's not fair. How come all of a sudden everyone thinks they can control our lives, decide who we can and can't see? It's bullshit!"

"I know," Gloria said. "But they threatened to ground me if I disobeyed them." She paused before adding, "For the whole summer, Toby."

"What?"

"I can see you once a week—during the day—and that's it. Anymore and they'll ground me."

"This is..." Toby didn't have the words to describe how he was feeling. Chest tight, mouth dry, he could only say, "Not fair. I can't see you, I can't see Mr. Joseph. Frankie's dead and..." Tears started dripping from his eyes.

"Toby," Gloria said, voice wavering. "I'm sorry."

"Me too," he said and then hung up.

"I'm sorry, kid," a voice from behind said.

Toby turned and faced his dad, who was standing just inside the kitchen doorway. "I didn't mean to eavesdrop, but I heard some of your conversation. I'm really sorry, Toby."

"Sorry?" Toby said, chin trembling. He wiped his eyes. "Bullshit, you're sorry."

"Hey," his dad said, voice not quite stern, but getting there. "There's no need..."

"You and Mom tell me I can't go over and see Mr. Joseph. The man who saved my life. And now I find out that I can only see Gloria once a week. Sorry doesn't cut it, Dad. I haven't done anything wrong. Gloria hasn't done anything wrong. Mr. Joseph hasn't done anything wrong. Yet we're all being punished. Does that sound fair?"

His dad sighed. “Toby, keep your voice down. Your mom’s upstairs, resting. This last month has been tough for her.”

“I don’t understand any of this. Mr. Joseph is a kind old man. Why do people seem so against our friendship?”

“It’s complicated...”

“I don’t understand why Mom told me I can’t go over and see him.”

“She worries about you, that’s all.”

“But there’s nothing to be worried about. He’s our neighbor. Don’t you talk with Mr. Klein? Go over to his house and, what is it you say, shoot the shit?”

“That’s different.”

“How?”

“We’re both adults. We’ve got stuff to talk about. Mr. Joseph’s an old man, you’re just a kid.”

“I’m not a kid,” Toby said.

His dad, looking pale and gaunt in the bright kitchen light, nodded. His shoulders slumped. “Right. I know you’re not. You’re growing up. But still, what have you got to talk about? What could you two possibly have in common?”

Toby could’ve argued with his father about how Mr. Joseph was an interesting person with an interesting past, that talking with him had helped ease the pain of Frankie’s death. But that wasn’t the real issue here. “It’s because he’s black, isn’t it?”

His dad blinked—noticeably, almost comically, twice.

“If Mr. Joseph was an old white man living across the street, you wouldn’t think anything of it if I were to go over and spend time with him. You’d think it a kind gesture. No one would have a problem with it; not you, Mom, Gloria’s parents, or even the kids in town.”

“You... you think I’m a racist?” His dad spoke softly, breathlessly.

Toby wasn’t sure if his old man was more shocked or saddened by Toby’s startling remark.

“I never thought so before, but now...I’m not so sure. Are you?” It was a bold move to ask his dad outright.

"No, I'm not," his dad said. The look of shock was still etched on his face. "My thoughts concerning you and Mr. Joseph have nothing to do with him being black."

Toby was tempted to say, "Are you sure?" but he didn't want to press his luck. Besides, he wanted to believe his dad was telling the truth.

"Okay, I'm sorry."

His dad half-smiled. At least he wasn't angry. He shook his head. "Don't be. You can talk to me about anything, you know that. No secrets. But I can assure you one hundred percent, I'm not a racist."

Toby nodded. He had his doubts.

His dad wandered over to the fridge and grabbed a can of Coors. He cracked open the lid and took a healthy swig. "Your mom and I just want you to be happy and safe. That's all. So I want you to respect our wishes, even if you don't agree with them."

"Sure, whatever," Toby said. "Anyway, I'm tired. I'm going up to bed. Good night."

"Night, Toby. And I am sorry about Gloria. Her parents are probably doing what they think's right, but for the record, I agree with you—I think it's bull. And unfair."

Toby sauntered out of the kitchen.

"Oh, and Toby?"

Toby turned and faced his dad.

"You know I love you, right?"

Toby shot his dad a half-cocked smile. "Sure. But twenty bucks would show me even more."

His dad gave him a tired smile. "Go on, get out of here."

Up in his room, Toby threw off his clothes and wearing only his boxer shorts, hopped into bed.

It was only half-past-eight, but he hadn't been lying when he told his dad he was tired. His mom would flip if she knew he had gone to bed without brushing his teeth, but what she didn't know wouldn't kill her.

After today, Toby was glad he hadn't told his parents the truth about Mr. Joseph. He'd feared they wouldn't understand—it seemed those fears were justified.

Can't trust anyone. It was a cold, sobering thought.

💀 💀 💀

He was in darkness.

He felt around. Cold, hard wood.

Not again, he thought. *How the hell did I get in here?*

This time, his hand fell on something small and hard. He picked it up. Judging by its size and shape, it was a cigarette lighter, similar to the one Warrick had when he and Frankie had camped out in Toby's backyard a hundred years ago.

He flicked it on, managed to ignite a flame first go. He screamed.

Frankie was lying in the cramped box beside him, his neck bent at an impossible angle, a large open wound running the length of his face, yellow and red pus seeping from the fissure. He was wearing an old battered black hat and dark sunglasses. Blood was seeping down his face from under the rim.

Frankie opened his mouth and with blood trickling down his chin, said, cackling, "Hey scaredy-cat, how's it hanging? Have you remembered yet?"

Toby jolted awake. He sat up, heart thumping, sweat flicking off his body.

Only a dream, he thought.

But it had felt so real, and that costume Frankie was wearing had seemed so familiar.

As did his laughter.

But it wasn't Frankie's laughter; not his belly-laugh, but a nasty, grating high-pitched cackle.

Remembering the sound made his gut clench tight. Though he wasn't sure why, or even why the laugh seemed familiar.

He glanced at the clock. A little after three. Swinging his legs off the bed, he placed them on the floor and walked over to the open window, wiping the sweat from his eyes. He gazed down at the street. Not surprisingly, his light was the only one on in Pineview, so it stuck out like a fireball.

Toby moved his gaze from the old house across the street to the shed behind. He could only make out a small portion of it, but staring down at the make-shift vodou temple, which too had seemed so familiar, its façade looking so ominous in the tranquil early morning haze, Toby shivered.

CHAPTER FOURTEEN

Toby was woken the next morning by his parents' voices. They carried through the house, up to his bedroom; loud, angry talking.

Sitting up in bed, Toby wondered—*were they having a fight?*

It wasn't like them to fight.

Toby wiped the sleep from his eyes and turned to the clock-radio. It was just after 7:30.

As Toby eased himself out of bed, he thought, *I bet they're arguing about me. Maybe Dad has had a change of heart, but Mom doesn't want to back down on the Mr. Joseph issue.*

Toby slipped on yesterday's shirt and shorts that were flung over his desk chair and headed for the bedroom door.

In the bathroom he drained his bladder, splashed cold water on his face and then headed downstairs. His parents' voices grew louder and clearer, and he realized they weren't fighting—they were angry, but not with each other.

When he stepped into the kitchen, his mom, sitting at the kitchen table with a cup of tea, and his dad, leaning against the bench, mug of steaming black coffee clenched in his hand, stopped talking and shot their gaze towards Toby.

"Good morning," his mom said, face creased with worry.

"Morning, champ," his dad said and took a quick sip of coffee.

"What's going on? I could hear you guys from upstairs."

"Sorry, did we wake you?" his mom said.

"No," Toby lied. He headed to the fridge, took out the orange juice.

Silence filled the room and when Toby turned around, he caught his parents trading shifty eyes.

Toby filled a glass with juice and after taking a thirsty gulp, said, "Will someone please tell me what's going on?"

His dad sighed. "We may as well tell him, Nancy. He's gonna find out soon enough."

Toby's gut clenched. His first thought was, *Oh God, they've found Warrick's body.*

His mom nodded. "Toby," she began, "there was some vandalism last night."

"We only just found out about it, and were discussing whether or not to call the police."

"You mean vandalism to our house? What kind?"

"Graffiti," his mom said.

"I saw it when I went out to get the paper." His dad shook his head, muttered, "Damn monkey-fuck kids."

"David," his mom said, though her displeasure at her husband's comment didn't carry much bite. He had simply voiced what his mom was too embarrassed to say.

Toby set down his half-finished glass of juice and strode out of the kitchen.

"Toby," his mom said, getting to her feet, but his dad said, "Leave him, Nancy. He's old enough to see it for himself."

As if you guys could stop me, Toby thought as he made his way down the hall and out the front door.

With bare feet, he stepped across the lawn, noticing some of the neighbors across the street were gawking at his house. When he reached the edge of the lawn, he turned around.

Staring back at him, in two-foot-high black letters painted on the left side of the house, was: COXSUCKING NIGGA LOVA

"Why don't you take a picture," his dad shouted at the neighbors as his parents stepped outside.

"Toby, come inside," his mom said.

Toby pried his eyes away from the graffiti. He turned and gazed down the street, towards Mr. Joseph's house. He wondered if the vandals had targeted his house as well.

He started walking.

"Toby," his mom said. "Please, don't."

Toby ignored his mother's plea.

"Let him go," his dad said.

Toby crossed the street and pushing past nosy neighbors, made his way to Mr. Joseph's. When he arrived, he saw that the vandals had indeed defaced Mr. Joseph's house. Sprayed in red graffiti on one side of the wall was: COXSUCKING NIGGA CHILD MOLESTA

"Jesus," Toby muttered. He started down the side of the house, heading for the kitchen.

At the back door, he knocked. "Mr. Joseph? It's Toby."

Silence. Then: "Come in."

Toby pushed open the door and stepped inside.

A familiar sight greeted him. Mr. Joseph sitting at the kitchen table with a bottle of Barbancourt white rum.

"I saw the graffiti. I'm sorry."

Mr. Joseph nodded. "Did they get your house, too?"

"Yeah," Toby said. "Bastards. My parents are trying to decide whether or not to call the cops."

"They needn't bother. The police have never caught the culprits in the past."

"I think I know who's responsible."

Mr. Joseph angled his head and gazed up at Toby. "You do?"

Toby nodded. "I'm sure it was Dwayne Marcos and his gang."

"Dwayne Marcos? Why do you suspect him of the graffiti?"

"I probably should have told you this sooner, but with everything else that's been happening, I guessed it sorta slipped my mind. I saw who graffitied your house and left the dead chicken that night about a month ago. It was Dwayne and his friends."

Mr. Joseph, still clutching the bottle of rum, said, "You know about that?"

"I watched the whole thing from my bedroom window. I couldn't sleep that night. I saw Deb Mayfour and Leah Wilmont graffiti your house, Sam Bickley kill the chicken, and Scotty Hammond throw the eggs."

"And Dwayne?"

"Sat in his car and watched."

"You didn't tell anyone about this?"

"No," Toby said. "I was scared. Scared that if I told, Dwayne would find out who squealed, and then I'd be in trouble. Also, I didn't want to get Leah in trouble. She's always been like a big sister to me. So you see why I suspect Dwayne?"

Mr. Joseph nodded. His eyes narrowed, his lips drew tight. "Yes, I see. Did you want to sit down?"

"No, I really should be getting back. Mom will probably have a heart attack if I don't come home soon."

"So they know?"

"Yeah," Toby sighed. "The whole town does by now."

"What did they say?"

"They reckon it's best if maybe I don't see you at the moment. Until all this blows over."

"I doubt it ever will," Mr. Joseph said.

Toby paused to contemplate that statement. "Yeah, well, they can't tell me what to do. They can't stop me from coming over and seeing you."

"You shouldn't go against your parents' wishes, Toby. You saw what was written on my house. I've caused you enough problems as it is. Maybe you should only come back when your parents say it's okay."

Toby was taken aback. "You agree with my parents that I shouldn't come around anymore?"

Mr. Joseph seemed to choose his words carefully. "Like I said, you shouldn't go against your parents' wishes."

"What if I told you that my parents just suggested it might be for the best I didn't come around, rather than specifically ordering me not to?"

"Well..." Mr. Joseph took a swig of rum. "If that's true, then I guess it's okay. I guess then it's up to you and me to decide what we're going to do about this situation."

"I want to keep coming around," Toby said. "I don't see anything wrong with it, and I won't let others intimidate me."

"If you're sure."

"I am."

"I just don't want an angry father on my doorstep, threatening me to leave his son alone."

"You don't have to worry about that."

Mr. Joseph nodded. "Okay."

"I should probably get back. But I might be by later in the afternoon. Again, I'm sorry about the graffiti."

"It's not your fault," Mr. Joseph said, and Toby left the old man's house.

Back home, Toby wandered into the kitchen. His mom was by the phone, his dad was sitting at the table finishing his second—or maybe it was his third—mug of coffee. "I called the police," his mom said, "they said there wasn't much they could do, but they're sending someone out." She added, almost as an afterthought: "How was Mr. Joseph?"

"What do you care?"

"Toby, be nice," his dad said, and he stood, picking up his briefcase. "Okay, I'm off. Toby, after the police have been, I want you to clean the filth off our house. We're out of turpentine, so you're gonna have to go to the store to buy some more."

"Chores?" Toby said.

His dad kissed his mom on the cheek, then ruffled Toby's hair as he walked past. "Yes, chores. See you guys tonight."

"Bye, David."

After his dad had left, his mom said, "So, did the hoodlums graffiti Mr. Joseph's house, too?"

"Yeah."

"Oh dear. Well, remind me to tell the police about Mr. Joseph's house as well."

"Don't bother," Toby said. "Mr. Joseph doesn't deal with the police."

His mom strolled over, put an arm around him. "I know you're upset, but try not to let all this get to you. It will all blow over soon."

"Yeah? Try telling that to Gloria's mom."

"Your father told me about what happened. I'm sorry, Toby. You may think I'm being unfair, overprotective, but even I think that's going a bit far. Want me to have a word with Helen?"

"God, no," Toby said.

"Okay. Hopefully Gloria's parents will see sense."

"This has been the worst summer ever," Toby muttered and the comment earned him a long, tight squeeze from his mom.

"Well," she said, taking her arm from around Toby's shoulder. "I should probably call work and tell them I'll be in late."

"Why?"

"I should wait for the police to arrive. Did you want me to make you some breakfast?"

"No, I'm not hungry," Toby said, and sauntered out of the kitchen.

An hour later—and with no sign of the police—Toby headed off to the hardware store. He took his time walking, but when he reached the township, he ducked in and out of Tim's Hardware. He was crossing over Main Street, bag containing the bottle of turpentine dangling from one hand, when he spotted Rusty Helm and Scotty Hammond up ahead.

As Toby stepped onto the sidewalk, he kept his head down, hoping they would pass him by.

No such luck.

"Well, looky what we got here," Scotty said. "If it ain't the nigger lover. Hey there, nigger lover, sucked any nigger cocks lately?"

Toby stopped as the two older teens blocked the road ahead.

"Scotty asked you a question," Rusty said, his tall, muscular body towering over Toby.

"Whatcha got there?" Scotty said, his short-cropped blond hair glinting with sweat.

"Nothin'," Toby answered, heart racing.

"Give it here," Scotty said and grabbed for the bag.

Toby pulled the bag away. "It's just turpentine," he said. "Just leave me alone, okay?" He started forward, but Rusty put out an arm and gripped Toby by his T-shirt.

"Where do you think you're going?" he said, a mean smirk on his face. "We're just being friendly."

"Yeah, it's not like we want to hurt you or anything," Scotty sniggered.

Rusty eyed his chunky friend with thuggish glee. "So," he said, turning his gaze back to Toby. "Tell me something. What does nigger cock taste like? Chicken?"

Scotty chortled, proud of his friend's remarkable wit.

"Why don't you ask Warrick," Toby muttered, and hoped—prayed—they hadn't heard him.

"What did you say?" Rusty said, leaning forward.

"Nothing," Toby said, turning his face towards the fence to get out of the firing line of Rusty's hot stinking breath.

"What the fuck has Warrick got to do with anything? What do you know?"

Rusty nodded to his cohort. Scotty moved behind Toby and grabbed his arms; the bag of turpentine dropped to the ground.

Toby struggled, but a swift punch to the gut from Rusty put an end to that.

It wasn't a hard punch, but still Toby doubled over, straining for breath.

(the sound of gravel crunching as feet kicked him in the stomach, screaming, laughter—laughter?!—and white hot pain)

"What do you know, Fairchild?" Rusty growled. "Huh? What the hell do you think you're playing at?"

Toby shook his head. "Nothing."

"You talked to him the other day. Apparently you were one of the last. What did he say to you?"

Rusty grabbed a clump of Toby's hair and jerked his head up. "I'm talking to you. What did he say?"

"Nothing," Toby repeated. "Just that he was sorry."

"About what?"

"About what happened to Frankie. And that he hadn't come and seen me since I got out of the hospital."

"That all?"

Toby nodded.

"Warrick's our friend, and we're worried about him, that's all," Rusty said, still gripping Toby's hair.

I seriously doubt that, Toby thought.

"We wanna find out what happened to him, ya know?"

Toby shrugged.

"So why d'ya make that remark about Warrick and nigger cock?"

"It's just something Warrick said once. About what a..."

A voice interrupted Toby. "Hey, let the boy go."

All heads turned to Mr. Joseph across the street, standing by the entrance of Barb's.

"This ain't none of your concern, freak," Rusty said.

"I'll make it my business if you two don't leave him alone."

Rusty and Scotty exchanged a look—Toby noticed, with a small amount of satisfaction, that it was a look of uncertainty, even fear.

Toby saw Rusty nod and Toby was let go.

Glaring at Toby, Rusty said, "Well, you be careful now. Associating with the likes of that nigger, you might get your head bitten off."

"Or some people might think you're as queer as he is," Scotty said, quietly.

"See you 'round, Fairchild." Rusty gave Toby a final hard stare and then the two thugs moved away, glancing once at Mr. Joseph still standing by the door, leaving Toby shaking, his stomach sore.

"Assholes," Toby muttered and then he bent down and picked up the bag. Mr. Joseph was still standing by the door. Toby gave him a small nod of thanks. Mr. Joseph waved, then he headed back inside Barb's. Toby continued walking.

When he arrived home, a uniformed cop was standing outside with Toby's mom. They were on the front lawn, looking at the graffiti.

Toby walked over to them.

"Toby. This is Officer Reilly."

The policeman, a young, fresh-faced guy, nodded. "Hey there." He was holding a notepad and pencil. "So Toby, did you see or hear anything last night?"

Toby shook his head.

"Any ideas about who may have done this? Anyone with a grudge against you, or Mr. Joseph?"

Sure, they just socked me in the gut ten minutes ago.

"Just about every kid in town has it in for Mr. Joseph," he told the policeman. "And I'm not the most popular person right now, so that narrows it down to oh... only about a thousand people."

"Toby, don't be smart," his mom said.

"It's all right Mrs. Fairchild. I know what Toby's saying." He winked at Toby and then flicked the notepad closed, pocketed the pencil. "Well, that about does it. If either of you remember anything, don't hesitate to call us. Now, did you say that Mr. Joseph had some graffiti, too?"

"Yes," Toby's mom said.

"Hmmm, well I should go over and talk to..."

"No, don't bother," Toby interrupted. "He didn't see or hear anything, either. I spoke with him earlier. Besides, he's not at home, he's working. But I'll tell him to give you guys a call if he does remember something."

Officer Reilly mulled this over for a momentous few seconds. "Okay. But you tell him to call us if he remembers anything—anything at all."

"I will," Toby said.

The policeman nodded. "Well, have a good day, the both of you."

He started towards his patrol car.

"Oh, Officer?"

He stopped, turned around. "Yes, Ma'am?"

"Can we wash off the graffiti?"

"Sure. Don't want that filth spoiling the neighborhood. Good day."

After the policeman was gone, Toby's mom said, "Nice man," then she said to Toby, "Well, there's no point in going to work now. Besides, I think with everything that's happened, it would be best if someone stayed home and looked after you."

"I don't need a babysitter," Toby said, grinding his teeth together.

"I know you don't. But today, you've got one. Now you get started on the graffiti while I go and call work. Make sure you scrub all the paint off and wear some gloves." As she turned to head back inside, she muttered, "Maybe we should think about repainting the house."

Toby groaned, thought, *I bet I know who'll get stuck with that job.*

He started towards the shed to get some gloves and rags.

An hour later, finished scrubbing the graffiti off the wall, Toby pulled off the gloves and tossed them to the ground.

“Talk about slave labor,” he muttered and as he rubbed his aching shoulders, thought about the filth sprayed across the front of Mr. Joseph’s house.

Toby felt bad that the old man would have to struggle to clean the paint. So, with a fresh bag of rags and the half-empty bottle of turpentine, he headed over to Mr. Joseph’s.

Back home and having taken a cool shower, Toby was lying on his bed, relaxing his aching muscles, when the doorbell rang.

He didn’t feel like moving, but he figured his mom was probably busy doing housecleaning, or whatever it was she did when she took the day off, so he sat up and eased his stiff body off the bed. He opened his door, stepped out into the hallway, but stopped when he heard his mom’s voice downstairs.

“Oh, hello, Mr. Joseph.”

Toby’s mouth went dry.

What’s he doing here?

Toby stopped short of the stairs, staying out of sight behind the wall, listening.

“Hello Mrs. Fairchild. I was wondering if I could have a quick word with Toby.”

“Sorry, he’s resting,” Toby’s mom answered quickly. “Is there anything I can do for you?”

“Oh, ah, yes. Would you please tell him thanks? I appreciate what he did.”

Toby’s mom laughed; a small, polite laugh that Toby knew masked her true unease. “I’m sorry, I’m not sure what you mean. Thank him for what?”

“For cleaning the graffiti off my house.”

A pause. “He did?”

“Um, yes, Ma’am. I take it he didn’t tell you?”

“Well, er, no, he didn’t.”

“When I arrived back from work, I noticed the wall was clean. Maybe I’m wrong, maybe it wasn’t Toby who cleaned it. If he didn’t, then I apologize for bothering you.”

“No bother,” Toby’s mom said. “But since you’re here, Mr. Joseph, I was wondering if we could have a word?”

Toby's gut tightened. He wanted to intervene, wanted to put a stop to this encounter between his mother and Mr. Joseph. But he remained where he was.

"Of course," Mr. Joseph said.

Toby waited for his mom to invite Mr. Joseph in, but the invitation didn't come.

"Mr. Joseph—Toby's a very sensitive boy. He's been through a lot this past month. Toby's dad and I, we're both... extremely grateful for what you did, we really are, but maybe it's for the best if you... well, you know... Toby doesn't need any more stress right now. I'm afraid that by allowing him into your home, it's done more harm than good."

There was a long silence.

Toby's jaw hurt from so much grinding.

How dare she...

"What does Toby have to say about it?"

"Well, you know how boys are, stubborn as mules. He says he'll do what he wants, but he doesn't know what he wants. No boy at his age does. His father and I know what's best for him, and that, I'm sorry to say, is that he no longer associates with you for the moment. Nothing personal, you understand."

"It seems to me that you've got a pretty smart kid there. A good head on his shoulders. Pardon me for saying so, Mrs. Fairchild, but I don't think you or your husband give Toby enough credit. He's strong, probably stronger than you realize. Don't you think it's up to him to decide what he wants? After all, he's the one who has to deal with all the grief that comes with associating with me. I think that gives him the right to decide, don't you?"

Toby almost screamed with delight—he loved his mom, but to hear someone put her in her place like that, well, he'd be lying if he said it didn't give him any satisfaction.

"You're entitled to your opinion Mr. Joseph," his mom said, after a moment's silence, "but I must say I have to disagree. And I'm sure my husband would, too. We know our son, and at the moment, it's not good for him to be under this kind of stress. So please, I'm asking you nicely, could you refrain from seeing my son? If he comes over, just politely tell him that you think it's best if he goes away."

"Did you know I used to be married?"

Toby's mom cleared her throat. "Um, no, I didn't know that."

"Yes, back in Haiti. I was married for almost forty years. Mangela, that was my wife, her parents didn't want her to marry me, they thought I was too old, too common, not educated—which was funny, since they were peasant farmers themselves. But anyway, if Mangela had listened to her parents, we would never have married, I would never have had all those years with her, and we would never have had Felicia or Rachel."

"Are they your daughters?"

"Felicia was, Rachel was our granddaughter. I've always believed that kids should listen and respect their elders, but sometimes, it's best not to."

"What are you saying Mr. Joseph? That Toby should wantonly disobey his father and me?"

"All I'm saying is that sometimes it pays to listen to the child for a change. Sometimes, those things which cause us the most pain are the most rewarding. Well anyway, I've said enough. Again, please tell Toby thanks. Bonswa, Mrs. Fairchild."

If Toby's mom said goodbye to Mr. Joseph, Toby didn't hear it. The door closed and he heard his mom sigh.

Toby crept back to his bedroom, closed the door and lay on his bed.

A short time later, his mom knocked on the door. "Yeah?"

She opened the door and smiled in at him.

"Who was that at the door?" he asked.

"It was Mr. Joseph."

Toby sat up, feigning surprise. "What did he want?"

"To thank you for cleaning the graffiti off his house."

"Oh."

His mom smiled, briefly. "That was a kind gesture. He appreciated it."

Toby nodded. "Well, I didn't have much else to do today. Is that all he wanted?"

Her smile faltered. "We also had a chat about the current situation, and we both agreed it was best if you stopped going over to his house—at least until this whole thing blows over."

Toby swallowed. "He agreed?"

"Yes. Sorry, but it's for your own good. So you won't go over there anymore, not unless your dad and I say so?"

So much for listening to the child. "Well, if Mr. Joseph said it's for the best, then I have no choice."

Her smile broadened; it was a smile full of relief. "Good, I'm glad. Okay, that makes me feel a whole lot better. I'm sure this mess will be over with soon, the people in town will forget about it, and then things can go back to normal."

"Sure, normal."

His mom left.

So you won't go over there anymore, not unless your dad and I say so?

Sure, he wouldn't go over there—at least, not for the rest of the day. But tomorrow, when his mom was back at work...

Toby grinned.

After all, I didn't promise I would stay away from Mr. Joseph's.

That evening, while Toby was in the family room watching TV and his dad was out in the shed, tinkering with some old, broken appliance (he was spending more and more time in the shed, or out playing poker), the phone rang. His mom was in the kitchen, reading, cradling a glass of wine, so after three rings, she answered the phone. Toby lowered the volume of the TV and heard his mom say, "Hi Suzie. Not much, just catching up on some reading." After that, her voice lowered, which meant she was talking about something she didn't want Toby to hear. But that made him all the more curious, so keeping the TV on low, he crept up to the kitchen and, like earlier, stayed out of sight while he listened to his mom talk.

"...know, it's horrible. Toby spent half the day cleaning it off, including Mr. Joseph's...

"Yes, that's right, his too...

"Of course I'm worried. I know what kids can be like, I heard them laughing about it at work yesterday...

"Hmmm? Oh, I don't want to repeat what they were saying, Suzie. All I'll say is that it had to do with chickens and, um, sex...

"Don't laugh. Poor Toby, he doesn't have many friends, he hardly sees anyone. He doesn't talk to me, and David's, well, I'm worried about David, too...

"Well, maybe another time. Not on the phone. Anyway, guess who came over today? Mr. Joseph...

"Yep, that's right...

"Well, to thank Toby for cleaning the graffiti off his house. But, get this, he also had the nerve to tell me how to raise Toby...

"I swear, he did. He stood there and told me that I don't know what's best for my boy, that it's perfectly fine to let a fourteen-year-old spend time at an old man's house...

"Yeah, but that's not all, Suzie. He told me about his wife and child, back in Jamaica, or Haiti, or someplace. Like I really care... and... huh?... yes, I've had a few drinks tonight, so what, that's not allowed...?

"Right, I know, I know. Anyway, he essentially said that kids shouldn't listen to their parents, that it should be us listening to them, and doing whatever they wanted...

"Yes, I'm telling the truth. Honest...

"What? Well, I told Toby that he was not to go around there anymore, that Mr. Joseph agreed it was for the best...

"No, I know, but he doesn't need to know that. Toby's soft, he's too sensitive, if he keeps on going around there, the kids in this town will tear him apart, cause him to have a nervous breakdown or something...

"No, I'm not being overly dramatic. That's how I see it. It's already started, and I'll bet there's been more things happening than just the graffiti that Toby's not telling me...

"Oh, I don't know, I'm sure kids are teasing him, maybe even prank-calling him. They like to do that...

"Yes, I know. But it really pisses me off. Kids acting like this. If it wasn't for a bunch of hooligans teasing that old hobo...

"Yes, I'm sorry Suzie...

"But do you know what was really strange? Mr. Joseph himself..."

A small, whispery chuckle.

"Yes, even more strange. Well, I realized I've never actually looked at him before, you know? Never really taken a good hard look at him...

"I know, that's what I'm saying. And there was something really unusual about him...

"Huh? Oh, I can't put my finger on it, but there's something... not right...

"No, I don't just mean those things. I mean... oh, I don't know... he gave me the creeps, to tell you the truth... I'm glad I told Toby not to go around there... if David felt what I felt standing there, talking to the man...

"Yes, exactly. I mean, I feel bad talking this way, after what he did for Toby...

"Yes, I know, I know. So how are you doing, Suzie?"

His mom's voice returned to normal volume again. Toby remained standing just inside the family room entryway, heart thumping, thinking about what his mom had said.

She sensed something was different about Mr. Joseph. What if she...?

No, Toby thought. *Mr. Joseph's secret hasn't been discovered for over ninety years.*

Still...

"...want to speak to him? Well, I'll go and ask him. Hang on."

Toby scurried back to the couch, had just sat down when his mom appeared. Walking over to him, she smiled. "It's Suzie on the phone. She wants to have a word with you."

"What about?"

"I don't know. Probably just wants to see how you're doing."

"Take a message," Toby said.

His mom sighed. "This is ridiculous. I don't know what happened between you two, but whatever it was, sort it out. I'm sure it wasn't anything to ruin your friendship over. Besides..."

"I haven't got any other friends?" Toby gazed up at his mom.

"No," she answered. "Well, maybe. You need to talk with someone about everything that's going on. And you and Suzie used to be so close."

"Yeah, used to be," Toby said.

"So you won't talk to her?"

"Not tonight," Toby said.

With a shake of her head, his mom turned and strode back into the kitchen.

Toby didn't bother eavesdropping on the rest of the conversation.

CHAPTER FIFTEEN

At around ten the next morning—his mom safely at work—Toby headed over to Mr. Joseph's. He didn't see anyone out in the street as he crossed Pineview, though he did wonder if there were any neighbors watching from inside their houses, hidden behind curtains, fingers itching to use their telephones.

When he arrived at Mr. Joseph's, he walked up the porch steps and at the front door, knocked. He waited. When there was no answer, he knocked again. Nothing.

He headed around to the back. As he neared the back door, he heard soft singing coming from inside the shed.

Toby stepped up to the shed and listened. He heard Mr. Joseph singing in some strange language—Creole? Toby wondered. Toby stayed by the shed, listening to the sound of Mr. Joseph's voice, entranced by the lilting melody.

When it became apparent that Mr. Joseph wasn't coming out anytime soon, Toby headed back home.

After lunch Toby was relaxing in front of the TV when the doorbell rang.

Toby peeled himself out of the couch, and as he ambled towards the front door, heard a car door slam and then a car skid away.

Nerves tingled in Toby's gut.

Relax. Probably nothing at all to do with me...

When he opened the door, he saw a small parcel on the porch, sitting halfway between the door and the steps.

Toby stepped out, reached down and picked it up. Before he closed the door, he looked up and down the street, but Pineview was like a ghost town.

Back inside, he looked over the box. The parcel had no address or name written on it; it was just a plain box, taped shut.

Toby considered throwing it straight into the trash, but curiosity got the better of him. He took the parcel into the kitchen and placing it on top of the table, sliced the tape with a pair of scissors and then tugged open the box.

The smell hit him immediately; a putrid meaty smell. With some hesitation, he opened the box fully and gazed inside.

His gut surged and before he puked up the hotdogs he'd eaten for lunch, he closed the box, not wanting to look at the severed chicken's head for a second longer.

"Sick fucks," Toby muttered, wiping his eyes. It was a good thing his mom wasn't home; she would have driven straight over to the police, no arguments.

He had a mind to go over to Dwayne's house and throw the damn box at his front door—but he didn't have the balls to do such a thing.

Besides, he didn't have proof it was Dwayne and his gang. Just like he didn't have proof they were the ones responsible for the graffiti on his and Mr. Joseph's house. Most of the kids in Belford knew of the stupid rumor that circulated a month ago, so it could've been any one of them.

But Toby knew better. He would've bet his left nut that this was Dwayne's doing.

Staring at the box with its horrid present inside, Toby thought about what to do with it. He wanted to throw it in the trash—that's where it belonged—but he worried his parents would discover it, and then he'd have a hell of a lot of explaining to do.

I should take it around to Mr. Joseph's. He knows about disposing of these things.

Tentatively picking up the box, Toby carried it over to Mr. Joseph's house.

This time when he knocked, the door opened.

"Monsieur Fairchild." Mr. Joseph frowned down at the parcel Toby was holding at arm's length. "What's that?"

“Mind if I come in?”

The frown remained as Mr. Joseph stepped aside and let Toby in.

Sitting at the kitchen table, Mr. Joseph opened the box. His face turned grave, he shook his head.

“Someone dropped it off at my house ten minutes ago. I heard a car drive away, fast. Don’t suppose you saw anything?”

Mr. Joseph shook his head. “I haven’t been inside much today, sorry.”

“You’ve been in your shed?”

Mr. Joseph looked surprised. “How did you know?”

“I came over earlier, but you didn’t answer. When I went around to the back, I heard you in the shed.”

“Oh, I see.”

“What were you sing...?”

“Any idea who might’ve left the box?” Mr. Joseph said, cutting off Toby.

Toby nodded. “Dwayne, or at least, one of his gang. I’m sure it was them.”

Mr. Joseph’s eyes narrowed, his brow furrowed. “That doesn’t surprise me. Little bastards,” he said, voice like thick black venom. “I have a mind to...” He stopped, gazed at Toby.

Toby saw hate in his face—for the first time Toby could remember, he saw genuine loathing.

“Is everything okay?”

Mr. Joseph blinked, the darkness lifted, and he shook his head. “Sorry?”

“I said, is everything okay?”

“I’m fine,” Mr. Joseph said. “So, what shall we do about this?” He nodded to the box.

“I was hoping you could get rid of it. I don’t want my parents finding it in the trash.”

“You don’t want to take it to the police?”

Toby was surprised by Mr. Joseph’s suggestion. “I didn’t think you trusted the police?”

“I have reason not to trust anyone in authority, but this, well, maybe you should report this.”

"Why? It's just a stupid prank. And telling the police would only worry my mom, and she's worried enough—too much, if you ask me."

"Yes, I was meaning to ask you about that. Did your mom tell you I came around to see you yesterday?"

Toby nodded.

"Good. The way things were left, I wasn't sure she would. So... she's okay with you coming over here?"

Toby swallowed, looked to the table when he answered. "Yeah, she trusts me to make the right decision. She said something about listening to the child for a change." Toby hoped Mr. Joseph wasn't good at picking up on lies.

"Well, I must say I'm surprised. I didn't think anything I said to your mom got through. I thought all she would see was a strange old man who was the cause of her son's pain. I'm glad to hear she took on board your thoughts and feelings on the matter."

"Yeah, well, anyway, I don't want to go to the cops. Are you able to just throw it in your bin?"

"If you're sure..."

"I am."

"Okay."

Toby waited at the table while Mr. Joseph took the box outside. When he came back, he said, "You know, I was hoping I would see you again."

Toby frowned. "Why?"

Mr. Joseph shuffled over to the fridge, opened the door and pulled out a bottle of Coke. "Because otherwise this would've gone to waste."

Toby smiled.

Mr. Joseph filled a glass with the cola drink, then brought the glass over. "Here you go."

"Thanks." Toby took a big gulp. "I'm just glad you didn't buy diet; or else you would never have seen me again."

Mr. Joseph chuckled—the first hint of sun Toby had seen in his otherwise cloudy disposition. "You know, I've never tasted Coca-Cola before," he said.

Toby almost spat the drink over the table. "What?"

"Never had a mind to. But I've always been curious. Mind if I steal some of yours?"

"Go ahead."

Mr. Joseph got himself a glass, poured in a small amount, and then sunk it back. He coughed, made a face. "That stuff's like acid," he gasped. "It's worse than rum."

"I guess it takes some getting used to."

Mr. Joseph nodded. "I guess so." He placed the Coke back in the fridge, then rinsed out his glass. "I think I'll leave the Coke for you."

"Fine by me."

Mr. Joseph sat back down.

"You should've seen the look Mrs. Stein gave when I bought the Coke. She couldn't understand why I would buy such an item." Mr. Joseph smiled thinly and shook his head.

"Thanks," Toby said.

"What for?"

"For getting rid of the chicken. And for this." He held up the glass of Coke. "And for yesterday." Toby looked to the table.

"I saw the confrontation through the store's window. I hope those boys didn't hurt you too badly."

"No," Toby said.

"I just wish people would leave you alone."

Toby looked back up. "I was curious. What was all that about this morning in the shed?" he asked

Mr. Joseph's face turned sour again, his demeanor darkened.

"Sorry," Toby fumbled. "That was rude of me to ask."

"No, no, it's okay, you're curious. It's perfectly understandable. I was, well, I was speaking to the loa."

Toby's eyes widened. He swallowed the Coke, then said, "A spirit? You were talking to a vodou spirit?"

"Yes. Guédé Nimbo, to be precise."

"What did you say to it? What did it say to you?"

"Nothing important," Mr. Joseph said. "Nothing you need to worry about."

Toby could tell Mr. Joseph was holding back—what was it he wasn't telling him? What had the loa told him?

Though Toby desperately wanted to know, he didn't want to press it. He figured, if it was something truly important, Mr. Joseph would tell him in his own time.

Or so Toby hoped.

"So, got much on for the rest of the afternoon?" Mr. Joseph asked.

Toby huffed. "With the whole town laughing at me? Sure, I'm Mr. Popularity." Toby finished off his drink.

"Surely it's not that bad?"

"It's bad enough that Gloria's parents have all but banned us from seeing each other. She's only allowed to see me once a week—they reckon we were seeing too much of each other, but Gloria thinks it's really because of this situation with you and me."

"I'm sorry."

"Yeah, well, adults suck. No offense."

"None taken. Well, if you're free, how about indulging this adult for a few hours? There's still plenty more story to tell."

Toby nodded. "I'd like that. It'll help me forget about everything for a while."

"Good. Okay, so where were we..."

"I don't know how long I was the master's personal slave—it might have been a few weeks, or maybe a few months. I expect it was probably somewhere in between. It wasn't exciting work, but it was a lot easier than being out in the cane field, hacking away at the sugar cane all day. But I was at his beck and call. Night or day, it didn't matter—whatever the master wanted, I obeyed. Whether it was cassava bread in the middle of the night, or a cup of coffee in the morning; whenever that bell jingled, or his deep voice boomed, "Slave!" I would stop whatever it was I was doing—usually menial chores such as cleaning or washing dishes—and go to him.

I wasn't treated too badly; the master and his son weren't mean to me, but they weren't friendly, either. I was like a ghost, my presence felt, but it was like they couldn't see me. They hardly looked at me when they spoke. But I didn't care; in my state, I didn't think about anything; I just was. I did my job as instructed.

When I heard or saw things in the house, I didn't think anything about it; I didn't care that the master had two, sometimes three girls in his bedroom, or where the stacks of money that appeared seemingly out of nowhere came from—I just viewed these with detachment and disinterest. When I heard the cries coming from outside, somewhere in the cane field, I didn't think about how awful it was; I just heard them and went about my business.

It was the same with the dramas inside the house.

Not long after I was transferred to the main house, I started hearing the arguments. Day and night, Marc and his father fought. Often about money, or the Americans—Marc was afraid they had too many slaves on the plantation, and feared the marines would soon discover their peculiar brand of workers. Silva waved his son's fears away, saying they had nothing to worry about; they were far enough away from any towns and no gendarme ever patrolled this far up. But mostly, the fighting had to do with the business.

Over the course of my time in the house, I heard a lot of things said. I missed out on some of the details, and didn't properly comprehend a lot of what was said until after I had been awakened, but this was the crux of all the fighting: Silva didn't think Marc was strong enough to take over the plantation when he was gone. Marc, of course, disagreed, but the old man was unmoving in his position—another man was set to take over as boss of the sugar plantation.

That other man was Raoul. I got to see a lot more of him in the time I spent as the master's slave. He was at the house every day, spending just as much time inside as he did out in the field, abusing the workers. Whereas Marc had a gentle way about him, always asking me to do this or that with a kind voice, Raoul was brash and violent. He would often knock me over, laughing his cruel laugh, smoking his rotten cigar. He would order me to do something, and when I didn't obey—which was all the time, as I only obeyed my master and Marc—he would hit me, sometimes with his fists, usually with his stick. He got told off by the master for doing so, but I could tell, even in my trance-like state, that the master was easier on Raoul than he was on Marc, who hardly did anything wrong.

The master treated Raoul more like a son than he did Marc. Often I would find Marc staring out the window, looking out over the cane field, a sad look on his face, a glint of water in his eyes.

"Old man," he would say (never, "zombi," or "slave"), "I've worked my whole life on this plantation, helping my papa. And what's it all for?" Then he would shake his head, sigh, and get back to counting the money, or speaking to business associates.

Raoul, on the other hand, strode about the house like he owned it, which, I guess, when the time came, he would; drinking and smoking, spending a lot of time in the master's bedroom whenever the young girls were over and the master was away.

The day of the uprising, Marc and Raoul had a particularly heated argument. I'm not sure what prompted this exchange; all I could gather from the shouting was it had something to do with papers and ownership of the plantation. They shouted, even traded blows—I was outside working in the garden for most of the day, so I heard it and, later, saw the outcome.

Silva had to break them apart, and, as an added insult, he blamed Marc for the outburst, telling him to behave like an adult, not like a little kid, and besides, he should be respectful to his future boss.

Well, that was it for Marc. He stormed away, muttering under his breath. Raoul came out of the house shortly thereafter and as he went past, he looked at me and smiled, blood running down his nose, staining his white teeth. "When I'm boss, you're history, zombi. I'm gonna get me a nice young Mulatto girl to be my slave." The master came by soon after and told me to get back to work. I noticed he had extra lines on his face and he walked with heavy steps.

Later that evening, I had just poured the master a third glass of dark rum, when Marc came back. He entered the house with a sullen face.

"About time," the master huffed, sitting in his chair, smoking a thick cigar, drinking his rum. "You're responsible for the day-to-day running of the slaves, and it's past their meal time."

"I know, I'm sorry papa, I shouldn't have gotten so mad at Raoul. But I'm back now."

"No, you shouldn't have," the master said. "But at least you showed some fire, which is good. About time you displayed some guts."

To me, Marc said, "Go to the kitchen and wait for me." As the master slurped his rum, I turned and headed out of the large living room and into the kitchen.

There I waited.

When Marc came in, instead of ordering me to start boiling the plantains, he said, "I'll serve the workers tonight. You go into your room and wait." I did as I was told. After some time had passed, Marc opened the door and placed a bowl down on the floor.

"Old man, I hope you will forgive me for what I'm doing."

He spoke in a whisper.

"But I have no choice. This plantation should've been mine."

I looked up at my second master, noting the sadness in his eyes, the madness in his face. Here was a man resigned to his fate. He sighed, and the last thing he said to me was, "I'm sorry." Then he turned and leaving the door to the closet open, walked away.

At the time I didn't know why he felt the need to apologize, to tell me he was sorry. Now, thinking back, I think he felt bad for a few reasons. He knew what was to come, what his actions would result in. Not only the death and the violence, but what his injured pride and pain would mean for all of us zombis. Everyone in Haiti knows that if there's anything worse in this world than being a zombi, it's being aware that one is a zombi.

I also think—or at least, I like to think—that he was sorry for my state, and how he and his father had used us as slaves. Whatever the reason Marc said "I'm sorry," I'll never know for sure—I never got to ask him.

But all those thoughts were in the future. At that moment, I was still an unthinking zombi. And I was hungry.

So I grabbed the bowl and held it in my arms like I did every evening. Only this time something was different. I could smell the stuff in my bowl, and it wasn't the usual cold mushy plantains. This had a sweeter smell—sweeter at least to my dull senses. I was wary at first, but wariness quickly gave way to hunger. I plunged my hand into the bowl, grabbed a handful of the food and stuffed it into my mouth. The food even felt different in my mouth—crispier. I chewed the bits of food, enjoying the taste.

And then it happened.

I hadn't even finished the first mouthful when I felt a change. It was sudden, like a bullet firing out of a gun. One moment I was sitting there, content in my nothingness; the next, I was suddenly aware of myself and my surroundings.

It was the strangest feeling. Suddenly I had thoughts in my head, a million thoughts all vying for an answer. I knew where I was, what I had been through, and how I got there—there was nothing wrong with my memory—and I was angry. The floodgate of feeling and emotion was opened, and it was almost too much to bear all at once.

It seemed when I tasted the salt on the crackers, the part of me that was trapped was unleashed. The salt on those crumbled crackers was like the blood of life, and it shocked me awake—which, under the circumstances, wasn't a good thing.

I spat out the crackers and started crying, even though no tears came. I cried for a few minutes, strong, unabashed weeping.

And then I heard the sounds from outside, and I stopped.

I heard the master's voice; hurried, loud, but scared, shouting, "Marc, what have you done!" All other emotion left me then and what remained was anger.

Pure, red-hot anger.

I threw down the bowl, got to my feet and walked out of the closet. I still walked stiffly, slowly, but there was a purpose to the walk that wasn't present before.

For I knew nothing at that moment except the man I knew as master—Silva, in another life—was the man I wanted to kill. I had to seek revenge for turning me into an abomination, for I felt him responsible for my state.

I staggered through the kitchen and into the main room, where the master was standing by the front window.

Outside I heard the clamor of voices—mostly those getting used to using their voice box again, and the sound was strange, like that of a hundred cows being gutted alive—and they were getting closer.

Even amid all the noise, the master must've heard me, or maybe he sensed my dark presence, for he turned from the window and his face opened up with fear. "Devil," he breathed, the gun in his hand trembling by his side. "Devil, get away from me!"

I snarled and felt the vilest hatred for the man standing about ten feet in front of me. "You," I said. Talking again felt strange.

"The devil speaks," the master said and it seemed he remembered he was armed, for he shook his head, looked down at his right hand and then raised the revolver. "You're not going to take me," he said. "None of you are. You're not going to win, devil." The master closed his eyes, muttered a prayer, and then stuck the barrel in his mouth and pulled the trigger.

"No!" I cried as the master slumped to the floor, leaving a splatter of blood and brain on the wall behind him.

I was furious. I wanted to feel the master's life slip away as I ripped his eyes out of his head and then stripped away all flesh as he screamed to the heavens. But he had deprived me of that.

The raging bloodlust in me was suddenly vanquished. Still, I sauntered over to the master's body, looking like a bloody rag doll, and spat on him. "Rot in hell, demon," I said, still getting used to my vocal chords again—the muscles hurt.

I stepped up to the window, wiped away some of the blood splashed there, and peered out into the night. The moon was full and it lit the scene outside in a nightmarish glow. Then I realized it wasn't the moon, it was one of the huts; it was on fire. And all of the slaves that had been shuffling up to the main house to exact their revenge, machetes and hoes in hand, were now stumbling around, howling to the sky in anger. Like me, they wanted payback, but they all knew the master was dead—they would never get that small satisfaction of killing him.

I looked for Marc, but there was no sign of him.

Just then three horses appeared, galloping in from behind the house. Gunshots rang out as the men on the horses opened fire. One of them was Raoul; the other two were new to me.

The gunshots continued as two of the men stayed on their horses, firing at the slaves, while Raoul jumped down and dashed towards the house.

I reached down and pulled the gun from the master's hand. I had it up and pointed at the door by the time Raoul burst in. He stopped at the sight of the master lying dead on the floor, then his eyes went to me, then to the gun.

Raoul, gun by his side, seemed to be mulling things over—I guess deciding whether, as they say, to fight or flight. "You freak," he said, voice unusually soft. "This was supposed to be mine. Well you're not going to take it from me. Damn Marc, I'm gonna cut off his balls and shove 'em down his throat!"

I pulled the trigger.

It seemed my aim was off, because the bullet smacked into the doorframe, narrowly missing Raoul's head by inches.

Raoul shrieked and ducked back outside.

I stepped forward, meaning to go after him, but when I looked out, he was already among the throng of slaves, shooting alongside his two friends, and I figured, those slaves probably had more desire to seek their revenge against him than I did—they had put up with his abuses for a lot longer than me.

So I turned and started for the back door—the master's dog, continually barking, made me think of the poor zombi out back.

I walked through the house and out the back door. The dog, barking like a madman, was chained up, choking itself against the chain. I wasn't sure whether it was acting so crazy because it knew its master was dead, or because it was scared and wanted to run away. Either way, it knew the unnatural things had suddenly become even more unnatural, and when it saw me, it stopped trying to break free and it hunched back, baring its teeth.

I raised the gun and fired once at the dog, hitting it in the chest. The dog yelped and fell to the ground. It was still alive, so I went up to it and put it out of its misery.

Next I looked for the mangled zombi; found it groaning near one corner of the yard. Unlike its fellow zombi slaves, this poor specimen hadn't eaten salt, therefore hadn't awoken from its trance—it was still an unthinking slab of meat. And a slab of meat it resembled: its lower half was completely severed, leaving only a mash of shredded skin, flesh, meat and bone. Its upper portion and some of its head had clearly been chewed on; it was such a pitiful sight that I had absolutely no qualms about aiming the gun at its head and pulling the trigger. "You are free, now," I said, and then headed back inside.

Walking towards the front door, I passed the forbidden room. I stopped, turned towards it. I had to know what was behind that locked door. I tried the doorknob, just in case, but it held steady, so I shuffled into the kitchen where I grabbed a meat cleaver. I headed back to the forbidden room, slipped the gun into one of my pockets, and then raised the cleaver, bringing the hatchet down against the edge of the door. After three chops, the doorknob broke off, the area around it was splintered, and the door was ajar. I tossed the cleaver to the floor and pushed open the door.

Inside was dark. The room was windowless, so I wandered over to one of the lanterns in the dining area, reached up and took it down from its perch. Then I walked back to the forbidden room and entered.

The room was small, about half the size of the master's bedroom, and almost vacant. I expected perhaps a vodou altar room, or maybe a place for the master to stash all his money. But what was contained in this sparsely populated room was much more chilling than anything I could have anticipated.

There was a stone table, and sitting atop this table were around twenty jars—govis. These terracotta pots were unadorned, not like the usual govis which were sacred to the vodou religion, wrapped in colored cloth to symbolize whichever loa was housed within. No, these govis were naked. Clustered on the table, these clay pots looked old, some were chipped, all were dusty.

I knew what they were, and I admit, I was scared to walk over to the table and be near them. Inside those clay pots were the souls of twenty men. Not vodou gods, but simple men—farmers, servants, husbands, fathers.

I stood just inside the room until I was able to gather up the nerve to venture forward. Setting the lantern on the floor, I walked to the table, stopping and looking down upon the master's collection of souls. Here were the lives of twenty men, destroyed by greed, revenge, and bought for a price by a man who saw only cheap labor and greater profit.

I reached down and with hands shaking, took one of the govis in my hands. It was weighty, its surface was rough, and I wondered—was this my soul I had in my hands?

I knew one of these govis contained my soul—but which one?

I quickly decided it didn't matter. Nothing could be done about it now. My soul could never be free, not unless the bocor who had cursed me set it free himself. And that was never likely to happen.

But, I could at least stop anyone else from taking control of these souls, taking them to another bocor and paying their way for the souls to again be in the power of some other greedy plantation owner.

I threw down the govi I was holding. The clay shattered, and a gust of wind slapped me in the face. I heard a ghostly cry, and then it departed. The soul would remain on this earth, roaming, but at least it would be free—as free as a zombi's soul could ever possibly hope to be.

I picked up the next govi and smashed it to the floor, releasing the soul within. With an increasing sense of liberation, I threw each govi to the floor; and each time just after the terracotta burst into a hundred pieces, I felt a brief gust of wind, heard the ethereal howl of a tormented soul pass by my ears.

I threw the pots down fast, one after the other, pausing only once when the cry that came after the breaking of just another old pot screamed louder, the wind was more forceful, and for just a moment, I felt a chill as the soul passed right through me.

I was left shocked, for a second my brain felt like it was being squeezed, memories of my past life flashed before my eyes like a movie on fast forward, followed by strange visions, of distant lands and men with dark hats and glasses, blood and pain, and death. Then all pain and flashes of memory went away.

I continued releasing the souls, and by the time I had smashed all of the govis, there was a heap of broken terracotta on the floor, and dust was thick in the air.

I turned and left the forbidden room.

Before I stepped out into the battle outside, I checked the gun—I had two bullets left.

I expected death and mayhem—after all, I had heard plenty of shooting while I was tending to the dog and zombi out back—and though there was a fair amount of death, there wasn't the anarchy I was expecting.

Ex-slaves lay scattered about the ground—all with their heads exploded—though I counted only half the total number. The rest were nowhere to be seen. So there wasn't much action going on when I surveyed the area. All the huts were now ablaze, their straw roofs and wooden walls flaming. I knew it wouldn't be long before the fire spread to the main house and the entire plantation would be up in smoke. Also, I could hear the horses and mules in their nearby pens, crying and kicking; it seemed they, too, knew the imminent fire danger.

Then I noticed something going on by one of the large trees near the huts—the one the young zombi had been hanging from. I saw Raoul and one of his friends attempting to truss up a few more zombis.

Fire raged through me. I remembered how scared I was at the sight of the young zombi slowly being strangled—that even as a zombi, the knowledge of how horrible a torture it must've been for that young slave filled me with dread. And now, as a savane, as a thinking, feeling, awakened zombi, I knew I couldn't let such a thing happen again to any of my fellow zombis.

I started forward, working my way through the maze of dead zombis, their brains plastering the ground around them. I felt sorry for them, but also relief, for at least now they were at peace.

I was twenty feet from Raoul when I noticed Marc sprawled on the ground. I stopped and looked down at his ruined body. I shook my head. He had been shot in the head, as well as split down the middle, his guts spilling out like a bunch of pink snakes had been dumped inside his torso. I wasn't sure who was responsible for his death—the zombi slaves, seeking their revenge against the people who had oppressed them, or Raoul and his friends.

I left Marc and continued towards the tree.

As I got near, I heard Raoul talking. "You will hang there like your zombi friend until you agree to work for me, like you did Silva."

The two zombis they were tying with the ropes struggled and begged to be let go.

"I'm not about to lose all my slaves," Raoul was saying, voice quivering with anger and loss. "You will learn to obey me, even if you have been awakened."

Raoul and his friend had gotten the ropes around the two zombi's necks and were starting to pull on the ropes, raising their bodies off the ground.

One of the zombis was my old roommate; the other looked vaguely familiar.

I didn't know if Raoul and the other man had any bullets left in their guns, but I didn't care. I stopped about five feet from them. I was lucky they were too busy trying to hang the zombis to notice me. I took careful aim. I fired at Raoul's head and immediately the older zombi crashed to the ground. As the other man let go of the rope, and the second zombi crashed to the ground, I moved the gun and tore off Raoul's friend's scalp.

And with that, it was over. Half the slaves were dead, the other half would be scattered all over the north come morning.

"Thank you," the older zombi said, pulling the rope from around his neck and getting to his feet. "I didn't fancy..." he glanced down at the younger zombi, whose bloated black head now lay a few feet from his emaciated body. The rope which had held him for so long still hung from the tree.

I nodded. I thought about throwing the gun away, but I thought better of it, even though it was out of bullets. I figured I could get some more if I ever needed to. So I tucked the revolver into the pocket of my pants.

The other zombi, now on his feet and free of the rope, looked at me with wide, fearful eyes. "People will come," he said. "The Americans, they will see the fires and come and when they find us, we'll be tortured worse than what Raoul was fitting to do." He took off, his legs stumbling, but still he continued, until finally the night sucked him into her bosom and he was gone.

"I think he was half-crazy to begin with, before he became a zombi," the older zombi said. "But he's right. We should go. Maybe not the Americans, but someone will be here soon. That other friend of Raoul's rode away. Soon half the country will be looking for escaped zombis."

I nodded. "Okay. But where should we go?"

"Do you have any idea where we are?" the older zombi asked.

"Well, I know we're in the north, I vaguely recall heading north from where I used to live to get here, and I think we're near the coast—I remember seeing the ocean on the trip here with Silva. And I heard Silva, Raoul and Marc talk often of the towns of Limbé and Port Margo during my time as personal slave."

"That means nothing to me, I'm afraid. I come from St. Marc, I've never been this far north before. I am Jean-Philippe Donnez, by the way."

"Jacques Joseph." We nodded, neither of us smiled—we both knew the shame in each other's dead hearts, though it was good to at least be with someone who seemed friendly.

"So where to? The zombis that weren't destroyed took off in all directions."

"I guess the mountains in front of us are the safest bet," I said. "The marines find it harder to navigate and traverse the mountains."

"Why the ones in front? There are mountains behind us, too. And they're closer."

"I remember crossing a river to get to the plantation. I heard Marc and Raoul talk about Port Margot a lot, and by the way they spoke of it, and the way they used to come and go, I would say the town's behind us, and easier to reach. So if the marines or the Gendarmerie were to come, I'm thinking it would be from behind."

"So you're saying we should go forward and cross the river and head into the mountains ahead of us?" Though the mountains were steeped in darkness, Jean-Philippe still pointed towards the cane field.

"Seems the sensible plan to me—if there is indeed any sense left in our world."

"Sounds okay with me. Lead the way."

Before we left, I asked Jean-Philippe to help me unlock the pens, and together we watched the mules and horses take off.

"You're an old softy," Jean-Philippe said as we shuffled towards the cane field. With the night aflame, we stalked through the tall sugarcane, Jean-Philippe remarking that he hoped he never saw sugarcane ever again.

Once we were past the field, we..."

The phone jangled.

The sudden noise was jarring, especially in Mr. Joseph's house—it was usually so quiet.

"I hardly get calls," Mr. Joseph remarked. "When I do, it's always people trying to sell me things, or wrong numbers." The old man hopped up and shuffled over to the wall phone perched near the back door. He picked up the receiver. "Hello?"

Toby saw the old man's face drop immediately. "Who is this?" he said. "Listen, I..." He shook his head. "You're disgusting. How could you even...?" He gripped the phone tight, his nostrils flared. "Is this Dwayne?" he growled. "One of his goons? Well if it is, let me tell you something, you had better watch your back, got me? You'll pay, you little bastard." Mr. Joseph slammed the receiver on the cradle.

When he turned and looked over at Toby, his expression was still troubled. "Sorry about that," he said.

"Prank call?"

Mr. Joseph nodded. "I'm afraid so, yes."

"You think it was Dwayne?"

"Maybe. I guess it could've been anyone." Mr. Joseph walked over to the cupboard, took out the bottle of rum. Without bothering with a glass, he brought the rum with him back to the table. He placed the bottle down, was about to sit, when the phone rang again.

"Want me to...?"

"No," Mr. Joseph said and he sauntered over to the phone, lifted the receiver, pressed the button to hang up, and then left the receiver resting on the countertop. "Why won't they just leave me alone," Mr. Joseph muttered. He sat down at the table.

"You've been getting many prank calls?"

Mr. Joseph took a swig of rum. "At least ten a day, more at night."

"I'm sorry."

"It's all right, I can handle the prank calls. I've been tempted to just unplug the phone for good."

"Why haven't you?"

Mr. Joseph shrugged. "I'm not sure." He took another, longer drink. "Shall we continue with my story?"

Toby nodded. "Sure."

Mr. Joseph raised the bottle of rum, was about to take another swig, but stopped. "Where are my manners? Would you like another drink of Coke?"

"I'd love one."

Mr. Joseph started to rise.

"I'll get it," Toby said. Taking his empty glass, Toby wandered over to the fridge, where he took out the bottle of Coke. He filled his glass and as he placed the bottle back, noticed how empty, how white the inside of Mr. Joseph's fridge was. He closed the refrigerator door, sat back down and said, "Okay, I'm ready."

"As I was saying, once we were past the cane field, we soon came to the river. It was wide and muddy, its depth unknown. "This is the river we crossed coming here," I said. "But that was on mule-back." I stepped forward into the water. I waded out till I was in the middle, and the water went only up to my waist. So Jean-Philippe followed me in and together we crossed.

Once on the other side, our clothes dripping, we started across the wide open farmland. Only once did I stop to turn around. I saw flames and thick acrid smoke rising into the night sky. I nodded, and then we continued towards the mountains.

As we crossed the plain, we kept close to clumps of trees, trying to make as little noise as possible as we shambled past single huts and larger habitations.

I was relieved when we made it to a valley, and passing groups of sleeping huts, found a path leading up into the mountains.

This mountain range wasn't nearly as wild and rugged as the one Silva took me through to reach his plantation. It was still heavily wooded, but the slopes weren't as high, so it was thankfully easy going without a mule or donkey to ride on.

Jean-Philippe and I walked our stiff, broken walk through the mountains without talking and when it seemed like we were deep enough in, I said, "Do you want to stop here and rest? I think it will be dawn soon, and this looks like a good spot to hideout."

Jean-Philippe agreed, and so we left the narrow mountain path and headed into the forest. We trudged through scraggly bushes, past ferns and oaks, stopping when we reached the edge of a deep gully. We sat behind a large pine, so if a gendarme patrol came by on the path, they wouldn't see us sitting in the woods.

"So," Jean-Philippe said after a spell. "What are we going to do? Here we are, two zombi savanes on the run. We can't hide out in this mountain forever."

I sat contemplating our situation.

"Do you have family?" Jean-Philippe asked.

I didn't answer for a long time, the pain I felt was too much. "Yes," I finally answered. "I have a wife, a daughter and a granddaughter."

"I'm sorry."

I nodded.

"Where are they?"

"On a small plot near a town called Pignon, in the northern central plateau. I'm a farmer... was a farmer."

"Sounds nice. Me, I have no family. I never married, never had any kids. I ran a small hotel in St. Marc. It wasn't doing too well when I... left, so I'm not exactly keen to get back there. Not, of course, that I could ever run it again."

"What did happen to you? If you don't mind me asking?"

"I was a gambler."

I almost chuckled. "Isn't everybody in Haiti a gambler?"

Jean-Philippe did chuckle. "I suppose. But I had it worse than most. Cockfighting was my game. I loved to bet on the cockfights."

"I'm a card man myself." I caught myself, almost added *was a card man*, but decided not to. I'm sure I would be catching myself a lot in the time to come—it would do me no good to keep reminding myself of what a sad pathetic creature I had become.

"Anyway, one day I bet on this strutting black cock," Jean-Philippe continued. "I was sure it would win, it was up against some mangy looking red bird. Just before the fight I noticed the owner of the red cock smear something on its feathers. I had seen this done a number of times before. It was a hot, pepper-like liquid that didn't harm the cock's feathers, but would sting and blind a cock if it was to get into another cock's eyes. Which was the idea. It was cheating, and being I had a lot of money on this fight, I spoke up, accused the owner of cheating. Well, there was an uproar, people demanded their money back, and the old man was bitterly embarrassed and angry at me. I later learnt that this man was friendly with some old bocor, and as payback for losing money and for the public humiliation, he paid the bocor to punish me."

"I see," I said. "It's always about payback."

"You have a similar story?"

I told him about the three cacos, taking in Marcel, him raping my daughter, and me giving Marcel up to the police. Once I had finished telling Jean-Philippe my story, he laughed, saying how we both paid the price for standing up for our principles—only he said mine was much more virtuous than his.

I also told him about my three girls, the strong beauty of Mangela, the frail beauty of Felicia and the innocent beauty of Rachel. Talking about them was hard, but I liked Jean-Philippe a lot, he was a good listener. I told him how much I missed them, and that I was concerned for their wellbeing. Afterwards he said, "They sound like three special people. In another time, I would've loved to have known them. And you. I'm sure we would've been good friends."

"I would say we are, now."

"Yes, we are, but not under the best of circumstances."

This I had to agree with.

By this time dawn had arrived, and we heard the footsteps of mountain women walking along the nearby path, so we stopped our talking. Fearing being discovered by anyone, especially the Gendarmerie, we kept mostly quiet while the sun was in the sky. We talked sporadically, always softly, about our lives, growing up, the people we knew, and about life on the plantation. We didn't have to work hard at keeping our voices down when speaking about that—we both naturally spoke in whispers about that awful topic. I learnt, that as far as Jean-Philippe could remember, he died around March nineteen-eighteen—which meant he had been on the plantation a full nine months before I arrived.

I mentioned to him about what I had found in the forbidden room, told him what I had done, and he remarked, with a noticeable shift in tone, about how, while he was outside with

Raoul, he felt a chill wash through him, a pained wail rang in his ears, and he had visions that both scared him and soothed him.

The day passed slowly. A few times we heard gunshots in the distance. One time the gunshots sounded close, but it was hard to tell in the mountains. We heard the sound of hooves go by at around lunchtime, and judging by how many there were, we figured it was Gendarmerie, either doing a routine patrol, searching for cacos—if in fact the war was still being fought—or perhaps searching for stray zombis.

At one point we even heard the toot of a ship's horn.

"Looks like you were right about us being near the ocean," Jean-Philippe remarked.

I nodded.

Finally, dusk came, and then night, and the cover of darkness swept again over the land.

I knew we had to move, but the inevitable question remained—where would we move to?

Jean-Philippe was the one to bring up the subject.

He was a dim shape beside me when he said, "So, what now? Where are you thinking you'll head to?"

There was only one destination I had in mind, one place I wanted to go, but I knew that was not possible now.

I had been thinking about what to do, where to go, for the whole day—there was nothing else to do but think, sitting there under the pine tree—and it always came down to the same conclusion: wanting to see my girls.

"I don't know," I said.

"What about heading home? I know things have changed, but do you think...?"

"No," I answered. "No, I couldn't."

"I understand," Jean-Philippe said. "If I had a family, I don't think I could face them either, no matter how much I wanted to."

"What about you? Will you try and head south?"

"I don't see why. Like I said, I have no family, and I could never go back to the hotel. No, I think it's safe to say that I no longer have a home."

"Yes, I know what you mean."

The situation felt hopeless, overwhelming. I wondered what the other savanes were doing, what their plans were now they were free—or at least, free from the plantation.

"I tell you one thing," Jean-Philippe said. "I'm hungry. I could really go for some cassava bread, or a nice juicy mango."

"But no plantains."

"No, I never want to eat another plantain again for as long as I..."

The rest of Jean-Philippe's sentence hung in the deep mountain silence.

"Come on, we should be able to find something to eat."

We got to our feet and walked back to the path. There didn't seem to be anyone around, so we turned left and continued through the mountains.

The wind had sprung up, the moon was curtained behind some clouds; it looked like it would rain soon.

We trudged along the path, winding around bend after bend, walking up hills, down gullies and through streams. We didn't pass any peasants, which wasn't unusual at this time of night, and thankfully we had yet to encounter any gendarme or marines. I knew that if we saw a patrol coming, we could hide in the woods by the side of the path; but if we got caught and they saw us before we saw them, I shuddered to think what we would tell them—they were bound to notice we were not quite human if they looked at us long enough.

Soon we heard the deep beating of drums. A steady rhythm, it was neither a *rada* ceremony, *petro*, nor a Congo celebration.

"A secret sect ceremony," Jean-Philippe whispered, and I nodded.

A secret sect was something to fear—all peasants knew the stories of child sacrifices, even cannibalism at these secret ceremonies. These sects had less to do with the religion of vodou and more to do with black magic. Everyone knew that anyone caught out at night who wasn't part of the sect was stopped and, if deemed unworthy, shot—or worse.

"That's all we need," Jean-Philippe said, "to run into a secret sect."

I tried not to think about it, but it was hard not to when there were drums pounding through the mountains, sounding like they were just around the next bend. They weren't, but they sure sounded close.

The drums were still pounding when we came upon a solitary hut by the side of the path. There was the faintest hint of light inside, but all was quiet. We would've passed right by and kept on going, if not for the mango tree beside it.

"Finally, some luck," Jean-Philippe said, and just as he spoke those words, the sky opened up. Rain poured down; hard, thick drops.

Jean-Philippe shrugged and shuffled over to the mango tree. He plucked a mango, tore off its skin and bit into it. "Not quite ripe, but it'll do," he mumbled.

I shambled through the rain, to the tree and grabbed myself a mango. I did feel bad about taking the mango without asking or paying, but I hoped the owner would understand.

I roughly peeled back the skin and took a big bite of the green fruit. It tasted bitter, the flesh tough, but compared with the bland plantains I had been living off for the past few months or so, it tasted heavenly.

I had finished the mango and was reaching up to pluck another, when the door to the hut opened and a voice, high-pitched and sounding as old as time itself, said, "Who's out there?"

Jean-Philippe and I both froze, rain splashing down on us, mango juice trickling down our chins.

"Come on, I can hear you, even through this rain. Speak up, I won't bite."

I looked at Jean-Philippe, he just shrugged, so I said, against my better judgment, "Just us, ma'am. Two old peasants."

"You don't sound too old to me," the voice croaked. "But you'd better come in before you drown."

I didn't know what to say. The thought of getting out of the rain did sound inviting, but the moment this old crone took one look at us—me in particular—I knew she'd scream and tell us devils to get out. She may even go to the police.

It seemed, too, that Jean-Philippe was stuck for words.

"I won't scold you for eating my mangoes. I got plenty of them. There's a fire in here and proper hot food. Even rum and coffee. So come on in before I change my mind, or you get eaten by a *Loup Garou*—whichever happens first."

Jean-Philippe and I looked at each other and saw in each other's eyes the uncertainty, the fear, but also the temptation of rum and proper hot food, so we turned and staggered over to the door and entered the hut.

Out of the pelting rain, inside the small hut, light coming from a fire in which two pots were hanging over on wire racks, we could see the old woman, and she looked to be at least a hundred years old. She had lines on every inch of her face, which was like black leather, and her hair was as white as white can be. She had a slight stoop, but walked with purpose as she went over to the pots.

"Come, sit," she said, lighting an old tin cup fashioned into a lamp. The small hut grew a little brighter. "I've got some millet and chicken bubbling."

"Sounds good," Jean-Philippe said.

"Yes, sounds good."

"Rum? Coffee?"

"Rum," we both answered, and the old lady chuckled. "Brothers, are you?"

"Ah, no," I said, which made the old woman laugh even harder.

"I wasn't serious. By lord, you are strange ones."

We sat on two rickety chairs by a wobbly hand-crafted table, watching as the old woman poured us some clairin into two tin cups. She placed them down in front of us, shaking her head as she did so. "Damn secret sect," she muttered, "annoying me with their drumming. Don't they know I'm blind, not deaf?"

Jean-Philippe and I looked at each other, amazed at our good fortune. This century-old woman was blind?

It made sense, now that I thought about it. She hadn't remarked on my bizarre features, or our glassy eyes.

"So," the old woman said as she started spooning the millet and chicken into two bowls. "What were you two young 'uns doing out at this time of night?"

I sipped my rum; it was good. "Well..." I began.

"You see..." Jean-Philippe stumbled.

The old woman laughed again. "Sorry, I shouldn't have asked. I've put you two in an awkward position. Trying to explain why you're out at night, when it's obvious the reason."

"It is?" I said, gulping down the rum.

"Yes, my hearing is perfectly fine. You're both zombis, right? Savanes?"

I blinked, suddenly dumbstruck.

For a short while the only sounds were the rain pounding on the palm fronds and the booming of the drums.

"You don't have to worry. I won't tell anyone. Why would I? You're no threat to me."

"But how...?" Jean-Philippe stuttered.

"Like I said, my hearing." She brought over the two plates, setting them on the table with all the ease of someone with perfect vision. Up close, I could see her eyes—glassy, unfocused, like that of a zombi's. She sat down opposite us. "Go on, eat."

We both ate, and it was delicious.

"Firstly, it's your voices," she said. "Zombi savanes have nasally voices that are unnatural. You don't hear it yourselves, and most other people can't detect it, but I can hear it. And second, neither of you breathe. That should be fairly obvious to anyone—anyone listening, that is."

So there it was. This old woman, the first person we had encountered since leaving the plantation, had instantly recognized us for the monsters we were.

"So you've met zombi savanes before?" Jean-Philippe asked.

"Sure. You live as long as I do, in these mountains near that devil plantation, and you come into contact with lots of things. Zombis included. I take it that's where you've come from?"

"That's right," I said. "We escaped last night."

"The whole plantation has probably burnt to the ground by now," Jean-Philippe said.

"Good, I'm glad," the old woman said.

"So where are we exactly?" I asked. "I come from near Pignon, in the central plateau, and Jean-Philippe is from St. Marc."

"You're in Morne Toussaint, in the north. The Bay of Acul is close by, as is Le Cap."

"We're near Le Cap?"

"Well, near enough. A couple of hours on foot, give or take an hour depending on your age, but that's a lot nearer than either Pignon or St. Marc. If you keep on heading east, you'll eventually come out of the mountains, onto the Plaine du Nord, which leads to Cap Haitien. You can't miss it; it's a big town." She chuckled to herself.

"We were sort of lost—still are, I guess," I told her. "We don't know where to go."

"Perfectly understandable," the old woman said. "You both have family?"

"Jacques does, I don't."

"But..."

"You can't go back to them, the way you are?"

"Well I can't."

"Yes, it must be hard."

We both gave her a brief rundown of how we came to be zombis. I told her of my three girls, and the old woman just sat there, listening, nodding her head every now and again.

By the time I had finished telling her my story, the rain had stopped, and I realized so too had the drumming.

"Just in case you were wondering," the old woman said afterwards. "It's now February 1919."

I did the calculations. Two months I had been away from my family; two months I had been a zombi.

My insides turned cold. By the look on Jean-Philippe's face, he, too, found this hard to stomach.

"We'd better get going," Jean-Philippe said. "While it's still dark."

"Where will you go?"

"Who knows," I said as I got to my feet. "Thank you for the food and rum. And for the company."

"And the mangoes," Jean-Philippe added.

"You're most welcome." She got to her feet. "You know, you're both more than welcome to stay here. For as long as you need. I could use the company, as well as help in the garden, and the gendarme don't bother me at all, not that they come through here that often. This isn't a big mountain range, not like those further east, where those nasty cacos are hiding."

"So the war is still going on?" I asked.

"My, yes. It's growing more and more bloody by the day. Another reason to stay. You don't want to risk getting caught up in all that business."

The offer was tempting, and by the look on Jean-Philippe's face, he, too, was contemplating the offer. But it wasn't right. I couldn't put this kind old woman in danger, and Jean-Philippe must've felt the same way, because he said, "Thanks, that's awfully kind of you, but we couldn't do that to you."

Besides, I had other ideas.

"Well, the offer is there if you want it, but I understand your position."

We shuffled to the door, opened it and stepped back out into the darkness.

"Goodbye young 'uns," she said. "And good luck."

We both said our goodbyes, and then started sloshing our way up the path.

We were only a few miles down the mountain path when Jean-Philippe said, "You know, we never found out her name."

I nodded. "You're right. I feel bad about that. We never asked."

"But she never told."

"I guess so."

Then, "Where to now, Jacques?"

"Well, I've been thinking."

"Yes?"

"I can't go back to my family. And besides, we're in too much danger here. Both from the marines and the Gendarmerie, and those gangs that go around, searching for stray zombis. You can even add cacos into that mix. Haitians know too much about zombis, we're too conspicuous."

"So what are you suggesting?"

"Well, Le Cap is nearby. I was thinking of going there, seeing if I can get onto a boat, or a cargo ship."

Jean-Philippe halted. I stopped and turned to my fellow savane.

"You're not serious?" Jean-Philippe said. "You're trying to tell me that you're considering trekking to Le Cap, strolling onto a ship and going... where?"

"To America, where else?"

Jean-Philippe was silent. He stood there on the path, mud all around us, lost for words. Finally, he stumbled out: "Let's just say for a minute you make it to Le Cap, that you don't get caught by the gendarme on the way, or the marines stationed in the city, that people see your deformed neck and slow shuffle and aren't immediately curious, just say you find your way to the port, and somehow find a boat or ship that will take you, without any money mind you, all the way to America. Just forget all that for a moment, and let me ask you this—what about your family? What about your country? You can't just leave it all behind."

"Why not? I told you, I can't go back to my family. You said so yourself that if you had one to go back to, you wouldn't be able to face them the way you are. My family think I'm dead, at rest—if they saw me like this, this abomination..." I shook my head. "I couldn't do it to them. It'd kill Mangela. I know it would."

"Maybe," Jean-Philippe admitted. "But still, leaving Haiti altogether? Isn't that a bit drastic?"

"I can't stay," I said. "I've been thinking about it for the past few hours. And I don't just mean the danger—I know it'll be dangerous wherever I go. But at least in America they don't know about zombis, don't know the tell-tale signs. You saw what happened back there with that old woman—she knew straightaway what we were."

"She was... different. Not everyone will know."

"Most will. But it's not just that. Staying here would remind me too much of my family. Knowing they were so close, yet not being able to go to them. I couldn't do that. I'd go crazy."

"So going to another country altogether won't make you crazy?"

"Less crazy."

"This is ludicrous," Jean-Philippe said. "You'll never make it. How will you even get on a ship? You don't have any money to bribe someone with."

I fingered the revolver hanging heavy in my pocket. "I'll find a way," I said.

"Ludicrous," Jean-Philippe repeated.

"Why don't you come with me? It would be good to have a friend along."

Jean-Philippe smiled, and it wasn't a pretty sight—not because the old man was particularly ugly; no zombi looks good when he smiles.

"You know, I'm tempted. As ridiculous as the whole idea is, I'm tempted."

"Well then come on. You heard what the old lady said. Two, three hours and we're at Le Cap. If we can get onto a ship, in a few days we'll be in America."

Jean-Philippe shook his head. "No, I can't leave Haiti."

"But you have nothing to stay for."

"I have cockfighting," he said.

"Come on, come with me. If we go down, at least we go down together."

"I like you Jacques. I like you a whole lot. You saved my life, if you can call what we are a life worth saving, but you saved me from a lot of pain. I would be hanging from that tree right this moment, slowly strangling, if it wasn't for you. But I'm not like you. I have no desire to leave. You say I have nothing to stay for, that is true, but at the same time, I have nothing to make me leave, either. I love Haiti too much, and besides, I'm too tired and too old to be traveling to another country."

I reached out and placed a hand on Jean-Philippe's shoulder. It was bony and wet. "I understand. I guess if I didn't have my girls, I would stay too. There'd be no reason to leave."

"That's right."

I was disappointed, I would've liked to have gotten to know Jean-Philippe more. We had a connection, a kinship—though we had only known each other a short time, it felt like we had known each other our whole lives.

"So you've made up your mind? You're staying?"

"Yes. And you?"

"Leaving. At least, attempting to."

"Mind if I walk with you till we come to the end of these mountains?"

"I'd be honored."

We continued along the path, sloshing our way through the mud, avoiding the multitude of puddles that had formed during the brief, but powerful downpour.

"Judging by the night, I'd say it's only just past twelve, one o'clock at the latest. If I can make it to Le Cap by four, it still should be dark."

"So you're really going through with it," Jean-Philippe remarked. "I wonder if any of the other escaped zombis are as crazy as you and have the same notion."

"Wouldn't surprise me. Haiti isn't the safest place to be for an escaped zombi."

"Neither is Le Cap. Or America for that matter."

"True, true. Still, I have to do this."

We continued on for a while longer, the path winding through the lush hills, until, finally, the hills grew smaller and, from the moonlight now full in the sky above, we saw the wide open plains below, and the sparkling bay over on our left.

"Must be Acul Bay," I said.

"Beautiful," Jean-Philippe said. "Well, this is where I get off. According to the old lady, this is the Plaine du Nord, so Le Cap should be somewhere over those hills."

I turned to Jean-Philippe. Looked at his ashen skin and glassy eyes. "So, friend, where will you go? What will you do?"

"You know, it occurred to me as we were walking, about how I have no family and you have to leave yours behind. I know how hard this decision is for you, how much you're going to miss your three girls, and that you're concerned for them."

"Don't remind me. I feel bad enough about leaving them."

"So how about I travel down to where you used to live and keep an eye on them, make sure they're doing well and not in any danger?"

I blinked. Didn't know quite what to say. "You'd do that for me?"

"I guess I owe you. And like I said, I've got nowhere else to go; so really, it doesn't matter where I go to set up my farm and breed my cocks."

I laughed. "You're going to breed cocks?"

"Fighting cocks. I probably won't ever fight them, but still, you never know. It'll give me something to do. I've always wanted to breed cocks."

"Are you sure this is what you want to do?"

"Absolutely. Your family doesn't know me, has never seen me before. I'll keep far enough away so they won't need to have anything to do with me, but close enough so I can keep watch over them, in your absence. That way, if they do happen to see me, they won't know what I am, or that we knew each other."

"I... I don't know what to say. Thank you Jean-Philippe. Thank you so much."

"Don't mention it. I've always wanted to see the central plateau region."

I reached out and hugged him. I've never hugged any man before, not even my papa when he was still alive. But I felt compelled to at that moment, and doing so felt good, right. Jean-Philippe patted me on the back.

When I pulled back, I said, "You know I would take your place in a heartbeat, but it would be too risky. If they ever saw me, or came over for some reason..."

"You don't have to explain to me, I understand. But there is a small catch."

"Excuse me?"

"I've never had many friends during my life. I consider you one, a good one, though we've only known each other a short time. It would be a shame to waste that. How about I make you a deal?"

"Always the gambler," I said.

Jean-Philippe nodded. "When your family are gone, made that final journey to Guinée, I want to come for you and bring you back home, to Haiti."

"What? Now you sound like the crazy one."

"Please, let me do this. I want to look out for your family, but once that is over, I'll have nothing in my life again. Besides, wouldn't you like to know? Wouldn't you like to come back and be with your girls, finally, forever?"

I looked down to the wet earth. "Yes," I said. "There would be nothing more in this world that I would like."

"Then it's settled. I promise to look after your girls, and once that is done, I'll come for you."

I looked back up. "But how will you find me? That could very well be a long, long time from now."

"I'll find you. Somehow, I'll find you. Even if it takes me fifty years searching all over America, I'll find you."

We clasped each other's hand. "Thank you," I said.

"Of course, if I never show up, you know something has happened to me. But I'll try my hardest to get to you."

"I know you will."

"Well, time is clicking on. You should get going if you're to make it to Le Cap and on a boat by dawn."

I nodded. We unclasped our hands.

Just before we parted company, I told Jean-Philippe the route I took to get from my village to the plantation—or as best I could remember, considering the state I was in—and where my tiny habitation was in relation to Pignon. Lastly, I explained in greater detail about what my three girls looked like; but, being that they were the only three females living together in the area, they shouldn't be too hard to find.

With that, Jean-Philippe headed south, down another mountain path, off, hopefully, to look after my dear girls and keep them safe.

I watched him vanish into the thick night, wondered when, if at all, I would see him again, and then I turned and continued east down the path.

I soon reached the plains and began the long journey across the sparsely populated rice fields and coffee plantations, staying close to the bay and as far from any huts and villages as possible.

But soon the villages grew more frequent and I had to leave the coast and venture more inland. I came upon a road, a major piece of construction that I was sure the marines used frequently. Figuring it led right to Le Cap, I stayed near the road, while still remaining as much as I could in the fields.

Finally, the frequent but still individual villages became one great sea of huts. I had never seen so vast an array before, differing in size and shape, color, and even ones with metal roofs instead of straw thatched.

I was heading into Le Cap, and I knew things were going to get rough.

I followed the road through endless tin-roofed shacks and double-storied buildings. Though it was dark, and dimly lit, I was still overwhelmed by the sheer number of buildings, all side-by side, like a crowd of thousands standing shoulder-to-shoulder. Prior to this, the biggest town I had ever been in was Pignon; but that was a leaf compared to the massive Mapou tree that was Le Cap. It wasn't even that I could see the expanse of buildings too well—but I could feel them, could smell the stench of thousands upon thousands of people living in this cramped sea of habitation.

The more I walked, the better I felt about getting out of Haiti. The narrow road and even narrower side streets were quiet and dark. I imagined the port being this dark and quiet; I pictured lonely ships waiting in the harbor, and me just hopping on one and waiting below, until it set sail to America.

Pure fantasy, I know that now, and even as I made my way through the modern city, I think I knew, deep down, it wasn't going to be as easy as that—but I could hope.

Smells overwhelmed me as much as the view: rotting fruit, fish, effluent. It was a thousand-fold here compared with a small town like Pignon.

I hardly saw anyone as I made my way towards the city proper—just a few shady figures lingering in doorways, probably just as wary of me as I was of them, or perhaps warier, considering my hideous appearance. Twice, a group of Gendarmerie rode past—one on horseback, the other in a jeep—but I heard them coming, so I was able to duck down a side-street, or into one of the darkened doorways before they reached me.

I was beginning to think this forest of modern living was never going to end, that I was destined to wander through this dark wasteland forever. I started to worry that I was lost, that by following this main road, rather than leading me to the port, it was leading me round and round in circles.

But then the smell of fish started to grow stronger, as did the aroma of coffee roasting, and the lamp-light grew more frequent and suddenly I was at the center of chaos, and I knew I had made it to the city of Le Cap.

The noise and lights and smells assaulted my senses. Even though it must've been the early hours of the morning, there were people everywhere—mostly Americans—but also Mulattos and blacks wearing uniform. I immediately felt too conspicuous. I was sure the moment these people set their sights on me, they would know I was a zombi, one of the walking dead, an unholy abomination.

So I kept my eyes down and as I continued walking, past brightly lit hotels, dark churches, and noisy cafés, hoping they would see my ratty clothes and mistake me for just another peasant.

But I began hearing shouting, directed at me, and though I didn't know what the words meant at the time, I still knew that "Gook" and "Nigger" weren't cheers of greeting.

I passed groups of drunken marines with girls on both arms, sullen looking gendarme soldiers, and even sadder local peasants.

Finally, with the noise and the lights all around me, disorientating me even further, I had to admit to myself I was lost. I could smell the ocean, was sure that if all the noise was suddenly shut off, that I would be able to hear it, but there were too many side-streets, and I feared one wrong turn and I'd never make it out of this metropolis.

So when I spotted a lone gendarme soldier, idly watching the goings on, I decided to ask him for directions. I only prayed he wouldn't notice my glassy eyes and unmoving chest. I shuffled up to him and asked in Creole, "Excuse me sir, which way to the port?"

The Haitian gendarme barely looked at me when he pointed and said, "Straight down this street. You can take any street in this area running in that direction, and you'll end up at the water."

"Really?"

"Yes. Just keep going straight. You can't miss it."

"Thank you, sir," I said and turned and started down the street.

"Hey, wait."

I stopped, and turning around, I feared the worst—like his rifle pointed at my head. "Yes?"

"How did you get like that, old man?"

I gave the first answer that came to mind. "Got into a fight with a stubborn donkey—the donkey won."

The gendarme man frowned. "Ouch," he said, then turned away.

Relieved, I started up the narrow street.

As I walked, the double-story terraced buildings towering over me on all sides, I thought about how I was going to get onto a cargo ship bound for America.

Again I thought of the gun in my pocket. It had no bullets, but no one else knew that. I wasn't a violent person by nature, not even very confrontational, but the more I thought about the situation, the more it seemed the only way.

Until I came across a drunken marine lying by the side of the street.

The thing about Americans, is that they drink a little and almost always get drunk; whereas Haitians are always drinking but rarely get drunk. It was at that moment I was glad for that fact.

The marine was alone, and looked to be passed out. The building he had collapsed in front of was gently lit, but it wasn't a hotel, nor a café.

The idea came to me as I neared him and I saw a broken bottle of *Rhum Barbancourt* nearby. I thought what a waste of rum—it was the good stuff, not raw peasant clairin. Then it occurred to me; the sure way of getting aboard a ship was to pay. No Haitian could turn down an offer of money.

I looked around the darkened street.

I saw people going by on the main road above, but I couldn't see anyone walking down this street. So I ambled up to the sleeping marine, crouched and ransacked his pockets. I found a wallet, and inside fifty American dollars. I took the money, put back his wallet and straightened.

I felt bad for taking his money. I was no thief; prided myself on being a hard, honest worker, but desperate times called for desperate measures. I justified the stealing by telling myself that I needed the money more than he did. He would likely spend the money on more liquor and women; this cash was my ticket out of Haiti, and hopefully a ticket to a safer place.

I had just pocketed the money and was about to continue down the street, when a voice, American, yelled out. Being it was in

English, I didn't understand what he had said; whatever it was, it didn't sound nice.

I knew I couldn't outrun anyone, so I turned around. I saw two marines coming out of the building the marine I had stolen from was lying in front of.

One pointed to me and said something, by his tone it was accusatory, and the other suddenly turned sour and yelled something short and sharp at me—again, there was that word, "Nigger."

They came charging towards me.

I pulled the revolver from my pocket and aimed it at them.

They halted, put up their arms. I didn't know if they had forgotten to bring their guns, or had purposely left them when they went out for recreational fun. All I know is they were unarmed when I pointed my empty revolver at them. I spoke to them in my native language, and though I was sure neither could understand me, I still told them to stay where they were, don't move or else I'd shoot. I'm sure it was just a lot of rapid-fire mumbo-jumbo to them. But there was no mistaking my purpose. They nodded, said something to me, this time less angry and more reassuring. I started to back away.

When I was far enough away, when the marines were merely dim shapes in the distance, I turned and continued up the street.

At the next side-street I turned left, then right at the next, then left again. Then I ducked into a dark doorway of some two-story building. I pocketed the gun and hid there a while. I heard lots of feet pattering along the nearby streets, but whether they were marines or Gendarmerie looking for me, I couldn't say. For all I knew, the two marines I had pointed the gun at had simply turned, headed to the nearest hotel and drank themselves silly.

Sometime later, I left the doorway, walked a little way up the narrow street and when I came to another, turned right.

Soon I found myself at another, wider road and I could see the port before me, tall palm trees swaying against a gray sky. The ocean was a dark expanse of black glass.

I could see all types of boats in the harbor; from small fishing boats to large freighters. I knew I had to find a large freighter that was taking a cargo of coffee or sugar to America. And once I found that, hopefully I could bribe my way on and stow away to lands unknown.

I still needed to be careful. The area around the port looked just as busy as the main road, and judging by the color of the sky, I didn't have long before dawn arrived and this busy port would get even busier.

So, with the money in my pocket and the gun for backup, I started across the road, heading for the..."

Once again they were interrupted. Only this time, instead of the phone, it was someone knocking at Mr. Joseph's front door.

"I wonder who that could be," Mr. Joseph said.

Toby glanced down at his watch. It was almost five-thirty. "Oh no," he gasped. "I didn't realize it was so late."

"Is there a problem?" Mr. Joseph asked as he got to his feet.

"Well..."

The knocking came again—not hard, but firm.

Mr. Joseph eyed Toby as he left the kitchen.

"Shit," Toby breathed, positive it was his mom knocking. He was tempted to sneak out the kitchen door—but he knew there was no point hiding from his mom. She'd catch up with him sooner or later.

So he followed Mr. Joseph.

He reached the front door just as Mr. Joseph eased it open. Toby heard his mom say, "Mr. Joseph, is Toby here?"

"Yes," Toby said, stepping up to the open door.

His mom stared at Toby. "Get home," she said.

"Mom..." Toby began.

"Home," she said. "I'll deal with you later."

"I'm sorry, Mrs. Fairchild, I don't quite understand..."

"I thought you would have better sense. Allowing a child into your house is one thing, but blatantly disobeying a parent is another."

"Mom..." Toby pleaded. "It's not Mr. Joseph's..."

"Has there been some misunderstanding?" Mr. Joseph said.

"I specifically told Toby he was not to come around and see you," Toby's mom said. "But I see he has disobeyed me. And I'm disappointed in you, Mr. Joseph, for allowing this to happen."

"Well I am sorry. But I thought we agreed yesterday...?"

"We agreed on nothing," his mom said. "You told me your opinion on the matter, I politely listened, but we never agreed on anything. It was my decision to make, and I made it."

"Mom, stop it," Toby said. "This is my fault, okay? Not Mr. Joseph's. I told him you said it was okay, that it was my decision. I heard you and Mr. Joseph yesterday. Well, you never asked me what I thought about all this, just told me what to do like you always do. Well I'm sick of it, I'm sick of everyone telling me what to do all the time."

"You eavesdropped on our conversation?"

"Yeah, so?" Toby said.

"Toby, I'm very disappointed in you."

"The feeling's mutual"

"Toby!"

"Toby, I think you'd best go on home and discuss this with your mother."

"Why?" Toby said, looking up at Mr. Joseph. "She won't listen. Nobody listens, nobody except you. But I'm not allowed to see you. Damn it, it's not fair!"

"Toby!" his mom said. Then, to Mr. Joseph, "I'm sorry he lied to you, and I'm sorry for accusing you..."

"Oh, shut up," Toby barked. "You couldn't care less about Mr. Joseph's feelings, or mine."

His mom stood staring at Toby, eyes wide, mouth agape.

"Toby, that's no way to speak to your mother."

"Yes, you just wait till your father..."

"Screw him, and screw you. Screw everyone!" Toby pushed past Mr. Joseph, past his mom, rushed down the porch steps, across the lawn and stalked off down the street, his mom's cries washing over him like the tears flowing down his face.

Why can't everyone just leave me alone? Just let me live my life? I'm not hurting anyone, Mr. Joseph's not hurting anyone. Jesus how did things get so screwed up?

He walked blindly, unsure of where he was going, not wanting to face home, his parents and their accusations and disappointed stares. The way he was feeling at the moment he never wanted to go home again, he just wanted to leave Belford and wander around the country, like Mr. Joseph, moving from town to town whenever he grew tired of the place or the people.

I need to speak to Gloria, that's what I need to do.

He changed direction and soon he arrived at Gloria's, hoping that her mom would allow him to talk to Gloria, even if just for ten minutes.

At the front door, he rang the doorbell and waited. He brushed tears from his eyes, took some deep breaths.

Please, Gloria answer the door. God please let Gloria...

The door opened and Deb stood there, tight halter straining to contain her breasts, jeans fitting snugly around her curvaceous body. "Well, looky who it is," she said, gum-smacking mouth curving into a grin. "What the hell do you want, there's no creepy old men here to give you candy... or dead chickens." She cackled.

"I just want to speak with Gloria," Toby said.

"Gloria? Gee, I'm sorry, but I thought my parents banned your sorry ass from seeing her. Something about you being too pathetic for their little princess."

Toby snapped. "Fuck you, you slut. This is all your fault! You were the one who spread the gossip about me and Mr. Joseph. If you had kept your dick-sucking mouth shut, I wouldn't be in this mess!

"You little shit," Deb cried. "How dare you talk to me like that. If Dwayne were here, he'd beat your skinny ass to a pulp." She reached into her mouth, took out her gum and threw it at Toby.

The grape-flavored piece of gum smacked Toby on the cheek, leaving a wet spot.

"Get the fuck outta here, you weird chicken-fucking geek. Go on, get!"

"What's all this yelling...?" The moment Rudy Mayfour laid eyes on Toby, his face grew hard, his chest puffed out and he grew about two inches taller. "Toby, is there something I can...?"

"He called me a slut," Deb said, pouting like the actress she was.

Rudy glared at Toby. "You what?"

"Look, all I want is to speak to Gloria, just for a moment. Please, it's important."

"You called my daughter a slut?" Rudy, nostrils flaring, looked ready to tear the door apart.

"Rudy, what's going on?" Helen appeared at the door. "Oh, Toby. Look, if you're here to see Gloria, she's not in."

"Bullshit, she isn't," he said, and then, right on cue, he heard Gloria call down, "Mom, Dad, what's going on?"

"Get out of here you little shit," Rudy said. "I don't want you anywhere near my daughter, got me?"

Toby couldn't help himself. "You don't have to worry, Mr. Mayfour; I wouldn't touch Deb with a fifty-foot pole."

"Why you..."

"Rudy, no," Helen said, grabbing her husband by the arm.

Toby took off, not wanting to find out whether Helen's grip was as strong as Rudy's temper.

Though he desperately wanted to see Gloria, he knew there was no way on God's green hell that was going to happen now—not tonight, not next week; he'd probably blown any chance of seeing Gloria again until she was old enough to leave home, in about four years.

Fuck! he screamed in his head. *Why is this happening to me?*

He jogged for about five minutes, until his legs started hurting and his lungs and ribs started aching. He stopped, convinced Rudy wasn't following, baseball bat in hand, and sat on the curb, gasping for air. Then he put his head between his legs and cried good and hard.

Once he had spilled all his frustrations, anger, and embarrassment of the last few days, he wiped his puffy eyes and got to his feet.

He took some deep breaths and wondered, *Where to now?*

He still couldn't face home, and he didn't fancy wandering around town for hours.

Go back and apologize to the Mayfours? Maybe they would let me see Gloria if I explained to them...

Who am I kidding? Rudy's probably already put a bounty on my head. Forget them, I've got nothing to be sorry about.

And then Toby had a thought—what if he went and talked to Frankie? There was nothing stopping him. He might feel silly talking to a hunk of rock and earth, but isn't that why people buried their loved ones and erected headstones, so they had somewhere to go and talk to them if they needed to?

Toby started off for the cemetery.

By the time he reached Belford Cemetery, a mild breeze had sprung up.

He made his way through the maze of headstones, finally arriving at Frankie's grave. He sat beside it, hugging his knees to his chest.

"Hey Frankie," he said. "Me again. Yeah, I've been crying. Yeah, I know, I'm a big pansy. But fuck it, I don't care anymore." He stopped, feeling strange talking to himself. Luckily the cemetery seemed to be empty. Still, when he talked, it was barely louder than a whisper.

"I didn't get to talk to you properly before, Gloria being with me and all. But I need to talk to you now. A lot has happened since I was last here—some things you wouldn't believe. Man, where to begin? Okay, well, I guess the biggest thing is that I found out something incredible about Mr. Joseph. Yeah, I know what you thought about him, and you would've had a field day with this, but here it goes—Mr. Joseph is a zombi. Yep, the real-deal, the living dead. Now, I know what you're thinking, but it's not like in the movies. It's kinda complex, but basically, he's what's known as a zombi savane, that means he was turned into a zombi, but sort of brought out of it, kinda like he was brought out of a trance. He's still dead and all, but he can talk and think and feel. You see it has to do with vodou and Haiti and working on a slave plantation—like I said, it's very complex. He's been telling me about how he came to be a zombi, what it was like to actually be one, when he worked as a slave, what it was like to awaken—all kinds of stuff you wouldn't believe. I hardly believe it myself. I mean, can you imagine if anyone in this town ever found out the truth about him? I only found out by accident, and, well, I was close to telling either the police or my parents, but in the end I decided not to. He did save my life and all. I can guess what you're thinking, but I'm not crazy. He's not some flesh-eating monster, that's all bull. He's perfectly harmless. Still, I almost went bug-fuck crazy trying to decide what to do about it. I'm glad I didn't tell anyone, though."

He paused, taking some much-needed breaths.

"But anyway, that's not what I came here to tell you; well, not really. Everything's gone screwy; ever since you... well, ever since that night, nothing has felt right. I think you dying unbalanced the world or something. Things were going good between me and Gloria, we've kissed and... well, I'm not telling you everything. Some things a guy's gotta keep to himself, you know? But then her stupid sister overhears me telling Gloria about me befriending Mr. Joseph, and she spreads it all over town. And so now everyone's laughing at me, prank-calling me, and they're doing the same to Mr. Joseph. But that's not the worst of it. Because of all that, my parents think it's best I don't see Mr. Joseph. Even Gloria's parents have stopped us from seeing each other. That sucks the biggest. I mean, I'm not doing anything wrong, yet I've been told I'm not allowed to see Gloria or Mr. Joseph. Life sucks, but then you already know that."

Toby lay down on the ground, gazing up at Taylor's Hill in the distance.

"I don't know what to do," he continued. "You're gone, my parents don't listen, and the only two people left I can talk to have been taken away from me. I don't have any friends left, not really. Shit, Frankie, I feel so alone."

Afterwards, he lay with his eyes closed, until sometime later a voice broke the silence.

"Toby."

Toby gasped, sat up. He turned and gazed up at Suzie. Wearing creased tracksuit pants and an old, faded T-shirt, she looked haggard; still her face retained some of the old Suzie, some of the kindness he knew and loved so well.

"Your mom called, she was worried about you," Suzie said. "I told her I thought you'd be here. I guess I was right."

Toby turned back and faced Frankie's headstone.

A shadow passed over him, and then Suzie sat on the ground beside him. "It's peaceful here, isn't it? I often come here, sit and talk to Franklin. I feel closest to him here."

Toby chewed on his bottom lip, fighting the urge to cry.

"Your mom told me what happened."

"Yeah, I bet she did," Toby muttered.

"I'm not here to argue, or to pass judgment. I'm just here to see if you're okay."

Toby lost the battle. Tears fell from his eyes.

"And to say sorry. I know I haven't been the best company of late, I know what I said hurt you, and the way I acted... well, you shouldn't have to see that."

Toby swiped tears from his cheeks.

"I hardly know what day it is, I never see Leah anymore, God knows what she's getting into." Suzie sighed. "But I haven't come here to tell you all of my problems..."

"Didn't stop you before," Toby said, managing a weak smile.

Suzie chuckled. "No, I don't suppose it did. Still, I want us to be friends again. I'll try and get better, stop the drinking, if you promise not to be too angry at your mom. Deal?"

Toby turned to Suzie. "You're a sly one, you know that?"

Suzie grinned. "Think Frankie would've been proud?"

"I'm sure."

"So, deal?"

Toby sighed heavily. "Okay, deal."

"Your mom just loves and cares about you, that's all. We all know how overprotective she can be. She doesn't mean any harm."

"You agree with her about Mr. Joseph?"

"Honestly? No. And I told her as much. I know you're a tough kid—sensitive, but tough. And I also know you're smart. I'm pretty sure you know what you're doing most of the time."

"Gee, thanks."

Suzie reached over and patted him on the arm.

"I just wish my mom would see it that way. She thinks I'm just some dumb little kid who can't think for himself."

"You have to understand. Mothers are programmed to think that way. I'm sure Einstein's mom thought her son needed help tying his own shoelaces, and I'm sure Bruce Lee's mother gave him an extra bag of lunch, just in case the bullies took one of them."

Toby shook his head. "You're nuts, you know that?"

"And proud of it. You have to understand, I can see how incredibly brilliant and mature and handsome and tough you are—

your mom only sees how handsome you are, and that's it. In her mind, you'll always be five years old."

"That's silly."

"It's the law. I can't change the law."

"But how can I convince her that stopping me from seeing Mr. Joseph won't help things? I like spending time with him. I know it's going to be hard, but so what? If Mr. Joseph can deal with all the teasing and pranks, so can I."

"I'll have another talk with your mom, see if I can't break the law, just this once."

"Yeah?"

"Yeah."

"Thanks. Now can you please convince Gloria's mom to let us see each other, too?"

"Eh, I'm afraid you're on your own on that one. Rudy scares even me."

"Yeah, tell me about it."

"Why, what happened?" Suzie said.

"Well, I kinda pissed Rudy off earlier. And Helen and Deb."

Suzie looked at Toby with a sly grin. "What did you do, Tobes?"

"I called Deb a slut, and told Rudy I wouldn't touch her with a fifty-foot pole."

Suzie laughed, and it sent birds scattering from the trees, into the air. "Holy shit, Tobes, I would've loved to have seen Rudy's face when you said that." She slapped him on the back. "I'm proud of you. But don't tell anyone I said that."

"I kinda felt bad afterwards. I was mostly angry at my mom, but still, they wouldn't even let me see Gloria for five minutes."

"Sounds like they got what they deserved. I love Gloria, I think she's the sweetest kid, but as for the rest of the Mayfour clan..."

"Yeah, sometimes I think that maybe Gloria's adopted."

Suzie reached over and took a hold of Toby's hand. "So, friends again?"

Toby liked the feel of Suzie's touch; it felt... familiar. "Yeah, friends"

"Good. Now, I don't know about you, but I'm starting to get hungry. What say you come back to my place and I cook us some Spaghetti Bolognese?"

Toby hesitated.

"I promise I won't drink. And I've got plenty of Coke stacked in the fridge."

Toby nodded. "You said the magic word."

Suzie smiled and, letting go of Toby's hand, got to her feet. "You can call your mom from my place, let her know you're staying for dinner."

Toby made a face as he got to his feet.

"Or... I could call her for you."

"That sounds better."

"Okay, but you know you're gonna have to face them eventually."

"I know, but I'd rather it be later."

"Putting off the inevitable. Good to see you picked up some bad habits from Franklin."

Toby smiled. Looking down at Frankie's grave, he said, "Well, thanks for listening, Frankie. I'll be seeing you around, and remember, don't tell anyone what I told you. If you do, I'll tell everyone you cried at the end of *Titanic*."

"Frankie cried at the end of *Titanic*?" Suzie said, her smile widening. "My Frankie?"

"Yep. Like a baby. Of course, he said it was because he had something in his eye."

Suzie blew a kiss at the grave. "See you tomorrow, my love."

As they left Frankie's grave and walked towards the entrance, Suzie said, "So, what did you tell Franklin that you don't want anyone to know?"

"Oh, um, you know, just guy stuff."

"I see. So, *Titanic*, huh? Not even I cried at the end of *Titanic*." She paused, said, "Well, maybe a few tears. But I'm allowed. I'm a girl."

"So was Frankie."

They both laughed, and it felt good, like old times.

Suzie held true to her promise. She didn't touch a drop of alcohol for the entire night, which meant, rather than Toby's parents having to come and pick him up, Suzie was able to drive him home (Suzie wouldn't let him walk home alone, which was fine by him—he was much too full of spaghetti).

And being inside Suzie's house wasn't so bad this time—it still felt strange being there, no longer the familiar, comfortable house he knew and loved, but it was bearable, he didn't feel as claustrophobic and overwhelmed with sadness like the previous visit.

As they neared Toby's house, the sight of a police car parked outside his house sent waves of panic through his body. "Oh my God," he breathed.

"Relax, hon, I'm sure it's nothing serious," Suzie said.

Toby's heart pounded; he feared the worst. "Sure, there's always police in front of my house at ten o'clock on a Wednesday."

Suzie pulled her car up to the curb opposite his house, and Toby was out and hurrying across the street before she had turned off the engine. Neighbors were scattered about the street, on lawns, but Toby barely noticed them as he rushed up to the open front door.

"Mom? Dad?" he called, panic shaking his voice, and he was never so glad to hear his mom's voice when she said, "In the kitchen."

Toby hurried through the house and when he entered the kitchen, saw both his parents. His dad was standing near the kitchen table, talking to two uniformed cops, a male and a female. His mom, sitting at the table, got up and walked over when she saw Toby, a worried look on her face.

"What's going on?" Toby panted.

"That's some broken window," Suzie said, coming into the kitchen.

"Huh? Broken window?" Toby breathed.

"Someone threw a rock through our front window," his mom said.

"Oh," Toby said, relieved it was nothing serious, but also concerned that both his parents' faces appeared more worried than what a broken window warranted. "No one was hurt?"

"No, thank God. Dad was in the kitchen doing the dishes, I was reading in the bedroom."

"Must've given you two one hell of a fright."

His mom looked at Suzie and nodded. "You better believe it. Say, thanks for driving Toby home."

"Don't mention it. Anything I can do?"

"No. The police have already taken my statement. They're almost finished taking David's."

Toby looked over at his dad; he looked tired, and fed-up.

"What else happened?" Toby said, turning back to his mom.

"Hmm?"

"You both look too anxious for just a rock through the window."

"It was scary, Toby. Someone actually threw a rock through..."

"We're about done here," the female police officer said.

"This is Toby, my son."

The police officer, twenty-something, brunette, fairly attractive, said, "Hi there. I don't suppose you have any idea who might've done this?"

Toby swallowed. "Um, no, not really."

"Not really?"

"Well, it could've been anyone. A lot of kids have it in for me at the moment."

The officer frowned. "Why is that?"

Toby sighed. Did he really have to get into it now?

"He's friends with someone who isn't very well liked in town. Some of the kids have taken offense to that," his mom said.

"Oh, okay." The officer obviously wasn't a local. "Well, we'll take the rock and note, see if we can get anything from them. But I wouldn't hold my breath."

"Note?" Toby said to the officer.

"Yes, there was a note attached to the rock."

"What did it say?"

The officer glanced at Toby's mom. "Well, maybe I'll leave it up to your parents to tell you, if they think it's appropriate. Now, we'll interview the neighbors, see if anyone saw anything. But other than that, I'm afraid there's not a lot else we can do."

"I understand," his mom said. "Thank you officer."

The woman nodded, and then walked over to her partner—Toby recognized him as the young man from the other day, Officer Reilly—who was still talking with Toby's dad.

"A note?" Toby said, turning to his mom. "I knew there was something else going on."

"Told ya, he's a smart kid," Suzie said.

"We'll talk about it later," his mom said.

"Well, I'll get out of your hair," Suzie said. "I had a good night, Toby. Thanks for the company."

Toby nodded. "Yeah, me too. Thanks for dinner."

"You're most welcome. Nancy, call if there's anything you need."

"I will. Thanks."

The moment Suzie left, Toby turned to his mom. "So what did the note...?"

"Later," she reiterated.

With a sigh, Toby headed into the family room. Glass littered the carpet under the window, the curtains fluttered gently with the breeze.

Toby went outside to get a better look at the broken window. The hole was big, bigger than when Frankie and Warrick had thrown rocks through Mr. Joseph's windows.

While Toby stood looking at the broken window, the officers, followed by his parents, came outside. "If we find out anything, we'll be sure to let you know," the female officer said.

"Okay, thank you officers," Toby's dad said.

"Yes, thank you," his mom said.

"We're sorry about the inconvenience," Officer Reilly told them. "Goodnight."

The officers turned left and began their door-knocking at the Weisenburn's. There was still a number of neighbors milling about, watching the proceedings, including, Toby noticed, Mr. Joseph. The old man was standing by his front door, and though the porch light was off, the hallway light cast a dim glow on his form. "I'll be back in a minute," Toby told his parents.

"Where are you going?" his mom said.

"To speak to Mr. Joseph. Now, don't have a fit, I won't be long. I just want to apologize for earlier and tell him what happened."

"He'll find out when he speaks to the police."

"Nancy," his dad said. "Let him go." To Toby: "But don't be long."

Toby sighed, nodded, then crossed the street. He felt the wandering gaze of the neighbors following him as he walked over to Mr. Joseph's.

"Bonswa," Mr. Joseph said as Toby walked up the porch steps.

"Hey," Toby said, joining Mr. Joseph on the porch. "Someone threw a rock through our window."

"I'm sorry to hear. I hope nobody was hurt?"

"No. Apparently there was a note, but my parents won't tell me what it said. Typical."

"Hmmm," Mr. Joseph said.

"Look," Toby said, finding it difficult to see Mr. Joseph in the darkness. "I'm sorry about lying to you. It's just, well, I thought my parents were being unfair, and I didn't like being told who I could and couldn't see. But, I shouldn't have lied."

"I appreciate you coming over and apologizing. I was worried when you ran off like that, so was your mom. We had another chat after you left, and we agreed that, for the moment, maybe it's best you don't come around anymore."

"What? Are you serious?"

"Yes. Your mother doesn't want you spending time at my place, and whether or not I agree with her is beside the point. I need to obey your parents' wishes, and you should too."

Disappointed, Toby said, "Okay, whatever."

"I don't like the situation any more than you do, but that's the way I feel. Please respect that."

"Sure," Toby said.

"Good. Now, you'd best get back, Toby. Goodnight."

"I guess I'll see you around, then?"

"I guess," Mr. Joseph said, and then he walked inside and closed the door.

Toby sauntered back home, head down.

His parents were in the kitchen, sitting at the table, both clutching glasses of whiskey. "You'll be happy to know that Mr. Joseph thinks it's best if I no longer come over. You guys got what you wanted."

"Toby..." his mom said. "Sit down, let's talk."

"Not until you tell me what was in that letter."

"I will, if you tell me why I got an angry phone call tonight from Mrs. Mayfour, accusing you of abusing Deb."

"I didn't abuse her," Toby huffed. "I called her a slut, that's all."

His dad hiccupped, though it sounded suspiciously like a laugh.

"Toby, I'm ashamed of you. Why would you say such a thing?"

"Because it's true. She's the one who spread the gossip about me and Mr. Joseph around town. This is all her fault."

The fire in his mom's eyes faded. "Oh. Still, you shouldn't have called her that. I want you to call Mrs. Mayfour tomorrow and apologize."

"Okay," Toby sighed. "So what was in the letter?"

His mom sipped some whiskey. "Are you sure you don't want to have a seat?"

"I'm fine standing."

His mom took a deep, shaky breath. "Well it wasn't a note as such, just a piece of paper stuck to the rock. It said... watch your back, nigger lover." His mom took another sip.

"You don't have any idea who may have done this?" his dad asked.

Toby gritted his teeth. "No," he said, then turned to leave.

"Toby."

He glanced over his shoulder.

"This is the right thing to do," his mom said. "One day you'll understand that we're only doing this to look out for you. Because we love you."

Toby shifted his gaze from his mom, to his dad. They looked like strangers under the harsh glow of the kitchen light. Without a word, he turned and headed upstairs.

CHAPTER SIXTEEN

For the next couple of days, Toby did as everyone wanted and stayed away from Mr. Joseph. And, like always, Mr. Joseph stayed mostly out of sight; it was like he didn't exist.

The cops never found out who threw the rock and left the note. Even though Toby was certain he knew who was behind it, he didn't say anything. After all, he hadn't been home at the time, so he had no proof it was Dwayne. So, like the graffiti, it looked like Dwayne was going to get away with it.

But he won't get away with it forever, Toby found himself thinking. *No, he'll get his. One of these days, somehow, he'll get his.*

Gloria called once, briefly, to see how he was doing, and to tell him that she was sorry about what happened the other night at her house. She told him she missed him, but that it didn't look like her parents were going to change their minds about their relationship anytime soon (despite Toby calling and apologizing to Mrs. Mayfour about his behavior). The call added to his already gloomy disposition, but it was still good to hear Gloria's voice.

The pranks and the teasing started to ease—he still got the occasional strange look and chicken squawk directed at him, but otherwise, it seemed people were starting to get bored with the whole thing. Maybe his mom was right, after all. Maybe staying away had been for the best. Maybe he could even start going around and seeing Mr. Joseph again.

But then, three days after the rock was hurled through his window, as he was heading to Barb's to buy some groceries for his mom, Toby happened a glance at Mr. Joseph's. He stopped. Frowned.

"Now that's weird," he muttered.

Standing on the sidewalk opposite Mr. Joseph's, looking down the side of his house, Toby could see a small section of the backyard, including some of the shed. Toby knew Mr. Joseph always kept his shed locked; but the doors were presently hanging askew.

Toby crossed the street. He didn't care that he was supposed to stay away. He knew something was wrong, he had to check it out.

Toby hurried down the side of the house, and when he reached the backyard, stepped over to the shed.

He stopped by the open door. A stench like a public toilet wafted out. Nervously, he gazed in. "Oh Jesus."

The items that had sat on the altar now littered the floor, most of them smashed. The wooden cross itself lay broken. The strange, though strangely beautiful paintings that adorned the walls were now defiled by spray paint—COXSUCKING NIGGA CHILD MOLESTA was written on all three walls. And the wooden center-post was split in half, its top portion lying on the ground, over a smeared flour-drawn vèvè.

Toby turned away from the ruined hounfor and headed for the back door. He knocked, got no answer, tried the knob and found the door unlocked. He pushed it open and stepped inside. Except for an empty bottle of white rum sitting on the table, the kitchen was empty. "Mr. Joseph? It's Toby."

"In here," came the faint reply.

Toby followed the direction of Mr. Joseph's voice, through the family room, down the hall, and into the front room.

Mr. Joseph was hunched over a single bed. He was delicately folding clothes into an open suitcase.

"What are you doing?" Toby said.

"You shouldn't be here," Mr. Joseph said. He sounded tired, weak—old.

"Screw that. What are you doing?"

"It's time to go," the old man answered without turning around.

"Go? What do you mean? You're leaving?"

"Yes."

Done folding the clothes, Mr. Joseph faced Toby. The old man had told Toby he couldn't grow older, but standing there in the small, almost vacant room, Mr. Joseph looked at least ten years older. "I take it you saw my hounfor?"

Toby nodded. "I'm sorry."

Mr. Joseph's mouth twitched. "I was lying in here, resting on the bed, when I heard a noise outside. By the time I made it to the shed, the vandals had gone, though I did hear a car speeding off." He shook his head.

"But... but you can't leave. You haven't finished your story. I want to hear the rest of it."

"Oh Monsieur Fairchild. There's not much more to tell. I've told you what you needed to hear; the rest isn't that interesting. I bribed my way onto a ship and stowed away to America. The next ninety years after that followed basically the same pattern—working at menial farm or cleaning jobs, renting houses or apartments until it was time to move onto the next place. I only came here because I noticed, on the bus ride to somewhere else, that a nearby farm needed a farmhand. So I rented a house in town, the cheapest one I could afford, and I've been here ever since. I worked at the farm for over ten years, and then when the owner died, Mrs. Stein was kind enough to give me a part-time job at her store. The end."

"Where will you go?"

Mr. Joseph paused. "I don't know. But it's getting too dangerous here. You already know about me, and with everything that's been going on, it won't be long before someone else finds out. I have to leave Belford. Like I said, it's time to go." Mr. Joseph shuffled over to the open cupboard and took down some more shirts.

Toby swallowed. He felt betrayed yet again. "Were you even going to say goodbye?"

Mr. Joseph paused, shirts cradled in his arms. "Truthfully? No. I thought it would be easier that way. I was going to leave you a note." He dropped the shirts into the suitcase. "Cowardly of me, I know. You deserve better than that."

"When are you going?"

"Tonight. I've settled all my affairs. There's nothing left for me here. But I want to wait for the cover of darkness. I've always felt safer at night."

Toby didn't know what else to say.

"You had better go, Toby."

Toby nodded, was out the bedroom door, when Mr. Joseph said, "Toby, wait."

Toby turned around.

Mr. Joseph closed his eyes. Kept them closed for a long time. Finally, he opened them. "I know I shouldn't be asking you this, but... can you come around tonight, after your parents are asleep?"

Toby frowned. "Um, yeah, why?"

"There are some things I need to tell you. Important things. I was going to write them in the letter, but... well, they're too important for that. Can you meet me in the shed at, say, one o'clock? Could you do that for me? I don't like encouraging you to disobey your parents, but I have to this once. You know I wouldn't ask if I didn't think it was important."

"I'll be here," Toby said.

"Good," said Mr. Joseph. "Good."

It was nearing one o'clock in the morning.

Nerves danced around in Toby's gut. What did Mr. Joseph have to tell him? What was so important that he would ask Toby to not only deliberately go against his parents' wishes of not seeing him, but to meet in the dead of night?

When the numbers on the digital clock clicked over to 12:55, Toby hopped out of bed.

Though his parents had gone to bed over an hour ago, Toby maintained stealth as he slipped on his T-shirt and shorts and crept downstairs.

Like a replay of the night Toby found out the truth about his neighbor, Toby slipped through the kitchen, out the back door and into the cover of night.

It was an intensely clear, starry night, with hardly a breath of wind—the kind of night that made you realize how truly small you were in the scheme of things, how mammoth the earth and beyond was.

Toby's sneakers squeaked as he crossed the street. When he arrived at Mr. Joseph's house, he stepped onto the straw-like grass and started down the side, towards the backyard. The kitchen window curtain was drawn, a light glowed within. As he reached the backyard, he noticed light inside the shed as well, shining from beneath the door. He heard muttering coming from inside the shed. Toby headed towards it, winding around the piles of junk.

At the shed, he raised a hand to knock, but he paused.

What if it isn't Mr. Joseph in there?

Toby didn't know why he would think such a thing.

Who else would it be?

Toby rapped gently on the door. "Mr. Joseph?" he whispered. "It's Toby."

"Come in."

Toby turned the handle and pulled open the door.

Mr. Joseph was sitting cross-legged on the ground.

Toby stepped into the make-shift hounfor, closing the door behind him. There was no longer the stench of urine and excrement, but a rich, smoky aroma of incense. The temple had been cleaned, though it was now a lot emptier than when Toby had first seen it. The graffiti on the wall was still there, and the center-post was still broken.

Toby gazed down at Mr. Joseph. His eyes were closed, there was a half-empty bottle of *Rhum Barbancourt* beside him. Toby waited for instruction, but when a minute ticked by without any, Toby shrugged and sat on the ground opposite Mr. Joseph.

"Guédé Nimbo, behind the cross... Today I am troubled... call Guédé... I am troubled," the old man sung. He opened his eyes. "Remember when I told you about the Guédé, about how they are the spirits of the dead? That Guédé Nimbo is the master of the cemetery and is a special protector of the children?"

Toby nodded.

"He is a powerful loa, Toby. He can be mischievous, even crude, but when you ask him for help, he will grant you your wish, though at a price. I never told you the whole truth about the night of the attack. I never told anyone. I want to tell you the truth now."

Staring at the twisted, scarred zombi sitting opposite, Toby felt the air sucked from his lungs. Tears stung his eyes. "What truth?"

"When I found you that night, you were badly injured. Very badly injured. I don't know how you managed to stumble from the field to your street, the way you were hurt. You were close to death. You would've died, of that I'm sure, if I hadn't found you when I did."

"Yeah, I know," Toby said, mouth dry. He swallowed.

Mr. Joseph shook his head. "No, you don't. You were collapsed in the street, slipping in and out of consciousness. I knew that if I didn't attend to you straightaway, you would've died right there in the street. No ambulance would've been able to get to you in time. I didn't go straight to your parents like everyone thinks. I took you here, into my hounfor. I laid you on the ground, under the post, and invoked Guédé Nimbo for help. I asked him to save you. I pleaded with him to let you live, and to look after you. Well, he came to me. Though I didn't have time to procure all the traditional offerings, he came. He knows me well, Toby, because his brother, Baron Lakwa, is responsible for supervising all zombis, and his father, Baron Samedi—the head of all the Guédé—presides over the dead. It is the Baron whom the bocor must invoke and get permission from to make a zombi. So, Guédé Nimbo came and though I had no black goat to offer for sacrifice, I did have rum, and he was happy with that. He granted my request to save you. He healed your most life-threatening wounds, leaving you with some serious injuries and some not-so-serious; for he knew that healing you fully would've looked too suspicious. After the Guédé helped you—and helped himself to my rum—I placed you back in the street and then went to your parents."

Mr. Joseph looked at Toby. His glassy stare was penetrating. "You understand, Monsieur Fairchild?"

Toby nodded.

No wonder this shed felt familiar that day, Toby thought.

"You're saying I was saved by a spirit?"

Mr. Joseph nodded. "The Guédé is in you, protecting you, looking after you, making sure you find peace. I wanted to tell you so many times, but the time never seemed right."

Toby took a deep, quivering breath. To hear how truly close he was to death, to learn that a vodou spirit had helped him—he was scarcely able to comprehend these things. "Wow," he breathed. "I guess I really do owe you my life."

"And Guédé Nimbo."

"Right. And Guédé Nimbo. So, how do I thank it... him?"

"You don't have to. He's getting what he wants, and in return he is looking after you, which is what he does." Mr. Joseph grabbed the bottle of rum and took a quick swill.

"In my dreams I've sometimes seen a strange person wearing dark sunglasses, hat and clothes. Is that...?"

"Oui," Mr. Joseph said. "Like I said, he's looking out for you. Most of the time he visits in dreams. Usually, when he wants to communicate, he'll adopt the form of a human, one close to you, like a friend or a relative. The Guédé have powers you or I can only imagine. They are as much feared in Haiti as they are loved. For instance, they can bring out the souls of the dead and use them for their service. They can send expedition morts, in which the Guédé takes the souls of the dead and sends them to enemies to seek revenge. The souls attach themselves to the person and makes them crazy. Sometimes they grow ill, and even die. Even Baron Lakwa, the idiot brother, can kill or zombify a person—for a price, of course."

"What kind of price?"

"Well, money for one thing. Or goods. If it's a poor farmer who hasn't a lot of money, he may offer the loa his produce, if the loa desires it. Alcohol is another popular offering, or the person asking the loa for a service may have to alter their lifestyle, stop smoking for instance, or... leave, if the loa feels that it's for the best."

"Is that why you're leaving? Is that what the loa asked in exchange for saving my life?"

"Well, yes. Sort of. It's complex, Toby. I believe the loa had a hand in bringing us together. I'm not saying he orchestrated things—even the most powerful loa can't do that—but he did tell me, on that fateful night, that we will have a connection. The loa don't always tell you everything; often they talk in riddles, mostly appearing in dreams and revealing only parts of the truth. Since I can't dream, I'm limited in what the loa can show me. So I don't know what it all means, why he wants me to leave, but I have to do what the loa tells me, trust that it's for the best."

"So you knew you would be leaving all this time?"

"Yes, and no. I only knew for certain a few days ago."

Toby remembered. "Is that what you were doing in the shed?"

Mr. Joseph nodded. "I invoked the loa again to see if anything could be done about our problem, and to ask advice for which course of action to take. The Guédé had already told me that time a month ago that I would have to leave soon; but when I invoked the loa a few days ago, he told me that if I want to help, if I want to put an end to all these troubles, now is the time to leave. Guédé Nimbo told me not to be scared, that things will work out. The loa said he would give me a sign when I was to leave. And that sign has come." Mr. Joseph paused to gaze around at his ruined hounfor. "I have to honor my end of the agreement. So you understand now why I have to leave?"

Toby nodded. "It doesn't seem fair, though. You save my life, and in return you have to leave."

"Like I said, it's not the loa's doing, not really. I would've left soon anyway—it was time, I think. The loa knew this. He just gave me a nudge, that's all."

It still didn't seem fair, but at least Toby understood why Mr. Joseph was leaving.

"I hope you're not too upset with me for keeping these things from you."

"No, I'm not upset."

"Good. I'm glad. I can't imagine how I would've explained all this to you in a letter. This way was much better."

Looking at the old man, Toby couldn't help but feel that Mr. Joseph was still holding some things back. He looked troubled, like he had grave concerns pressing on his mind. Did the loa show him something else, something that Mr. Joseph didn't want to, or couldn't, share?

"Maybe it's best you head home, now. I've kept you up far too late already. You need rest, Monsieur Fairchild."

"So that's it? This is goodbye?"

Mr. Joseph stared long and hard at the cold concrete floor. "Yes, I'm afraid it is." He looked up. "Goodbye, Toby."

Toby got to his feet. "Will you send me a letter when you get to wherever you're going?"

"If I can, I will. But I can't promise anything."

Toby smiled thinly; tears stained his eyes. "Thanks for everything. I... I'm gonna miss you."

"And me, you. Don't worry about me, Toby. I'll be okay. Things happen for a reason, I've always believed that. Take care of yourself, and remember, the Guédé is looking after you."

Remember...

Toby opened the shed door.

As he stepped outside, he thought he heard Mr. Joseph start to speak, but there was only silence, so Toby closed the door and headed home.

After the boy left, the old man went for a walk.

Usually he walked around aimlessly, simply intent to enjoy the freedom, of being able to go wherever he liked without fear of ridicule or staring eyes. He must've walked every inch of this town over the years, always under the cloak of darkness, always without purpose, other than the simple freedom of the act.

Not tonight.

Tonight, for his last ever walk around Belford, he had a place in mind. A goal.   As he walked, suitcase in hand, he thought of the boy and what was to come.

The old man had wanted so much to tell him everything, all of what the loa had shown him. Despite what the Guédé had said, he thought the boy deserved to know the truth, then and there, and he was so close to letting it all spill from his lips. But he kept quiet.

The boy would learn the truth in time, the loa had said. It was every person's right to be in charge of their own lives, make their own decisions, be responsible for their own actions. The boy had to make that decision, he had to learn about life and death, maturity and responsibility on his own. The old man could only take him so far—the rest was up to him.

The old man understood all that, yet he was still afraid for the boy. The Guédé had assured the old man that the boy would be okay, that he would see to it that the boy would find peace and would come to no harm.

The old man had no choice but to trust the loa—after all, they never lied. They may do things in an unorthodox manner, but they never lied. They always held true to their promise. And Guédé Nimbo was a protector of children, so the old man had to believe the Guédé would do just that.

Which brought the old man to his own promise.

When the old man had invoked the loa a month ago, the Guédé had asked him for one very important offering. Not to leave, as he had told the boy—well, that was part of it, sure, the Guédé explained to him he would need to leave in order for things to work out; but more importantly, he asked the old man to finish what had been started so long ago, in another time, in another place. Along with copious amounts of rum, that was his payment; in lieu of a black goat, he would be the sacrifice.

The old man fingered the revolver, his old master's revolver, sitting deep in his pants pocket.

Once the old man had carried out this act, only then would the boy learn the truth and finally find his peace. That was the deal.

The old man was okay with that—he wasn't scared of death, or, more accurately, no longer existing on this earth. He was simply afraid for the boy. He wanted to be here for the boy, but he knew that was not possible.

But what was possible was saving the boy from potential harm. He wanted to see the bastards responsible for the destruction of his hounfor, responsible for all the pain this past month, pay for their crimes, which was why he stopped off at the house on his way out of town.

Because when he had invoked the loa the second time, to ask for guidance, the loa had felt it fitting that the old man know the truth, the truth the boy had for so long wanted to discover, for he had become a part of the boy's life when he had saved the boy that night. And as payment for learning such secrets, the loa had told him it was time to leave; time to fulfill his end of the deal.

But not before I do this last deed.

The house was in darkness, a sleeping giant, and standing in front of it, the old man set his suitcase down.

It would be so easy, the old man knew. No one locked their doors in Belford. He just had to walk in, find the appropriate room, rest the barrel against the sleeping murderer's head, and pull the trigger.

Or maybe he would wake the murderer first, tell him that he was going to die for all the pain he had caused an innocent boy, and the needless deaths of two more. The old man liked the idea of seeing the murderer's eyes, the fear in them, before he sent the bullet home.

The old man knew it wasn't his place to carry out such a deed. He knew what the Guédé had said, but damn it, the boy needed closure, and the sooner the better, in his opinion.

He took out the gun, his grip tight on the revolver. He took a step forward. Suddenly a strong wind gushed over him, like the hand of Le Bon Dieu Himself was reaching out. The wind whispered, "Not yet; it will be done, but not by your doing," and then blew away as suddenly as it had appeared. When the old man looked down, he saw he was holding nothing but the sultry night air.

He blinked, looked down to the ground, but knew there was no point in searching—the wind hadn't knocked the gun out of his hand, it had taken it. To where, the old man could only guess.

I'm sorry, he said to the invisible wind. *I should know not to disobey you. I should learn to take my own advice*. With shoulder's slumped, he picked up his suitcase.

He took one last look at the murderer's house, spat a curse to the one spared death, and continued his journey out of town.

Now without a gun, the old man wondered how he was going to hold up his end of the deal.

The Guédé will provide, he thought.

He guessed the time wasn't right for the old man to find peace, either. It looked like the Guédé had plans for him, too.

As he started on the road out of town, he thought about where he was going to go—to the south? Back to Florida? To the west coast?

No. He had already made up his mind about where he was going.

He hadn't been honest with the boy when the boy had asked him earlier where he was going. He did know; he just didn't want to give the boy false hope, in case he never arrived.

He had thought a lot about what he and the boy had talked about during their time spent together; had given much thought to the boy's willingness to accept him, to remain loyal to him even in the face of resistance and humiliation. Certain things the boy had said to him hit home and they rolled around in his mind now as he arrived at the sign telling him he was now leaving Belford, and please, come again.

Despite his reluctance, despite his fear, he knew, as sure as if the Guédé himself had spoken to him, that it was the right thing to do.

He had to face his fears.

Thank you, the old man said to the boy.

It would be a long journey, the destination of which he may very well never reach, but he knew the boy would want him to at least try.

The old man left the town behind and was soon swallowed up by the night.

CHAPTER SEVENTEEN

Toby awoke to early morning sunlight streaming through the window.

He sat up, looked at the clock. It was just past seven.

He wiped sleep from his eyes, swung his legs out of bed and placed his feet on the carpet.

He sat there a while, feeling the emptiness in his gut.

He knew. Somehow, he just knew. Mr. Joseph was gone.

Toby stood, slipped on the shorts and shirt he had worn yesterday and sauntered downstairs, trying not to wake his parents. He downed a glass of orange juice and then headed outside.

The sun was glaring, the morning air promising another hot summer's day. He walked down Pineview and when he arrived at the old man's house, stood staring at the chipped clapboard. The people of this town had driven Mr. Joseph away, no matter what he had said about loas and destiny. The people of Belford drove away a kind old man, and Toby felt sick to his stomach at the thought.

Toby knew the house was empty, yet he felt compelled to go inside and confirm what his gut was telling him. So he trekked down to the back of the house, to the kitchen door.

He noticed the shed was closed, the door padlocked.

Toby wasn't surprised to find the back door unlocked. Nobody would ever willingly enter this house—not unless it was a teenager on a dare. Even if someone did come in unannounced, there was nothing in here worth stealing.

Toby stepped into the kitchen. It was intensely quiet, for the life that imbues a house, gives it its heartbeat, didn't exist in here. Not for twenty years. A body lived here, but not a soul.

Toby wandered through the house. The books were still here—Mr. Joseph had taken nothing with him, only his clothes and his memories.

Back in the kitchen, Toby sat down at the table. There was no bottle of rum, no goodbye note, just an old, scratched wooden table.

Toby sat there for a long time. When he was ready to go, he got up, turned towards the back door—and stopped.

One of the kitchen drawers, the top one, was slightly open.

Toby stepped towards it. He pulled the drawer fully open and gazed inside. Three items lay within. Toby picked up the first: a key. A small, boringly normal key—the kind one might use to open a shed door.

Toby pocketed the key.

He picked up the second item. This was much heavier, and much more lethal.

Turning the revolver over in his hand, Toby felt a sense of sadness sweep over him, as if all of Mr. Joseph's private pain had seeped into its wood and metal. Toby opened the chamber. Empty. He clicked the chamber back.

The last item was a box of cartridges. Toby took it out, flipped it open and tipped five brass cartridges onto his palm. He studied them for a while before tipping them back into the box. As he placed the box into his pocket, he wondered why the old man hadn't taken the gun with him. Had he simply forgotten to take it when he left? Was it too risky carrying firearms where he was going?

Or maybe he no longer needed it.

Toby liked that last thought, but he knew, as he left the house, that it was the least likely of the three.

Back home, Toby headed up to his room and from the closet, took out the shoebox. He placed the gun, key and box of cartridges inside, then placed the shoebox back and went over to his chest of drawers. He pulled open the bottom drawer, lifted the stack of comic books, and took out the sheet of paper that was hidden underneath.

His parents still asleep, he took Mr. Joseph's letter downstairs, turned on one of the gas stove burners and touched one edge of the letter to the flame. He took the flaming letter over to the sink, where he watched a man's secrets burn. When the paper had all but disintegrated, he turned on the tap and watched the ash swirl down the drain.

Now, Mr. Joseph lived only in his mind.

ONE MONTH LATER

CHAPTER EIGHTEEN

Toby awoke to the sound of a single gunshot echoing in his head.

He sat up, breathless.

It was dark, middle-of-the-night dark, and as he hopped out of bed, a sense of déjà vu washed over him.

He went to the window, pulled back the curtain and gazed down at the old house across the street.

It was bathed in darkness.

Toby heaved a deep sigh.

After a spell, he wandered back to bed, closed his eyes, and fell asleep almost immediately.

CHAPTER NINETEEN

Toby sat on his bed, waiting for Gloria to arrive.

It was a Saturday night, the last Saturday before school started on Tuesday. An end-of-summer celebration had been organized up on Taylor's Hill, similar to the one that was held at the beginning of the summer—the one Toby and Frankie never made it to.

The party was bound to be huge, the not-to-be-missed party of the summer.

And Toby was scared to death about going.

Damn it, why did I have to say yes? She'll be here any moment, and what will I do?

He stood, walked to the window and gazed down at the street. Saw only hazy shadows cast by the rows of elms. Gloria said she would sneak out of her house and be at his place at around eleven-thirty—any earlier, she said, and they'd risk getting caught (which was true; Toby's parents had only gone to bed half an hour ago). And anyway, Gloria had said, the party would only just be getting started, so there was no need to get there any earlier.

Though life in Belford had returned to almost normal since Mr. Joseph left (except for Warrick still missing), Toby was still hesitant about seeing his peers after everything that had happened. Gloria, on the phone earlier, talking about the party, organizing their late-night rendezvous, had said it would be good for him to go, that it would send a message to everyone that he wasn't scared of them. She had also told him, with a hint of longing, that she missed him and wanted to see him, and that the party was a good chance for them to spend some time together.

How could he say no to that? So even though the mere thought of the party sent his gut into a nervous twitch and made his palms sweat, he had agreed.

But now, standing by the window, waiting for Gloria, he was beginning to have second thoughts.

What if his parents found out? They would ground him for the next ten years, maybe longer. Or Gloria's parents? He didn't want her getting in trouble.

He was deciding what to do when Toby noticed a shape moving around below. Looking down, he saw Gloria. She was creeping along the sidewalk, head darting this way and that. She stopped behind the hedge separating Toby's property from the Weisenburn's, craned her head around and looked up at Toby's room. Upon seeing him, she made an O shape with her thumb and forefinger, then raised her hands, asking him if everything was okay.

Seeing her made him realize just how much he had missed her, how much he wanted to spend time with her, so though he was nervous about going to the party, his heart won out. *Really*, he wondered, *what was there to be scared about?* Most of the people at the party would be too drunk to care about little ol' Toby Fairchild.

He nodded, raised a finger, telling her to wait a minute. As she ducked back behind the hedge, Toby turned and started towards his bedroom door.

He was about to leave, when he stopped, turned and looked over at his closet.

Go on, take it.

He hesitated, but then something in the back of his mind told him to take it. So he crept over to his closet. Inside he picked up the shoebox and took out the revolver and the box of cartridges. He placed the gun down the waistband of his shorts, covering it with his T-shirt, then stuffed the box of cartridges into one of the pockets. He placed the shoebox back and closed the closet door.

He wasn't sure why he felt the need to take the gun to the party—protection maybe? No, that wasn't it. He didn't feel that danger, per se, was imminent. Strangely enough, the word that came to mind was peace. But what that had to do with Mr. Joseph's old revolver Toby didn't know.

He left his bedroom and made his way downstairs, careful not to make a sound.

He snuck out the back door, and once outside, hurried over to Gloria.

"Hey," Gloria said, and when she smiled it lit Toby's insides.

"Hey yourself."

Gloria was wearing snug fitting jeans and a lacy shirt. She wore just the right amount of make-up and smelled divine, like apple-blossom.

"Sorry I'm a bit late. I wanted to make sure both my parents were asleep. Dad went to bed a little later than usual."

"That's okay. I'm just glad to see you."

Gloria smiled again. "Come on."

Hand-in-hand they started up Pineview.

"You nervous?" she asked, voice louder once they were away from Toby's house.

"Yeah, a little. You?"

"Sure, I guess," Gloria said, the warm breeze teasing her golden hair. "But I'm more nervous about Tuesday. I can't believe we start high school. Grade nine."

Toby sighed. "Yeah. Are you looking forward to starting?"

A pause. "I guess so. I mean, there was a time not so long ago when high school seemed so far away. It felt like we'd never get there, you know? But it's come up so fast. I don't know if I'm quite ready for it."

"Me either," he admitted. "High school. It sounds so... grown-up. And it's going to be extra weird for me."

Gloria frowned. But it didn't last long. "Oh." She offered a kind smile.

"I always thought that no matter what happened in life, that no matter how hard school was, I'd always have Frankie there with me. My partner in crime. We often talked about high school, about what we thought it would be like, what we'd be like, what we'd look like, about..." He stopped just before he said, "girls." There were certain things you only talked about with guys.

"About...?"

"Nothing. Just, we also used to talk about going to college together, sharing a dorm room, then finally living together afterwards. We had all these plans. And now Frankie's gone." He was surprised at the touch of anger he felt, along with the sadness. It was almost as if Frankie had just upped and left town or moved onto a new group of friends rather than died. It was silly and as they continued towards Taylor's Hill, Toby said a silent apology to Frankie.

"Well, you've still got some friends. So it won't be all bad, will it?"

Toby smiled. "No, I guess not." But his smile dropped as it occurred to him. He may have Gloria now, but once they started high school, how much longer would they stay together? How could he compete with the older high school boys? Compared with them, he was still just a small, clumsy kid. Toby wouldn't blame her for wanting to associate with more mature people. After all, girls matured faster than guys—or so they say. Toby could picture it now; for the first few weeks they would hang around together, stealing kisses here and there. But as they both got settled in, met new people, they would drift apart and Gloria would be picked up by the popular crowd, be ogled by every male in school. Toby would inevitably be pushed aside. Not out of spite or meanness, it was just the way things went. He wouldn't hate Gloria for it. He could never hate Gloria.

But, for the moment, they were together. He knew he had to make the most of the time he still had with her. If there was one thing he had learned over this tumultuous summer, with the loss of Frankie and listening to Mr. Joseph's story, it was that you had to cherish the here and now, cherish the time spent with the people you cared about. Because you never knew what tomorrow would bring.

So Toby stopped, bringing Gloria to a halt, and when she turned to him, he planted his mouth over hers.

Gloria opened her mouth and let Toby in, then her hand reached around to the back of his head and gently caressed his hair.

They kissed long, tenderly. It was very, very good.

Afterwards, Gloria exhaled and said, "Wow."

Toby smiled.

Sure, he may lose Gloria in the wilds of high school, but he would forever have the memory of this summer; the kisses, the talks, the one memorable, scary, exciting moment on the couch. He figured a lot of people were never so lucky to have such fond memories.

They continued walking, talking casually about what they had been up to, and the upcoming Labor Day picnic and barbecue in the town square. It was getting on midnight when they reached Taylor's Hill.

Cars were parked all around the base of the hill. Most were empty, though there was the odd group sitting on hoods passing a bottle of alcohol, or a joint back and forth. A few of the cars' windows were fogged-up, which made Toby feel both awkward and excited. Streams of people were either going up or coming down the path winding through the woods. Toby and Gloria joined the throng and started the trek up.

"I've never been to a party up here," Toby said to Gloria, who was now a gray shape beside him. The moonlight only broke through the tops of the trees in dabs.

"Don't worry, it'll be fun," Gloria said and gave Toby's hand a gentle squeeze.

They heard the music first, and then light broke through the trees.

The path leveled out, the trees fell away and the sight that greeted them was one of pure adolescent rapture.

Hundreds of teenagers were spread around the large open area, most concentrated around a raging bonfire. Music from the portable stereo thumped through the night. People danced, people mulled around, laughing, people were on the ground making out, people were having drinking contests. There were more shimmering bottles of booze than Toby had ever seen in his life.

"Wow, some party," Gloria said, smiling at Toby, and then, spotting Danielle and Emma near the fire, she said, "Come on," and pulled Toby towards them.

Smells washed past Toby as they made their way to Gloria's friends—the fresh earthiness of the woods gave way to smoke from the bonfire, and then all sorts of smells ebbed and flowed underneath: perfume, aftershave, beer, whiskey, cigarette, cigar, dope.

A far cry from the sleepovers and tree house parties he was used to.

When they reached Danielle and Emma, Gloria let go of Toby and hugged her friends. “Some party, huh?” Danielle said, taking a swill of beer. “We were wondering when you were gonna show.”

“Yeah, Drew’s already puked,” Emma said with a shake of her head. “Boy can’t hold his liquor.”

“Can’t wait till high school, when we get to be around real men, not boys.” Danielle looked at Toby and, looking slightly embarrassed, said, “Oh, hey Toby.”

Toby nodded hello to both girls.

“Gloria, you want a beer? There’s plenty on ice.”

“Sure.” She turned to Toby. “You want one?”

“Sure, why not.”

The heat from the bonfire was like standing next to an oven with its door open, so a cold drink—even a beer—was just the ticket.

Emma left.

“Hot, I know,” Danielle said with a chuckle. “But it is nice. And it does give good light.”

Over on the other side of the fire, a bunch of topless seventeen-year-old guys spat alcohol into the fire. The flames intensified briefly, as did their drunken laughter. “Look at her burn,” one of them cackled.

“Now there’s a good mix; fire and alcohol,” Toby commented, and Gloria and Danielle laughingly agreed.

Soon Emma returned with two frosty cans of Bud. She handed one to Gloria, the other to Toby.

The Bud was just as bitter as the Coors, but at least it was cold.

“Say, you guys wanna go someplace else?” Danielle said, looking from Gloria to Emma. “It’s getting too hot standing here.”

“I think me and Toby will just walk around, mingle a bit, check out what’s going on,” Gloria said. “Maybe we’ll catch you guys later?”

“Sure, whatever,” Emma said.

"Just don't go into the woods by yourself," Danielle said. "There are lots of drunken, horny guys around."

"Isn't that kinda the point in coming here?" Emma said, frowning at Danielle.

Danielle shrugged. "Well I'm just saying. Stay in the areas where there's light."

"Unless she wants to be alone with Toby," Emma said with a wink.

"Very funny," Gloria said. "Later."

Once they were away from Danielle and Emma, Toby said, "Thanks. I know your friends don't like me too much."

"Danny does. But Emma... I love her and all, but she can be a bitch when she wants to be. She thinks we should all be dating older guys. She thinks that dating anyone our age is demeaning or something. It's silly. I mean, she's still with Drew, and he's our age; at least, I think they're still together. It's hard to keep up with those two."

Hand-in-hand once again, they walked casually around the field, saying hello to friends and acquaintances (well, it was mostly Gloria who said the hellos), sipping their beers.

When they came across a very drunk Paul Rodriguez, Toby and Gloria stopped.

"Hey, Paul," Toby said.

The short, thin boy stopped chatting to a couple of guys Toby didn't know the names of, turned around and raised the can of beer he was holding. "Toby, my man, good to see you," he slurred. He reached out and draped an arm around Toby. He smelled of sweat and alcohol. "Some party, huh?" When his drunken gaze fell on Gloria, he said, "Shit, sorry Gloria, didn't mean to be rude. How are you this fine evening?"

Gloria smiled. "I'm doing all right, Paul. And how are you?"

Paul howled, and then took a long drink. "Me, I'm flying."

Toby glanced at Gloria and raised his eyebrows.

He had never seen Paul like this—come to think of it, he had never seen any of his ex-classmates like this. He had only ever seen Frankie and Warrick drunk.

"Actually, Toby, I'm surprised to see you here," Paul said.

"Yeah, why's that?" Toby said, feeling vaguely uncomfortable with Paul's arm around his shoulders.

"Well, I didn't think this would be your scene. Especially, you know, after everything that happened."

Toby frowned. "What do you mean?"

"You know, Frankie dying, the whole thing with that old freak." Paul leaned in, breathing hot beer-breath in Toby's face. "Tell me, what did you talk about when you went over to his house?"

Toby grabbed Paul's arm and unhooked it from around his shoulders. "Your mother," he spat.

Paul flinched, and a sudden look of shock came over his sweat-beaded face. "Hey, why so defensive, bro? I thought we were friends?"

"If we're friends, then how come you never came over to see me after I got back from the hospital?"

"I did," he said. "I came over to see if you wanted to play a game of baseball."

"In my condition? That was smart. I meant just to, you know, hang out."

Paul frowned. He shrugged. "Fucked if I know," he said, then laughed.

Toby sighed, and looking at Gloria, motioned with his head to keep moving.

"Asshole," Gloria said as they moved away from Paul.

"Hey, what I say?" he called, but Toby didn't turn back.

He just kept on walking.

"Hey, slow down," Gloria said and pulled Toby to a stop. "Toby? You wanna leave?"

He faced Gloria. In the glow of the firelight, her face looked like bronze. "No, we just got here. This is the last weekend of summer. I want you to have a good time tonight."

"And you. You deserve it more than anyone."

"Right, 'cos of Frankie dying and the whole thing with that old freak."

Gloria first broke into a smile, then she laughed.

Toby smiled back.

"You wanna sit somewhere, just talk?"

Toby nodded. “Yeah, that sounds good.” He scanned the field. “Over there,” he said, nodding to an empty space on the outer edges of the circle of light cast by the bonfire. They walked over, threading through the maze of bodies. They sat down, the grass bristly underneath. From here they had a good view of the party, without being in the heart of the drinking and the roughhousing. Behind them lay darkness, the end of the open area, and the continuation of the woods. There was probably more roughhousing going on behind the trees and in the bushes, though of a different sort.

“This is nice,” Gloria said, sipping her beer.

Toby nodded, shifted due to the way the handle of the revolver was sticking into his belly.

“You okay?”

Once the gun was no longer poking into him, he said, “Fine.”

“Hey, forget what Paul said. He’s just drunk.”

“That’s when people speak the most truth.”

Gloria nodded. “Yeah, I guess you’re right.”

Toby watched some jock light his fart; two girls making out (one of which was Leah); and some poor kid, no older than Toby, puking all over the ground. His first drinking experience? Toby wondered. He shivered at the remembrance of his own.

When he felt Gloria’s stare, he turned and smiled nervously. “What?”

“You miss him, don’t you?”

“Who, Frankie? Of course I do.”

“No, not Frankie. I know you miss him. I meant Mr. Joseph.”

Toby faced the bonfire and staring into the flames, said, “Yeah, I do,” and there was no one else in the world—not even Frankie, if he was still alive—that he would’ve admitted that to.

There had been no word from Mr. Joseph, which didn’t surprise Toby. He thought about him most days, wondered where he was; hoped that, wherever he had ended up, he was at peace—well, as much at peace as was possible.

Toby thought back to what had woken him in the middle of the night a week ago, could still hear the gunshot echoing in his head, but then Gloria talking jolted him back to the present.

“It’s okay, I understand,” she said.

Toby wanted to tell her that as much as he appreciated her kindness, she didn't understand. She couldn't possibly begin to understand half of what had transpired between him and the old man. It wasn't just a simple case of a lost teenager befriending a lonely old man; it went much, much deeper.

Toby finished off his beer, threw the can to the ground.

Maybe I should tell Gloria the truth about Mr. Joseph. What does it matter now? The old man is gone. Gloria's the only person I can trust, the only person who may understand what I went through this summer.

Though he had just polished off the beer, his mouth was sticky-dry when he turned to Gloria.

She turned, smiled at him. The smile quickly switched to a frown when she noticed Toby's pinched expression. "Toby, is everything okay?"

"There's something..." he started to say, but then a body was hovering over them. Looking up, Toby frowned. "Jesus, Paul, what do you want?"

"To apologize," he said, sounding even more drunk than he was just a few minutes ago. He stuck out an arm. Clasped in his hand was a bottle. "My peace offering."

"What is it?"

"Rum," he said.

"Rum?"

"That's what I said. I want you to have it, as my way of saying sorry."

"Where'd ya get it from?" Toby asked.

"I just found it on the ground," Paul said. "A full bottle, just sitting there. It didn't seem to belong to anyone, so it's yours, if you want it." He giggled to himself, as if remembering a private joke. "Well, I drank a teensy-weensy bit," he said, "so it's not totally full, but it's near enough."

Toby swallowed, remembering the taste. Still, he found himself intrigued by the bottle, drawn to the fiery promises it held.

"Tell the truth, who'd ya steal it from?" Gloria said.

"It just appeared, honest. I was tempted to keep it for myself, but then I remembered I don't like rum. I'm more of a beer and tequila kind of guy."

Toby knew he should decline the offer—he wasn't a fan of spirits. Beer was enough for him.

Yet he found himself reaching up for the bottle. "Okay, I'll have it."

Paul handed it down to him. "So, we cool?"

Toby nodded. "Yeah, we're cool."

"Great. Well, I'm all out of beer, so I'll leave you two crazy kids alone. Have fun. Oh, and enjoy the rum, too." He winked and then staggered away.

"Do you even like rum?" Gloria said.

Toby turned the bottle over in his hand. It was white rum, *Barbancourt*, just like what Mr. Joseph drank. "No, not really," he said. He unscrewed the cap and took a drink. He winced as the liquor cut a path of fire down his throat. He coughed.

"Can I try some?" Gloria said.

Toby passed her the bottle. She sniffed the drink, made a face, and then, taking a breath, placed the bottle to her lips and took a sip. She coughed, wiped her eyes. "That tastes terrible," she said. She followed it up with another swill.

After her second drink, she handed the bottle back to Toby. Toby put the lip of the bottle to his own mouth, thought about how Gloria's lips had just been on the bottle, and then he sunk back more of the clear white rum.

Wincing, he said, "Hard to imagine that some people drink this stuff all the time." Leaving the cap off, he rested the bottle on the ground.

"Like who?"

"Well, people from Jamaica and Haiti drink it all the time. Mr. Joseph drank it all the time."

"He did?"

Toby nodded. Remembered he was about to tell her about Mr. Joseph; but the moment had passed, and really, it was probably for the best he didn't tell her.

"Well, I think I'll stick to beer," Gloria said. "Speaking of which, I'm all out. I'm gonna go and see if there's any left." She got to her feet. "You want me to bring you back one?"

Toby shook his head.

"Okay. Well, don't go anywhere. I'll be right back."

Toby lifted the bottle. "I'll be here waiting." He took a sip and Gloria chuckled as she headed back into the ring of fire.

Gloria didn't come right back. Instead, she got caught chatting to some people. Toby watched her talk and laugh from where he sat, and, steadily sipping the rum, enjoyed the view from afar.

With his head buzzing from the alcohol, and the smell of the bonfire evoking simpler times when he, his dad and Frankie used to go camping, Toby's attention wavered between watching Gloria and everyone else around him enjoying their last vestige of freedom before the constraints of school bound them.

As he sat waiting for Gloria to come back, trying not think about school, or what his parents would do if they caught him sneaking home after the party, or smelled alcohol on his breath tomorrow morning—*Let them smell the alcohol. What do I care? What can they do? Ground me? Stop me from playing with Frankie after school?*—his attention was drawn to a person standing outside the light cast by the fire. Though the person was about fifteen feet away, and swamped by shadows, there was no mistaking the dark hat, clothes and sunglasses.

Toby frowned.

Guédé Nimbo? he thought.

But he knew that wasn't possible. He wasn't dreaming.

He figured it was just a party goer, for some reason wearing that unusual outfit. Still, though Toby couldn't see the person's face, he was sure the person was staring straight at him—he could feel their stare. He could also see the tiny light from the tip of a cigarette; it burned brightly for a brief moment before going dull.

Nobody seemed to notice the person; people walked past without so much as a glance or a "Hi."

Toby grew nervous.

Could it really be? he wondered. *If so, then what did the loa want? Why had he shown up here, now?*

A sudden breeze fluttered, flapping his clothes and hair, and a chill passed through him. The wind died and the coldness left him.

Maybe he wants some rum, Toby thought.

But when he looked down at his right hand, Toby found it empty.

But I was just holding it...

The stranger in the dark clothes turned and walked into the woods.

Toby sat there, baffled, scared, but also curious.

Did the stranger want him to follow?

Toby glanced over at Gloria, still chatting.

Do I dare? If it is Guédé Nimbo, then he must be here for a reason.

Getting to his feet, Toby headed for the area where the stranger had vanished.

He stepped around couples copulating on the ground, people lying drunk, stopping when he reached the spot. Swallowing his nerves, Toby stepped forward.

All light from the bonfire was soon gone and Toby was left to dodge tall trees and push past sharp branches and stinging twigs in almost total darkness. His only guide was the dabs of moonlight that managed to break through the foliage.

Just as Toby feared he had fallen into a trap, into some netherworld which consisted of nothing but trees and bushes, the woods ended and he found himself standing on the small, narrow clearing overlooking the cemetery.

Toby and Frankie had been up here many times over the years—though never after dark—and thrown rocks at the cemetery below. They used to single out a headstone and play 'who can hit the headstone first'. It was a difficult game to win; not only was the cemetery a good twenty feet away, but you had the steep hill directly below to contend with. So one wrong slip and you'd go tumbling all the way to the wad of bushes which hid the bottom of the thick iron cemetery gates.

It was a disrespectful, immature game, Toby knew that now. Especially as he thought of kids picking out Frankie's headstone and using that as target practice.

But he hadn't been brought here to play any games. Toby gazed around. There was no sign of the stranger.

So why had he been brought here?

Probably wasn't the Guédé after all. Probably just some senior playing a joke on me; or my imagination.

But when he sniffed the air, he thought he could smell cigarette smoke.

He was about to turn and head back, when he heard distant laughter from down in the cemetery. Toby squinted through the darkness; noticed a group of people sitting among the headstones, though at this distance he couldn't tell who they were.

He soon got his answer when he looked further down the cemetery, towards the entrance, and saw a car parked out front—Bruce, Dwayne's 1969 Chevy Camaro, looking remarkably like the animal it was named after, the way the moonlight glinted off its blue and white exterior, its front like a dark gaping maw.

Another burst of laughter, louder this time, the sound riding on the gentle breeze and floating up to where Toby stood. One laugh in particular stood out: a high-pitched cackle.

It was the laugh from his dream.

Fear, like a thousand icy worms wriggled into Toby's body.

Remember...

And then he did.

Like Moses parting the Red Sea, layers of murky waters were peeled back to reveal what lay buried beneath, and he was catapulted back almost three months to that horrible life-changing night...

Toby on the ground, trying desperately to shield himself against the onslaught of baseball bats, iron bar and kicks that sent shockwaves of pain through his body;

hearing the sound of Frankie grunting, of gravel crunching as his attackers (there was more than one!) feverishly assaulted them;

and the laughter.

Throughout it all, the laughter.

Cruel, vicious laughter.

But one laugh in particular: a high-pitched cackle that cut through Toby's pain like a machete through Jell-O. A laugh that belonged to one of Dwayne Marcos's thug puppets—Sam Bickley.

Standing on the narrow clearing overlooking the cemetery, Toby felt as if all air had been sucked out of his lungs. He found it difficult to breathe, his legs had turned to rubber, threatening to give way completely.

Head spinning, he staggered to the nearest tree where he hugged its rough skin, desperately drawing air into his lungs.

I don't... believe... it... all this time...

Dwayne, Toby thought, the name like poison on his tongue. *Dwayne was responsible.*

He knew there was at least one other participant, Sam, and most likely the other two thugs—but Toby knew with crystal-clear clarity that it was Dwayne's doing. It was his want, his will, his evil mind that was behind the attack.

When he got some of his composure back, Toby unhooked himself from around the trunk. Tears trickled down his cheeks. Now he knew the truth, what was he going to do about it? The obvious answer was go to the cops and tell them what he had remembered, that he knew who had killed his best friend.

But that idea didn't sit well with him. For one, he didn't trust them. They didn't try very hard to find the real murderers. Instead they were content to let an innocent man take the blame for Frankie's death; as Mr. Joseph had said, a dead black vagrant was the perfect scapegoat.

Even if he did tell them what he knew, that he had remembered a vital piece of information that he thought lost forever, the moment they smelled his breath, not only were they sure to dismiss his accusations as ramblings, but he'd be in big trouble, both with the law and his parents.

No, he couldn't go to the police.

Then why was I brought here? Why did Guédé Nimbo lead me to the murderers and reveal the truth?

Toby felt the pull of the gun tucked down the waistband of his pants.

Is that it? he wondered. *Is that why I felt the need to bring the gun with me tonight?*

But he was no hero—he had never stood up to Dwayne and his gang before, what made the Guédé think he could do it now?

Because they have to pay. Someone has to make them pay for what they did to me and Frankie.

Toby just wished that someone wasn't him.

You don't have to do anything. You could always run home and wake Mom and Dad, tell them of the situation.

No, this was his fight. He wasn't a kid anymore—those days were over. He had to take charge of his life, stand up for himself.

Besides, the Guédé wanted me to find out, wanted me to have the gun and seek revenge for Frankie. The loa knows all, so I guess this is how it has to be.

Scared, body shaking, Toby turned and headed back through the woods.

When he broke through to the large clearing, he was crying, but he didn't care if anyone saw. He didn't care about anything at that moment, other than seeing those bastards pay for what they did.

In the cold distant echoes of his mind, Toby heard Gloria calling out to him. "Toby, where are you going? Toby, is everything okay?"

She didn't see the smile through the tears, a smile full of pain, anger and relief.

Yes, everything is going to be okay, he thought as he started down the path that lead down from Taylor's Hill.

He bumped into drunken teenagers on his way down, ignoring the cries of, "Hey, watch it," and, "Looks like someone's had too much to drink."

When he reached flat land, the dark woods giving way to bright moonlight that shone over the parked cars making their chrome exteriors glitter, he headed left.

As he strode towards the cemetery, Toby thought about Mr. Joseph. Had he known the truth about who the attackers were? Is that what the Guédé told him that day? If so, then why didn't he tell Toby?

There must've been a reason. Maybe he knew I had to find out for myself. Maybe the Guédé told him to keep the truth a secret. Perhaps I need to face this particular fear alone. Need to find my own peace.

Toby was thinking about all this when he arrived at Belford Cemetery.

With the sounds of the party up on Taylor's Hill distant, the hooting of owls and the whisper of the breeze now filling his ears, he slipped the revolver out from under his shirt and strode through the entrance.

He pulled the box of cartridges from his pocket and as he plunged deeper into the cemetery, tears still flowing, he plugged the chamber with the bullets. Once filled, he snapped the chamber in place and pocketed the empty box.

Soon he heard the wicked laughter, smelt the sweet, pungent odor of dope.

He saw them up ahead. Scotty Hammond was standing in front of a grave, pissing on the headstone. Sam Bickley and Deb Mayfour were sitting nearby, laughing; Sam was cackling the hardest. There was no sign of Dwayne or Rusty Helm.

"How'd ya like that, fat-boy?" Scotty laughed, his strong stream splashing against the white stone. "Drink up, Frankie."

"That's disgusting," Deb Mayfour said, laughing, smoking a joint. "You're a pig, you know that? It's sac... sacri... against God to do that. He'll punish you for it."

"Fuck God," Scotty said, finishing up. "And Fuck Frankie."

"Yeah, fuck Frankie," Sam said, swilling from a bottle of whiskey.

Scotty had just zipped up when Toby stepped forward, aiming the gun at the group of misfit teenagers. "No, fuck all of you," he said, voice wavering.

Deb, taking a hit of Mary Jane, coughed out smoke and said, giggling, "Toby? Jesus, what the fuck are you doing here?"

"What is that, a cap-gun?" Scotty said, a wonky smile on his chubby face.

"You bastards," Toby said, pushing the words past his constricted throat. "You killed Frankie. You fucking bastards."

The laughter stopped.

Toby stepped closer, swinging the gun back and forth between the three older teenagers. He was unable to stop his hand from shaking. "Who else was there? I know you were there, Sam. And I'm sure Dwayne was, too. Who else? All of you?"

"What the fuck's he talking about?" Deb said.

Sam got to his feet. "You drunk, Toby? 'Cos I don't know what the fuck you're talking about."

"Hey man, that gun looks real," Scotty said, his gaze fixed on the revolver. "Is that fucking thing real?"

"It's real," Toby said.

Scotty huffed, suddenly looking nervous. "Well shit, why you got your knickers all in a knot, huh?"

"Because you killed Frankie!" Toby cried, and he was unable to stop the torrent of tears from washing down his face.

"You're crazy, Toby," Deb said, getting to her feet, brushing grass and leaves off her skirt. "Just put the gun down, huh? I don't know what you think..."

"I remembered," Toby said, his bitter voice cutting off Deb. "Guédé Nimbo brought me to you, so I could hear Sam's laugh. Then I remembered. The night of the attack. It came back to me. So tell me right now, who was involved? And where the fuck is Dwayne? He needs to be here."

They all looked at Toby, eyes pooled with fear and confusion.

"Tell me! Or else I'll kill all of you, even if you weren't involved."

"It was all Dwayne's doing," Sam blurted, his face twitching. "He made us do it."

"It's true," Scotty said. "We didn't mean for Frankie to die. Honest. Yeah, we wanted to hurt you two, give you some payback, but not kill. But Dwayne took it too far. He got carried away."

"Yeah, it was... an accident, that's all," Sam said.

Toby turned the gun on Sam. The teenager took a step backwards, shock and fear etched on his thin face. "Accident? Accident my ass. Now just tell me where Dwayne is."

"You're not serious?" Deb cried, flicking the tiny cigarette away. "Guys, don't lie just to save your skin. Tell Toby the truth, you weren't involved. It was that homeless bum, he was the one who did it." She turned to Toby. "Toby, come on. Be reasonable. Dwayne and the guys didn't have anything to do with the attack. They're just saying they did because they're afraid." She took a step forward.

Toby aimed the gun at her. She stopped in her tracks. "Don't come any closer."

"Or what? You'll shoot me?"

"If I have to."

The world fell quiet.

Then Deb muttered, "Jesus."

"Dwayne," Toby breathed. "Where the hell is he?"

"He's not here," Scotty said.

"Bullshit. I saw his car out front. Where's he hiding?"

"He's not hiding," Scotty said. "He and Rusty went up to the party to get some more beers."

"You're lying! I was up there. I didn't see them."

"Well shit Toby, I don't know what to tell you. That's where they went, honest to God."

"Deb?"

Deb, looking scared and in shock, said, "It's true. They went up to get beers."

A distant voice: "Toby? Toby, you in here?"

Oh no!

"Gloria, go away," Toby cried.

"Gloria, help! He's got a gun and he's going to shoot us!" Deb cried.

"Shut up!" Toby told her.

"Deb?" Gloria said, her voice closer.

Toby turned towards Gloria's voice. He didn't want her here. He didn't want her to witness this. "Gloria, you have to..."

An arm grabbed Toby around his neck. Strong, slick with sweat; it wrapped around Toby's throat, choking him. The gun flew from Toby's hand, and then a deep, familiar voice tickled Toby's left ear. "Surprise, Fairchild."

Toby hadn't heard Dwayne coming; no leaves crunching, no twigs snapping. It was like he just appeared out of nowhere—a silent hunter.

"Scotty, pick up the gun," Dwayne ordered.

Scotty ventured forward, bent down and picked the revolver up off the ground. Holding it in his hands, he turned the gun over, studying it, like he was checking to make sure it was real.

From off to one side, Rusty Helm stepped out of the shadows, half a dozen beers cradled in his arms. "Shit, we was sure Toby was going to shoot you guys." He dropped the beers to the ground.

"How long have you two been hiding?" Sam asked.

"Long enough," Dwayne said.

The grip around Toby's throat tightened; he couldn't breathe.

"Bad mistake coming here, Fairchild," Dwayne said into Toby's ear. "A real bad mistake."

The grip loosened and then Toby was pushed forward. He landed on the ground, his head smacking into the dirt.

Gloria appeared. She started to say, "Toby, I heard you shouting and I..." but she stopped, gasped. "My god Toby, are you all right?"

Gloria rushed to Toby's side.

Toby turned away from Gloria, spat out dirt, and then, with her help, got to his feet.

"What the hell's going on?" Gloria asked no one in particular.

"Your boyfriend here crashed our party, accusing Dwayne and the others of killing Frankie. He reckons he was going to kill us all." Deb spoke fast, breathlessly.

"What?" Gloria turned to Toby. "Is that true?"

Toby nodded.

"What on earth makes you think they were responsible for Frankie's death?"

"Because it's the truth."

The world once again fell silent.

Then: "Shit Dwayne, what are you doing?" Scotty cried.

"Yeah, we have the gun, we don't have to play his games anymore," Rusty said.

Toby looked over at Dwayne. Wearing jeans and a polo shirt, he looked like the all-American jock. His smooth, chiseled face was covered in a light sheen of sweat, his short dirty blond hair looked like yellow needles in the moon's light. He strolled over to Scotty and took the gun from his friend. He clicked open the chamber. Half smiling, half frowning, he flipped the chamber back into place. "What's the point in hiding it? He knows," Dwayne answered, voice cold and flat. His gaze shifted between Scotty and Sam. "But you two fuckers were quick to make sure his suspicions were confirmed. And quick to lay the blame on me."

Scotty and Sam exchanged nervous looks.

"But the little fucker will go to the police now that he's remembered," Rusty said.

"If he was going to go to the cops, he would've already gone," Dwayne said. "Besides, there's no evidence. We're still in the clear. As long as we get rid of the excess baggage, we should be fine."

"Jesus!" Deb cried. "I don't believe this. I covered for you. I told the cops that you were with me the whole night. You and your pathetic loser friends. And all this time you bastard."

Dwayne turned to Deb. He grinned, only slightly, but it contained so much darkness it looked like a black hole had been cut across his face. "Grab her," he said, turning to Scotty and Rusty.

Deb, eyes wide, turned and started running as fast as her drunken, stoned legs could manage.

"Grab her!" Dwayne bellowed, and Scotty and Rusty dashed after her. They quickly caught up with her.

"Let go, fuckers!" she cried as they grabbed her.

"Let her go!" Gloria gasped.

"Dwayne..." Toby said, but stopped when the murdering teenager pointed Mr. Joseph's gun at Toby.

"You be quiet. And if either of you think about trying to run away, think again." Then he called to Rusty and Scotty, "Bring the bitch back."

"Get your hands off me, you fuck-heads!" Deb cried, bucking, as Scotty and Rusty dragged her back to Dwayne.

When they had Deb back in front of Dwayne, she cried, "What the fuck do you think you're doing?"

"Bitch, bitch, bitch, that's all you do. Well, that and gossip. I couldn't let you go."

Debbie's face contorted into a visage of fear. "What... what do you mean?"

Dwayne, still keeping the gun trained on Toby, shook his head. "You really are a stupid cow. A great lay with a great set of tits, but dumb as a cucumber." Then, with his free hand, he socked her in the face.

Toby heard the sickening smack of knuckle against flesh.

"Deb!" Gloria cried.

Next Dwayne punched Deb in the gut. She doubled over and Dwayne stepped back as vomit sprayed forth.

"You bastard," Gloria whimpered.

Toby felt powerless. And useless. He had come here to avenge Frankie's death, and he couldn't even do that right. And what's worse, he had put Gloria in danger.

He wanted to do something, wanted to stop Dwayne, but what could he do? Dwayne now held the gun.

Scotty and Rusty let go of Deb. She dropped to the ground, gasping for air.

"Watch her," Dwayne ordered. "Don't let her get away."

"Are you sure we should be doing this?" Sam whispered to Dwayne. He looked scared.

"We have no choice. And we have Fairchild to thank for it. Don't we?"

Toby looked over at Dwayne. "You attacked me and Frankie. You killed my best friend. This is all your fault."

Dwayne snarled. "That's where you're wrong, Fairchild. This is your fault. Yours and Wilmont's. So I'm not to blame for all this. You started it."

"I don't know what you're talking about," Toby said.

"Sure you do. You think I don't know? I know everything you little shit-heel. Your little water bomb stunt? I know it was you. You and your fat fuck of a friend. Well, he paid. He paid real good."

Tears flowed freely down Toby's cheeks. "You killed Frankie just because we water bombed your car?"

"I couldn't let that slide. Not with my rep. No fucking way. I had to pay you two back. But it wasn't just the water bombing. I also know about you spying on us that night when we egged Mr. Joseph's house, and that your little pervert of a friend saw Deb's tits. Damn little pervert. Yeah, I know everything, and you two shits had it coming."

"Dwayne," Toby said. "Please, just let us go. We promise we won't say anything."

"Yes, just leave us alone," Gloria muttered. "Jesus, haven't you done enough?"

"Let you go?" Dwayne huffed. "You really think I'm gonna do that? Fuck no, Fairchild. You know too much. You're gonna have to pay. Gloria and Deb are gonna have to pay."

The realization of what Dwayne meant hit Toby full-force.

The realization apparently hit Debbie then, too.

She got to her feet and, still dazed from the two punches, lunged at Dwayne.

Dwayne turned and fired two shots.

The gunfire was short, sharp. The bullets smacked into Debbie's chest and gut. She stumbled, falling near an old, chipped headstone.

Gloria screamed and it was louder and more piercing than the gun blasts.

She rushed over to her sister.

"Debbie!" she cried. "Debbie!"

"Gloria..." Toby started, but then Dwayne turned the gun back on him.

Toby looked over at Gloria, wailing beside her sister, and noticed that Deb was still alive—he could hear her sharp wheezing breaths.

Toby turned away and puked up the rum, beer, and the barbecue ribs he had eaten for dinner.

"Scotty, grab the little cunt," Dwayne said, "and bring her over to me."

Toby watched through teary eyes as the fat oaf waddled over and grabbed a hold of Gloria. Like her sister, she fought, but she was no match for Scotty. He dragged her kicking and screaming to Dwayne. Dwayne smiled, licked his lips. "I've always wanted to have a go at Deb's little sister. Now I'll get my chance." He raised the revolver and brought the butt of the gun down across Gloria's face and she fell quiet, her body flopping like a rag doll in Scotty's arms.

"No," Toby choked.

"Put her down and keep an eye on her," Dwayne told Scotty.

As Scotty dragged her away, Toby noticed with a sickening blow to the gut where one of his hands was cupped. He dumped her on the ground nearby, straightened and then readjusted his crotch. It didn't take a genius to figure out what they planned to do to Gloria. It was up to Toby to make sure they didn't get the chance. Even if it meant death, somehow he would make sure these filthy sickos didn't do that to Gloria.

"Finally, a bit of peace and quiet," Dwayne said. "Damn broads, pain in the ass if you ask me. They're only good for two things.

Laying on their backs, and using their mouths as vacuum cleaners. Isn't that right big boy?" Dwayne winked at Toby, picked up the bottle of whiskey from off the ground and took a long drink. When he had drained the bottle, he threw it to the ground. "So tell me. Man to boy. I know you've felt her tits, Warrick told me all about it, but the question is, have you fucked her? Has she sucked your pecker? Have you eaten her...?"

"People will come," Toby interrupted. "They would've heard the gunshots."

"Not with the party going on. Besides, even if someone did hear, they'll think it was just firecrackers, or a car backfiring. No one's saving you, Fairchild. Still..." Dwayne turned to Rusty and Sam. "You two, go to the front gate and keep an eye out, just in case some nosy fucker did hear and decides to call the cops. If you guys see anything or anyone, come straight back."

"Sure," they both said, and then hurried off through the graveyard.

"I don't want to be disturbed while I have my fun with Gloria," Dwayne said, facing Toby. "And you're gonna watch me, before I end your pathetic life."

"Please Dwayne," Toby said. "Just leave Gloria out of this. This is between you and me, she has nothing to do with any of this. Do what you want with me, but please don't hurt Gloria."

Dwayne giggled; a drunken, almost girlish giggle. "You really think that pathetic pleading's going to work? She knows too much now. I can't let her live, just like I can't let you live. But don't worry, the guys and I will have some fun with her before her time is up. You may not have been man enough to pop her cherry, but we'll make sure she's had a taste of Dwayne before she bites the dust."

"You won't get away with this, you know that, don't you? You don't have that old hobo to take the blame for you this time. Luck's not on your side tonight."

"Luck? You think it was a simple case of luck? Shit, give us some credit, Fairchild. We planned on getting you and Wilmont back for the water bombing, the spying, the perving, but we weren't sure when. We were biding our time for the right moment. When that homeless fuck arrived in town, we knew we had to capitalize on him being here. We figured if we did it while he was here, everyone would think it was him who attacked you and Wilmont. And we were right. That stupid cock-sucking nigger took all the heat off us. We were still smart, mind you. We made sure there were no witnesses, no evidence like fingerprints and shit. And with Deb as our alibi... I knew we wouldn't be caught. The cops questioned us and everything. They had no fucking clue. You got lucky that night my friend. Damn lucky. Lucky that nigger boyfriend of yours came along when he did. But it was all over. Everyone thought that hobo was responsible, there was nothing linking us to the crime, you hardly remembered anything about that night, so we left it at that. But now you've gone and fucked everything up." He glanced at Gloria, slumped on the ground. He grinned. "But at least I'm gonna finally get me taste of her."

In a flash decision, Toby lunged at Dwayne. He knew he stood a good chance of getting shot, but at that moment, he didn't care. All he cared about was stopping Dwayne from hurting Gloria.

Toby managed one clumsy punch. It connected with Dwayne's jaw, but the punch probably hurt Toby more than it did Dwayne—Toby's right hand roared with pain. Dwayne stepped back, looking more stunned than hurt, and once the initial surprise of the sudden attack had worn off, he jacked up his right knee and busted Toby's nose open.

Toby collapsed to the ground.

The pain was immense, the coppery taste of blood was strong, sickening.

"Hey, you all right, Dwayne?" Scotty called, still standing watch over Gloria.

"Yeah, I'm fine," Dwayne said. "Nothing I can't handle. You just stay with Gloria and make sure the princess doesn't escape."

Toby lay on the ground, heaving. He spotted the empty whiskey bottle lying a few feet away, pictured smashing the bottle open and using one jagged half to open Dwayne's throat. Toby started crawling towards it, but before he was able to grab it, Dwayne snarled, "You stupid little shit," and kicked the bottle away. Toby's only chance of survival, at saving Gloria, had just skipped away, coming to a stop near Debbie's motionless body.

"You're pathetic," Dwayne said and kicked Toby in the gut.

The wind was knocked out of him and he struggled for breath.

"You fight like a goddamn girl. No, worse than a girl. A faggot."

Dwayne spat and Toby felt the thick glob of phlegm paste itself to his face.

"Just remember, this is your fault. You and your idiot friend had to act like a couple of fucking infants. So you brought this on yourself." Dwayne huffed. "It was a good thing you and Wilmont were stupid enough to fall for Warrick's charms. Well, that and the beer and whiskey."

With blood streaming from his nose and into his mouth, Toby gazed up at Dwayne. "What are you saying? That you gave Warrick the alcohol?"

"Fuck no, as if I'd waste booze on him. Nah, he swiped all that shit from his old man; got a good beating because of it, too. But it was worth it—at least, for me. Warrick told me everything. All of what you and Wilmont said during that fucking sleepover." He chuckled. "A sleepover. God, what a pair of pussies."

Toby spat blood from his mouth.

Warrick had betrayed them? He had told Dwayne all of what they had told him in confidence? Toby felt bitterly disappointed, sad; but not, unfortunately, surprised.

"Poor, poor Warrick. So desperate to be liked, to be part of the cool crowd. Once we had learnt who it was that had water bombed my car, he knew we were after yours and Wilmont's blood, that's why he told us that you and Wilmont were going off to get your bike that night. I knew, then and there, that it was the perfect moment to strike. Pity Warrick had to grow a conscience and a loose tongue. We were watching him closely, I know he didn't tell you anything, but still, we couldn't take the chance that he eventually would."

Suddenly it all made sense. "You killed Warrick," Toby breathed.

"Didn't want to. We had to."

"Because he knew. Was he with you that night?"

"Yeah, but he stayed in the car. He didn't participate, if that's what you're wondering—he was much too big of a wimp for that; but he was a witness, so he knew he had to keep quiet. But he had to grow a conscience, the fool. So, he had to go."

"And I bet you were the ones who sprayed graffiti on mine and Mr. Joseph's house and sent me the chicken's head?"

Dwayne smiled, showing off his pearly whites. "Guilty as charged."

Toby gazed up into Dwayne's eyes. The very eyes that so many girls had swooned over, had called 'dreamy'. If only they knew the monster lurking behind those eyes.

Is that why Warrick came to see me that day? To confess?

"You're crazy," Toby said, choking back blood and tears.

"What's so crazy about self-preservation? That's all this is; self-preservation. Now, I have to piss, so don't move, or else I'll put a bullet through your faggoty little head. Got me?"

Sprawled on the ground, Toby watched Dwayne stagger over to Frankie's grave. Moments later he heard what sounded like water splashing against the headstone.

"Ah, that's better," Dwayne sighed.

Bastard, Toby thought.

But he saw another opportunity. It wasn't much of an opportunity, but he knew he had to seize any that came along. He glanced back at Scotty, saw where his eyes were fixated—and they weren't on Toby—so Toby started creeping along the ground. Like a wounded animal, he dragged his body, trying to make as little noise as possible.

Toby inched towards the bottle of Jim Beam.

When he reached the bottle, trying not to look at Deb's body before him, he grabbed the bottle by its neck, and then started crawling back towards Dwayne.

Dwayne was still busy relieving himself when Toby got within two feet—the smell of Dwayne's acrid urine was sickening.

But something alerted Dwayne. Toby wasn't sure whether it was a twig breaking, Toby's breathing, or just a general sense of someone close by. Dwayne looked over his shoulder and at the sight of Toby, spun around.

Fortunately, he had stopped peeing, or else Toby would have gotten sprayed, but Toby did catch a glimpse of the older teenager's pecker and he chuckled. Dwayne's face went from dark amusement at Toby's pitiful attempt at a sneak attack, to enraged madman and he didn't bother tucking in his pinkie-sized cock as he kicked Toby in the head.

Just before he passed out, Toby heard Dwayne tell Scotty, "Start getting that bitch undressed."

And then he fell into darkness.

"Toby? Hey Toby, wake up."

Through the swirl of pain and darkness, Toby thought the voice sounded like Frankie's, albeit more nasally—but he knew that was impossible.

"Toby, wakey, wakey."

A gentle slap on the cheek and Toby's eyes fluttered open. "Frankie?" he groaned.

"That's my name, don't wear it out."

Gazing up at the round, smiling face of Frankie, Toby blinked, figured he must be dreaming.

But the pain felt real; an intense, skull-splitting headache and a general feeling of sickness through his body. He tried to move, but the pain and exhaustion was too much. So he gave up, remaining on the ground and looking up at Frankie; Frankie, his best friend, dead almost three months, but looking just the same as he always did—except for his dark clothes. And the dark sunglasses.

And the bottle in his hand. And the cigarette dangling between his lips.

"Frankie?" Toby said again. "But it... it can't be you."

Frankie took a swill from the bottle of white *Barbancourt* rum; took a drag of his cigarette without taking it from his mouth or using his hands. "It is, and it isn't." He flicked the rim of the dusty old top hat, with a skull and crossbones painted in white on the front. Then he straightened and wiggled his dark coat and stretched out his dark pants. "Like my new threads? Pretty nifty, huh?"

Toby frowned, or at least that's what he meant to do; whether or not he achieved it he couldn't tell. "What's... what's going on? Where's Gloria?"

Frankie bent down again and looking at Toby through the dark shades, said, "Toby, we have to be quick. The sinners must be punished."

A cloud of cigarette smoke blew against Toby's face. "I tried," Toby murmured. "I tried, but I failed."

Frankie made a clicking sound with his tongue. "Oh Toby, you silly boy. We both know you could never kill anyone. It's not in your nature. You weren't brought here to kill anyone yourself; you didn't fail—things happen for a reason. I needed to communicate with you, in order to help you. In order to give you peace. After all, that's what I was asked to do, that's the deal I made with the zombi."

"Mr. Joseph?"

Frankie smiled, and it was a dark, sly smile. He nodded, drank more rum. "Now that he's kept his end of the bargain, I'm here to fulfill mine. The first part is done. I've shown you the truth. Of course, it was always in you, but you forgot, or blocked it out, whatever, it doesn't matter now. The important thing is, you've remembered. And now, you must decide what to do about it."

"I don't understand."

"Yes you do," Frankie said, drawing heavily on the cigarette. "How do you want me to punish the sinners?"

Toby swallowed. So much pain, so damn tired. "Huh?"

"Dwayne, Sam, the other two—do you want them dead?"

Toby faltered. "I, ah..."

"Or I could turn them into zombis. Or I could give them a serious illness. Or I could turn them mad. It doesn't matter to me; it's all the same. But it's up to you, Toby. It's your choice."

"My choice?"

Through the gray cloud of his mind, Toby heard shouts and laughter. The shouts belonged to a female, the laughter, males.

Gloria?

"Oh Jesus, help Gloria," Toby breathed. "Please, Frankie, help Gloria."

"I will. But what of the others? Hurry, time is running out."

Toby dearly wanted Dwayne and the others to pay for what they had done—Toby thought he wanted them dead, but Frankie was right; he was no murderer. He could never kill and he couldn't order for them to be killed, either. There had been too much death already.

"I don't want them dead," Toby said. "I just want them to pay for what they did. I want everyone to know what they did to you, Frankie. And I want everyone to know that Dwayne is crazy."

Toby started weeping.

"Okay," Frankie said, taking a long drink of rum. "It will be done."

Frankie straightened, turned and started walking away.

Toby watched through the narrow slits of his eyes as Frankie, decked out in old back hat and black clothes, strolled over to Deb Mayfour's body. She almost looked like she was sleeping, except for her blood-stained shirt and the red splashes on her face.

Finished with the rum, Frankie hurled the bottle into the night. Toby waited for the inevitable smash, but it didn't come. Frankie then reached down and picked up Deb's body.

Or at least, that's what Toby thought he was doing; but as he gazed at the body slumped in Frankie's arms, Toby saw it was translucent. Looking back down, he saw Deb's body still lying on the ground.

Then, like someone letting go a dove, Frankie tossed the Deb-spirit into the air and the ghostly body sailed up into the sky.

When the ghostly form reached the tops of the trees, it flew back towards the ground, but before it crashed into the earth, it swooped sideways, to somewhere out of Toby's narrow range of sight.

For a brief moment the night was still, dead, but then a shrill cry shattered the stillness like a rock through glass.

Then Toby saw a sight the likes of which he had never seen, and would likely never, ever forget.

He saw Dwayne running around, screaming, wailing like a banshee, tearing at his clothes like they were on fire. "Get off me!" he cried. "Get off me!"

Slithering over his body, like a silky, transparent human sheet, was the ghostly presence of Deb. It was whispering to him—and though Toby couldn't hear what she was saying, he was sure they weren't sweet nothings.

Frankie, looking satisfied, marched towards one of the gravesites. He stopped, turned around, looked at Toby, saluted, winked and then disappeared into the ground.

Toby opened his mouth to say *No, come back Frankie, I miss you*, but it was no use. He was too tired to speak.

He fought to keep his eyes open, but they closed and sleep overtook him.

"Toby? Toby, wake up."

Not Frankie this time, but Gloria.

"Toby, we have to get out of here. Dwayne's gone crazy."

Toby opened his eyes. He sat up. He was still in great pain, but he quickly forgot about that when he heard the shouting. Then a gunshot.

Toby looked up at Gloria. Her hair was messed, the makeup on her face was smudged, and her eyes were wide with fear. She gripped Toby by the arm and pulled him to his feet.

Toby glanced around the cemetery. There was no sign of Frankie, but there were two bodies lying nearby.

Two?

One was Deb; the other, Toby saw, was Scotty. The boy was lying on his back, gently groaning. "What happened?" Toby breathed.

"Like I said, Dwayne all of a sudden went nuts. Started ripping at his clothes, screaming for something to get off him, and then he freaked out even more, saying that they were all against him."

"They?"

"Scotty, Sam, and Rusty. He shot Scotty. Just like that. And then he took off, I guess to go after the other two."

Toby stared at Gloria. She had tears in her eyes. Her shirt was torn on one shoulder, exposing her tender skin. "Are you hurt? Did they...?"

"No," Gloria said, looking to the ground. "No, Dwayne went nuts before they could do anything."

Toby reached out and hugged her.

It was only a brief hug. Another gunshot shocked them apart.

"Oh God," Gloria gasped.

"We should hide," Toby said. "Who knows where Dwayne is. He could come back, looking for us."

Gloria nodded, and together they headed towards the mausoleum.

There they waited, huddled behind its ancient stone, holding each other.

They didn't move from their hiding spot until a policeman's flashlight found them, fifteen minutes later.

CHAPTER TWENTY

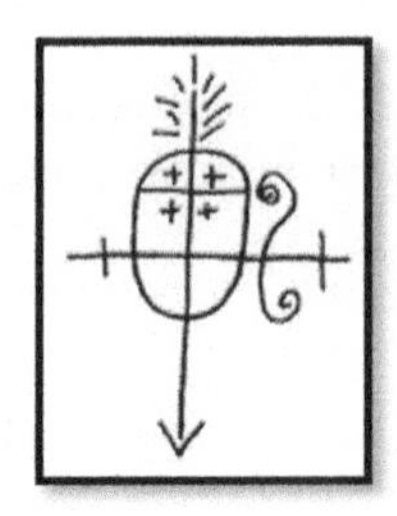

The bell rang and everyone was up and out the door before Mr. Mooney, the grade nine English teacher, could stutter out: "G-goodbye c-c-class."

Toby was the last one out. At the door, he stopped, turned and looked at the small, slightly hunched gray-haired old man collecting his papers, stopping every so often to push his glasses up his face. "Have a good weekend Mr. Mooney," Toby said.

Mr. Mooney looked up, squinted and said, "Ah, y-y-yes, have a g-g-good weekend...er..."

"Toby, sir. Toby Fairchild."

"Of c-c-course. Sorry T-T-Toby."

Toby nodded and left the classroom.

It was only the end of the first week of the new school year, so most of the teachers at Holt High hadn't yet committed to memory many of the new kids' names. Sure, they knew the naughtier kids, or the brainy ones that always seemed to have their hands in the air, but when it came to kids like Toby, the quiet ones, the ones who just blended in with the crowd, it would take the teachers longer to remember their names.

So far, high school was as overwhelming and intimidating as Toby had feared it would be. He felt lost, alone, like he was a tiny boat floating in a seemingly endless ocean. At least most of the teachers were nice enough, though none were as nice as Miss Wilson.

Toby missed her. He missed a lot of things about Holt Middle School. He missed the classrooms, the smells; he missed seeing the old familiar faces, he even missed Warrick's juvenile antics.

And of course he missed Frankie.

Already the halls were as empty as an old ghost town. At his locker, Toby grabbed his bag, and then headed out the front door, his footsteps clacking against the hard floor.

He strolled down the large stone steps and started down the path.

Groups of kids were hanging around, some chatting to friends, others walking along casually, lost in thought, perhaps dreaming about that elusive guy or girl they had a major crush on. Toby still couldn't get used to seeing so many older kids. He felt young, like a baby; yet, in many ways, he felt older than all of them, knew he had seen more and learned more about life these past few months than some people do in a lifetime—the kinds of lessons you couldn't learn from a text book or a bored teacher.

As Toby meandered towards the bus stop, his thoughts drifted to Gloria.

Gloria and her family were having a hard time dealing with the loss of Deb. Toby could only imagine how Gloria must be coping with what happened that night—and also with what almost happened. He still wasn't sure when Gloria would begin her high school year.

Toby had noticed a darkness in Gloria's eyes now, and there were lines on her face, faint though they may be, that Toby knew hadn't been there just a few weeks ago. They hadn't spoken much since that night. Which was a shame, but in truth, Toby didn't mind. He knew it could never be the same between them, not after what they had been through. Some experiences brought people closer together; others caused a rift that was beyond repair.

Toby never told Gloria the whole truth about what happened that night. He told her most of it—hearing the laughter, remembering the night of the attack, and then going down to the cemetery to confront Dwayne and his gang. As to the events later, Toby just had to shrug and pretend he agreed with the general consensus that Dwayne must've suddenly, inextricably, gone mad. Maybe it was killing his girlfriend that pushed him over the line—

after all, he was now currently in the state hospital mumbling about Deb and ghosts, his body racked with fingernail scars.

His sudden madness was also used to explain why he had gone after his three best friends with the gun (Scotty had been shot in the shoulder, but was making a good recovery; Sam and Rusty had managed to escape Dwayne's wrath, but they had been so frightened, they confessed everything to the police—including where to find Warrick's body; about a mile out of town, buried in a small patch of woods off the dead-end Hurston Road, along with three baseball bats and a crowbar). All four were currently awaiting trial for the murders of Frankie and Warrick (as well as Deb, in Dwayne's case).

The story Toby told the police was basically the truth—he only omitted the parts about watching Frankie send Deb's spirit to make sure Dwayne and the others got what they deserved, and about getting the gun from Mr. Joseph (he told them he found the gun and box of cartridges a week ago wrapped up in cloth, while out walking in the woods near the cemetery. The police had been suspicious of his story, and rightly so, but it was the best explanation he could come up with, without implicating Mr. Joseph. Both his parents and the police were severely disappointed with Toby, but because he didn't actually shoot the gun, he got off with a stern lecture from both parties).

Toby's parents had been a big help this past week. His mom still fussed over him too much, but he didn't put up much of a fight. For once, he didn't mind her overprotective ways. His dad still looked too thin, but he was slowly getting better, healthier. Suzie had all but stopped her drinking. Her pain was far from over, but it was a start. Toby had to admire her for that.

Toby suspected that for both his parents and especially for Suzie, finally knowing who was responsible for the attack offered some closure, even if those responsible hadn't turned out to be who they wanted it to be—not some stranger, but someone close to them, living in their own town.

That, Toby knew, hit them hard; it had hit the entire town hard. The Labor Day celebrations had been canceled due to the tragic events, and though Belford may be slowly getting back to normal after the murders, whether it would ever truly recover, only time would tell.

Toby was still recovering, too. Though his physical injuries were close to healed—aside from the newly broken nose—his emotional pain still had a long way to go. Helping him in this regard was Pastor Wakefield; he had been a strong support, listening to Toby's pain, offering invaluable words of advice. But most of all, he had been a good friend. At least Toby could think about the good times he had shared with Frankie, Gloria, even Warrick, and no longer cry; well, not cry as much.

He still had nightmares, though the ones containing strangers in dark clothing, hat and sunglasses had stopped. He'd had a particularly strange dream just the other night, in which he was inside the high school, except the school had no windows or doors. He ran around, trying to find a way out, but couldn't find one. All of a sudden the walls and ceiling started contracting. He screamed for someone to help him, to get him out, but nobody came. Slowly, the building grew smaller, the walls closed in on him, the ceiling got lower. The lights blew out, he was left in utter darkness, and he couldn't do anything except wait in the pitch black, until he was crushed like a bug under a shoe. Toby couldn't remember the outcome, whether he was crushed or not; all he could remember was waking up in a cold sweat, feeling like he couldn't breathe.

He kept himself busy weekends working at Barb's, stocking the shelves and pricing the stock. It was good, simple, honest work—and as a bonus, he got loads of free candy, so it was the perfect job for the time being. He was sure both Frankie and Mr. Joseph would agree.

Mr. Joseph.

Toby missed the old man—though it wasn't a deep sense of loss like it was with Frankie. He missed Mr. Joseph's company, but ultimately Toby couldn't be sad about the old man leaving, for he knew the zombi savane's pain was now at an end.

A few days ago, Toby had received a postcard. It was from Haiti, and was dated a week before the big end-of-summer-party up on Taylor's Hill.

It read:

Dear Monsieur Fairchild.

Bonjour! I hope this postcard finds you well. I wanted to write to you to tell you that I'm safe and, as you probably already guessed by the card you're holding, back in my homeland. Yes, I decided to return to Haiti and face my fears. I have met my great-grand-children and great-great-grand-children—My, do the girls look like Felicia and Rachel! They were surprised, but happy enough to see me, though some of the adults regarded me with trepidation and suspicion—which is perfectly understandable. Still, they opened their homes to me and for that, I am grateful. I am grateful to you, too, Toby. For if it wasn't for you, I would never have had the courage to come back home. But, like you said, if you could accept me, then maybe others would, too. So I thank you, for giving an old man a second chance.

It was great to have known you. I will never forget you, and I sincerely hope you find your peace—though I have a feeling you will. And soon.

I am heading off to find my own peace, and to honor my end of the bargain, so this will be the last time you hear from me.

Goodbye for now.

Your friend,
Jacques Joseph

Instead of hiding the postcard in the drawer, he had tacked it on the edge of his desk, for all to see.

He felt he owed Mr. Joseph that much—after all, the man had saved his life.

The school bus arrived, a great big yellow beast of a machine that Toby was sure he would come to know intimately once his days at Holt High were over—which seemed so far away. But then again, so did high school not so long ago.

Toby followed the line of students onto the bus.

He chose a seat near the back. By the time the bus started off with a lurch, no one had sat next to him.

Which didn't bother Toby. He didn't mind being by himself. He wasn't ready for a new best friend yet anyway. Maybe in the future. But for now he was content to live his life one day at a time. Once he got through one day, then he would concentrate on the next.

As the bus gained speed, Toby turned and gazed out the window.

It wasn't an overly warm day. Still, Toby unlatched the window and pulled it down. Fresh fall breeze blew against his face and hair. The sensation invigorated him, and as he sat watching the world speed by, he savored the simple pleasure of being alive.

And free.

THE END

ABOUT THE AUTHOR

Brett McBean is an award-winning horror and thriller author. His books, which include *The Mother*, *The Last Motel*, *Wolf Creek: Desolation Game*, and *The Invasion*, have been published in Australia, the US, and Germany. He's been nominated for the Aurealis, Ditmar, and Ned Kelly awards, and he won the 2011 Australian Shadows Award for his collection, *Tales of Sin and Madness*. He lives in Melbourne with his wife and daughter. Find out more at: brettmcbean.com

NO VAMPIRES . . . NO WEREWOLVES . . .
NO ZOMBIES . . . BEEN THERE. DONE THAT.

You've heard their stories before and you're screaming for a different breed of horror. Say "Hello" to the ones that are still hidden by the shadows. The ones that peer from behind the gravestones with multi-faceted eyes and crawl from the sewers on slime-covered tentacles. The ones that stain the pages within this tome with the blood of their victims . . .

NOT YOUR AVERAGE MONSTER:
A BESTIARY OF HORRORS

THIS AIN'T YOUR DADDY'S NIGHTMARE!

Available in paperback or Kindle on Amazon.com

ISBN-13: 978-0692567937

JUST WHEN YOU THOUGHT YOU COULD
VENTURE OUT OF YOUR HIDING PLACES,
HERE COMES ANOTHER HORDE OF HORRORS

Slithering, wriggling, lurking, and creeping. Leaving slick trails of pustulent slime behind them. These aren't your run-of-the-mill monsters populating the pages of this tome. No, these critters feed on the fear that bubbles up inside you when all appears lost and the scent of blood is on the wind. Now is the time to face these demons and read on . . .

NOT YOUR AVERAGE MONSTER, VOL. 2:
A MENAGERIE OF VILE BEASTS

THIS NIGHTMARE HAS JUST BEGUN!

Available in paperback or Kindle on Amazon.com

ISBN-13: 978-0692644737

ON THE HORIZON FROM BLOODSHOT BOOKS

2016

The Frighteners – Stephen Laws

Vyrmin – Gene Lazuta

Blood Mother: A Novel of Terror – Pete Kahle

Tunnelvision – R. Patrick Gates

Odd Man Out – James Newman

2017*

Eternal Darkness – Tom Deady

Shadow Child – Joseph A. Citro

The Boulevard Monster – Jeremy Hepler

The Breeze Horror – Candace Caponegro

The Abomination (The Riders Saga, Book 2) – Pete Kahle

Not Your Average Monster, Volume 3

2018*

The Horsemen (The Riders Saga, Book 3) – Pete Kahle

* other titles to be added when confirmed

Made in the USA
Monee, IL
11 May 2023